Ellery Queen was the pseudonym of writers Frederic Dannay (1905–82) and Manfred Bennington Lee (1905–71), two cousins who were working in New York as advertising agents in the late 1920s, as well as the name of one of the most successful classical detective "figures" in the history of American detective fiction. Dannay and Lee's masterfully plotted stories, in which the mystery was always far more important than the characterization, social relevance, or great writing, and their efforts to nurture and promote detective fiction gave rise to one of the most famous quotes in the history of the genre, and one of the truest: "Ellery Queen is the American detective story."

Ellery Queen's

JAPANESE
MYSTERY STORIES

from Japan's Greatest Detective & Crime Writers

Edited, with an introduction by
Ellery Queen

TUTTLE Publishing
Tokyo | Rutland, Vermont | Singapore

The Tuttle Story
"Books to Span the East and West"

Our core mission at Tuttle Publishing is to create books which bring people together one page at a time. Tuttle was founded in 1832 in the small New England town of Rutland, Vermont (USA). Our fundamental values remain as strong today as they were then—to publish best-in-class books informing the English-speaking world about the countries and peoples of Asia. The world has become a smaller place today and Asia's economic, cultural and political influence has expanded, yet the need for meaningful dialogue and information about this diverse region has never been greater. Since 1948, Tuttle has been a leader in publishing books on the cultures, arts, cuisines, languages and literatures of Asia. Our authors and photographers have won numerous awards and Tuttle has published thousands of books on subjects ranging from martial arts to paper crafts. We welcome you to explore the wealth of information available on Asia at **www.tuttlepublishing.com.**

Published by Tuttle Publishing, an imprint of Periplus Editions (HK) Ltd

www.tuttlepublishing.com

Copyright © 1978, 2020 by Charles E. Tuttle Company, Inc.
First Tuttle edition, 1978
First published in 1978 as *Japanese Golden Dozen*

Library of Congress Control Number: 77816031 ISBN 978-4-8053-1552-1

Printed in Malaysia   2003VP

23 22 21 20   10 9 8 7 6 5 4 3 2 1

Distributed by

North America, Latin America & Europe
Tuttle Publishing
364 Innovation Drive
North Clarendon, VT 05759-9436 U.S.A.
Tel: (802) 773-8930; Fax: (802) 773-6993
info@tuttlepublishing.com
www.tuttlepublishing.com

Japan
Tuttle Publishing
Yaekari Building, 3rd Floor
5-4-12 Osaki, Shinagawa-ku
Tokyo 141 0032
Tel: (81) 3 5437-0171
Fax: (81) 3 5437-0755
sales@tuttle.co.jp; www.tuttle.co.jp

Asia Pacific
Berkeley Books Pte. Ltd.
3 Kallang Sector
#04-01, Singapore 349278
Tel: (65) 6741-2178; Fax: (65) 6741-2179
inquiries@periplus.com.sg
www.tuttlepublishing.com

CONTENTS

FOREWORD

Japan has been and continues to be a land of mysteries. From pulp fiction and foreign translations to primetime dramas and comic books, stories of crime and detection abound the life of the Japanese. And in this land of mysteries, Ellery Queen is king to Agatha Christie's queen, as the most famous non-Japanese writers of the genre. For example, *The Tragedy of Y* topped the 1985 survey of top 100 non-Japanese detective novels conducted by a major weekly magazine *Shûkan shunjû*; in the 2012 survey, it came in second only after *And Then There Were None*. So it is no surprise that Frederic Dannay, one half of the Ellery Queen duo, was treated like royalty when he visited Japan in September 1977, even if he himself was shocked, as his wife Rose who accompanied him on the trip later recalls, at the reception he received. And it is also no surprise that the project to have Ellery Queen select Japanese detective stories for publication saw great success in Japan despite the fact that these stories had already been published elsewhere. In fact, Dannay's visit to Japan was to celebrate the Japanese publication of the second volume of *Ellery Queen's Japanese Golden Dozen* (the original English title of this collection), which was never published in the United States.

In his introduction to this volume, retitled *Ellery Queen's Japanese Mystery Stories*, Mr. Dannay refers to the twelve short stories in this collection, written in the first half of the 1970s, as belonging to the "neo-social" era. As he readily admits, this information came from his Japanese informants, but the "neo-social" works did not make enough of a mark for this designation to become a part of literary history. Rather, the 1970s is often seen as a period of transition in the history of Japanese detective fiction, sandwiched between the Social School boom in the late 1950s to the mid-1960s and the emergence of the Neo-Orthodox School in the late 1980s headed by the likes of Ayatsuji Yukito, Norizuki Rintarô, and Arisugawa Arisu, all of whom were deeply influenced by the works of Ellery Queen. This is not to say that the "neo-social" designation is insignificant, as it reveals the historical lineage within which its organizers sought to position this project. And such positioning certainly makes sense considering that one of the principal organizers of the project was Matsumoto Seichô, the founder of the Social School who exerted significant influence within the publishing industry.

It was the late 1950s when Matsumoto Seichô's *Ten to sen* (Points and Lines, 1958), *Me no kabe* (Walls of Eyes, 1958), and *Zero no shôten* (Zero Focus, 1959) quickly fashioned a Seichô boom in Japan to usher in the age of the Social School. By then, Japan had made major strides in its recovery from the devastation in World War II with the support of the United States. The Korean War, in particular, functioned to boost the Japanese economy as producers of goods necessary to support U.S. involvement in the conflict. As a result, Japan entered a period of high economic growth starting in 1954, and, in 1956, *Keizai hakusho* (White Paper on Economy) published annually by the Japanese ministry famously declared that "it is no longer postwar." Buttressed by big government and big corporations, prosperity was becoming the norm for the Japanese. And befitting of such a society, the "suiri" stories of the Social School--what might be called social mysteries--that described the world of salary men and veteran cops and focused on the criminality that lurks in the shadows of the everyday became the favorite reading material of the Japanese who found excitement in the possibility that their mundane life may be turned on its head.

But the realistic approach of the Social School, which Dannay aptly describes in the introduction, naturally led to the loosening of the rules of the detective story, and, as the generic boundary between detective fiction and other literary genres became increasingly blurry, the appeal of the detective story as extraordinary mysteries and entertaining puzzles waned. By the mid-1960s, when the 1964 Tokyo Olympics symbolized Japan's return to the international scene, the works of the Social School had deteriorated to a point that even Matsumo Seichô was calling for social mysteries to incorporate elements of what the Japanese call *honkaku* (orthodox) detective fiction exemplified by the classical tradition of Agatha Christie and Ellery Queen. The result of such call was his editorial supervision of *Shin honkaku suiri shôsetsu zenshû* (Collection of New Orthodox Suiri Novels), a ten-volume collection published in 1966 and 1967, which included three writers whose works are contained in this collection, namely, Sano Yô, Miyoshi Tohru, and Togawa Masako.

Other publishing companies were also quick to jump on the opportunity created by the dissolution of the Social School and the accompanying sentiment against its realism. And it was to the past that the publishers turned to fill the void, whether because of convenience or necessity, reprinting various works of mystery and fantasy, including many from the prewar. Most importantly, in 1968, Yokomizo Seishi's *Yatsuhakamura* (Village of Eight Graves) was made into a comic book and gained immediate popularity. Serialized originally in the magazines *Shinseinen* from 1949 to 1950 and *Hôseki* from 1950 to 1951, *Yatsuhakamura* was a part of Yokomizo's detective Kindaichi Kôsuke series that had ignited an orthodox detective story boom in the immediate postwar. Not to miss out on the success of this work, the publisher Kadokawa shoten created a pocket book version of this story in 1971 as the first story in a series of works by Yokomizo who had basically stopped writing in the early 1960s thanks to the popularity of the Social School. Appealing to a younger generation of readers with the help of their movie versions, the Kadokawa pocket book series brought on a massive Yokomizo Seishi boom in the 1970s with over 40 million copies of the series sold by 1979.

It is against this backdrop of the dissolution of the Social School and the rise of the revivalist movement that the stories in this collection were produced, tasked to negotiate the tenuous relationship between social mystery and orthodox detective fiction. And if such negotiation was to take place within the realistic approach, which many of the writers in this collection were apt to do given their roots in the Social School, then they must have been aware that things had changed since its heyday, as the late

1960s and early 1970s Japan experienced many stumbling blocks in its path of postwar prosperity. Major student protests against corrupt practices of school administration spread like wild fire, often turning violent, and shut down universities across Japan. The United States began to see Japan more as an economic rival, detaching yen from the dollar in 1971 and levying an export embargo on soybeans--needed to make tofu, miso paste, and soy sauce among other Japanese staples--in 1973. And the Oil Shock of 1973 reminded Japan, a land with scant natural resources, that it was wholly dependent on the whims of international economy, as OPEC's decision led to major consumer issues in Japan.

Interestingly, the stories in this collection do not appear to contain markers of such social turmoil during which they were written (perhaps with the exception of the Molotov cocktail, which was used by student protesters). Company gossiping gone too far, insider trading and insurance fraud, struggles of a small business owner, housewives trying to keep up with the Joneses, parental pressure to excel at school--such topics suggest that the normalcy of the period of high economic growth remains in tact. Or one could even argue that many of these stories already foreshadow the blossoming of consumer society in the 1980s when Japan overcame the issues in the 1970s to emerge as a true economic rival of the United States. And precisely by their continued telling of the criminality lurking in the mundane despite the social conditions, these stories, representative detective stories of the first half of the 1970s, seem to reveal the ideological characteristic of social mysteries as that of perpetuating the worldview of normalcy as Japanese prosperity and progress.

Perhaps, it is for this reason that the works of the "neo-social" era would have a long life in the popular consciousness of the Japanese, especially as they were incorporated into the expanding TV industry. Although detective stories had been turned into TV dramas since the late 1960s, it was in the late 1970s and the early 1980s that they became quite popular in Japan when they became two-hour stand-alone works and were shown during primetime. Nishimura's "The Kindly Blackmailer" and Kusano's "Facial Restoration" from this collection were one of the first mysteries to be dramatized for the first of such drama series called "Saturday Nights at the Mysteries," which started in 1977. And in the summer of 1980, Matsumoto Seichô utilized the Japanese boycott of Moscow Summer Olympics to promote a drama series based on this collection (as well as other collections that had been published as a result of collaboration between Japanese publisher and Dannay by then) called *Kessaku Suiri Gekijô* (Night with Mystery Masterpieces) with Dannay appearing at the start of each show in vein of the American TV series *Alfred Hitchcock Presents* (1955-65).

Although the series was not extended beyond the following summer (total of 24 episodes), this series along with the "Saturday Nights at the Mysteries" functioned to establish mystery dramas as a staple of Japanese television during the 1980s and beyond with series such as "Tuesday Nights of Suspense" (Nihon TV, 1981), "The Suspense" (TBS, 1982), and "Monday Night of Drama" (Asahi TV, 1982) quickly following suit. Many if not all of the writers of this collection provided their stories, both new and old, for these primetime dramas that the Japanese people could not get enough of. In particular, Natsuki Shizuko and Nishimura Kyôtarô were the queen and king of primetime TV dramas, with the latter establishing his own genre of so-called travel or train mysteries, which became a huge success in print and on TV from the late 1970s after the success of his 1978 *Blue Train satsujin jiken* (The Murder Case on the Blue Train) about a murder on an overnight train.

Frederic Dannay left Japan after a public interview with Matsumoto Seichô that appeared in the 1978 inaugural issue of *EQ*, renamed as such after a publisher change of the Japanese version of the *Ellery Queen Mystery Magazine* from Hayakawa shôbô to Kôbunsha, that latter being the publisher responsible for the Japanese version of this collection. But even after his departure, the relationship between Ellery Queen and Japan would continue, including Dannay's aforementioned appearance in the TV drama series. After two successful volumes, Kôbunsha would publish the third volume of *Ellery Queen's Japanese Golden Dozen* in 1982. Much to the joy of the project organizers, the third volume was produced at the request not by the publisher but by Dannay who expressed his approval of the detective stories of the "neo-social" era, writing an introduction for the volume titled "The American, English, French Writers Will Learn from the Japanese." And Natsuki Shizuko, who developed a close relationship with Dannay thanks to his visit to Japan, would write her masterpiece *The Tragedy of W*, an homage to the Drury Lane series originally published under Barnaby Ross, in 1982. As if to reciprocate, numerous works by Natsuki were translated into English, appearing in *Ellery Queen Mystery Magazine* throughout the 1980s and beyond.

-Saito Satoru

INTRODUCTION

Dear Reader

When the Suedit Corporation of Tokyo asked me to select twelve stories for the compilation of this volume I asked myself: What do I know about the Japanese detective story? And I had to answer truthfully: almost nothing.

I dug into my memory. I was aware of the short stories written by Edogawa Rampo (pseudonym of Taro Hirai, often called "father of the Japanese mystery"), and had mentioned his work in *Queen's Quorum*, the history I wrote in 1951, and updated in 1969, of the detective-crime short story of the United States, England, and Continental Europe. Edogawa Rampo's name has a familiar sound to Western ears; if one says the name aloud, and keeps repeating it, the names becomes a verbal translation of the Japanese pronunciation of Edgar Allan Poe.

What else did I know of Japanese detective stories?

Nothing.

Confronting the challenge the Suedit Corporation had given me, I ransacked my memory. More than thirty years ago Vincent Starrett, the famous bibliophile, had told me of his researches in the Chinese detective story. I consulted long-forgotten notes and refreshed my memory.

The detective story, as we know it today, was apparently unknown in China until the first translation of the Sherlock Holmes saga, probably in the 1890s. After Holmes (sometimes called Fu-erh-mo-hsi), the deluge. The Chinese writers pitted Sherlock against their beloved ghosts, fox-women, and tiger-men, turning Holmes into a popular hero in their literature for the masses. (How different things are today!)

But in old China, centuries before Poe and Doyle, storytellers had woven tales of criminal investigation and "detective" solutions. For the most part the "detectives" were just and upright magistrates with a passion for righting wrong, for correcting the errors of society and the injustices of fate. The stories, however, were too deeply rooted in the supernatural to be called detective stories as we understand the term today.

Did Japanese detective stories resemble or follow the Chinese tradition? Or did Japanese stories resemble or follow the Occidental tradition?

I asked myself: Have Japanese writers originated detectives of their own in the analytical and deductive school of Poe's Dupin, Doyle's Sherlock Holmes, and Ellery Queen? Are there tough Japanese private eyes like Dashiell Hammett's Sam Spade, Raymond Chandler's Philip Marlowe, and Ross Macdonald's Lew Archer? Have Japanese writers created super-sleuths like Agatha Christie's Hercule Poirot and Rex Stout's Nero Wolfe? A courtroom detective like Erle Stanley Gardner's Perry Mason? A priest detective like G. K. Chesterton's Father Brown? A scientific detective like R. Austin Freeman's Dr. Thorndyke? Are the official detectives of Japanese fiction like George Simenon's Inspector Maigret or more procedural like John Ball's Virgil Tibbs or the men of Ed McBain's 87th Precinct?

There was only one way for me to find out: read whatever histories of the Japanese detective story I could locate, and perhaps more relevant, read the stories sent to me by the Suedit Corporation from which I was to prepare this volume.

From James B. Harris' Preface to Edogawa Rampo's *Japanese Tales of Mystery and Imagination* and from Katsuo Jinka's "Mystery Stories in Japan" (in the February 1976 issue of The Armchair Detective), I learned that until 1923 "no Japanese writer had attempted a modern detective story".

In the beginning the old-style mystery story was known in Japan only through the tales of court trials imported from China. But as long ago as 1660 Japanese writers began to fashion similar tales; the most famous was Saikaku Ihara's *Records of Trials Held Beneath a Cherry Tree* (1689).

So far there was merely a duplication of the Chinese tradition. But in the Meiji period (1868–1912), Japanese writers broke with the Chinese tradition and a new era began. Still no native Japanese stories were written, but the Chinese imports gave way to a flood of translations of Western detective classics—the works of Poe and Doyle, of course, and of Wilkie Collins, Emile Gaboriau, Anna Katharine Green, R. Austin Freeman, G. K. Chesterton, and others, most of these translations appearing as serials in Japanese newspapers. Apparently, in the mystery field, there was no fear of the blending of cultures, no attempt to protect Japanese writers and readers from the intrusion of a foreign influence.

Then, in 1923, Edogawa Rampo founded a native Japanese school. "The first original Japanese mystery story", according to James B. Harris, was Rampo's short story "Nisen Doka" (The Two-Sen Copper Coin), which appeared in *Shin-seinen* (New Youth), the only mystery magazine published in all Japan at that time. The detective tie with China, if not with the West, was broken forever.

Next we studied the historical data supplied by the Suedit Corporation. The modern Japanese detective story can be divided into three periods. The first began with Edogawa Rampo in 1923 and ended just before World War II. It is called the Tantei era; Tantei means "to solve a puzzle", and the emphasis in this period was on the qualities that distinguished The Golden Age of the Detective Story in the West (1920–40)—pure puzzles stressing ingenuity, complexity, bafflement, and surprise.

The middle period shifted the emphasis from "unrealistic" puzzles to "social" detective stories. This second period is called the Suiri era; Suiri means "to reason". In these social detective stories, with the work of Seicho Matsumoto the dominant influence, a more literary and more realistic approach took over. Greater attention was paid to credible motivation, to the dictates of human nature, and to the events of everyday life. The nature of crime also changed. No longer was the crime of or by the individual the focal point; instead, the stories dealt with political crimes, corruption in high places and in industry, gangster organizations, and social evils. It might be said that the Japanese detective story had come of age.

The third period, still in process, is in essence a continuation, a further development and growth of the social detective story.

This is usually called the Neo-Social era—detective fiction of today and tomorrow (until the stories of a fourth period begin to emerge). The writers in this collection belong to the third period. Examples of their work, chosen from more than 2500 short stories published in Japan since 1970, were gathered by a special Japanese Mystery Committee, and the twelve stories finally selected by Ellery Queen for this volume represent a cross-section of the contemporary Japanese genre.

The publication of mystery stories in Japan is more than a flourishing business—it is experiencing an extraordinary boom. Each month an average of 30 books and 40 short stories are published. Ten years ago the sale of mystery books totaled approximately 14,000,000 copies; this year it is estimated that more than 20,000,000 copies of hardcover and paperback mysteries will be published by Japanese devotees of the detective story. One of the reasons for this tremendous popularity is that "mysteries provide an escape from Japan's nervous urban life". But another reason will strike Western readers as unusual: most Japanese commute to work by train, and their favorite reading, as relaxation before and after the serious problems of the day, is a good detective story.

The major Japanese writers today are considered to be Yoh Sano, Seiichi Morimura, and Shizuko Natsuki, together with the above-mentioned Seicho Matsumoto, all of whom are contributors to this anthology; but the older writers, Edogawa Rampo and Masahi Yokomizo, still have a large number of loyal fans. Masashi Yokomizo published *The Honjin Murder Case* in 1947, and last year his books sold 3,000,000 copies; at the age of 71 he was still an active writer.

The most popular Western detective writers are Agatha Christie and Ellery Queen, followed by Freeman Wills Crofts (a rather surprising favorite), John Dickson Carr, G. K. Chesterton, Erie Stanley Gardner, and S. S. Van Dine (another surprise); but most of the important Western detective writers are translated and widely read. Whereas *Shin-seinen* (New Youth) was the only mystery magazine in Japan in 1923 (it was founded in 1920 and continued publication until 1950), there are now ten major publishers in the Japanese detective field. Mystery magazines include *Hoseki* (The Jewel) *Lock*, *The Phantom Castle*, and *Shosetsu Gendai*; the Japanese edition of *Ellery Queen's Mystery Magazine* is 20 years young and still going strong.

In the United States we have an organization called the Mystery Writers of America; in England there is the Crime Writers Association: and in Japan there is the Association of Mystery Writers of Japan[*] (Nihon Suiri Sakka Kyokai), founded by Edogawa Rampo. The Japanese association gives two annual awards comparable to the American Edgar and to the English Gold Dagger—the Edogawa Rampo Memorial Award to a new writer and the A.M.W.J. Award to the best Japanese mystery novel of the year.

And now let us consider the stories in this volume. The ideal detective-crime-mystery story of today, in the eyes of Japanese writers and critics, is "one which, although written around a believable framework, is first and foremost a detective fiction". And that definition is exemplified and adhered to in most of the stories that make this volume.

The twelve stories in this book offer you detection of all types—deductive, intuitional, and procedural—and a "compleat calendar of crime" ranging from theft and poisoning to blackmail and murder. You will meet a variety of crime investigators, of both official and amateur, including legal, journalist, and scientific detectives, in locales as different as a police inquest, a barber shop, a hospital, and a luxurious hotel. You will find in the diverse styles humor and horror, in the diverse plots "vampires" and villains—hours of excitement and escape, of suspense and suspension of disbelief, days of entertainment and adventure,

---

[*] There is confusion in my mind as to the correct name of the Japanese counterpart of Mystery Writers of America, and the correct names of its annual awards. In my research I have come upon no less that ten different versions, four of the organization and six of the awards. Whatever the reason for so many variants, I have used the names as they appeared in the translations available to me.

and weeks of afterthoughts about the serious problems of modem living.

Only a few Japanese detective stories, perhaps less than a dozen, have been translated into English and published in the United States; and probably no more than that in Europe. The Japanese mystery is therefore unknown to almost all American readers, and Western critics have had little or no opportunity to judge its qualities. As a result, the influence of the Japanese mystery has been negligible, if not nonexistent. It is hoped that the publication of this volume will prove to be a breakthrough in the current history of the Eastern detective-crime story.

" Ellery Queen "
Frederic Dannay

Ellery Queen's Japanese Mystery Stories
from Japan's Greatest Detective and Crime Writers

EITARO ISHIZAWA

Too Much About Too Many

Eitaro Ishizawa was born in Manchuria and began to write detective stories in 1963. He is noted for his ingenuity and for the wide range of his source material, which includes art, biology, history, and archeology. Although he has published relatively few books so far, each one is a fine work written with carefully developed plot and ideas.

His story introduces Police Inspector Kono in the case of a murder that occurred on Friday the 13th during an end-of-year party—a murder with 13 witnesses. The victim is a good man, respected and trusted, the soul of discretion, the Father Confessor of the 13 suspects—not at all the sort of man who kills or is killed. A baffling mystery—but Inspector Kono is a cool, patient criminologist. . . .

WHEN POLICE INSPECTOR KONO got into the car in F, where the prefectural capital was located, he said to himself, "This case will drag on for a long time."

Since the war, scientific investigation had become the byword of the police world. Mention of such things as the sixth sense was avoided. Still, Kono knew that what was called intuition was really the result of many years' accumulated experience. Though he did not oppose the principle of system, which condemns putting too much emphasis on experience, Kono knew that intuition was at work in a police investigation.

Officer Satohara had come in the car to meet Kono from the local police branch office in S Spa, where the incident had occurred. Kono asked him, "Where'd they set up investigation headquarters?"

He meant the headquarters that had been established for investigation of the murder of Taro Usami.

Satohara gripped the wheel firmly. "They've rented a house not far from the Happiness Inn."

"A house, eh?"

"Yeah. The garden house of a local rich man named Sakai."

"That's real nice."

The death had taken place at the inn. It was impossible to set up investigations in a commercial lodging, and the local police office in S Spa was too small. Happily, they found a suitable place to investigate a murder that had ironically occurred in a place called Happiness Inn.

Officer Satohara said, "Chief Takahashi's eager to see you."

"Oh?"

If Satohara's words had been uttered by an experienced detective, they might have been taken for gross flattery that could only be ignored. But Kono glanced at Satohara's childish, tense face in the rearview mirror and thought how it could only be maybe two years since this young man was appointed a police officer. He had probably gone into police school immediately after graduating from high school and had been in a front-line police office now for no more than eighteen months. Innocently, he probably believed and tried to practice the motto that police exist for the sake of citizens and swallowed everything his seniors told him. In fact, he likely deified his seniors and had a dazzling image of Kono, Kono judged these things from the stiffness of movements and the flushed color of the young man's face.

"How d'you like working in a police branch office?"

"Very interesting. I mean, I enjoy my work."

"That's real nice."

Trying to use soft words to relax Satohara, Kono recalled what Chief Inspector Kimura had said to him that morning. Depending on how they were taken, his words, too, could be regarded as flattery. Kimura told Kono that he was sending him to act as assistant head inspector in the case of the death of Taro Usami, which had taken place the night before. "The boys down there figure the case is solved once you've been assigned to it. Especially, Takahashi. I guess it's a case of leaving anything connected with big business to you. Do your best."

There are two ways of using people: cajolery and pressure. Kimura adopted the first. His policy was to praise.

But Kimura did not make up the part about big business, and the inference to Kono's aptitude. Kono enjoyed this reputation throughout the entire group in the prefectural department. It was said that in a hundred percent of all cases, if a murder involved the internal conditions of some business concern, Kono would find who did it.

Kono had a long career in the second department, which dealt with corruption, fraud, and similar offenses and which handled cases connected with government organs and commercial enterprises. A man in charge of this department for ten years has no choice but to become a specialist in company organizations and the mental attitudes and reactions of executives and employees. Kono had been transferred to the first department, handling homicide cases, four years ago. His long experience in the second department stood him in good stead. Aside from spontaneous killings, murders taking place within companies often bore connections with grudges and ill will. Kono's knowledge of the inside and outside of white-collar workers' minds was valuable.

It was nine in the morning when the car pulled out of the city of F and headed for S Spa. The police car was caught in the heavy traffic of the rush hour. This gave Kono time to think about the death of Taro Usami. From Kimura, Kono knew the general outline of the case. But he thought, "Still, they've acted fast."

The incident had occurred at nine thirty, Friday night, December 13. Chief Takahashi of the S branch office had set up investigation headquarters at eight the next morning. This was fast work, in spite of the close communications maintained with prefectural headquarters.

Kono regarded the chief's action as especially astute, because it required courage to determine whether death had been murder or suicide in cases of this kind. On the other hand, he had misgivings about hasty judgment.

The facts were simple. The general business office of the Sanei Electrical Thermal Engineering Company, located in the city of F, had been holding an end-of-year party in the main room of the Happiness Inn at S Spa. Thirteen staff members and the company managing director attended. It was the right time of year for such a party: employees had received their bonuses only five days earlier.

The party began at seven and reached a peak by nine. Formalities were set aside in the generally relaxed mood. Though the S Spa is only thirty minutes from the city, most of the men decided to spend the night. Word had it that the waitresses in the hotels and hostesses in bars in this resort town would sleep with customers for low rates.

Suddenly, Taro Usami, head of the personnel department, showed signs of acute suffering and was dead in five minutes. A great commotion followed.

Chief Takahashi was called at once. He immediately initiated investigations by questioning thirteen witnesses.

In questioning, he determined that death had been murder and that the employees in the inn kitchen were not responsible. He made contact with prefectural headquarters and set up local headquarters for the investigation of the murder. The direct cause of death had been a highball containing potassium cyanide. Usami had only one more year before retirement.

"Fast work," Kono thought. It took courage to decide the killer was one of the thirteen other participants at the party. Kono believed the solution to a case often depended on the speed of initial investigation and quick decision on whether the death was accidental or murder. But for some reason, when he got into the car that morning, he had the notion the case would drag on for a long time.

He recalled a case in which he had stumbled years ago. He had been on the force only seven years, and had just been made an assistant police inspector. Immediately after promotion he had been lax, and this case developed. It was an instance of youthful error. Thanks to the warm help of his superior, Inspector Takami, the matter concluded without serious consequences. But even now, thinking about it, he broke into a cold sweat.

"It's stupid," he muttered, shaking his head to rid himself of the mean memory.

The car pulled into S Spa. Kono saw the sign on the door of the rented private house: "Investigation Headquarters."

2

Kono sensed a fever of activity as he stepped into the entrance hall. Inspector Takahashi greeted him. They had met before. Still, being met personally by the man in charge gave him a heavy awareness of what the staff expected of him.

"We're running through secondary inquiries, right now," Takahashi said quickly, leading Kono into a small room next to the entrance hall. He told him the general results of the first inquiries. Nodding, Kono said from time to time, "I see," and "Oh, really?"

What Takahashi had to say boiled down to two main points. First, Taro Usami was not the type person that anyone in the company would resent or hold a grudge against. Second, each of the other thirteen people in the room at the time had had a chance to pop the potassium cyanide into Usami's highball.

"The party began at seven. By nine thirty, nobody was feeling any pain. None can recall when Usami drank the drink. That gets me."

"Who made the drink?"

"Well, there's a shortage of waitresses. So these people did a kind of self-service. They all brought bottles and put 'em in one corner of the room. Anybody who wanted a drink helped himself."

"I see."

"But what worries me is Usami's personality. Everybody praised him. I don't think they're lying, either. They really liked him. I can't lay my hands on a motive." He made a face. "But, you know, that company's really piling up loot. I was surprised to hear how much bonus they pay. The bonus of an office girl at Sanei is equal to mine."

"Yeah. An interesting company."

"You know something about it?"

"A little. Seven years ago, there was a case of corruption in the local city office. Sparks flew around Sanei. I ran an internal check on 'em."

"You really know your companies, don't you?"

Kono realized he knew more about Sanei than anybody else on the police. After all, it was a firm he'd had his eyes on since his days in the second department. His remark that Sanei was an interesting company reflected experience and knowledge.

Sanei belonged to a contradictory business type, frequent among companies having demonstrated rapid economic growth, in which business is very good but the company unstable. It paid good dividends and still had a sound internal reserve. The cancer eating away at the company and making it unstable was a two-cause result: strife and factionalism among the executives and conflicts on the labor-union front. On two occasions in five years, presidents and managing directors had been dramatically forced out. Not many companies have such a tempestuous domestic life. Within the sixty staff members, there were two labor unions, each violently opposed to the other.

The major cause of this situation was the nature of the company itself. It had been formed fifteen years earlier by ten small electrical companies who were just beginning to develop. Each company came equipped with its own set of executives and labor unions. Labor unions tend to split up in companies that are new and lack tradition. There seemed no hope of compromise between the two groups at Sanei. The first union called the second the Establishment, and the second criticized the first for being radicals. It was only the steady supply of outstanding, independent technicians, attracted by high salaries, who worked for the company that enabled Sanei to show good business results.

Kono knew these details because of his experience with the second department.

Takahashi said, "Come, sit in on the second interrogation."

"O.K." Kono followed Takahashi from the room.

The purpose of the second questioning was to track down discrepancies in testimony given at the first, which had taken place from two to ten in the morning.

Kono glanced over the brief history of Taro Usami and the list of thirteen suspects that Takahashi had given him. He then read the history of Taro Usami with special care. There were too many names on the list for him to form any images without personal meetings. Still, he made mental notes of some of their vital statistics:

> Managing Director, Kenzo Yokomizo, age 58, 5 years in firm.
> Business Bureau Chief, Yozo Misumi, 40, 5 years with firm.
> Business Department Chief, Akira Atsuta, 33, 4 years in firm.
> Saburo Matsushita, 29, 5 years with firm.
> Shinkichi Harada, 28, 2 years with Sanei.
> Yoshio Ozaki, 28, also 2 years.
> Haruko Nagai, 28, 2 years with firm.
> Personnel Department staff:
> Shiro Shibaura, 31, 5 years with firm.
> Yuzo Nakanishi, 31, 5 years in firm.
> Junichi Murayama, 29, 2 years.
> Tetsu Nakajima, 26, 1 year.
> Yasuko Ikenami, 25, 1 year.
> And typist, Yumiko Murase, 33, 5 years with firm.

3

One by one, each of the thirteen was summoned from the Happiness Inn, not far away. They were subjected to penetrating questioning. Some seemed nervous, others quite calm. As Kono listened, Taro Usami, the victim, was the thing most firmly fixed in his mind. He believed that, without a clear understanding of the victim's authority and place in the company and of his personality, it was impossible to form an image of the murderer. Whenever he asked a question, it invariably pertained to Usami.

To Kenzo Yokomizo: "Mr. Usami was with the company for ten years, longer than any of you. He was a college graduate. Can you suggest any reason for his slow rise in the firm?"

To Yozo Misumi: "Mr. Usami was the head of the personnel department for seven years. Why did he remain in this position so long?"

To Akira Atsuta: "Was Mr. Usami popular among the technicians?"

To Saburo Matsushita: "Did Mr. Usami seem to favor one or the other of the two labor unions?"

To Yumiko Murase: "Was Mr. Usami popular with the women employees?"

From the answers to such questions, Kono developed a clear image of Usami's personality and learned why, in spite of new executive staffs every five years, Usami had not moved from the position of chief of the personnel department. Of others who had entered the company at the same time as Usami, not one person remained. Many had been forced to leave as a consequence of becoming enmeshed in the factions surrounding the executive positions. Throughout all this turmoil, Usami had persisted in being neutral: See no evil, hear no evil, speak no evil.

Why should someone who tried to remain unbiased and fair in all things fail to advance? A company was a living thing with an elaborate interweaving of subtle emotions. The man who tried to remain in the neutral position in conflicts was disliked by both sides. He was labeled unreliable. He could even be thought a double-dealer or timeserver. Though not forced to leave the company with the followers of the defeated executive team, he was not regarded seriously by the winning group. Because of conditions of this kind, Usami had remained the head of the personnel department. There was nothing to indicate whether Usami adopted this policy of neutrality out of principle or for utilitarian reasons.

But it was part of his personality, or so it seemed. He had entered Sanei Thermal Engineering at forty-five. For twenty years before that, he had been a white-collar worker for another firm. Thirty years of work in business probably made it a habit to want peace at any price. As simple proof, Kono pointed out to himself Usami's office nickname: the Quiet Man.

Although slow to speak, Usami had not been narrowminded. This was suggested by his willingness to listen to anybody's complaints, dissatisfactions, secrets. People often carried their griefs to him because they knew they were safe in telling Usami. The Quiet Man would never repeat anything he heard to a third party. Kono was strongly impressed with this aspect during questioning.

Kenzo Yokomizo said, "I trusted him entirely. He was the closest-mouthed man I've ever known."

Shinkichi Harada said, "It's not so much that I relied on him. But he'd listen to any complaint no matter what. Often, I met him on the way home, talked, and got what was troubling me off my chest. He was completely good."

Haruko Nagi remembered him fondly. "Oh, in that sense, you could trust him entirely. Mr. Usami'd never repeat anything you told him."

But there were others who were critical. For instance, Yuzo Nakanishi said, "Oh, sure, he'd listen to you. But he never suggested anything, or gave advice. He'd just sit and listen. In that sense, you couldn't rely on him. But since most people already have an answer to their problem before they tell anybody about it, they're generally content to have a listening partner. Even if you criticized the top execs, you knew you were safe talking with Usami." Though he made the comment that it was not possible, in a sense, to rely on Usami, he ended by praising him.

A man to whom everyone told his troubles. A man everybody trusted, because he would not betray them. Is this the kind of man that gets murdered?

Chief Takahashi decided it was murder. He did so on the basis of Usami's attitude displayed until he began suffering from the poison. A person intending to kill himself usually reveals excitement of one kind or another. Everybody said Usami had been enjoying drinking. This was not the nature of a suicide. The high opinion held of Usami flustered Takahashi. The investigation team noted this.

By four that afternoon, all employees of Sanei had returned to their homes.

In a scholarly tone, but with a certain excitement, Chief Takahashi said, "Usami's family life was peaceful and content. He had no outstanding debts. His hobby was the inexpensive one of gardening. He was liked by his neighbors. In other words, he was a fine member of society about whom nobody had anything bad to say. I know of only one case of murder like this."

"What's that?" Assistant Inspector Iizuka asked, with a look of disbelief. The other members of the investigation team shared this look.

"It's in my imagination. Somebody in the company tells Usami an important secret. Later, he thinks, 'I've done it, now. If Usami spills that, it's all up with me.' Then this guy gets the idea of killing Usami. . . ."

One of the team objected, "But Usami was famous for keeping secrets."

"Yes. But if the secret was very important, the person who told it might become the victim of terrible doubts," Kono said, thinking that Takahashi had something.

Another of the team said, "I can't help thinking the police chief's explanation relies too much on imagination."

There was some substantiation to this objection. Takahashi, disgruntled, said no more. An uncomfortable silence ensued.

Could it have been suicide? Kono felt this doubt among the members of the group. No one voiced it. They had investigated the case as murder to this point.

Pressure of duties had made administrative employees kill themselves. Often these suicides paid no attention to their surroundings. During rush hour, they leaped in front of oncoming trains, or hurled themselves from office windows during work hours. Usami might fit this category.

A veteran detective named Hosobe, asked, "Chief, couldn't it be suicide?" It was a brave gesture under the circumstances. Kono had heard that Takahashi and Hosobe did not get along well.

Takahashi said clearly, "Right now, I'm not considering suicide. In the first place, there's nothing in Usami's daily life to warrant suicide. In the second place, potassium cyanide looks like a planned killing. There was no suicide note. And, two days before the party, Usami himself bought plane tickets for a business trip to Tokyo. . . ."

"I see." Hosobe seemed convinced for the moment. The investigation was ploughing ahead for murder, and Hosobe lacked sufficient confidence to try to call it to a halt.

Turning to Kono, Takahashi said, "How d'you make it?"

"You mean murder or suicide?"

"Yeah."

Kono folded his arms. "I think the chief's right. It seems like it's murder. Forgive me for being vague."

Takahashi asked, "I get the feeling the investigation's bogged down in questioning. What d'you say?"

"Earlier, you said everybody was prepared for Usami to keep

their secrets. Maybe it's related to the heart of the matter. I'm not saying it points directly to a conclusion, but it might be a good notion to examine the issue from the viewpoint of what's happened in the company." Kono glanced around, scowling, then said, "Right now, the idea of self-defense is especially strong in commercial enterprises and their staffs. To give a simple example— a bank where embezzlement's occurred. It's possible to make preparations. Let's say the amount is five million yen. The bank will certainly deal with this within the limits of its own organization and not let word leak to the outside. After all, banks require the customers' trust. If Usami'd heard an important company secret—and if this is the cause from which the crime grew, the investigation . . ." Kono paused. Then he slowly added, "Will be very difficult."

One of the investigation team had come in and was whispering something to Takahashi. Wrinkling his forehead, Takahashi said, "The lab report says the only clear prints on the glass are Usami's. There are other smears, can't be identified. Another thing, potassium cyanide is used by Sanei. Strictly controlled, but an employee could probably get it if he wanted it bad enough."

The room was heavy with silence.

That night, Kono found it difficult to sleep. His mind was busy with the Usami case. His intuition told him it was murder. But he was convinced some secret was concealed behind the matter. He had talked of self-defense in commercial enterprises and their staffs. He'd given a bank as an example. But cases like this were not limited to banks. They could be found in the police department itself. Instances of embezzling occurred in the police and were dealt with without publicity. The police, too, required the trust of the people. While uncovering crime, they had to eliminate such from within their own ranks. Kono recalled the mistake he'd made in his youth. It embarrassed him to think of it, though it could not really be called a crime. . . .

Just promoted to assistant inspector, he went through a brief period when he lowered his standards slightly. As the person in charge of economics-related crime, he had to deal with illegal practices in horse and bicycle racing. This meant he often traveled to the tracks. One day—he must have been bewitched—

he suddenly found he'd bought bets on a race and that he'd made a large winning. Although he realized it could be the start of involvement with other kinds of gambling, he began taking a lively interest in horse races and bicycle races. There was no rule that a policeman must not gamble. But there was an unwritten law that they should exercise self-control. Because he had a guilty conscience, Kono avoided the tracks in F city and attended regional ones.

One day, when he had lost all the money he'd brought with him, he felt someone tapping his shoulder. Turning, he saw Wakamoto, the head of a small loan-company.

"The afternoon race is the big one," he said casually. "Want me to let you have some money?"

Wakamoto had noticed that Kono's funds had run out.

"Maybe—"

This was his mistake. Once this kind of borrowing starts, it becomes habit and debts snowball. A policeman is the best kind of customer a small loan-shark can have. Because of his work, he cannot kick back. Before Kono knew it, he had borrowed more than he could pay off. Interest piled up, and the debt increased. He knew he must do something. The days rolled relentlessly by.

One day, his superior, Inspector Takami, called him. The two went to an out-of-the-way restaurant. Seated, Takami said, "I consider you a talented man. Your promotion to assistant inspector was the fastest in the department, ever. It makes me proud of you. But you've got into debt, right?"

"What?"

"You're dealing with a nasty customer. Wakamoto's tied up with gang financing."

The blood drained from Kono's face. Takami knew everything.

"How much can you scrape up from friends and relatives?"

The conversation swept on, and Kono was powerless to resist. After all stones were turned, Kono was still short one million yen. Takami lent it to him out of his own pocket, saving him from a bad predicament. Kono considered Takami a great benefactor from that time on.

Takami had happened to spot Kono's name in Wakamoto's books when he was making a check. His foresight saved Kono from a serious black mark, both in and out of the police force. He'd certainly have been disgraced if he'd been publicly exposed in the books of a petty loan-shark.

Kono learned from the mistake. First, he gained a true understanding of what it meant to be a policeman. Second, he saw the police as an organization that acted speedily to cover whatever unfortunate events occurred within its limits. Kono realized that Takami had also taken the step to protect his own position as a ranking officer on the force. Unreliable people in the department would have brought a black mark against him as well.

Since then, Kono had been so severe on ethical points that he'd earned the nickname, the Hard Guy. His mistake proved a good tonic that later brought him immense trust. He had to grow to the point where he could take a cool, professional look at everything happening above him in the organization. Kono understood the self-defense syndrome in big business. He suspected Taro Usami's death was connected in some way with the self-defense feelings of the company or someone on its staff. A sense of smell developed through years of experience led him to this belief. Difficulty in falling asleep, because of the Usami case, was shared with Kono by all thirteen of the people who had been questioned.

Kenzo Yokomizo was wide awake. "I didn't lie. That's certain. It's just that I didn't volunteer information on some things. Still . . ." He tossed, turned. "Why'd I shoot my mouth off about a secret to Usami? I knew what he said wouldn't do any good. He had no talent. He wasn't forceful. All he did was work hard. But, whenever I was alone with him, I always wanted to talk. Must've been because I knew he'd never tell what I said. That day, on the way home from work, I met him—invited him to a restaurant, and after a few drinks, started talking."

"Promise not to tell anybody, but . . ."

A month before, representatives of the large electrical firm K had held a secret discussion with Yokomizo. It was a sounding out on the subject of merger. The K company was weak in the heating and air-conditioning department and had its eye on Sanei's outstanding technical staff.

K Company, knowing that Kiyose, the president of Sanei, hated the idea of big firms, put feelers out to Yokomizo. Terms were good. For bait they offered him a director's chair. Obviously, he took the bait. He was already at a deadlock with Kiyose anyway.

Their strategy demanded secrecy. Using an affiliate's name, the K company would buy up miscellaneous Sanei shares. Then, at a general stockholders' meeting, they would demand the resignation of President Kiyose, work out something to conciliate the executive staff, etc. This project was already deeply, silently underway.

Yokomizo bit his lip. Why had he let Usami in on such an important secret? Of course, he couldn't tell anyone about the letter he'd received from Usami on the eighth, about what he'd done to comply with that letter. If he let that out, he would become an important suspect in the Usami murder.

A sleepless night visited Yozo Misumi: "Usami was probably murdered, but I didn't kill him. But why—why did I tell him about *that?*"

The whole affair had ended in four months. It was only a game for her, a way to work out her frustrations because her diabetic husband couldn't satisfy her. It wasn't the first time Misumi had been to bed with another man's wife. But all the other affairs had ended with nobody the wiser. If this one should be known, it would be fatal for Misumi. He had picked the wrong woman.

That day, driving down a busy street, he glanced out the window and saw a woman wave to him.

"Give you a lift?" he asked. She was carrying a shopping bag.

"That's great."

"Get in, then."

She did, then said, "Why, it's not even three o'clock." She smiled. "On a day like this, I bet the country air's fresh and clean." When he thought back, Misumi knew what a clever invitation it had been.

"Why not drive out to the Cape?" he said.

"What about your work?"

"Conference just ended. It's O.K.," he said, turning the wheel.

"I hear you're real cool with the girls."

He said nothing.

"My husband told me."

Then, the conversation took a softer turn.

Many of the men said she was too good for her old man. As the rumors suggested, she had a youthful, fresh body.

Misumi thought he would never tell. The only person who had known she was Shigeko Kiyose, the wife of the company president, was Taro Usami. He knew because Misumi told him.

He no longer had anything to do with her. When they passed on the street they pretended not to know each other. Still, though it was all over, if it were ever discovered . . . After all, she was the president's wife. This meant the issue wouldn't be settled on the basis of individual privacy alone. He certainly couldn't tell anyone about the letter—dated the eighth—that he'd received from Usami. If that got out, he would be a suspect in a murder case.

Saburo Matsushita, of the business staff, had an introspective personality. His reflective thinking tended to be gloomy. He, too, suffered because he'd told Usami something he should never have mentioned.

"It's tragic. . . ." That was how he started; then he told Usami everything.

Matsushita had homosexual tendencies. It wasn't that he was completely uninterested in women. He swung both ways. But, if his ideal type man appeared, that was a strong magnet, and he was iron filings.

"My trouble's I'm not attracted to gay men. They turn me off. For me, a man has to be normal. What does this mean? No sex. Because normal men find gays repulsive.

"But my ideal has turned up. Promise not to tell this to anyone, but it's the head of the business department, Akira Atsuta. He's a sportsman, efficient and good at his work. He's my ideal. But how's this for irony? He wants me to marry his niece. Of course, I'll marry her. That way I'll have him with me always, as a relative."

Matsushita berated himself. Why had he made such a personal confession to a department head—the head of the personnel department, at that. And the wedding was scheduled for the following spring! Then, there was that confidential letter from Usami, dated the eighth.

Sometimes Matsushita had wanted to kill Usami. Then Usami died. The thought that he had for a moment wished his death tormented Matsushita. "I didn't kill him. But . . ."

Shiro Shibaura, of the personnel department, was deeply happy that Usami died. If he'd gone on living and had sent more of those letters, Shibaura might have killed himself.

He had vowed never to tell anybody about that, not at the cost of his own life. Then, why had he told Usami? It must have been because Usami reminded him of a priest. A priest is forbidden to tell what he hears in a confessional. At the time, he felt as if he were confessing to a priest.

"Please—listen . . ." he had sobbed. Then he virtually clung to Usami, telling him about the hit-and-run killing.

He hadn't been to blame, that much was clear. He was on his way home from a bar. Near an apartment building, a fat man suddenly jumped in front of him. It happened quickly. Though he'd had only one beer, he had been drinking. Almost without thinking, he started the engine again. He did not look back.

The following morning, he looked at the paper. He remembered reading the item timidly. To his surprise, the victim had been a managing director of the S Commercial Company, one of Sanei's important customers. Not only that, he'd been coming to the apartment building where his secret girlfriend lived. For a time rumors ran rampant. But the scandal about the director grew to such proportions that almost everybody lost interest in it as an incident of hit-and-run.

If he'd kept the matter to himself, it would have ended there. The other guy was clearly wrong. Shibaura had little feeling of guilt except for having driven away from the scene. He had been the only one who knew about it. Why, then, did he feel like confessing to Usami? Psychologically, he felt confession would bring absolution. That was it. Usami had only said, "Yes," and "I see," like a priest. Shibaura had been grateful to Usami.

The confidential letter dated the eighth shocked him, frightened him, and made him want to kill Usami. He had died. Someone had killed him. But wild horses could never drag the story out of Shibaura.

The typist, Yumiko Murase, may have handled the matter in a cooler way than anybody else. She read the letter, dated the eighth, at seven on the evening of the ninth. Because she lived in a small satellite town of the city F, it took a day for the letter to reach her. It arrived in the morning while she was at work. She read it that evening:

"A need for money has come up. Please transfer one hundred thousand yen to general account 821–5613 at the S bank, no later than December eleventh."

It was signed Taro Usami. There were two days left before the deadline for the transfer.

On the morning of the eleventh, Yumiko phoned the office saying she'd be late. At nine ten, she pushed open the door of the local branch where she did her banking. The Sanei company made transfers of salaries and bonuses to its employees' banks. Yumiko's end-of-year bonus should have been transferred to her account December 7.

Filling out a form with her own account number and indicating she wanted one hundred thousand yen transferred to general account 821–5613 of the S bank, Yumiko hurried to the counter. As she left the bank, she saw a man on the opposite side of the street. It was Akira Atsuta, chief of the business department. He was hurrying and looked pale. No need to be a detective to figure it out. He must have received one of those elegant blackmailing letters from Usami, too, and probably was on his way to do whatever he'd been asked to do.

Yumiko thought, "I wonder what Atsuta told Usami?" In her own case, it had been the kind of man-woman relationship that happens in all companies between high-ranking men and lower-ranking women.

A year before, Yumiko had fallen in love with Mr. S of the technical staff. He was married and had children. From the beginning, it was clear he had no intention of marrying Yumiko. But, he was exciting, attractive—the type Yumiko admired. She was already an old maid at thirty-three and not so pretty, either. The words S used to entice her were of the driest. Late one night, when they were in a bar, both having drunk too much, S said, "Looks like I'll have to spend the night away from home. What d'you say? Lending it to me won't wear it out."

His rude words thrilled her, and they immediately went to

a hotel. They had sex until they were tired of each other's bodies. Then, Yumiko discovered herself pregnant. Handing her two hundred thousand yen for an abortion, S said, "Pretty high rent. This ends everything between us."

Then the humiliation, the suspicious hospital, and the position she had been forced to assume on the surgical table. Then a man—even though a doctor—she'd never seen before did what he liked with the part of her body he should never have touched. The scalpel, which she feared, invaded her body. While understanding she was paying for something she had done, she suffered a festering wound.

Even an old maid left on the shelf has her pride. It was to cleanse herself of the resentment she felt for S that Yumiko confessed the ugly truth to Usami. Then she received that nonchalant letter. She had no choice but to comply with his demand.

For those who received the official-looking blackmail letters, Usami's death was a shock. Nor were Yokomizo, Misumi, Matsushita, and Shibaura the only recipients. There were also Atsuta, Nakanishi, Murayama, Nakajima. . . .

All had two things in common. First, they suspected someone had murdered Usami and suffered both anger and fear at the sight of Usami's odd right-slanting script, in which the letters were written. Second, they had made up their minds to remain eternally silent about what they had confessed to him and about the way they had complied with the demands in the letters. If any one of them were pushed to extremes and mentioned either of these things, he would become a murder suspect.

4

Six months after the incident, headquarters for the Taro Usami murder case was closed. It had been a cold winter. Now it was late May, with the greenery of trees inviting the eye to rest. As the investigation dragged out, the notion that the death was suicide gained more acceptance. This further retarded the search for a solution, since it lowered morale and robbed men of the enthusiasm essential to a successful investigation. Sarcastic investigators said it bogged down because of rotten luck: the murder took place on Friday the 13th; there were thirteen suspects.

Before the final closing of investigation headquarters, there was a meeting of Takahashi, Kono, and Kimura. Kimura was eager to close headquarters. There was much work in the department, many cases, and tying up too many men on a job that showed no signs of coming to a conclusion seemed a waste. "Calling it murder must've been a miscalculation," he said with regret. Takahashi and Kono were silent, neither agreeing nor disagreeing. But Takahashi looked wretched.

Kono said, "I've no objections to closing headquarters. I don't think new facts will turn up. Still—I don't think we should give up, either. Let's simply reduce the scale of the operation. Put me in charge."

"You mean, you still don't want to give it up?" Kimura asked.

"Yeah. That's right."

"Stubborn?"

"Nope. I'm adopting a waiting policy. Let the other guy tip his hand. I think that's the way—"

"Waiting policy?"

"Yeah. Let me have Shibata and Kawanishi."

"O.K.," Kimura said. "You've got it."

Yumiko Murase, the typist with Sanei, gave notice six months after the murder. She said her mother had died and there was no one at home to look after her father, who had grown old.

It was a fact; her mother had died. Further, the only person home with her father was a third son, who was a second-year student in high school. Under these circumstances, it was hard to block her request. But she was an excellent typist, and they would have liked her to remain. Yumiko persisted, and the company accepted her resignation.

But she had said to a fellow worker, "I don't like the gloomy feeling around here. The murder isn't solved, and everybody suspects everybody else. I can't stand working in such an atmosphere." Maybe this was her true reason.

The day of her resignation, with nothing but a suitcase, she left her apartment. She had given her stereo and TV to one of the girls in the office. She flagged a taxi, and told the driver to take her to the airport. When people from the office who had come to see her off heard this, they must have thought it strange.

Yumiko's home town was a small village in the mountains, three hours by train and another two by bus.

An hour later, she was on a plane. As she watched the city of F receding through the small, round window, she thought without regret, "Well, goodbye to that—"

Yumiko's home town was so small she could not tolerate it even for a day. The city of F was only a provincial town, too, where rumors were always plentiful. The plane was headed for Tokyo, A vast city of twelve million. A cold city where a corpse might not be noticed for a year by neighbors in the next apartment. A good city to hide in. "Crime." A cool smile played over Yumiko's face. She smiled with pride at the thought of the perfect crime she had committed. She touched the case in her lap, the reward. There were a lot of zeros after the first figures in the four bank books in that case. They represented the triumph of the mind.

She had come upon the notion for the crime about a year ago, at the time when there was talk of her marrying. She had begun thinking like a murder novel. Usami knew about S and her abortion. Suppose he should demand money for keeping her secret? Yumiko knew she would probably make the utmost efforts to get that money.

When the marriage fell through, Yumiko expanded the idea. "Now—look at this. . . ." Usami was a money tree. He was just full of private secrets. For one like Usami, who would never get ahead—maybe even precisely because he wouldn't—it would be wonderful to turn all these confessions into money. Next, Yumiko thought, "If he won't do it, why don't I turn them into money myself?"

For a year she made preparations. The most difficult thing was copying Usami's strange right-slanted handwriting. It took a year to do that. The next thing was knowing how much to ask each person for. Finally, she decided to ask for more in the upper echelons of the company. This seemed in keeping with principles of social justice and with ideas of the chivalrous bandit. She would keep the text as simple as possible—and be suggestive. . . .

"A need for money has come up. Please transfer ___ yen to general account 821–5613 at the S bank no later than December eleventh." She signed *Taro Usami*. Taking up her pen, in the letter to Kenzo Yokomizo, she wrote "five million yen." Stopping, she asked herself if this might be too much. Then, with a toss of her head, tightening her abdomen, she said, "Nope. It's a gamble. With gambling, courage is necessary."

Although she knew little about business, lately she had noticed something suspicious about Yokomizo. She did not know what it was, but she felt certain he was up to something. If it were a business secret, he would be willing to pay that much.

Finally, intelligently, she wrote a blackmail letter to herself as a coverup. She wrote in figures for one hundred thousand yen.

Total: thirty-two million one hundred and seventy thousand yen.

On the twelfth of December, she went to the bank to check the account in the name of Taro Usami. All thirteen people—including herself—had paid in the amount she counted on. With the automatic disbursement machine, it was a simple matter to draw the money out.

"A pity about Taro Usami," Yumiko thought. But to make her crime perfect, he must die. When the end-of-year party was a little noisy, taking care to leave no fingerprints, Yumiko set a highball containing potassium cyanide on the table before Usami.

But as the plane swung over Tokyo International Airport, Yumiko murmured, "Stop thinking about the past. The future is ahead of you."

* * *

Inspector Kono was listening to a report by Detective Shibata in an official phone call from Tokyo. Shibata's voice was clearly excited.

"Yumiko Murase's activities since arriving in Tokyo. At a real estate office, she sublet an apartment—two rooms and a dining-kitchen. The building's in Shinjuku Ward, fifteen minutes from the Kabuki-cho entertainment district. She paid deposits and a year's rent, totaling five hundred thousand yen. Next, she negotiated to purchase the management rights and equipment of a nearby coffee shop. Total expenditure was fifteen million yen.

"When she left Sanei, because of outstanding debts, her retirement fund came to only three million yen. Looks as if you're

SEICHO MATSUMOTO

The Cooperative Defendant

Seicho Matsumoto was the first chairman of the Association of Mystery Writers of Japan. He ushered in the second period in the history of the modern Japanese detective story. His novels epitomize the contemporary themes of social problems, with emphasis on realism in the characters and in their motivations. He was the first to establish this social-detective-story genre in Japan, and his books are consistently among the best sellers of the country. He won the Detective Story Writers' Club Prize for his work titled The Face and Other Stories.*

The story he gives us now is representative of his technique and thematic outlook. The victim is a merciless moneylender, the accused a young owner of a noodle shop. The crime is murder, the investigator a legal detective. The style is "documentary real-life"—with a surprise twist at the end. . . .

THE CASE SEEMED SIMPLE. . . .

On an autumn night, a sixty-two-year-old moneylender was clubbed to death in his own home by a twenty-eight-year-old man. The murderer stole a cashbox from the victim's house and fled. The box contained twenty-two promissory notes. Of these notes, the killer stole five, then threw the cashbox into a nearby irrigation pond. The murdered moneylender's house was located in a western part of Tokyo that was beginning to prosper architecturally, but at the time of the killing, the immediate vicinity was still roughly half agricultural fields.

When the young lawyer, Naomi Harajima, received word from his lawyers' association that he had been designated court-assigned counsel for the case, he did not much like the idea and was on the verge of refusing. He already had three private cases on his hands, and they were keeping him occupied.

The president of Harajima's lawyers' association argued that he would very much like him to take the case. It appeared that one other lawyer had already been appointed but had suddenly taken ill. The trial was scheduled for an early date. The court would obviously be embarrassed if no legal representative for the defendant was found.

The president said, "Besides, Harajima—this case is nothing much. Come on, now, man—at least give it the once over. All right?"

Section 3 of Article 7 of the Japanese Constitution makes provision for state-assigned legal counsel in cases where the defendant is too poor or for some other reason unable to procure legal advice (Article 36, Criminal Legal Procedural Code).

Since the state pays, the legal fee is extremely low; busy lawyers usually do not want these cases, though sometimes humane reasons for aiding a defendant enter in. The association attempts to divide these duties among its members on a rotational basis, but any attorney is free to refuse. But something must be done. . . .

Accordingly, cases like this usually find their way into the hands of lawyers who are quite young, or who are not too busy.

Because the fee is small, handling of such cases often becomes less careful than it might otherwise be.

Recently the reputation of the system has improved slightly. But actually, these men, often disinterested or very busy, may do no more than give the case a brief run-through before the trial and meet the defendant for the first time in the courtroom. Things will never be completely remedied until fees for court-assigned counsel are raised.

Harajima was urged to defend Torao Ueki in the case of the murder of Jin Yamagishi, because the work was simple. He finally agreed.

In reading the documents pertaining to the indictment, the records of the criminal investigation, Harajima learned the following things.

Originally, the victim, Jin Yamagishi, had owned a rather large amount of agricultural land. But he had sold this to a realtor. With the money accrued, he built a two-story house and immediately opened a small-scale financing business. This had happened ten years ago. At the time of the murder, Yamagishi lived alone. Childless, his wife had died three years before. Yamagishi rented the second floor of his house to a young primary-school teacher and his wife. The rent was not high, though the old moneylender had a reputation for being greedy. He was impressed because the schoolteacher had a second-dan black belt in judo. In other words, the young man would be a combination tenant and guard.

Any elderly person living alone might want protection. In this case, it was still more important for Yamagishi, since he had made a bad name by charging high interest on the money he lent. Many of his customers were small businessmen trying hard to succeed in a newly developing part of Tokyo. The neighborhood was along one of the private commuter train lines. A good location. But population growth had been slow, and business was not thriving. Some of the people who paid Yamagishi's high rates went bankrupt. There were cases in which older people used their retirement funds to open stores. They put shop and land down as security for loans from Yamagishi. He took everything when they could no longer keep up their payments.

Customers in other districts along the same train line suffered because of Yamagishi's behavior. It was not alone fear of thieves but also the knowledge of the many people who hated him that encouraged the moneylender to install the young judo expert and his wife in the upstairs apartment.

On October 15, the young teacher received word that his mother was close to death. He and his wife left that day for their hometown. The murder took place on October 18, and Yamagishi's body was discovered by a neighbor on the morning of October 19. This person found the front door open (later it was disclosed that all other windows and doors were firmly secured with rain shutters that were locked from within), entered the hallway, and immediately saw Yamagishi stretched out face down in the adjacent room. Fearful, he called out. There was no answer from the inert form.

He reported the matter to the police.

Autopsy revealed the cause of death to be brain concussion and cerebral hemorrhage, caused by a blow on the head. An area about as large as the palm of an adult hand was caved in and flattened at the back of the skull. The wound had been fatal. Yamagishi had tumbled forward and expired in a crawling position. He had apparently been struck from behind and, after falling, had crawled a short distance on hands and knees.

From the contents of the victim's stomach, it was ascertained that he had died about three hours after his last meal. Yamagishi, who cooked for himself, was in the habit of eating dinner around six. This would mean that the murder took place between nine and ten, an assumption that agreed with the autopsy doctor's estimation of lapse of postmortem time.

Nothing in the room was disturbed. In a smaller bedroom next to the one in which the corpse was discovered, a sliding cupboard door was open. The black-painted steel cashbox in which Yamagishi kept his customers' promissory notes and other documents was missing. Japanese-style bedding was spread out on the floor of this room. The top quilt was pulled partly back. The sheets and pillowcase were wrinkled but not violently disordered. This suggested that Yamagishi must have gotten out of bed and walked into the next room. He habitually retired at nine o'clock (testimony of the young teacher and his wife).

It was apparent that Yamagishi had opened the front door of the house himself, letting the murderer in. Usually the door was locked by means of a stout wooden pole forced against the frame in such a way as to make opening from the outside impossible. When the body was discovered this pole stood in the entranceway beside the door. Only Yamagishi could have removed it and opened up from inside.

Someone Yamagishi knew and who knew his habits well must have come to visit.

Why was the greedy, suspicious old man willing to get out of bed and admit someone at the hour of nine o'clock at night?

There were no reported rumors about Jin Yamagishi's masculinity. He was not prohibitively old. But perhaps because of his curious personality or stinginess, from his youth he hadn't much been interested in women. The person who called at nine that night must have been a man.

Not one of the neighbors had heard anybody knocking on the old moneylender's door or calling out to him on the night of the murder. If he had already gone to sleep, anyone who called loud enough to wake him in the inner sleeping room would have been heard. Possibly the telephone had roused him. The instrument stood on a small table in a corner of the room where he slept. The murderer could have called Yamagishi first to tell him he was coming. Yamagishi then removed the pole from the front door and waited. He must have been quite familiar with the person, if this were true. He did not know he waited for his death.

The stolen cashbox gave some hints about the killer. It contained promissory notes from the people who had borrowed from Yamagishi, plus renewals for payment of interest and other promissory contracts. The murderer obviously knew both the contents and the location of the cashbox. His purpose had been to steal the promissory notes.

Under a Buddhist shrine in the house, the detectives discovered 150,000 yen in cash. But nothing was disturbed; there was no trace of the killer's having tried to find it.

Two days after the crime, the police had arrested Torao Ueki.

One of the investigators learned that a Mr. Nakamura, while looking out of his bathroom window, had seen a man hurrying at a run down the street in the direction of Yamagishi's house. This man looked very much like the proprietor of a noodle shop near the train station.

Torao Ueki had opened a noodle shop next to the train station three years earlier. About a year ago, he had purchased some of the neighboring land and expanded and remodeled his shop, not because business was on the upswing, but because he wanted to compete with a new noodle shop in the vicinity. He had hoped that by enlarging and improving his place he would attract more customers. He did not. The number of customers decreased. But to purchase the land and make renovations, he had borrowed money from Yamagishi at a high rate of interest.

With the interest and the drop in business, Ueki was in a tight spot. But he had a hunch that, in a bit, the number of houses in

the neighborhood would increase, causing a rise in daily com-
muters on the trains. His shop was in front of the station, an
excellent location. He decided to stick it out. But Yamagishi's
exorbitant interest payments were getting the better of him. He
couldn't sit back calmly and wait for a brighter tomorrow. From
the age of eighteen till twenty-five, he had worked in a second-
hand bookshop in the center of town. The restaurant business
was completely new to him.

Ueki had suffered deeply because of his connection with Yamagishi. The moneylender was merciless in exacting his due. The
note had been renewed a number of times, and the interest came
to four times the original loan. When the murder took place, Ueki
owed Yamagishi seven and a half million yen. Yamagishi felt that
if the debt rose still more, Ueki would never be able to repay, so
he would assume ownership of the land and shop, which had
been put up as security. This disturbed Ueki terribly and had recently caused trouble. Ueki hated Yamagishi. He told certain persons that he would like to "kill that old man!"

2

There were many other people who hated Yamagishi enough
to kill him. But to be a suspect, there had to be the lack of an
alibi for the hour from nine till ten on the night of the crime.
The suspect had to be known to the victim and have knowledge
that the schoolteacher and his wife were out of town. He had to
posses detailed knowledge concerning the layout of Yamagishi's
house and the exact location of the cashbox. And, judging from
the brutal wound on the back of the victim's head, he had to be
quite strong.

No fingerprints belonging to the killer were discovered. There
were numerous other fingerprints, but they were smeared, except
for some belonging to the couple upstairs. They, though, had the
clear alibi of being in Kyushu at the time of the murder. The
remaining prints probably were those of people who came to see
Yamagishi on financial business. All the prints were old.

The killer left no weapon behind. No suspicious footprints
were found, and the entrance hall was floored with concrete, so
such prints were unlikely. The pole that latched the front door

was considered as a possible murder weapon, yet it seemed too lightweight, slender, to have caused the fatal wound. The only prints on it were Yamagishi's. Yamagishi had been almost completely bald, and had bled little. Neither blood nor hair would be found on the weapon.

Under the eaves at the back of the house was a stack of pine logs, cut for fuel. Town gas had not yet been piped to the area. Most of the residents used bottled propane. Yamagishi, however, in his miserliness and accustomed to farmhouse ways, fired his cooking stove with wood. The pine logs had been carefully split into pieces with roughly triangular cross sections some four centimeters to a side. It seemed that several blows with such a log could cause the kind of wound that killed Yamagishi. Detectives checked the top ten of perhaps thirty bundles of firewood in the stack, but the rough surfaces made it difficult to trace prints. It was, in fact, next to impossible. There were no findings of blood or hair.

With this information on the condition of the body and scene of the crime in his mind, Harajima read the report of the confession made by Ueki:

"Must have been nearly two years ago, I got money from Jin Yamagishi. It was at a damned high rate of interest. Since that time, I suffered because of the debt. Just lately, he made a threat—said he'd auction off my shop and land; they were put up as security for the loan. Everything I had was used to buy the land and open the noodle shop. Later on, I borrowed money from Yamagishi to enlarge and improve my shop. But business didn't go so well. I thought it would be better. That and Yamagishi's crazy demands drove me to despair. Yes. I decided my wife and children, and I, would commit suicide together. But, by God, before I died, I wanted to kill that old man. It would at least be something for the sake of all the other people he brought to grief.

"October 18, I was in the Manpaiso mahjong parlor, maybe two hundred meters from the train station. From maybe seven in the evening, with friends—Nakada, Maeda, and Nishikawa—playing mahjong. Lately, seeing how we don't have many customers, I leave the shop to my wife in the evening, and play mahjong or kill the time one way or the other. We played maybe three games, I think, when Shibata came in and started watching. He comes to the mahjong parlor pretty often. He wanted to join the game. I said, 'Look, I've got to run home for something. Why don't you sit in for me?' It made him happy. I left the Manpaiso at maybe nine o'clock.

"But I didn't go home. I went over to the phone booth in front of the station and called Yamagishi. After a time, he answered. I told him I wanted to talk about him taking my property. I told him I'd managed to get together two million yen and I'd bring it with me right now. I said maybe he could postpone his claim on the land and shop, we could talk. At first he was kind of angry, interrupting, saying he'd gone to bed. Then he smoothed out, changed his mind when I mentioned the money. 'Okay, c'mon over. I'm waiting.' He sounded even impatient.

"It's about a half a mile to Yamagihsi's. After a bit there aren't many houses, only fields and two irrigation ponds. I didn't meet anybody. There are twelve or thirteen houses along by Yamagishi's. But Mr. Nakamura's house is off the street a ways, some distance. I had no idea he'd be able to see me from his toilet window. He eats at our noodle shop.

"Just like he said he would, Yamagishi had opened the door. I knew the teacher and his woman had gone to Kyushu three or four days ago. The teacher eats at the shop. He told me himself.

"Before I went to the door, I went around behind the house. I hunted around and found a chunk of wood from the pile I knew was there. Nobody was home upstairs, either—I made sure. All the windows were shuttered. No sign of light anywhere through the cracks.

"So I went to the door. I stepped into the hallway and called to Yamagishi. He came to meet me. There was a light in the other room. I held the hunk of wood behind me. It was shadowy.

"'You know, it's late,' he said. But he was grinning and didn't seem upset. He was sure as the devil thinking about the two million. 'It's okay, though,' he said. 'C'mon, in.'

"I tried to stall, thinking about the piece of wood. I said something about being sorry to disturb him so late, and all. Told him I'd managed to get together two million yen. I didn't want to leave it home for fear of thieves.

"'C'mon, c'mon,' he said, moving into the next room. He pulled two seat cushions from a stack in the corner and put them by a table. I kept the wood behind me as I stepped up into the main part of the house from the hall. The second I sat on the cushion, I stuck it underneath, behind me, and said, 'I brought the money; how's for writing me a receipt?' I figured the subject of money would keep his attention. I let him see the fake newspaper-wrapped parcel I'd fixed, bulging from my front pocket. He figured it was the money, okay. He jumped up to go into the next room, probably for blank receipts.

"I thought, this is it, and leaped up, too. In one move I smashed him on the back of his bald head with the chunk of wood. I gave it everything. He gave a hell of a yell and fell on his face. I bent down and smashed him three more times on the back of the head. He lay there on his face and didn't move. Then, to make it look like I'd been a thief and not a guest, I put the two cushions back on the pile in the corner.

"Then I went into the next room to look for the cashbox. I found it in the cupboard. I wanted to take it out and tear up the notes like he'd made me suffer, but I didn't know the combination to the lock. I decided to take the box with me. After I left the house, I put the piece of wood on the pile in back. I don't remember exactly where. It was dark. It took maybe thirty minutes, all told.

"The moon was coming up now. I went down the road a little ways, then walked off it into a clump of deep grass. I hunted around, found a large stone, and cracked the lock on the cashbox. I looked quickly through the promissory notes, took the ones with my name on them, along with five or six others. I put these in my pocket. It was hard to see, but I'd been able to make out the names in the pale moonlight. I tossed the box into the irrigation pond on my right. Then I went along to the playground of a life-insurance company, not far away, where I lit a match and burned the notes I'd been carrying in my pocket. I scuffed the ashes into the ground.

"I was plenty surprised when the police told me they had recovered the cashbox from the pond, and that my notes were still there. It turned out that Yamagishi's account book had a customer with a name like mine: Tomio Inoki. The police claimed I must've been mistaken, thinking his notes were mine, in the dark. I'd destroyed the wrong ones. Inoki's notes were missing from the box. I was very excited at the time, so it could have been like that.

"After I'd done all this, I went back to the Manpaiso, where my friends were still playing mahjong. I watched maybe ten minutes, till Nakada won the round. Then I took Shibata's place and played a round myself. None of them knew I'd just murdered a man. If I say so, I was very calm. I guess it was because I had no guilt feelings about having killed Yamagishi.

"I slept well that night. I had burned the notes. Yamagishi had no heirs. The debts would be canceled. I felt happy and relieved.

"The next day, the news of the death caused a big stir in the neighborhood. But there was no one to feel sorry about it. I felt fine when people said it was good he was gone, that he got what was coming to him.

"Two days later, I was watching television in the shop, when two detectives came. They asked me to come to the station. They had a few things to ask me. At the time, I knew it might be the end. Maybe it was wrong to kill him. But he deserved it. I made up my mind to tell the police everything. Of course, if I could, I wanted to make it look like I wasn't guilty."

Reading all this, Harajima got the impression that the case was indeed simple. It could arouse little interest in any lawyer, private or court-assigned. The best he could do would be to ask for clemency on the basis of extenuating circumstances. But as he went on with the case report, he was surprised. Ueki abruptly changed, and claimed to have nothing to do with the murder. He insisted the confession had been the result of psychological torment and leading questions, plus a promise of leniency on the part of police investigators. Of course, defendants like Ueki made this kind of claim often, especially in cases involving heavy punishment.

Just the same, from the evidence in these documents, Harajima felt reasonably sure Ueki was guilty. The written confession sounded natural and unforced. It agreed with the results of the police investigation on the murder site and environs. It did not appear to have been made under police pressure, as Ueki claimed.

Nonetheless, in front of the public prosecutor, Torao Ueki had issued another deposition containing the following information.

3

"It's true, as stated before, I was playing mahjong with Naka-da, Maeda, and Nishikawa in the Manpaiso and that, after two games, Shibata took my place. It's true, I went over to the phone booth in front of the station, called Jin Yamagishi, and told him I had to talk about the securities involved in the loan. It's also true he told me he was up and waiting—and that I went to his house. The rest of the statement I made at the police station, it's untrue.

"I didn't tell Yamagishi on the phone that I'd scraped together two million yen. I could never find that much money. God. But the police kept on insisting Yamagishi wouldn't get out of bed to see me 'less I'd brought money. They claimed, if I'd just told him I wanted to see him, he'd say to wait till the next day. They said I put something in my pocket that looked like a bundle of money, before going to the house. So I thought about what they said. On the basis of Yamagishi's personality, a third person would see eye-to-eye with the police. So I agreed they were right.

"Actually, I simply told Yamagishi I wanted him to wait before taking possession of the securities. If I lost the land and shop, my whole family would have nothing to live on. I said I had an idea for a solution, and I wanted him to listen. He said possession of the securities wasn't really what he wanted—he'd only decided to take such a step because he didn't think there was any hope of my repaying the money. If I had some proposal, he'd consider it. He said I was to come, and that he'd leave the front door open.

"So I walked close to his house, but couldn't go in. I didn't have any damned proposal to make. I was so damned worried about the loss of the land and shop, all I wanted to do was ask him to wait. But I knew this would only make him angrier than ever. I couldn't bring myself to confront him. I felt bad. I just wandered around the neighborhood for maybe thirty minutes, then started back.

"I didn't feel like playing mahjong. I wandered around the playground of the life-insurance company, while thinking over my troubles. It's a country road. I didn't meet anybody. I must've wandered like that for an hour before I went back to the mahjong parlor. The game was nearly over. I took Shibata's place and played for a while. Since I'd done nothing wrong, I was calm.

My friends testified to that. My wife says I slept well that night. After all, there was nothing on my conscience. This is really what happened that night. I'll say this about the false confession I gave earlier:

"First off, I told the police I didn't kill Yamagishi. They wouldn't listen. One after the other, detectives came into the room. They said it'd do no good to lie. Said they had all the proof they needed. According to their side, the stolen cashbox had been recovered from one of the two irrigation ponds. The combination lock was smashed. Inside, they found twenty-two water-soaked promissory notes, including mine—for seven and a half million yen. God. They said they compared the contents with Yamagishi's account book. They said promissory notes of a man named Tomio Inoki were missing. They said I'd made a mistake. Intending to steal my own notes, I'd misread the name Tomio Inoki for Torao Ueki. They said it happened because the characters used to write the names are similar. And, also, because there was only a little moonlight that night.

"Then another detective came in. He said did I know Yoshiya Nakamura? I said, sure, because he's a customer at my shop. Then he said Nakamura must know my face pretty well, and I said, sure, that's right. The detective looked real proud of himself then, as if he'd won something, and told me Nakamura had testified to seeing my hurrying in the direction of Yamagishi's house about five minutes after nine, on the night of the murder. Nakamura was looking out his toilet window. The detective was all grins. He said I probably hadn't been aware of Nakamura's watching me, but it was too late to evade. Now they had testimony of a man who'd seen me in the vicinity, the evidence of the cashbox—and my own admission of a motive. They said it was 'unshakable evidence.' God. Then they said they sympathized with me. If I'd confess, they'd have the public prosecutor release me, arrange to have the case dropped. They were very pleasant to me when they said that I probably wanted to go home to my family and my work as soon as I could.

"I tried to explain why Nakamura had seen me through the window. They wouldn't listen. They kept on promising to have the case dropped if I'd make a false confession. Well, I finally said, all right, I committed the murder. God. They were so happy they let me have cigarettes and ordered in food for me. So then I wrote a confession to their instructions. They wanted something else. A map of the interior of Yamagishi's house. So, I did that.

"Writing, I ran into problems. First, I didn't know what kind of weapon to say I used. One of the detectives said, looking at me like an owl, straight-faced, 'How about the stuff used for fuel in a stove?' I said, 'Sure, I beat Yamagishi to death with a chip of coal.' The detective called me a fool, and said, 'Stump-head. The longish stuff they bring from mountain forests. About this long.' He gestured. 'Oh,' I said. 'Split logs?' 'That's right,' he said. 'You smacked his shiny old bald pate with a hunk of firewood.' Then he said, 'C'mon, where's it kept?' I didn't know, you see. So I said, 'A corner in the kitchen.' Well, he got mad then. He shouted at me, 'No! It's a place where rain falls on it. But only drops of rain. Drop, drop, drop!' He was probably trying to be highly descriptive. 'Under the eaves?' I said. 'Right as rain!' he called out.

"But what is written in the investigation report and that first deposition makes a different impression: 'Before I went to the door, I went around behind the house, I hunted around and found a chunk of wood from the pile I knew was there. . . . So I went to the door, I stepped into the hallway and called to Yamagishi.' It's true, the general meaning of the two statements is similar. On the end of the confession is the sentence, 'I affix my signature to certify that this transcription is identical in content to my oral testimony.'

"The detectives took me behind Yamagishi's place and asked me to show them the piece of firewood I used for the murder weapon. But I hadn't murdered anybody! I was at a loss. 'How's for this one?' asked a detective, picking a log from about the second row on top. I think he had it in mind from the start. I said, 'All right,' and it was identified as the murder weapon. Then I said, 'But there's no blood or hair on it.' They explained that there had been no exterior bleeding and Yamagishi'd been bald. So, obviously there was no blood or hair. Then, like they were making fun of me, one said, 'If Yamagishi'd bled, we'd've been forced to paint blood of his type on the log.' When I asked about lack of my fingerprints, another said, 'Prints can't be detected on a rough surface like that.' So he wrapped the log in cloth as a piece of material evidence.

"Then they asked how we'd been sitting when I killed Yamagishi. I said I'd hid the piece of wood in my hand, come in the hallway, and told him I had two million yen with me. He asked me in. I took off my shoes, stepped up into the main part of the house, and abruptly smashed him on the back of the head with the piece of firewood.

"The detectives said it was impossible. So, they had a version. Since I was a guest, Yamagishi must've taken out two cushions, like he would. When I told him I'd come to pay two million, he probably rose to go into the next room for receipt blanks. That was, according to them, when I hit him on the back of the head. They added that I'd put the cushions back in the pile by the wall to suggest the murderer hadn't been a person received as a guest. By this time, I was damned tired of arguing, and just said, 'Sure. That's how it was.' But they insisted I repeat it all, like they'd said it. So, I did that. Not very well, actually. But I did like I was told.

"Next thing, they asked me how many times I struck him. 'Once,' I said. They said it wasn't enough to kill. 'How many times?' 'Six or seven.' But that was too many. If I'd hit him that many times he'd have bled more. 'Let's see,' one said. 'You just don't remember, but it's three times, right? Three times.' He spoke as if I were a child. Then he muttered, 'Three blows with a piece of firewood would make a wound like the one described in the autopsy report.'

"Then came the cashbox, breaking it open, taking the notes, mistaking Tomio Inoki's name for mine—all of that was the detectives' suggestion. They asked about the pond where I threw the cashbox. I said, 'The one to the left.' They told me to think again. 'After all, there're only two.' So, I said the one on the right. Now, if the real killer's prints could be found on that box, I'd be okay. The investigators said it was impossible to take prints from it, because it got coated with mud from the pond. According to them, I deliberately threw the box in the mud to obscure fingerprints.

"Of course, I didn't know about the ashes they say they found in the weeds in the playground of the life-insurance company.

Maybe the police burned some paper like the notes on their own. You can't read printing or writing on ashes.

"I was so eager to go home, I fell into the police trap. They promised to have the public prosecutor release me and have the case dismissed, if I confessed. They said they sympathized with my motive and wanted to help me as much as they could. I believed them.

"They took me right from the jail to the detention house. The detectives said to tell the public prosecutor exactly what I'd said to them. If I said anything different, they threatened to return me to the police and start all over. 'This time, we'll really let you have it. You try denying the confession in court, we'll see you get the limit. Play it smart, Ueki.'

"They frightened me. So, I told the public prosecutor the things like they're written in the false confession. Then, finally, I found their promises about dropping the case, letting me go home, it was all a lie. I decided to come out with the truth."

4

After reading this deposition, Harajima couldn't decide whether the claim that the confession had been made under police pressure was exaggerated or true. The first confession sounded unforced, natural. But, in its way, so did the second. There were still some policemen who might resort to tactics of the kind Ueki described. As a lawyer, Harajima was tempted to lean toward the second confession.

The public prosecutor's indictment refused to recognize the second deposition, insisting on considering the confession made before the police as evidence. The constitution (Article 38) states that confessions obtained by means of coercion, torture, or threats, and confessions obtained after unduly long detention are inadmissible as evidence. Confessions given as a result of deceptive interrogation—for instance, claiming that an accomplice has admitted guilt when he has not—or as an outcome of leading questions slanted in favor of the interrogator, are to be regarded as forced. Such evidence is insufficient to establish guilt.

Defendants often plead their confessions were forced in an attempt to prove their innocence. In such cases, corroborating evidence is of the greatest importance in establishing guilt. Such evidence includes material evidence, and testimonies of third parties. It can be divided into direct and indirect, or circumstantial, evidence.

Torao Ueki had borrowed money at high interest from Jin Yamagishi. Unable to pay, he faced the threat of having his securities seized. His desire for murder was circumstantial evidence, He had no alibi for the time of the crime. Testimonies of his friends, Nakada, Maeda, Nishikawa, and Shibata, and the manager and personnel of the Manpaiso mahjong parlor, established the fact that he had left the premises at around nine in the evening and had returned at ten.

Yoshiya Nakamura testifed that, shortly after the time Ueki left the Manpaiso, he had been looking out of the window and had seen Ueki. He had not witnessed Ueki's entry into Yamagishi's house, or the murder. Therefore, his evidence was indirect.

Material evidence included the piece of firewood, and the cashbox fished out of the irrigation pond. In searching, the police had dragged the pond and recovered it. Ueki's fingerprints were not on the box. This has been explained. The following police report covers the question of prints on the firewood:

"Question: With what did you strike Jin Yamagishi on the back of the head?

"Answer: A chunk of pine log. Like they use in old-fashioned stoves.

"Question: About how long was the piece of wood?

"Answer: Maybe thirty centimeters.

"Question: Where was it?

"Answer: What?

"Question: Where was the wood kept?

"Answer: Oh. Piled under the eaves behind Yamagishi's place. I'd been thinking of using it ever since I got the idea of killing him.

"Question: You mean you knew there was firewood piled in that place?

"Answer: Yes.

"Question: What did you do with the wood after the crime?

"Answer: I put it back where I got it.

"Question: If we went back to where the wood is stored, could you pick out the piece you used?

"Answer: Sure, if nobody moved it.

"Question: Since the discovery of the body, the house has been in police custody. Everything's just as it was."

"Answer: Sure, then if I went there, I could pick out the piece."

In this report there are no traces of the association-game hints Ueki claimed were forced on him in the second confession. The defendant was taken back to Yamagishi's house, as the following report reveals.

"The defendant was taken behind Yamagishi's house, where he examined a pile of about thirty-five bundles of wood stacked under the eaves. He promptly picked out a piece from the second row from the top. He said, 'This is it. This is the one I used.'

"An investigator put on gloves and took the piece indicated. The defendant, too, was given gloves and held the wood in his right hand. Then he swung it two or three times to the right and left and made five or six downstrikes with it. He said, 'This is it, all right. I guess once you've used something like this, you know the feel of it, don't you?'

"In offering this evidence, the defendant was most cooperative."

Torao Ueki's efforts to help made it look almost as if he were currying favor with the police.

Harajima had not seen the full initial investigation report. He took time from his busy schedule to visit the police station. From the report, he learned that the police had narrowed their search to Ueki from the moment they received Nakamura's testimony about having seen Ueki from his bathroom window. Ueki confessed immediately after arrest. The police had been comfortably able to send in an early report.

Realizing Harajima was court-appointed counsel, the officer in charge was clearly angry when he said, "I understand the defendant's now denying his confession. What's he trying to do? It's ridiculous. The police can't be accused of using strong-arm tactics. We'd never promise to set a man free or have the case dropped if he agreed to sign a confession. We don't threaten to fight for the death penalty when a defendant denies his confession in court. When Ueki first came in here, he sat right down—

told us everything about the murder, how he went in and talked to Yamagishi, how he killed him. He drew a map of Yamagishi's house, explaining it all on his own. The whole thing about the murder weapon was just as it's written up. He pointed it out to us, made a few swings with it, said he recalled the knot. He even asked us to find out if his fingerprints were on the log. He was friendly. I really don't think he could have described things so well unless he knew what he was talking about."

This business of Ueki being "friendly" made Harajima frown. Sometimes defendants cooperate with the police so they can be sent to the detention house quickly. Once there, they change their tune, claiming what they said for the police was made under duress. Maybe this was how Ueki figured things. Still he might pretend friendliness, believing the police would free him and drop the case. He certainly had cooperated.

The trial was drawing near. Stealing time from other cases, Harajima made a trip to the detention house to talk with Ueki.

Ueki was tall, reedy, with a pale, femininely gentle face. Both his shoulders and eyebrows slanted downward, giving him a kind of parallel semblance of rejection. Thin-lipped, he had a tight, narrow forehead, but he was quite polite when he met Harajima, expressing respect and gratitude that the lawyer was representing him. Especially since there was no fee. There was a certain meekness about Ueki, though none of this was in his words.

Harajima was of two minds about the man. Could such a weak-looking fellow commit murder? Still, that girlish face might conceal brutality and cunning. Although he had looked into the eyes of hundreds of defendants, Harajima wasn't always able to tell whether they were sincere.

"Torao, I've taken your case. You want the right kind of defense, you'll have to be completely frank."

"Sure, yes—understood."

Harajima hesitated, then said, "Do you still claim your first confession was a lie?"

Ueki was quick, direct. "Absolutely. Damn it, I was tricked by the police."

"Then, it's true, about the leading questions, all that?"

"Yes, yes—"

"They claim you cooperated with them, went so far as to point out the firewood to the investigators."

Ueki shook his head, "That's not so. It's like I said in the second deposition. The detectives told me just what to say."

"You'll testify to that?"

"Certainly."

"Okay, then. We'll work out a defense on those lines."

Ueki's tone changed. "Mr. Harajima? I can prove the confession I made was forced from me."

"Prove?"

"Yes."

5

A smile touched Ueki's lips. "I thought of it last night in bed. I'm sure it's because you've been chosen to defend me—God graciously jogged my memory."

Harajima sighed. "What d'you mean?"

"Sure. It's about what happened before I'm supposed to have killed the old man. I heard he was on his face, turned in the direction of the next room. Lying there, like that, I mean. When I first talked with the police, I made it up that after Yamagishi'd seen me, he said a couple of words, then invited me in. That he turned to go into the other room. This is when I said I hit him with the log. Well, the police said that story wasn't any good. They kept insisting I must've sat on a cushion Yamagishi pulled out for me. Then I'd put the cushion back after the murder. So it'd look like the crime was by someone who broke in, not by a guest. They kept at it, and finally I went along. But listen—the truth is Jin Yamagishi never offered cushions to people who came to borrow money. I was there a lot and he never gave me one. You'd have to know him. Must've been like that with everybody, I bet. You can ask around."

"Why'd he have the pile of cushions in the comer?"

"For show, see? None of his customers ever sat on one. If they sat down, they'd stay too long. He liked us to leave right away, after he'd forced his conditions on us. Okay, if the talk lasted a while, then he might maybe show some kind of human feeling. Of course, that's not saying he didn't give a cushion to ordinary visitors. The detectives didn't know this."

"You have any other proof?"

"The cashbox, Mr. Harajima. I didn't know where it had been found. They said something about 'water,' so I remembered the irrigation ponds. But when I said the one on the left, they called me a fool. So I told them the one to the right. That's in the deposition I made after meeting the prosecutor. Damn it, Mr. Harajima, the fact my promissory notes were still there, in the box, should prove I didn't kill him. They said I misread Inoki for Ueki. But, hell—now, would somebody who'd murdered to get those notes back fail to check the names on them? The police said it was dark. But I'm supposed to have burned five notes in the playground a little later. This means I had matches, right? I could've checked the names when I struck a match. Anyway, my prints weren't found on the cashbox."

"Well. Anything else?"

"Yes. It's important, too. How about this—does the hunk of wood used as the murder weapon match the wound on Yamagishi's head?"

"How d'you mean?"

"Listen, I read the medical report. A copy, that is. There was a flattened spot on the back of Yamagishi's skull, maybe the size of a human palm. The bone was dented in. The log the detectives made me select was triangular, Mr. Harajima—in cross-section, I mean—about four centimeters wide on a side." Ueki shook his head. "I just don't think three smacks would leave something like that. I mean, the fractures would've been uneven. He must've been hit with something larger, once." He blinked. "Naturally, it's only my guess. But, still, you might check it."

Ueki had been speaking quietly, but with an undercurrent of hope.

Harajima took a taxi home from the detention house. On the way, he thought over what Ueki had said, and could not help becoming excited. Finally, he concluded Ueki's words had considerable significance.

Back at the office, he read the case record over with a different eye. He saw that when the viewpoint alters, so does the impression one gets from the materials. Other possibilities hadn't been investigated. Ueki had confessed, immediately upon arrest. The police had relaxed and consequently were careless about making certain of their evidence. Happy over success, they'd been lax in their very first investigations.

Harajima questioned some ten customers of Yamagishi's about the cushions. He learned that the moneylender never provided them with one when they were at his house. From the young teacher upstairs, however, he found that Yamagishi did, indeed, give courteous hospitality to those who visited on other than business. He seemed to enjoy sitting and chatting. Other associates of Yamagishi attested to this.

The police had considered it only common sense to assume Yamagishi brought out cushions for customers. They required the suspect admit doing this—returning the cushion to the pile after the murder—to suggest the act had been committed by a thief.

Next, Harajima took the coroners' report to a friend who was a doctor of forensic medicine, and asked his opinion.

"It's supposition, remember," the doctor said. "But to make a wound of the kind that killed Yamagishi would require a single blow with a weapon more than eight centimeters wide." Shaking his head, he said, "It's odd the police don't see this. But, of course, they place more importance on their own intuition and experience than on what we say. They think our reports little more than reference material." He made a clucking sound with his tongue. "They actually look down on us doctors," he said, smiling quickly.

It would seem that one of the detectives had simply decided the murder weapon should be a split log, lacking anything else suitable. The excitement of conducting an investigation immediately after Ueki confessed probably accounted for much of the laxity. It was different from times when a criminal left so much evidence behind that it confused the police with its very abundance. Nothing was as open to error or powerful prejudice as the educated hunch of an over-confident detective.

Harajima had some notes about this, right on his desk, taken from *Ascertaining the Facts*, by the Judicial Research and Training Institute. It was interesting, and a parallel: "There have been many cases in which police officers, operating on the basis of a preformed notion, have failed to take into consideration facts that remove suspicions and have used undue methods to force confessions. Almost all judges with long experience have encountered one or two such incidents. Written works on criminal matters often refer to cases of the kind. For instance, mention is made of police officers who carelessly and hastily overlook facts that prove innocence. In addition, there are remarks to the effect that there is much falsehood in confessions made before police."

Harajima became enthusiastic. This very case might just be a stroke of good luck. In court, he called the forensic medical expert to give an opinion about the wound. As new witnesses, he summoned several persons who had associations with Jin Yamagishi. He questioned the four police officers who had interrogated Ueki. They all testified that the confession had been given willingly.

—Did you tell the defendant, Mr. Ueki, "We know you killed Yamagishi. You won't get off now. But, if you confess, we'll let you free and get the public prosecutor to drop the case"?

—Witness A: Listen, I never said anything like that.

—In order to prompt a confession, did you allow the defendant to smoke as much as he liked in the interrogation room? And after the confession, did you order food for him on three occasions?

—Witness B: It's customary to allow a defendant two or three cigarettes during questioning. This isn't to "prompt a confession." We ordered food once.

—During questioning, did you instruct the defendant with hints about having to put the cushions back in the original place?

—Witness C: No. He told us that, offered it on his own.

—Did you suggest the firewood, exhibit one, as the murder weapon? And, did you lead the defendant to select the log shown here—and to say he struck the victim on the back of the head with it, three times?

—Witness D: Of course not. He confessed all that himself. He chose that piece of wood himself. He said, "This is it," or something, and swung it around. Then he said, "No mistake about it." He was very cooperative.

Ueki was quite disturbed, indignant, about the testimony of these men during cross-questioning.

"See? They said what I told you. How the devil can they lie

like that? Just to make themselves look good. They don't give a damn about who's guilty."

There was a deadlock. The police officers strongly denied Ueki's accusations.

Three months later, the verdict was handed down. Not guilty, for lack of sufficient evidence.

The verdict was reached for the following reasons:

1. The piece of wood presented to the court as the murder weapon is four centimeters wide at the broadest point. According to testimonies of the autopsy doctor and one other, flattening of the victim's skull would require a weapon at least as wide as an adult palm, eight or nine centimeters. (A report by an expert from a large medical university confirmed this.) Therefore, the pine log offered as evidence cannot have been the murder weapon.

2. Fingerprints of the defendant were not found on the piece of pine log, nor on the cashbox belonging to Jin Yamagishi.

3. According to the confession, the defendant took five of the twenty-two promissory notes from the cashbox. He took these to the playground of a life-insurance company some two hundred meters from the irrigation pond and burned them. Among notes left in the box were those in the name of the defendant, Torao Ueki. It was assumed, after investigation, that the five notes burned had been in the name of Tomio Inoki. The judicial police insist that, in the dark, the defendant must have misread the name Tomio Inoki as his own, Torao Ueki.

This seems likely, but the defense attorney's insistence is also convincing: if the defendant is in fact the murderer, then recovery of the notes would have been his primary concern. He would have made certain he had the right ones.

4. Examination of the written confessions reveals no trace of coercion or undue detention by the judicial police to force the defendant to confess. However, there is an impression that deception and leading questions were employed. The series of depositions submitted by the defendant to this court strongly claim such methods were used. This is not enough to convince the court that the crime was not committed by the defendant. The defendant is unable to account convincingly for his actions and whereabouts for the hour from the time he left the Manpaiso mahjong parlor

to the time when he returned. There is doubt because Yoshiya Nakamura testifies to having seen the defendant near the victim's house around that time. This substantiates the first confession.

5. This court has considered the evidence, and come to the following decision. The court concludes that there is insufficient evidence of guilt and, in accordance with Article 336 of the Criminal Actions Law, pronounces a verdict of not guilty.

6

A year passed. Naomi Harajima was in the habit of reading legal volumes during his free time. One night, as he glanced through *Studies of Not-Guilty Verdicts* by the English judge James Hind, his eyes locked on an arresting section. He sat bolt upright in his chair. He read on and experienced an unpleasant thumping in his chest.

In 1923, Peter Cammerton, a worker in a sail factory in Manchester, England, was arrested and charged with murdering a wealthy widow, Mrs. Hammersham, and then setting fire to her home. Because he was in need of money, Cammerton planned to kill her and steal whatever he could. Going to her house around seven in the evening, he struck her several times in the face with an iron rod, about fifty centimeters long. He then strangled her with his leather belt, took one hundred and fifty pounds in cash, along with some jewelry from her room, and fled.

To conceal traces of his act, he returned about nine in the evening, intending to burn her house. Lighting a kerosene lamp, he placed it on a book atop the bureau. Half of the lamp-base projected over the edge of the book. The lamp leaned because of unstable support. On the floor, he piled waste paper and clothing, which would ignite when the lamp fell. The fire would spread to the entire house. He knew the lamp would tumble when a freight train passed on tracks behind Mrs. Hammersham's house in the next hour. The ground and house foundation trembled whenever a train came along. Three hours later, the house was in flames. Firetrucks raced to the scene. They were unable to extinguish the blaze.

Peter Cammerton was arrested soon after. He confessed, but later denied his confession. He was pronounced not guilty through lack of evidence.

Was Peter Cammerton, in fact, the person who robbed and killed the woman and set fire to the house?

There were no fingerprints or other objective evidence to link him with the crime. More, there was little circumstantial evidence to establish his guilt. Many of his friends testified that he had said and done nothing unusual between the time of the crime and his arrest. On the day of the murder, he had taken a pleasure trip to London. He returned eagerly to Manchester, knowing full well he would undergo a police investigation. This spoke in his favor.

Cammerton confessed to the police, but later denied the confession, claiming he had been coerced into making it. The court uncovered no foundation for coercion and ruled the confession acceptable as evidence.

But close examination of the confession, in comparison with other evidence, revealed serious discrepancies. In the confession, he said Mrs. Hammersham first opened the door only a crack. He had waited to strike her with the iron bar when she put her whole face out of the door. Two days after, he claimed she invited him into the house and that they sat opposite each other and talked. He waited for her to be off her guard and then struck her.

When he struck her was a point of major importance. Cammerton would not forget such a major action. Why would he lie? This conflict of statements was difficult to understand.

At first, Cammerton said he struck Mrs. Hammersham once in the face with the iron bar. Two days later, he said it had been twice. One week later, he claimed he struck her with all his might once and that, as she lowered her head, he hit her again four or five times, A medical expert said the condition of the bones in the victim's face verified the assumption that the attack really consisted of only one blow.

So, what Cammerton said later also did not agree with his original confession. Lapse of memory was unthinkable. Increasing the number of times he struck the victim could scarcely be to the defendant's advantage. Still, there was little reason to suspect him of deliberately falsifying. All of this cast serious doubt on the veracity of the initial confession.

Immediately upon arrest, the police confronted Cammerton with the steel rod and asked if he'd ever seen it. He said he thought his fingerprints would be on it. He seemed to recall the rod, but there had been several where he picked up the weapon. He could not be certain. Holding the rod, he placed it under his right arm, measured its length, and finally said there could be no mistake—it was the one he had used.

The wound in the victim's face was measured and found to be three times as wide as the rod (2.5 centimeters). This meant that the rod could not be the murder weapon. Why had Cammerton claimed it was? Would the real killer be unable to recognize his weapon? The fact that Cammerton claimed the rod as the weapon and also mentioned fingerprints awakened the possibility that he identified the weapon to please the police, even though he knew it was unrelated to the crime. Why would he do this?

Investigations failed to reveal traces of the kerosene lamp on the floor by the bureau. If it had been there, even though it may not have started the fire, it could scarcely have been overlooked. Had there been no lamp? Many questions remained unanswered. The judge pronounced the defendant not guilty, due to insufficient evidence.

Finished reading this passage, Harajima felt as if the words on the page had leaped out and struck him in the face. The two cases closely resembled each other. Coincidence? It was too close for that. A strong gut feeling told him Torao Ueki had read the same book.

From eighteen to twenty-five, Torao Ueki had worked in a second-hand book store, opening the noodle shop only after getting married.

Harajima checked a copy of the case record, found the name of the book store. He then called a book collector friend, and learned the store specialized in legal volumes. They would certainly have Hind's *Studies of Not-Guilty Verdicts*, which had been translated into Japanese before World War II. As an employee of the shop, Ueki would have had ample time to read it.

It is not easy for a criminal to escape the police. Many criminals have been executed or imprisoned because they have become entangled in their own clever subterfuges. Those who do escape detection often lead lives of anxiety and suffering in some ways worse than a long prison sentence. The ideal thing is to allow the police to make an arrest, then be declared not guilty. When he decided to kill Jin Yamagishi, the moneylender who had caused him much grief, Torao Ueki must have considered this and recalled the volume he once read in a second-hand bookshop.

In the Manchester case, Peter Cammerton claimed that a piece of iron rod the wrong size was the murder weapon. Believing him, the police admitted the wrong item as evidence. Ueki had done the same thing with the firewood. After his arrest, Cammerton identified the iron rod, measured its length under his arm, and suggested his fingerprints would be on it. Ueki had done something very similar with the piece of wood. Learning much from the English murder case, Ueki made self-incriminating statements in his confession, which he later denied. He then created the impression that the confession was made under police pressure.

As the inspector said, Ueki had been cooperative and friendly. The police fell for this and were too pleased with the way things were going to substantiate their evidence. Both Cammerton and Ueki changed the number of times they claimed to have struck their victims. In each case, only one blow had been used. Ueki's knowledge of Yamagishi's habit of never offering cushions to business customers was put to his own advantage when he said he'd been offered such a cushion and had returned it to its corner pile. He had employed the trick of leaving his own promissory notes in the cashbox to convince police he would not have done so if he'd been the murderer. It made no difference that the notes weren't destroyed. Yamagishi had no children, no relatives for heirs. At his death, all debts would be canceled.

What would the police think if they knew Harajima's notions of the truth? In court, when Ueki indignantly accused them of coercing a confession, tricking him with leading questions, bribing him, why had the police allowed it to end in a draw? Had they given up before Ueki's tremendous brass? It was true, when he observed the staunch courage with which Ueki testified, Harajima had become convinced the confession had not been freely given.

Harajima was very nervous. He paced back and forth in his study. At length, trying to calm himself, he removed a slender volume from the bookshelf and thumbed through the pages.

"Never judge the truth or falseness of a defendant's confession on the basis of the excitement he shows in making depositions about the crime, or *by the courage with which he faces police witnesses in court*. Make judgement on the basis of (1) whether the content of the confession agrees with known facts, (2) the personality and nature of the defendant, and (3) the motive that may have induced him to confess. But, after thorough investigation of all evidence, if there is no trace of the defendant's attempting to obscure the uncovering of the truth about his confession, *do not be deceived by distinctive character traits or by the falseness of a servile personality into believing the confession has been forced*. (Special Criminal Report of the Superior Court, March 16, 1944. Kanazawa Branch, Nagoya Superior Court)"

Ueki's whereabouts are unknown. After the trial, he sold his shop and land to a realtor for a good price, and went away. He did not come to thank Harajima. He phoned, instead: "Can't thank you enough, for getting me out of a tight spot. Mr. Harajima, you're tops. The only thing is, I'm embarrassed having to call on your services without paying you." After a few more inconsequential words he was gone.

If Torao Ueki were killed in a traffic accident, it would be no more than just punishment, or perhaps divine retribution. This, however, is somehow unlikely.

TOHRU MIYOSHI

A Letter From The Dead

Tohru Miyoshi is perhaps Japan's leading spy writer. He is one of the contemporary "social novelists" who came on the scene after Seicho Matsumoto, and his books deal with national and international politics, revolutionary movements, and worldwide points of view. He is especially interested in "pursuing the thought behind the crime."

His story is more than just a well-written detective story. Through the character Wakizaka it portrays the faces of human nature and some of the pain that can be dealt by a maddening twist of fate.

Imagine a newspaperman of today receiving a letter "from the banks of the Styx." It has often been said that "dead men tell no tales." It follows that "dead men do not write letters" — and therein lies the provocative problem. . . .

EARLY IN APRIL, the curious letter arrived in the readers' column section of the newspaper office. The readers' column, a branch of the editorial section, was responsible for selecting material submitted by subscribers for publication, and for answering questions about news items. Its staff was small and did less flashy work than the local news or political sections. Most of the employees on the readers' column were older. Their work consisted in going through piles of letters delivered daily, reading them, working them up into printable form. When work was light, or when some of the staff finished early, no one complained if they took long coffee breaks or killed time somewhere. On the other hand, there was little chance of making a scoop or stepping into the limelight on the readers' column.

Shunya Wakizaka was unhappy with his daily grind. All the people who worked with him were over forty and interested in nothing but raises in salary and promotions. Oda, who sat next to him, had five or six years left before retirement, but the first thing he did every morning was open the paper to the stock report.

Wakizaka was only thirty. He had transferred from a provincial branch of the paper to the Tokyo readers' column six months ago. He wanted desperately to be put in the local-news section. First, he could not get used to what he considered old folk's work. Then, he was envious of friends who had joined the newspaper at the same time as he and who were now doing exciting work in other sections.

Still, he must do his work. So, on that April day, he turned to the pile of letters on his desk and began opening them.

"What the hell kind of joker's this?" Oda growled, waving a letter around in front of him.

"What's the matter?" Wakizaka asked.

Oda signaled one of the office girls to bring him a cup of tea, then said, "I'm pretty good-natured most of the time. But it gets under my skin when people try to make a fool of me. What's this guy mean, 'I'm writing this letter from the banks of the River Styx'?"

"The banks of the River Styx?"

"Yeah."

"Lemme see —"

"It's nutty. When you're finished, toss it in the basket."

Oda began slurping the tea the girl brought. Wakizaka read the letter:

"I am writing this letter from the banks of the River Styx. My body no longer exists in this world. In the words of mortals, I have died. I was given a splendid funeral. My fellow workers at the company, my friends, and relatives all paid their condolences. They expressed their sympathy at my death. But I was murdered. It was neither suicide nor accident. The only ones who know are the murderer and myself. Unfortunately, I was unable to see who the killer was. He came up on me from behind. Desire for revenge is keeping me on the banks of the Styx. I can't cross to the other side. Probably you think dead people can't write letters. You're mistaken. I didn't know it when I was mortal, but there are many things that can't be scientifically explained. Ghosts and spirits exist. All around me are many who cannot cross the Styx because they left things unfinished in the world, and are disturbed about them. My own spirit is operating on a certain person, causing this letter to be written. It may take a long time, but it will reach the world of the living."

Oda, who was waiting for Wakizaka to finish, said, "How about that? Beautiful, huh?"

"It's certainly strange."

"Strange. It's crazy. These cranks get me, writing trash like that."

Wakizaka looked at the address on the envelope. It gave only the name of the newspaper company, then "Central Ward, Tokyo." No street or number. Of course, it would be delivered. The envelope bore the proper stamp, which had been canceled. The return address was Shiro Kureha, Okuzawa, Setagaya Ward, Tokyo.

Oda was still bitching. "Wow."

"Yeah, but what can he be getting at, sending a letter like this?"

"A little leg-pulling."

Maybe. But to Wakizaka, it looked too elaborate for a practical joke. He had an idea, and glanced at the cancellation mark on the stamp. The letter had been posted at the seaside town of Atami, three hours' train ride from Tokyo. February 8th. Wakizaka knew it was April, but looked at the calendar anyway.

Well, sometimes mail took longer than it used to. Four or five days were frequently needed for letters within the city. Still, two months from Atami to Tokyo was a long time. A little time might be allowed because the address of the newspaper had been given incompletely. Just the same, two months . . .

Wakizaka recalled what the letter said: "It may take a long time." He arrested his hand halfway to the wastebasket. The cancellation date stopped him. Could there be something here that was not explained by means of ordinary common sense? He yanked the phone directory toward him, checking to see something, flipping the pages. There it was: Shiro Kureha, same address. Wakizaka grabbed the phone and dialed.

A woman answered.

"This the Kureha residence?" he asked.

"Well —"

"It isn't?"

"Actually, this used to be the Kureha house. But Mrs. Kureha has moved."

"When?"

"The end of last month."

"You happen to know where she moved?"

"Yes. It's an apartment near here."

"Could you tell me her phone number?"

"I've heard she doesn't have a phone."

"You may think this's a strange question, but could you tell me if Mr. Kureha's in good health?"

There was a pause. Then, the woman said, "I heard her husband died."

"Dead? You know when?" Wakizaka was excited now. Hesitating, the woman asked suspiciously the name of the person with whom she was speaking. Wakizaka told her. He added, "I wanted to ask Mr. Kureha something. I didn't know he'd passed away."

"I'm afraid I don't know any of the details," the woman said. "But I think it was some time ago. Maybe three months?"

"Excuse me. But have you known them long, the Kurehas?"

"No. We only know what we found out when we bought this place."

"I see. Well, forgive me for disturbing you. Thanks for the information."

2

Oda said, "What's that about?"

"The man who wrote that letter is dead. He died three months ago."

Oda stared. "Murdered?"

"I don't know, for God's sake. The woman I spoke with said she bought the Kureha house after his death."

"Calm down," Oda said, "Don't get so hot. No matter when the guy died, this letter's a joke. Dead men don't write letters."

"I'm not excited. Not much anyway. But doesn't it puzzle

you? I'd like to know what's behind it."

"Drop it flat. Let it lay. It's crazy, I tell you."

"Yeah. But it took two months to reach the office. How you figure that?"

"I don't know, pal. But you mess around with shit like this, you'll be wasting your time."

Wakizaka pursed his lips, but said nothing.

He was perfectly aware that dead men don't write letters to the living from the banks of the River Styx. First, there was no River Styx. Did he want people to think he was bananas? But he could not repress a desire to solve the riddle. As he left that evening, he slipped the letter into his pocket and went to the former Kureha house, which was located in a quiet residential district.

The new owner was named Kamimura. When Wakizaka rang the bell, a dignified lady of something over fifty answered. She was disturbed to find that she was dealing with the person who had made the phone call.

She said, "The only connection we have with the Kurehas is that we bought this house. You want more than that, I suggest you ask Mrs. Kureha herself. She lives right near."

Wakizaka walked the short distance to the two-story wooden apartment building. On the door of the end apartment on the first floor was tacked a small piece of paper: Kureha.

His heart pounded as he rang the bell.

A woman pushed aside a small curtain in the door window, revealing only a pair of eyes. "Who is it?"

Wakizaka told her, mentioning the paper.

"I'm already taking a newspaper. I don't need any."

"I'm not selling subscriptions. It's just that I heard of your husband's death. There's something I don't understand —"

"What?" She sounded suspicious.

"Yes, You see, your husband sent a letter to our office."

"My husband?"

"Yes."

"What *are* you talking about?"

"It true he died three months ago?"

She did not answer, but the eyes peering at him through the door signaled assent.

"Well — even though he's dead, he still sent a letter to our office."

"What?"

Wakizaka repeated everything. He wondered if she suspected him of the crime? Mrs. Kureha — he later learned her name was Reiko — looked highly disturbed and made no offer to open the door. It wasn't surprising, but still, he persevered.

He said, nervously, "Your husband was dead before February 8th. But our office received the letter dated that day. Look at this, please."

"This is lunacy." She paused. "You really from the newspaper?"

"Believe me. I understand how you feel. But, just take a glance at this."

Wakizaka slipped his card and the letter into the mail slot. A few moments passed, then there came a low moaning voice from the other side of the door.

"What's wrong?"

There was a gasp. He held his breath, frowning, wondering what she would say.

Her voice was weak. "This — this letter . . ." She seemed unable to continue.

"Yes? What is it?"

"It can't be. It can't."

"Mrs. Kureha. Please open the door."

"Did this letter really and truly arrive at your newspaper office?"

"Yes, really and truly. But, please — the door."

"All right. Yes —"

The chain slipped, clattering from the latch. The door opened. A woman of twenty-seven or -eight was leaning against the vestibule wall. She gripped the letter in one hand. She glanced at Wakizaka as he entered. He took in the apartment at a glance. Sliding paper doors concealed what must be the Japanese-style room beyond.

Mrs. Kureha sank into the chair by the table in the small room. Then, oblivious of Wakizaka, she read the letter. She was riveted to the paper. She reread it.

Wakizaka said, "Mrs. Kureha. D'you have any ideas about this?"

"Ideas?"

She raised her eyes. Wakizaka's question seemed to recall her to the present from another world.

"What d'you mean, ideas?"

"The contents. The writing. Who do you think it is?"

"It's amazing."

"What?"

"But my husband committed suicide. He can't have been murdered. All this business about the River Styx. Something's wrong. But . . ." She closed her lips. She paused, then said, "The writing's my husband's."

3

Wakizaka thought, this is nonsense. Dead men can't write letters. If they could, the sun would rise in the west, men would bear children, there'd be moon maidens.

He said, "Mrs. Kureha. Is this really your husband's writing?"

She nodded, blinking.

"Forgive me, but when did he die?"

"January fifteenth."

"You said suicide?"

"Yes. While he was in Atami. He threw himself into the sea."

"At Atami?"

"Yes."

"Mind telling me how it happened?"

"But — please . . ."

Wakizaka urged her on.

She spoke slowly. Shiro Kureha had been a director in the advertising department of Tozai Electric, an important manufacturer of electronic parts. He had married Reiko ten years ago and was thirty-three when he died. The fifteenth of January was a holiday. On the evening of the fourteenth, six men from the advertising department traveled to Atami for a party and to spend the night. They did this each year to mark the end of the New Year's holiday and to play mahjong. The following day they usually fished or played golf. In their work, everybody played mahjong. If a person didn't know how to play when he was first assigned to the department, he soon learned. Everyone connected with advertising was supposed to know how to play the game.

There were six men: department chief Oba; assistant chief Sakamoto; staff members Nakaya, Sada, Murai; and Kureha. They arrived in Atami at seven in the evening on the fourteenth of January. It took about two hours for baths and dinner. The game began at nine.

Four persons are required for the game of mahjong. There were six in the party. This meant two would sit out each game. Kureha said he had a headache and didn't feel like playing. He had looked pale and worried since leaving Tokyo. The group all agreed to this when they later testified to the police.

Oba was worried when he asked Kureha, "You okay?"

"Yes. I'm fine. I think I'll order a masseur in the room." Kureha left. He shared a room with Nakaya.

There was still one too many, but the game commenced. A roll of the dice determined who would sit out. Oba got the lowest number and sat out the first round.

By the time the third round ended, it was twelve o'clock.

"I'm tired," Oba said. "Must be getting old. Think I'll turn in."

"Don't quit when you're winning," Murai said.

"I want to be in shape for golf tomorrow." Then he said, "Suppose I wake up Kureha and get him to join you?" They hadn't thought of Kureha till then. The others said no. If he came back, there would be an extra. All four men wanted to go on playing.

They played till five in the morning. Even then, the losers wanted to continue, but they all needed sleep.

When Nakaya entered the room, Kureha wasn't to be seen. He wasn't in the bath or toilet. The bed nearer the window was rumpled. That must be where he had slept.

Nakaya was concerned about where Kureha might be, but he was tired; he fell asleep and didn't wake until breakfast. Kureha still had not returned. Now Nakaya was still more worried. Hastily washing, he hurried to where breakfast was set out. Kureha was not here, either.

"Where's Kureha?" Nakaya asked the group.

Sakamoto spoke up. "Isn't he with you?"

"He wasn't in the room all night."

"Funny," Oba said. "I felt concerned about him. On the way

to my room, I glanced in. He was sleeping soundly, then."

Sakamoto suggested Kureha might have gone for a walk. Oba disagreed. It was still too dark at five in the morning. Something must have happened.

"Maybe he went to the golf course," Nakaya said. He took a quick gulp of coffee and hurried back to the room to check Kureha's things. A suit was missing. When Nakaya reported this finding, the other members came to the room to examine it thoroughly. Kureha's overcoat, shaving kit, and golf bag were all there. His shoes had been checked at the desk, as is the custom in Japanese inns. They had remained untouched. He couldn't have gone out barefoot. It later turned out that he'd put on wooden clogs the inn provided at the garden door.

Of course, the day's golf was off. Leaving Sakamoto at the inn, the others returned to Tokyo. Before leaving, Oba reported to the police, who investigated. Oba said he could think of no reason for the disappearance, though Kureha had seemed curiously listless, almost neurotic during the past week or so.

Reiko was informed. She arrived in Atami at one o'clock in the afternoon on January fifteenth. Sakamoto met her at the station and they took a cab to the police office. Oba, who was waiting there, tried to console Reiko, but she was little interested in what he had to say. Worried only about her husband, she told the police to "Please, find him as fast as possible. . . ."

"We're trying. That's why we'd like to ask you a few things. First, have you noticed anything different about your husband lately?"

"I don't understand." Reiko was slightly pale.

"I don't like to frighten you, Mrs. Kureha. But, I've got to say it — we feel disappearances like this are caused by one of two things. Death by murder or accident, or death by suicide." He paused, then said rather officiously, "Can you tell us anything?"

Reiko argued that the alternatives suggested were not the only possible ones. If it had to be one of the two, accidental death was more likely. Her husband might have gone for a walk, slipping on wooden clogs. He was struck by an automobile and the driver transported his body somewhere; there were many irresponsible drivers.

But the officer had been in contact with police in surrounding towns. No bodies had been reported. He said that, in investigations of this type, accurate information was paramount.

"I know how you must feel," he said. "I'm only trying to do my job. Now. D'you think your husband might've had a motive for disappearing or committing suicide?"

Reiko's voice was tight. "Suicides always leave notes, don't they?"

"Usually. Not always. Sometimes they act on impulse."

"I can't believe he'd kill himself." There was a certainty in her tone.

Shiro Kureha and Reiko had been happy together. He hadn't progressed professionally as fast as he might. He was no more than a director. Certainly he'd been dissatisfied with some things at work, but that was scarcely motive for suicide.

Sakamoto, in Atami, said Kureha had some small troubles at the office, but then, so did others.

Suddenly, new information came from a taxi driver named Maezawa. At two in the morning on the fifteenth, he had picked up a fare, a man, in front of the inn where the group had stayed. The man wore a suit. When the passenger got out, the driver noticed that he wore wooden clogs. The man had asked Maezawa to drive him "somewhere."

"Somewhere? I'll have to know more than that."

"Anywhere," the man said.

Young couples often wanted to drive around, but it seemed strange for a lone man to make this request. Still, it was no reason to turn him down.

"Would you like to go to the mountains, or the seaside?"

"Makes no difference. Let's make it the seaside."

Starting toward Ito, the driver checked the man in the rearview mirror. He sat, apparently absorbed in thought, with arms folded. Occasionally, he looked out the left window. He didn't seem to be watching for anything. Anyway, there was only black sea and a few lights from fishing boats.

As they turned into the main street of Ito, the driver suggested they start back. He felt uncomfortable with this silent passenger. The man told him to drive on.

"Listen — you okay?" the driver asked, unable to restrain himself any longer.

"I have money."

"It's not the fare that worries me."

"What is it, then?"

"I simply want to know where you want to go."

"I want to drive, that's all."

"But — damn it. . . ."

"If you don't like it, let me out."

The passenger seemed to have made up his mind about something. The driver, an odd, self-centered fellow, irritated, said, "Okay, then. Get out." He stopped the car. The passenger paid him and got out. Now, the driver rather regretted his actions. The passenger did not wait for change, but started stumbling away in the dark, as if he were drunk. The driver was concerned, but turned back toward Atami.

Maezawa's description of his passenger agreed with that of Kureha. It seemed certain Shiro Kureha had made up his mind to kill himself. Even Reiko had no idea why he should do such a thing.

4

Wakizaka said, "Then you don't know if your husband really died. If the writing in this letter is his, couldn't he be alive somewhere, right now?"

Reiko's voice was faint. "A week later, his body washed up on the beach, just beyond Ito."

Wakizaka stared at Reiko. But he put several questions to himself. What did the letter mean? If the cancellation mark was correct, it had been mailed after Kureha died. But since dead men do not write letters, someone alive must have written it.

"Mrs. Kureha. Are you certain this is your husband's writing?"

She looked steadily at the letter, then, staggering up, disappeared into an inner room, to return with a diary. She opened the book and showed it to Wakizaka. The writing was the same methodical script as in the letter. Wakizaka examined the book. A perfectly ordinary diary with entries beginning January 1 of that year, ending on the thirteenth.

"May I read it?"

"Yes. Go ahead."

None of the entries was long, but they were all suggestive, especially certain ones.

"January 5 — I'm sick of it. I've been betrayed. I can't believe anyone, now. What shall I do?

"January 8 — What I was afraid would happen has happened. But I'm trying to look on the bright side. Strange creature. I'm being used. But this isn't enough to get me down. I'll put up a real fight with the people who are trying to get rid of me. I'm the only one who knows the truth.

"January 12 — Someone's after me. I like to think it's just my imagination, but can't. I must keep my guard up. It's hard to believe, but a lot of unbelievable things happen. And once they happen, it's too late to do anything about them.

"January 13 — The department head and the managing director are having secret talks almost every day. I don't know what they're talking about. But I have an idea. That operation. Someday that trick is going to be discovered. But when the time comes to pay, I'll bet they are not the sacrifices. It'll be someone else. Tomorrow's the party at Atami. But I don't feel like drinking. Really, our accounting boys are something. Is this what is called a 'top company'? Don't make me laugh. They're all rotten. I wonder what would happen if the police found out?"

The diary ended here. On the fourteenth, he had gone to Atami and had been unable to make an entry. The writing in the two documents certainly looked the same. Wakizaka had no knowledge of handwriting identification, but if the letter were a forgery, it was skillful.

Wakizaka said, "But you said your husband killed himself. On the basis of these diary entries, I'd say there's reason to suspect he was murdered. After all, he says someone's after him —"

"I found the diary only recently. I hadn't the heart to clear up his desk. I left things as they were. Then, not long ago, I decided to steel myself and do what I must. When the body was found, I knew nothing of this diary. The police concluded it was suicide."

"What d'you believe now?"

She lowered her gaze. "I don't know what to do or think. Since reading the diary, I've begun having doubts."

"The police performed an autopsy."

"Yes."

"The verdict?"

"He had swallowed seawater. They decided it was suicide by drowning. Then there was the testimony that he'd been neurotic."

"Who made that testimony?"

"Somebody from the company."

"Who?"

"I don't remember."

"As his wife, would you say he was neurotic?"

"Since the end of last year, he seemed to've been displeased with something to do about his work. But I wouldn't say he was neurotic."

"He says someone's after him. Did he ever mention anything like that?"

"I don't recall that he did."

"He says something's wrong at work. You ever hear him discuss this more clearly?"

"He rarely talked about his work."

"Have you showed the diary to anyone else? The police, or anybody at the company?"

"I didn't know what to do. I still don't. What do you think?"

Most of the thirteen entries in the diary were random thoughts. But the ones for January fifth, eighth, twelfth, and thirteenth were definitely out of the ordinary. These suggested Kureha had suspected danger or smelled death. He had known a company secret. He had been indignant about the way the executives were behaving and sensed someone would become a victim.

Wakizaka felt it necessary to reinvestigate the entire case. At the same time, he was aware of what the case could mean to him professionally. He was dog tired of desk work on the readers' column. He felt that a journalist who doesn't gather news and write articles is no journalist at all. He didn't want to become like Oda.

"Mrs. Kureha, would you be good enough to lend me the diary?"

"What will you do with it?"

"I'd like to investigate this thoroughly. If they'd known about the diary, the police probably wouldn't have been so quick to give a suicide verdict. Any way you look at it, there's something damned odd about the way your husband died. I think it has something to do with the company. I won't abuse your confidence or the diary. I only ask you to rely on our newspaper."

"Are you going to write an article about this?"

"I don't know yet. If I'm able to throw new light on your husband's death, I'd like to write it up."

"I'm not sure I want the newspaper to write all kinds of things."

"But, since it's murder — I mean — if —"

Reiko was silent. Instead of replying, she handed the diary to Wakizaka.

5

The next day, after listening to Wakizaka's story, Kamei, who was in charge of the readers' column, said, "That's a damned odd tale. But it's got nothing to do with this department. Better tell the local-news people about it — leave it up to them."

"Local news?"

"That gripe you? Look, this is no time for ghost stories in the readers' column."

"Yeah — but . . ."

Kamei was saying that dead men don't write letters. But a man had died, and the letter had been delivered to the newspaper. Moreover, new evidence had turned up in a case that had been closed with a verdict of suicide. Clearly, it was something worth investigating.

Wakizaka did not want anyone else handling the story. He had hoped Kamei would tell him to investigate. But probably Kamei was so accustomed to desk work that he didn't want to undertake more than he had to. He was cool, now, as he stared at Wakizaka.

Wakizaka returned to his desk. It was piled with the usual letters. He felt curiously out of luck. It would have been better to remain in the provincial branch than to be stuck with this job. He had no notion why he'd been assigned to the readers' column. Fickle fate. The sight of the letters on his desk depressed him still more. "Just another damned cog in the wheel," he thought angrily.

"What's wrong?" Oda wanted to know.

"That letter that came yesterday."

"What about it?"

"I checked out the address and found some new stuff."

Oda sipped tea while listening to Wakizaka's story, then asked, "He worked at that company, right?"

"You know anybody at Tozai Electric?"

"Why would I know anybody?"

Wakizaka sighed. "It's just that when I heard you say 'that company' I thought maybe you might know someone there."

Oda shook his head. "But I know about the stir the company made."

"Stir?"

"Don't you read the papers?"

Wakizaka grimaced.

"It was in the stock-market report."

"Never read it."

"Well, you ought to. It's the most valuable thing in the paper. Regular stuff about elections, murders, homeruns — nothing to do with practical daily life.

Oda was sounding off. Wakizaka never read the stock reports. He had neither inclination nor money to play the market.

"You know what Tozai Electric's worth now?"

"No."

"Closing price yesterday was one thirty-five, ten yen less than last week."

"That so?"

"But last year, that stock took off. Until then, it hung around a hundred and forty yen. Then, at the last market of the year, it went above two hundred. Can you guess why?"

"A rush of buyers?"

"Of course. But what's important is why the rush?"

Wakizaka tightened his lips, shook his head.

Oda said, "Right after the market opened, word got out that Tozai had developed a new television shadow mask that could be produced for about half the cost of the older ones. This meant that production of color sets would be drastically cut. Now, Tozai doesn't make sets itself, but some of the big makers use their parts. Consumer groups had been attacking color TV makers and prices dropped some. But this was only the result of holding down the excess profits the makers'd been pulling in. But, if this new shadow mask was that cheap, it'd mean makers could cut the consumer price of their sets without reducing profits. The minute the session opened, there was a run on the stock. It went up more than sixty yen in half a day. A few days before, I'd sold my Tozai because it hadn't been moving. When I looked at the stock report that evening, I got sick."

"You play the market?"

"Only in a small way."

"Well, what happened then?"

"The first session of the new year, the bottom fell out. The stock dropped. People had found out that the rumor about the new product was a fat lie."

"What made them lie?"

"Some sharpy pulling a fast one. It's happened before, but usually over weekends. Stock-market gamblers are funny. They try to make money spreading false information. But they always control themselves, not using the break between the last session of the year and the first of the coming year. That's what fooled everybody this time."

"Anybody know who handed out the phony info?"

"They say people in the know have an idea. But there's no proof. Well, it's because of the rush that people got interested in Tozai. But what you say suggests Kureha's odd death may be related."

"I'm certain of it."

"Who knows? If he really was murdered, then there'd seem to be a tie-up."

"Kamei says to leave it to local news."

"You'd better listen, then. Those boys know how to get information in cases like this."

Oda turned back to work.

To investigate further, Wakizaka would have to go to Atami. He'd need Kamei's permission. He didn't want the case to fall into someone else's hands, so he was willing to pay his own way to the seaside resort. If he could prove Kureha had been murdered, Kamei would be interested. The editor would be impressed, and there might be a transfer to the local-news section.

6

He found no free time till around three in the afternoon. Instead of the usual coffee break, he hailed a cab and went to the Stock Exchange Press Club. Takegaki, hired at the same time as Wakizaka, was in charge of the stock-market news. As Wakizaka entered the club, Takegaki, who'd been writing a report, raised his eyes. "Well, look who's here."

"Something I want to ask you. Could you come outside?"

"Okay. Wait'll I finish this — a minute."

Wakizaka looked on enviously as his friend resumed work. Wakizaka felt sorry for himself. In a few minutes, Takegaki said, "Let's go."

As he slipped on his jacket, a parcel fell from the inner pocket. A bundle of money, maybe a million yen, projected from the packet. As they entered a nearby coffee shop, Wakizaka said, "You must be in great financial shape."

"That's money I'm keeping for a guy who asked me to buy him some stock. By the way, how's work on the readers' column?"

"Fed up. I really envy you guys."

Takegaki looked satisfied, "What'd you want?"

"It's about Tozai Electric stock."

"You thinking of playing with that?"

"No. But I heard it did some strange things the beginning of the year. Checking it out."

"Yeah. People were tricked that time."

"I know the gist of it. Anybody know who came up with the false information?"

"Not for sure, but the company's responsible."

"How come?"

"When the rumor about the new product began floating around, I called Tozai. I got this guy in advertising who handed me a lot of pretty vague information."

"You checked yourself?"

"Yeah. The minute buying opened, the rumor about the product began. Right off, there were orders for three hundred thousand shares."

According to Takegaki, since about a year before, Tozai stock had been gradually dropping. Strangely, some stocks become popular and others do not, just as some baseball players are more popular than others with the same batting average. No one knows why.

A year earlier, the price of Tozai stock had been about 160 yen. It might or might not do better. While the general market grew active, Tozai lost value. The only possible reason was popularity. A day's sales usually involved only forty or fifty thousand shares.

Then there was an order for thirty thousand shares to be purchased at any price. This captured the attention of the entire stock market. A small, apparently independent, securities company called Kanto Securities had placed the order. This meant that even the big people who controlled the market couldn't immediately find out who was behind the order.

Stock prices reflect the balance between purchases and sales. If sales are numerous and purchases few, the price drops, and vice versa. As a result of the order for thirty thousand shares at any price, Tozai went up to ten yen. If there had been no further purchases, the stock value would not have advanced further, and the order for thirty thousand shares would have been assimilated. But, as Takegaki explained, there was soon another unlimited-price order for fifty thousand shares of the same stock.

"It happened about ten o'clock. As a matter of common sense, there has to be something behind buying of this kind. So I phoned Kanto Securities. They said that they placed the order on instructions from a customer. When I said there must be something else, they stuck to their story. Big companies make orders like that, but it seemed funny for small fry like Kanto. I couldn't help thinking something was up, so I called the company."

"You called Tozai?"

"Yeah. Usually, with something like this, the managing director handles things. But they said he was in conference, and the advertising guy took the call. Ordinarily, I go directly to the office to check on this kind of thing, but it was the last market session of the year — it would be over by noon. There was no time. I decided to clear it up by phone. But the guy made a big mystery. 'It's not us — must be somebody else.'"

Remembering the incident, Takegaki looked insulted. Changes in the price of a company's stock usually meant something was altering in their way of doing business. Since he had no time, Takegaki decided to come directly to the point.

"It sounds like excuses, but I really didn't expect much. Even when they've perfected a new product, companies usually try to announce strategically to take advantage of good timing. But this guy said, 'There's going to be a conference to explain the new product after the opening of the new year. But I don't have details.'"

"He admitted there'd be a new product?"

"He said there'd be a meeting to explain it. That's the touchy point. He didn't say a new product had been developed. This caused problems later."

"What about the stock price?"

"Steadily up. Because the new product was supposed to be a real breakthrough, buying concentrated on this stock. In half a day, three million five hundred thousand shares were sold. The results for that day's buying were about one hundred million. Of the total, Tozai accounted for three and a half percent. That's a lot."

"The stock went suddenly up by sixty yen?"

"Yes. Stockbrokers never want to miss the boat. They get all hot and bothered and start screaming 'buy' and 'sell.' They never look at things calmly. What they hate most is missing a good deal. But it didn't take long for people to see that this new-product story was suspicious."

"A lie?"

"The company said they'd scheduled a meeting to explain the product. Just for fun, I checked. The conference was actually to be held in a hotel in Tokyo. But that was soon forgotten. At the first market of the new year, selling concentrated. Other words, things were back where they'd started."

Takegaki sounded irritated.

"Sounds like the company was trying to pull a fast one."

"We checked. They admitted nothing except that the meeting

had been scheduled. They said they hadn't given out any information."

"What about the new product?"

"The meeting was supposed to take place January 6th. Then,
they claimed that because of the upset, it was postponed. They
took this step to avoid misunderstanding, they claimed."

"But they finally announced the product?"

"No. Indefinite postponement. Said they found a defect in the
product."

"Too pat. You remember the name of the guy from the advertising department?"

"Nope. When I wanted to investigate further, they said they
didn't know who I talked to. They asked me to forgive them and
apologized for the misunderstanding."

"Was the name Kureha?"

"I just can't remember. I was in a rush. Any rate, there's still
no proof it was all a trick to affect prices. But the guy who worked
it made a cool one hundred and fifty million."

"Wow."

"Sure. Three million more shares were active that day than
usual. At first, about eight hundred thousand shares were bought.
But the man behind it was selling. Probably, up till then, he'd
been accumulating Tozai shares by buying inconspicuous blocks,
thirty or fifty thousand a day. When the big rush hit, he sold.
There may've been some small sellers involved, too. So this guy
may not have sold all three million shares. But he was probably
responsible for two and a half million. He made a profit of sixty
yen a share, or a total of one hundred and fifty million. At the
very least, I'd say he must've made one hundred million."

"But to buy like he did takes big capital." Wakizaka was dubi-
ous. "It'd mean an outlay of about three hundred and fifty million."

"No," Takegaki said. "They were trust shares. Of course, capital was needed, but only about one-third of the total amount."

"Even so, that's too much for an individual purchaser."

"Huh! There're plenty guys hanging around with one or two
hundred million to use. That kind of money's nothing."

Wakizaka sighed. "Well, no matter whether it was an organization or an individual, isn't there some way to pin down the guy

at Tozai who made the one hundred million?"

"Hold on, now. What I've been telling you's only my personal opinion. I don't really know whether somebody slipped a hundred million in his pocket. Don't write anything about this. Anyway, where d'you get off? Some letter from a dead man?"

"I think you've about hit the nail on the head. Here, look at this."

Wakizaka handed the diary to Takegaki.

7

The next day, Wakizaka called Kamei to say he had a cold, and went to Atami. If the case became public, the lie would be exposed. He'd face that problem when it came up.

At the Atami police station, he spoke with police chief Nojiri, who said, "Yes. There was a case like that. But I don't believe it was murder."

"Any definite proof of suicide?" Wakizaka asked.

"There was nothing to lead us to suspect murder. For instance, he left the hotel on his own. There was no phone to call him out."

"The killer could've planned it so as to meet Kureha at some specific place. He could've trusted the killer and went out without any suspicion about what would happen. Just because he had seawater in his lungs doesn't mean he drowned himself."

"Yeah, but if he'd made an agreement to meet anybody, he wouldn't've driven around the way he did. After all, it was late. He'd probably have gone straight to wherever he was going."

"Maybe he wanted it to look as if he were out for a drive."

Nojiri frowned at Wakizaka's persistence.

"We had testimony to the fact that he'd been neurotic about his work. He certainly could get out of the taxi and throw himself into the sea."

"What about the diary?"

Nojiri's scowl deepened.

"That diary looks like proof of neurosis to me. He claims somebody's after him."

Wakizaka was convinced the policeman didn't want to go to the trouble of reopening the case. If it turned out to be murder, the police error in declaring the death suicide would come to light. All of this could be avoided by clinging to the suicide verdict.

Wakizaka was frowning, now. "How about identification of the corpse? Kureha's body was in the water for a week. Wasn't it hard to identify him?"

"There was damage, sure. The body beat against boulders. But the face was in pretty good shape. The autopsy showed the wounds had been made after death. A man from his office identified him."

"Didn't his wife see him?"

"She couldn't take it. We relied on a man from the office. His name was Sakamoto."

Wakizaka believed Kureha hadn't died early on the morning of January 15, but had actually written the letter and died afterwards. This was the only answer to the riddle of the letter.

"Did Sakamoto say Kureha was neurotic?"

"He wasn't the only one. Several said the same thing."

"Okay. Look at this letter. The cancellation date's February eighth. It arrived at our office only a couple days ago. What d'you make of that?"

"It's a long time, but it could happen."

"Okay. Suppose the delay might be that long. Still, the letter's in Kureha's handwriting. What about that?"

"It's a forgery. Besides, he's got to be joking about the River Styx."

"All right. Dead men don't write letters. But I don't admit the deal involved is pure coincidence."

"You got me."

"How's for reinvestigation?"

"It's not that I want to avoid trouble, mind you. But can you understand what another investigation would involve?"

"But you've got to admit it looks as if somebody at Tozai Electric was up to something tricky."

Nojiri hesitated. "Well — maybe . . ."

Wakizaka rose. The only thing was to expose a few facts in the paper and force the police to act.

Back in Tokyo, he called Takegaki, He asked the man to follow up the movement of the stock shares and let him know the outcome. "Anything more on the case we were talking about the other day?"

"Oh, that. Look, a lot of time's passed since then. It's not easy to find these things. Wait a bit."

"When can you know?" Wakizaka was eager.

"It'll take at least a week."

"No faster?"

"I'll try, chum. But don't get your hopes up. You ask me, you won't get much of a story out of this." Takegaki was cool.

Wakizaka knew what it was. From Takegaki's standpoint, the case had nothing to do with financial news. He wasn't really interested. Wakizaka couldn't force it. On the other hand he wouldn't give up.

The next day, he took all the information to the city desk. The man in charge, Takishita, sat smoking his pipe as he listened. Wakizaka gave him the diary when he finished speaking.

"Hm. Letter from the dead. Not a bad headline. Let's give this a try."

Takishita called a roving reporter, Fujimoto, and explained things. "Find who wrote this letter. Maybe somebody in the office feels sorry for Mrs. Kureha and copied her husband's writing. There should be plenty of things Kureha wrote lying around."

Wakizaka and Fujimoto visited Reiko Kureha. Wakizaka was excited; he sensed a conclusion. During the same day, the local news section verified everything Wakizaka had so far uncovered. For a starter, they drew up an article dealing with the mysterious letter to the newspaper and the contents of the diary and tied this in with the fluctuation of stock prices. At the end of the article was a vague hint that murder might have been committed. This was the first shot.

Driving to Reiko Kureha's, Fujimoto said to Wakizaka, "I think the chief's right about this letter from the River Styx. I bet it was Oba who did it. He's the only one without an alibi. He could've slipped to a phone and ordered Kureha to go out. Then he could've tailed him in the taxi. As far's the stock deal goes, Oba was in a position to tell Kureha what to say when the newspapers called."

Wakizaka agreed. Now all they had to do was clear up the riddle of the delay in delivery of the letter.

Reiko Kureha was not at home. The woman next door didn't know where she'd gone. Wakizaka and Fujimoto waited until nearly midnight for her.

"Maybe she went home to her parents," Fujimoto said. "Anyway, you've already got information from her. Why not just use that?"

"Yeah. But — let's wait a bit longer. You go back and write this up."

"Okay." Fujimoto departed.

Wakizaka continued waiting in the dark. Reiko did not return until nearly one. Wakizaka surprised her.

He called, "Mrs. Kureha. It's me — Wakizaka."

"Oh! You startled me."

"Sorry. Just wanted to tell you the story'll be in the morning paper. As it turns out, your husband was the victim of a shady stock deal."

"Who did it?"

"Well, we're certain of the stock deal, but there're some doubtful points to clear up about the cause of death and that letter."

"Is it really going to appear in the paper?"

"Yep. It's being written up right now."

Reiko sighed and asked Wakizaka inside. Wakizaka explained what he had discovered. They talked until well after three.

". . . and that's why we'll have to write a follow-up. We'll want your cooperation."

Reiko nodded.

Wakizaka said, "I'll call the paper." He did, and the presses were already rolling. He told Reiko, who smiled.

She said simply, "You told me you were still puzzled by the cancellation date on the letter. Shall I explain it to you?"

"Explain it?"

"Yes. First I wrote my own address on the letter in pencil. Then, when it arrived, I erased it and wrote in the newspaper's address. Two months later, I handed it to the girl at the reception desk in your building."

Wakizaka was silent.

"My husband killed himself. The reason was a person at your newspaper named Takegaki. He put out information that Tozai Electric had developed a new product and in that way artificially raised the price of Tozai stock. Of course, there was a group with plenty of money. Although he was principal actor in the scheme, he made it look as if it were my husband's fault. The Tozai executives reprimanded my husband. He was a meek man, and this blame worried him so much that finally, one dark night, he took his life. The men from the office were right to say he was neurotic."

Wakizaka could not speak. In his mind's eye, he saw the packet of money lying on the floor at Takegaki's feet.

Reiko went on. "I decided to avenge my husband. I wrote the diary myself and mailed the letter. I knew it'd be ignored unless I was careful. So I went to Atami and mailed several envelopes. I selected the one with the clearest cancellation mark. My husband was very unlucky. If only he'd not answered the phone when Takegaki called. All Takegaki's supposed to have asked is whether it was true the company planned to hold a conference to explain a new product. Such a meeting was planned, but for a very ordinary, unimportant new product. My husband told him about that. It was used against him. He kept saying over and over how unlucky he was. . . ."

Wakizaka still could not speak. He wanted to cry out, "Your fool husband's not the only person with rotten luck!" But he lacked the strength.

SEIICHI MORIMURA

Devil Of A Boy

In 1969 Seiichi Morimura published A Dead Angle of the Skyscraper *and won the 15th Edogawa Rampo Memorial Award.*

Compared with their American or European counterparts, Japanese writers are generally prolific. Morimura is representative of this particular phenomenon, and with his remarkable energy he has published a great number of novels and short stories in a short period of time. Though most of his works belong to the genre of the pure detective story, he has also written some prominent stories dealing with abnormal mentality and psychoanalysis.

"Devil of A Boy" explores the malice and cruelty of ten-year-old primary-school students — crimes of poisoning, arson, even murder. One of the child characters "has a positive genius for wickedness. . . ."

RETURNING FROM THE SUPERMARKET, Makiko Sagara witnessed something frightening. Usually the maid did the shopping, but since it was the girl's day off, Makiko decided to go to the market herself for the first time in a long while.

On her way home, she had to cross a two-lane road. Although the street passed through a residential area, drivers were in the habit of speeding here because of the good pavement. Up ahead, on the sidewalk, Makiko noticed a cluster of five or six primary-school children.

Our Masao's age, Makiko thought. As she approached the group, she made a mental comparison between them and her own small son. From behind, an automobile passed her, moving swiftly in the direction of the children. Just before it reached them, a child suddenly darted out in front of the car.

"Look out!" screamed Makiko, closing her eyes.

The driver slammed on the brakes and tires screeched horribly.

"What you doing?" the driver shouted. "You want to get killed?"

The child will be all right, Makiko thought as she fearfully opened her eyes. The little boy who had run in front of the car was standing safe on the other side of the road, grinning shyly.

Seeing that he was dealing with children and that scolding would do no good, the driver drove off.

Makiko's heart was still beating fast as she asked, "Haven't you been warned about playing in the road?"

A voice called from the cluster of children: "Oh, you're Masao's mother, aren't you?"

Makiko looked closely and recognized Soichi Ono, one of Masao's classmates, about whom there were unpleasant rumors.

"Ah, Soichi Ono — right?"

"I bet you were surprised just now, huh?"

"Of course. I thought my heart would stop."

"It's called the street-crossing game. Everybody's doing it."

"Street-crossing game?"

"Yeah. You wait till a car's right on you. Then you jump out in front and run across the street. The one who cuts closest wins. Tanaka just ran in front of that car. Everybody's been calling him a coward because he wouldn't play. Now he's shown us all up. Well — I guess that's what you can expect from Doctor Physical Education. He can do it if he wants to."

Little Tanaka was especially good at physical education.

"I don't believe it." It was too much for Makiko; she was confounded. Then she was seized with fresh fear when she began asking herself whether her own son might be playing this dangerous game. "You must never do it again. It's horrible. Nobody'd be a coward for refusing to play. If you don't stop, I'll tell your teacher —"

"What's wrong? We're only trying to see how brave we are."

Soichio Ono gave Makiko a disgruntled look. A strong little boy, he was notorious as the prankster and troublemaker of his class. His father worked as a guard in the company where

Makiko's husband was president.

"That's no way to test courage. You do what I tell you, or I'll see your father."

Some of the impudence went out of Soichi's face. Evidently he was afraid of his father.

"Mama? What's the matter?"

Makiko recognized the voice and turned to see her son Masao standing behind her, smiling. He was on his way home from the piano lessons he'd recently started taking. In contrast to Soichi Ono, Masao was a studious boy and always at the top of his class. In primary school good students had authority. Even a little toughie like Soichi seemed to give in to Masao at first glance.

In his right hand, Masao was carrying a rather large bundle. With his left hand, he was leading an old lady with a bent back.

"Masao, who's this?" Makiko asked, as she looked suspiciously at the old woman.

"Oh, are you this little gentleman's mother? I was on my way to a house near here when I asked him the way. He was sweet enough to say he'd take me, since it was close to where he was going. The dear thing carried my package all the way. A fine little boy." The old woman's face wrinkled with gratitude. She bowed several times in appreciation.

"Why, thank you. I'm happy he's been of some help." Makiko was proud, especially since she had just been scolding someone else's child for doing bad things. "My boy is different," she said to herself.

Makiko was proud about everything. As a matter of fact, it made her a little unhappy that her son's good deed was performed where no one else could see and appreciate it. She wished his school teacher had happened along just then. Although she wanted to tell those other bad little children to learn a lesson from her Masao, she repressed the desire.

But, by way of driving her point home, she turned to the children and said, "Now listen. Don't you ever let me catch you playing that game again." And with this, she parted from the old lady and started home with Masao.

"What's the matter, Mama?" Masao asked.

"Just now, Ono and the others were playing the street-crossing game. Masao? You don't play that game, do you?"

"Oh, Mama — really. I thought they were playing that game. Teacher told them they shouldn't do it again. OK, tomorrow I'll report them to the class committee."

"But, if you do that — won't Ono and the others try to get back at you some way?"

Makiko was worried about this. There was something wily and treacherous about that Ono boy, something unchildlike. The impudent way he'd looked at her when she was scolding him — it was no expression to find on the face of a fourth-grade pupil. If a terrible little boy like that should hold a grudge against Masao, her own child whom she protected from everything, there was no telling what might happen.

The world of children was cruel, more cruel than the adult world. A child's cruelty was completely open. Children ostracized and oppressed the weak members of their group. The thought prejudices and exclusivism added to the fun of the game. The order prevailing in the child's world was stricter and more all-pervasive than the order in the world of adults. No matter how much a child was teased or tormented, he must never carry tales to his parents or teachers. If he did, he would be severely punished. Adults were only sometimes threatened with disgrace, but intimidation ran throughout the lives of children.

Makiko did not think anyone would intimidate or torment Masao. Still, the dangerous party in this case was Soichi Ono, who could not be judged by standards applicable to other children.

"Now, Mama, don't worry so much," Masao said with a laugh.

"But — that Ono's a devil of a boy."

"It's no reason to stand by and watch him do bad things. No matter how strong he is, if you're brave, you won't let the other guy do things he shouldn't do. Isn't that right?"

"Yes. That's true. That's the meaning of real bravery."

Of course, that was true courage. It was something different from that wild street-crossing game. Her boy had true courage. Makiko loved him so much she could have squeezed him, right there.

2

The first incident that marked Soichi Ono as a no-good had taken place some six months earlier. Hitomi Sagawa, a girl in the same class as Masao and Soichi, saw Soichi teasing some younger school children and told the teacher. Soichi denied it at once, and a few days passed without further incident.

Then, one day, Tommy, Hitomi Sagawa's pet cat, disappeared. Hitomi looked for him everywhere until it got dark, but Tommy did not come home. On the following morning a housewife from a neighboring apartment took her trash to the incinerator to burn. When she got there she saw a cardboard box crammed inside.

The woman frowned. Everyone who used the incinerator was supposed to make certain his trash was completely burned. It was an apartment rule that no trash could be burned at night. Some thoughtless people who came too late simply put things in the door and left them there. This caused a great deal of trouble for the next person who wanted to use the incinerator.

Grumbling, the housewife decided that, since she did not know who the guilty party was, she would burn this leftover trash together with her own. She lit the fire. There was nothing but paper in the compartment, and soon the flames seethed brightly.

Closing the incinerator door, the woman started away when she heard a savage howl. Something inside the incinerator was struggling desperately. She was terrified. Suppose someone were inside!

The thumping and shrieking continued, but by now it was clearly not a human being, but some kind of animal, being burned alive. The fuel in the furnace flamed fiercely, and there was nothing the housewife could do.

When the fire died down, she assembled some of her neighbors. They slowly opened the door of the burner compartment. The stench of burned flesh belching from the incinerator sickened some of the women so much they ran off.

Inside, was the charred body of a cat. Owing to a lack of fuel, the body had not been completely destroyed. From the horribly disfigured remains, it was possible to identify Tommy.

One of the women remembered seeing Soichi Ono loitering around the incinerator the night before. There could be no doubt that he had put the cat in the box, tied it to prevent its escape, and left it to die terribly in the incinerator.

Soichi flatly denied the accusation: "I don't know anything about it."

"If you're really telling the truth, look me straight in the eye." The teacher questioning him was perturbed.

With no sign of fear, Soichi looked directly into the teacher's eyes. It was the teacher who finally looked away.

Makiko recalled this incident.

"Masao? Did anything happen at school today between Soichi and little Tanaka?"

"Ono and Tanaka?"

"Yes. Maybe it wasn't today. But in the past few days, have they had a fight, or anything?"

"Well, now you mention it . . ."

Masao looked as if he remembered something.

"What is it?"

"Ono was in charge of cleanup, but he didn't do his work. Tanaka told the teacher on him. The teacher bawled Ono out."

"I thought there was something."

"What do you mean?"

"Nothing. But don't you play with that Ono anymore."

"All right. Anyway, he's not in my group."

"Even if he gets put in your group, don't you play with him."

"But why, Mama?"

"Never mind why. Just do what Mama tells you."

"OK. But you're funny today."

"And don't say anything about this to Ono."

Makiko was thinking. What a frightful child that Soichi Ono is. He had conveniently ignored his own guilt about not doing his work, and had taken this dangerous and sneaky way of revenging himself on the boy who tattled on him to the teacher. Fortunately, little Tanaka was unharmed. But if he'd been struck by the car, it might have been a case of skillfully arranged murder. What's more, the murderer would have been a pupil in the fourth grade of primary school. Even with murder, a child that young could not be held responsible for his actions. Had Ono calculated all of this? If so, he was dreadful indeed.

That night, after Masao was in bed, Makiko casually brought up the subject of Soichi Ono's father to her husband.

"Ono? He's serious and responsible. Works very hard. Why d'you ask?"

Makiko told him about Soichi Ono.

"He sounds like a problem child, all right. But, you've got to remember, children can be very cruel. When I was a kid, I used to dissect frogs and lizards. Don't take it too seriously. He'll grow out of it."

"But it's different, killing frogs and lizards. That boy could have been plotting murder."

"Don't exaggerate," Sagara said. "Remember, too, his father's accident and disability are bound to have shadowed the boy's personality."

Sagara sipped tea as he reproved Makiko gently.

Soichi Ono's father had operated a taxi. A reckless driver crashed into his cab. Ono was so seriously hurt that he lost the use of both legs. Sagara had felt sorry for him and employed him in his company as a guard. Of course, the company contracted professional guards for building security. Ono's work consisted of simple checks and acting as a kind of information clerk. If Sagara had not given him this job, Ono and his entire family would have been homeless and destitute. Well aware of his debt to Sagara, Ono worked to the very best of his abilities.

"Don't worry so much about other people's children," Sagara said. "Think about Masao."

"Nothing's wrong with Masao. Really, sometimes I worry about him because he's too good."

Makiko told her husband about Masao and the old woman.

"That so?" Sagara nodded and grinned with pleasure. Though known as a shrewd businessman, he was completely soft on the subject of his only child.

Makiko suddenly thought of something else, something that disturbed her. It had nothing to do with Masao, or Soichi Ono, and she felt a trace of guilt as she watched Sagara through veiled eyes.

Sagara was her husband. . . . She must remember that.

. . . . And Masao was their child.

3

Hiroshi Naito's tropical fish were famous. In the large tank he kept at home, he had angelfish, guppies, black tetras, and Sumatras — the types of fish beginners usually had. His tank was outfitted with thermostatic heater, air-pump, and filters, along with several different kinds of colorful aquatic plants. Hiroshi prepared a balanced diet for his pets by combining live and dried foods. For a primary-school child, he was much more serious about his hobby than might be expected.

In his class at school there was a tank with some angelfish and guppies that he had donated. A fishkeeper was appointed on a rotational basis to feed the class pets. But it was Hiroshi Naito who was most diligent in their care. The food these fish ate was usually a compound prepared by Hiroshi.

Lately, something unexpected was occurring. The tropical fish seemed to go more for food Soichi Ono brought than for Hiroshi's preparation. Ono's food was a compound different from commercial brands, and he had his own recipe. Since eating Ono's food, the fish were clearly growing larger.

The children in class began to take a different view of Ono. In the past, his image had been decidedly bad. Children were little adults. A child's standing among his classmates was determined more by his grades than by physical strength. A rough child who was strong and boastful, but who remained scholastically at the bottom of the heap, was despised and shut out.

In Ono's class, several children were recognized authorities in given fields. One was the champion at handstands. Another knew most about animals. One was the bug expert. Still another was the outstanding runner. Hiroshi Naito was the unquestionable authority in the field of tropical fish. This position had won him the nickname Doctor Fish.

But since he had discovered an apparently better fishfood, Ono seemed to be challenging Hiroshi's claim to the title.

Hiroshi tried hard to maintain his position, but no matter what new food he devised, at feeding time the fish always clustered around Ono's recipe. These fish were frank: they made their preference known with a candor verging on cruelty.

"Boy! That's really something, Ono."

"How'd you make the food?"

"Teach me!"

"I didn't know Ono was such a great fishfood maker."

"From now on, Ono's Doctor Fish."

Once the outcast, Soichi Ono was now the center of class popularity. Hiroshi Naito could do nothing. He stood on the sidelines and watched as his own position gradually shifted from that of star to has-been. For a Doctor Fish, this was the depth of humiliation.

Some days later, Hiroshi Naito heard Soichi Ono call to him as he walked home from school. Their houses lay in different directions and they never met each other this way. Evidently Ono had been following him.

"Naito. Could I see you a minute?"

Soichi said this after looking around to make certain none of their classmates were near.

"What d'you want?"

Hiroshi was a little frightened. He did not like Soichi. This was not only because Soichi had recently made incursions into the tropical-fish field. Soichi always tried to make his point with brute-force tactics: a kick, a karate chop. To Hiroshi, this was a barbarous way to behave. In primary school there was no room for violence. Children who used it were regarded with fear, as if they were animals.

Ono spoke now in a strange, wheedling voice.

"What would you think if I gave you that goldfish food I made?"

Hiroshi was perplexed. He couldn't believe his ears. He stared at Soichi.

"Look, to tell the truth," Soichi said, "I'm not really interested in goldfish — tropical fish, I mean. I didn't make that food, anyway. A college guy who lived in our neighborhood made it for me. I don't know how to make it. Now he's moved away, there won't be any more. Before my supply runs out, I thought I'd give the rest to you. See, I brought it with me. You're Doctor Fish — you can probably make some more."

Soichi held up a plastic bag filled with fishfood.

"You're giving it to me — really?"

It was so sudden that Hiroshi half believed and half distrusted Soichi. There were times when he'd thought of asking Soichi to share his fishfood with him, but his pride did not allow it. Asking would have constituted abandoning authority as Doctor Fish. This would have been tantamount to total defeat. Now, here was Soichi offering him the food. But he had chosen a time when no one else was near. Hiroshi became uneasy. Maybe Soichi was setting some kind of trap.

"Don't you dare tell anybody about this. I'd feel like a fool if people found out I didn't really make it."

Soichi's tone had become rough. This change led Hiroshi to believe that Soichi was truly being himself now. His uneasiness was dispelled. Hiroshi would be ridiculed worse than Soichi if the transaction were known in class. By imposing silence, Soichi was actually acting in Hiroshi's best interests.

"I really shouldn't take all this."

"Go ahead. I've given up goldfish." Soichi lifted a hand. "Well, so long."

"Bye. And — thanks."

Hiroshi was elated when he got home. His authority as Doctor Fish was safe. The sudden intruder into his realm had lost interest and gone away. Now he could find out what was in Ono's food and prepare a better kind that would surprise everybody. The thought made him happy. The unhappiness came the next day.

"Hiroshi! Come quickly! All your fish are floating."

Hiroshi was still in bed when his mother's shrill voice startled him. He leaped to the floor and dashed to his fish tank.

All of his treasured tropical fish were floating upside down on the water's surface. They were all dead.

"Mama —" he said in a tearful voice, "what's happened?"

"I don't know. Did you give them something bad to eat last night?" His mother's voice trembled.

The thermostat and air-pump were working normally.

"No. Only the regular fishfood. . . ."

Hiroshi stopped. It was his custom to feed the fish three times a day, each time giving them only as much as they could consume in about ten minutes. Last night, at their final feeding, he had used Soichi Ono's fishfood. The "something bad" could only be that food. But the fish at school had eaten the same food, and thrived. Was it the same food Ono had given him? Hiroshi had believed Ono and had accepted the food on the strength of what he'd said. What if Ono had mixed poison with the food? It was frightening. Why would Ono do a thing like that?

He had an idea. Ono had once asked Hiroshi to lend him his monster book. The book was a rarity, containing all of the old familiar monsters like Godzilla and Angilas, as well as the new ones, like Ultraman, Mirrorman, and the Masked Rider. It gave their heights, weights, dates of birth, weapons, and family histories. All the children he knew were dying to have that book, but it had gone out of print. The only way to obtain a copy was to rummage in old-book stores. Hiroshi was afraid that, if he loaned it to Ono, he might have trouble getting it back. He had heard of other classmates complaining that Ono borrowed things and never returned them. Hiroshi was unwilling to lend his treasured book to such a dangerous character. He refused Ono's request. That might have made Ono so angry that he took his terrible revenge.

There had been no reason for Ono to give the fishfood to him; he should have offered to trade it for the monster book. Hiroshi might have suspected some trick, but now it was too late. All of his precious fish were dead.

Hiroshi screamed as he stamped his feet. "Ono, you rat! You dirty bum — I wish you'd drop dead!"

"Ono?" Hiroshi's mother said, "What's he got to do with this?"

Hiroshi told her everything. She at once decided that the matter must not rest. It was too wicked to be merely a childish prank.

She told her husband, who had just gotten up.

"We've got to do something," she said.

Hiroshi's father took a calm view of the situation. He spoke to his son. "D'you still have any of the food you got from Ono?"

His father took the evidence to school. The teachers and staff were surprised. Seriously doubting the likelihood of such a trick, the science teacher analyzed the fishfood. He discovered traces of an organic phosphate, a mildly toxic substance used in insecticides. He claimed it was probably strong enough to kill delicate tropical fish.

The school authorities now took a more serious view of the case. Deliberately mixing insecticide into fishfood with the intent of killing a classmate's pets was a bit too sophisticated a plot for the ordinary primary-school pupil. Still more serious, since there are some who have a habit of tasting food before giving it to animals, it was conceivable that a human being might have taken the poison. The principal, the faculty head, and the class teacher summoned Ono and questioned him. He calmly denied everything.

"I never gave Naito any fishfood," he told them. "He's jealous because my food was better than his. That's why he's lying about me."

Ono insisted this was true. Since no one had witnessed his giving the food to Naito, it was impossible to press him further on the matter. The school authorities then had no choice but to have Ono turn over to them all of the remaining food; not surprisingly, there was no poison in it. A strong suspicion persisted that Ono had poisoned only part of the food, that which he'd given to Hiroshi Naito. There was no way to prove this. No one really thought Hiroshi Naito had lied. On the other hand, it was a fact that Ono's new fishfood had lowered Hiroshi's position as Doctor Fish. Undeniably he had been, as Ono insisted, jealous.

The teachers didn't know how to handle the matter. While tending to believe Soichi Ono guilty, they could not afford to make a rash statement. There was no actual proof. The matter remained unresolved.

But the image of Soichi Ono as a horrible little boy became firmly fixed in the teachers' minds.

4

Masao was in the garden. He quickly spotted his mother through the living-room window.

"Mama — where've you been?"

Makiko was surprised. "You're home early today?" she said. This was the day Masao had extra classes.

"She let us out early. She had a special study project to do today. But where've you been?"

"Shopping. Why're you so filthy? You're covered with mud."

"We're making a cemetery."

"A cemetery? What for? Don't you go burying a lot of strange things in the yard."

"For the fish, Mama."

"Fish?"

Masao's friend, who had been digging with him, looked toward the mother and son.

Makiko recognized him. "Hello, Hiroshi."

"Hi, Mrs. Sagara."

"Mama. All Hiroshi's tropical fish died."

"I know."

Makiko was prompted to say she knew about Ono's poisoning them, but she stopped herself. The story was discussed among the parents and families of Ono's classmates, but it was still up in the air because of lack of proof.

"Hiroshi lives in an apartment building and doesn't have a yard. He didn't want to bury his fish out in a field somewhere. I offered him our garden."

"I see."

"If you don't mind, Mrs. Sagara." Hiroshi Naito hung his head.

Makiko was happy over her boy's thoughtfulness in "offering" their yard as a cemetery for his friend's pets.

"Of course, I don't mind. Make a nice little grave for them." Makiko nodded with satisfaction, and started for another room, but stopped as Masao called.

"Mama, I didn't tell you before, but —" He hesitated.

"What is it, Masao?"

"Well, you see —"

"What is it, Masao? Say it."

Makiko had been out a little longer than she had expected and was hurrying to make preparations before her husband came home.

"It's about Hitomi Sagawa's cat."

"What about the cat?"

That must have been the cat Ono burned to death.

Masao went on, "I didn't say anything about it, but I let her bury the cat in our yard. Hitomi lives in an apartment, too. I offered her our yard."

"Well, now!"

"Sorry I didn't tell you. But the cat was in bad shape — worse than the fish. I thought I'd better be quiet about it."

"It's all right. I forgive you. But always tell Mama about these things. And — don't bury the fish next to the cat, or the cat'll eat them up."

"We'll bury them a little way apart. OK?"

"When the funeral's over, come in and have a snack. But wash your hands first."

5

Three months passed after the disturbance over the tropical fish. The dry, cold weather typical of the Tokyo winter set in. For sixty days, no rain fell. This broke all previous records for dry spells. In the arid weather, fires were frequent. Sometimes several occurred in one day. People were worried over the dangers.

The air was so dry that merely walking around a room generated static electricty in the form of flying sparks whenever a person touched metal. Many persons seriously consulted the fire department to learn whether static-electrical sparks could cause a fire.

Makiko Sagara lived about an hour's train ride from the heart of Tokyo, in a region that, until quite recently, had retained a rural mood but that was rapidly being built up with apartments and factories. In the dry weather, fires were numerous here, too. Once a fire broke out, it spread so rapidly that all the fire department could do was struggle to halt its progress. Usually they could not save the flaming building. People were resigned to the idea that fire meant total loss.

During this particular dry winter, some unpleasant occurrences intensified the anxiety of the local population. Leaflets bearing childish writing were delivered by mail to some five houses. The leaflets said, "Condolences on the fire," "Beware of fires," or "Handle all flammable substances with caution."

At first, they seemed nothing but warnings. People who received them paid little attention, assuming some acquaintance had sent them. The leaflets were not signed. Probably someone was merely urging caution in the long rainless period.

All these leaflets said the same thing. They were delivered every two or three days, until people began to worry, because fires were breaking out almost daily in the vicinity.

What could it mean?

People who received leaflets reading "Condolences on the fire" were most upset.

"Maybe it's a threat of arson," some said. They took the leaflets to the police, who started an investigation at once. If this was some kind of practical joke, it was in very bad taste.

The postmarks on the leaflets were from the local office. This pointed to a local person as the culprit, unless the leaflets were deliberately transported from somewhere else.

The handwriting proved interesting. The letters were quite childish, with many mistakes of the kind a small child might make. A handwriting specialist examined the leaflets and said he could detect no attempts to use childlike writing as a coverup. "Looks more like the writing of a primary-school child. It may well be," the investigator said.

Next the police tried to uncover something in common among the recipients of the leaflets. All the families had children who attended the nearby primary school, and the children were in the same class. This simplified the investigation.

It didn't take long to weed out Soichi Ono, whose handwriting perfectly matched that of the leaflets. Ono was called in for questioning and confronted with the facts. He was a boy of ten. Under the stern interrogation, Ono said only that he had wanted to caution some of his classmates about the danger of fire in the dry winter.

"Then why didn't you sign your name?"

"I sent them to girls' homes. I was too embarrassed to sign my name."

"Why'd you send so many leaflets?"

"There were fires every day. It worried me. I was going to keep sending them till it rained."

The suspect was a child. If he insisted his story was true, it would be difficult to prove malicious intentions. The contents of the leaflets were no more than caution; nothing in them violated any law. It was true that, during this dry spell, repeated messages of this type aroused fear of arson. Ono claimed he was simply trying to show how much he liked the girls. Indeed, these were girls in whom he regularly showed interest. Perhaps it was a bit early for Soichi to be concerning himself with the opposite sex, but the way he chose to reveal his feelings was precisely what might be expected of such a child. It was hard to find traces of menace in what he had done. Even if he were threatening the families, he was a child of ten and not liable to criminal prosecution.

"If that boy knows enough about the law to realize he can make threats without paying for it, he's plenty sharp."

"What're you saying? He's only a fourth-grader. Our boy's the same age — practically a baby."

"It's pretty frightening to think he sent warnings about fire to his girl friends in place of love letters."

Having found out who was sending the leaflets, the police decided nothing criminal had been perpetrated. The five girls in Ono's class told their story.

"Soichi Ono asked us to lend him our science notes."

"We were afraid if we lent them to him, he wouldn't give 'em back."

"Maybe it made him angry. Then he pulled that trick on us."

This looked like motive for threat, but since all the girls were top students, many other little boys probably wanted to borrow their notes. Even if Ono had been angry because of the girls refusals, it was impossible to tie this in to the fire warnings. Ono's past record had no influence with the police.

But the faculty and the parents involved were irritated with him. "He has a genius for wickedness," one teacher said. Though they were certain that the cat barbeque, the incident of the tropical fish, and now the fire warnings were all Ono's doing, they couldn't pin him down. He hadn't been seen in the act of putting the cat in the incinerator, or mixing poison with the fishfood. He had evaded blame easily. He may not have had detailed knowledge about the law, but it looked as if he were counting on getting off because he was a child.

Makiko Sagara had remained quiet about the street-crossing game. But with the premeditated malice involved in that incident, Ono had committed four perfect crimes. He truly had a knack for wickedness. The situation was grave. But there was no proof against Ono. At school he was regarded as something of a live bomb.

6

"We can't continue meeting this way."

Makiko spoke to Obata in a cool voice. Their sweating bodies were still hungrily entwined, but the echoes of pleasure were receding. Having sated her desires as a female, Makiko turned to an awareness of herself as a mother.

"Why?" Obata asked. "Does your husband suspect something?" The lovemaking was over, but the young man still spoke with lingering tenderness as he stroked Makiko's full breasts.

"No. It's hard to fool Masao. More difficult all the time. It seems like only yesterday he was a little baby. Now he's almost an adult. He knows things. The other day when I came home after meeting you, he said, 'You go out a lot these days don't you, Mama?' It startled me."

"I don't think it means so much."

Obata was thinking of what would happen if this woman left him. Until now all he had to do was ask, and she generously let him have her luscious body. Of course, it cost him nothing. As a matter of fact, after he'd satisfied himself with her, she gave him spending money.

"I'm certain he thinks something's wrong with me. He's always asking where I've been. The supermarket and beauty shop don't work anymore. The other day when I said I'd been to the shop, he asked why my hair looked the same as when I'd went out. It frightened me."

"Ah, you worry too much."

Obata would do anything to put Makiko's mind at rest.

"I'm sure he knows what's between us."

"C'mon, he's only a kid."

"Before, he used to talk about you a lot in front of his father. Lately, he never mentions your name. He's perceptive. I think he senses something."

"He's just interested in someone new now. To Masao, I'm a person in the past. Let's not talk about that anymore. Let's do it again."

"No. Not now. I've got to go, Masao comes home early today."

"Doesn't he go to private classes today?"

"His teacher's off on a trip. She asked Masao to come another time. Didn't you listen to what I said?"

"Sorry. It's only that I need it."

"You're spoiled. You better change, or I may have to say good-bye for good. Anyway, no more for today."

Makiko slipped out of bed and began dressing. He watched as the sweet female flesh that had been panting under his body was gradually covered with clothes, transforming her into another man's wife. Now she was out of his reach, sobered to her role as wife and mother. There was longing in his eyes as he watched her move away.

"When can we see each other again?"

"I'll be in touch. Don't call me. Lots of eyes are watching what I do. Get dressed. You can drive me to the taxi."

Obata was sexually powerful, precisely what Makiko needed to quench the passion of physical hunger that her tired husband was unable to satisfy. The young man was principally concerned with his own sexual appetite and was careful not to do anything that might endanger the convenient relation. The affair had assumed a contractural nature, the calculated renting of a body.

Obata was in financial difficulties. There was no question of their belonging to each other. Both enjoyed the meetings. It was only natural that the one with the money should pay — a kind of rental of his flesh. Makiko defrayed all costs of their dates. She paid him each time. This not only took care of the rent for his body, but also provided Makiko with safety insurance.

He abided by the conditions, never exceeding the limits of a physical rental relation. It suited him. First, he never felt the maddening sexual hunger that plagued many of his bachelor friends. Second, he had spending money in addition to sexual satisfaction. For the sake of extra money, some of his friends worked part-time in the so-called host clubs and sold their bodies to women. They could not pick and choose. He was better off. He enjoyed a perfect female and was financially rewarded in the bargain. Hard to find a better setup than that.

He really desired Makiko strongly. Their dates were pure physical pleasure, and had been going on for two years. The absence of psychological attachment made the pleasure all the greater.

Recently there had been a change. In the past they had met regularly at a certain time and place, without making specific dates. Sometimes something prevented Makiko from coming, even though she wanted to. As Masao grew up, he made it difficult for Makiko to take advantage of her husband's absences as much as she wanted. Her son's private school and the P.T.A. interfered from time to time. Her husband was home more, now that he was successful. All these things made incursions on the time available for her secret dates.

The balance of supply and demand broke down. From Makiko's standpoint, Obata was never anything more than a stand-in for her husband, an accent in married life, which might fall into a rut. Reduction of the number of times she met Obata did not mean frustration for her. For him, however, the situation was different. Makiko was his sole sexual outlet. Deprived of her, he would be physically starved. He would find himself in a financial crisis, too. This difference upset things.

Makiko said to herself, "I think the time's come to part with Obata."

Thinking back, she knew they had both enjoyed their time together. Though not as softly skillful at lovemaking as her husband, the young man was an inexhaustible fountain of sexual energy. For this reason, he'd been capable of calming her own overwhelming female passions. But if she remained infatuated with the pleasure and acted like a glutton she might do irreparable damage. No. Far better to stop now, while her husband was still unaware, while she and the young man had nothing but pleasant memories. Yes, she thought. The time has come for goodbye.

After their dates, the young man drove Makiko from the motel to a cab. It was always the same place, and safer than calling a taxi to come to the motel. It made no difference if she was seen riding in Obata's car. The important thing was not to be seen entering or leaving the motel.

"I'll get out just before the pedestrian bridge, up there."

While the car was leaving the motel, Makiko crouched in the back seat. She sat up when they reached what she considered the safety zone.

"Looks like an accident up ahead."

A police motorcycle and an ambulance were parked just at the bridge.

"Damn!" Makiko said, frowning.

"It's OK. I'll drop you just beyond the bridge."

Appearances would prove them guilty of nothing. But after having deceived her husband, Makiko felt strange about being seen by the police. Obata seemed to share her feelings, and speeded up.

7

Soichi Ono waited in the cold on top of the bridge. A blue Corolla was supposed to come by before too long. He had memorized the license number, and was supposed to receive further contact when the car drew near.

Below, a constant stream of automobiles passed. It was calm on the bridge. As he watched, it seemed as if the cars were being transported on a conveyor belt. From time to time a pedestrian would cross the bridge. They paid no heed to Soichi: "Probably just another car-crazy kid."

"Hello. Hello, Car's coming. Blue Corolla. Number Shinagawa 116–654. Approaching bridge. Stand by!"

The voice came from a small portable transceiver hanging around Soichi's neck.

Soichi answered. Then he readied something held close to his chest.

Makiko and Obata approached the bridge. A figure standing in the middle of the bridge caught Makiko's eye. It seemed to be a child. Then, as the car moved directly beneath, Makiko lost sight of the figure. At that instant, a small, black object fell from the child's hand, hurtling toward the car.

"Look out!"

As she shouted, the black object struck the hood and burst with a flash of showering flame. Brakes shrieked and the Corolla crossed the center line into the path of an oncoming vehicle. A violent crash was followed by a soaring column of fire. Makiko lost consciousness. At the moment when a voice from the transceiver called, "Stop! Stop!" the Molotov cocktail had already left Soichi Ono's hands, making a direct hit on the car.

Soichi was confused to see that a small act of his own could have such horrendous results. Then the whistle of the police and the siren of the ambulance broke through his lethargy, and he ran. A minor traffic accident had occurred nearby, and the police, who had come to investigate, caught Soichi Ono.

Obata was rushed to the hospital, but he was dead on arrival. The driver of the other car was so seriously hurt that he would be hospitalized for months. Makiko escaped with only minor scratches. The effect of the crash had been minimized for her since she was crouching in the rear seat to avoid being seen by the police. The psychological shock, however, was great.

When questioned by the police, Soichi Ono would say no more than that he'd been playing with a Molotov cocktail. As a result of this child's play, injury or death had come to three people.

The police checked Soichi's transceiver. It was a good instrument, capable of making communications over two kilometers in the city and a radius of twenty kilometers in open country. If he had a transceiver, he must have been talking with someone. That someone became a subject of concern.

The police believed Ono had the transceiver so he could receive a signal telling him when to drop the Molotov cocktail. Suppose the person on the other end of the communication were an adult? Using a child to commit murder was an ugly thought. There seemed to be no adult who might put Soichi up to the act. There was no reason to believe Soichi hated any of the people involved in the crash. The police decided to investigate everyone in the vicinity who owned transceivers in hopes of finding someone who might accidently have intercepted the conversation between Ono and the other party. They were certain this communication contained the key to the identity of the person who had used Ono as a tool.

8

Three days after the accident, two detectives called on Makiko. One was the chief detective from the local police department.

After expressing regrets about the tragic occurrence, he came to the point. "There are a couple of questions —"

Makiko had expected this. When she had entered the emergency hospital, a policeman asked her a few simple things, but no further inquiries had been made until now.

Makiko prepared herself. "What do you want?"

"First, what were your relations with Mr. Obata, who was killed?"

"I've already explained that. Mr. Obata was a graduate student at Waseda University. A year or so ago, he tutored my son."

"Why were you in his car?"

"He gave me a lift."

She had told the same story to her husband.

"Quite by coincidence?"

The faint smile on the detective's lips made Makiko uncomfortable. Does he suspect something? she wondered.

"Mrs. Sagara, we have no intention of intruding on your privacy. But, just the same, we'd like the truth."

"I'm telling you the truth." Somehow she kept up the pretense.

"Mrs. Sagara, in one of Obata's pockets we found a box of matches from a motel. We've already talked with the people there."

Saying this, the man took out a cigarette and lit it with a match from a box given at the motel. Makiko paled.

"You and he'd been seeing each other for some time, right?"

The detective exhaled a cloud of pale smoke.

Makiko's poise gave way. "I didn't mean to hide anything. But — please keep this from my husband."

"We don't want to interfere. That's why we came when we knew your husband wouldn't be in."

"What else do you want?" She felt relieved, realizing that her relation with Obata was not the main purpose of their visit.

"Do you have any reason to suspect your son knew about you and Obata?"

"He may. He's very perceptive." Makiko thought of the recent suspicion in Masao's eyes. "Why do you ask?"

"If your son knew, d'you think he'd hate Obata?"

She frowned. "I don't know —" What was he getting at? She sensed what was behind his words. "You can't mean my son would do something like that!"

"Well, we don't like to think so, but —"

"Ono said something to make you suspicious."

"Ono had a transceiver."

"That has nothing to do with my son."

"We've learned that Ono was in contact with your boy Masao, just before the accident."

"But I was in the car. No matter how much he might hate Obata, he wouldn't drag me into it. Masao's a gentle boy."

The man was making a ridiculous mistake. He must be out of his head. He would have to be crazy to cast suspicion on Masao. Makiko became indignant.

The detective took no notice. He said, "We know there are rumors about Soichi Ono. We called together all the people involved in the incidents caused by him. We came up with a new lead."

"Does it have anything to do with Masao?"

"Unfortunately, yes." He eyed her. "First, there's Hiroshi Naito, whose tropical fish ate poisoned food. He's first in science in the class. Your son is second."

"So?"

"Please, listen. Hitomi Sagawa, whose cat was burned alive, is first in arithmetic. Your son is second. And the five little girls whose families received the fire warnings are all better in music than your boy."

"So what? Masao's no superman. He can't be tops in everything."

"Right, I agree. Usually, Masao is always best in the class. But he's second or lower in some fields. Read this," he said, holding out a piece of paper. "It's a composition written by Masao."

Wondering why the chief detective brought such a thing, Makiko took the paper and read:

"When I grow up, I want to be president of the company, like my dad. The president is number one. I only like to be first. I would rather be last than second. I will study as hard as I can to be first in language, arithmetic, science, music, physical education, and everything."

Makiko suddenly thought of something. Little Tanaka, who had been playing the dangerous "street-crossing game," was very good in physical education. The class called him Doctor Physical Education. So, behind that game, too . . .

She began to draw a fearful mental picture. Masao's father had always urged him to be first. Masao could do almost anything he wanted to do, but he was not the type to demonstrate brilliant abilities in one field. Instead, he was good at everything. Although he was often second or even third in some subject, his average was always tops. But he hated this. He had to be first in everything. Recently, he had started taking private piano lessons in hopes of overtaking the girls in his class who were better at music than he.

In the fourth grade, children began to be competitive. To stimulate them to their best efforts, the school encouraged competition by giving out gold and silver seals for achievement. The children collected the seals and boasted about the numbers and kinds they had. Masao had more than anyone else in his class. Feeling that his fever to be always on top was abnormal, Makiko had tried to convince her son to worry less and play more, like other children his age. Masao would not listen. Still, the police must be wrong to think Masao would try to get rid of his rivals by enticing Soichi Ono to help him.

"Certainly, you can't say Masao's wanting to be first in everything has some relation to the things Soichi Ono's done. That would be groundless suspicion that could damage the innocent mind of a child."

"It's not groundless, Mrs. Sagara, We have proof."

"Proof?"

"Ono had a transceiver. We reasoned he must have been in contact with someone immediately before the accident. We checked all the people in the vicinity who own transceivers."

The detective looked at Makiko as if asking permission to continue. She nodded abstractedly.

"Some restaurants and stores use transceivers. We interviewed all the places in the neighborhood of the site of the accident. We found that just before the crash, some owners of transceivers heard a child's voice saying, 'Blue Corolla. Number Shinagawa 116–654. Approaching bridge. Stand by.' But the next words said are the important ones." He paused.

"What words?" Makiko was impatient.

"No! Mama's in the car. Stop — stop, I tell you. Stop!"

Makiko felt helpless. She remembered she hadn't gotten out of the car in the usual place, because the police were there. Masao had intended to kill only Obata. When he found his mother was in the car, he had frantically tried to stop Ono from dropping the Molotov cocktail.

"The license number is that of Obata's car. Masao is only a child. No one else would refer to you as Mama."

"But, why? Why?"

Makiko's eyes went dim. She heard the detective's voice as if in darkness, struggling with herself. She could not believe that her Masao — a boy who helped old ladies and who let his friends make a cemetery for their dead pets in his yard — could have done this horrible thing.

"Mrs. Sagara. I'm not going to preach. But I do ask you to give some thought to your own actions. Think how hard it is for a young boy to recover from the shock he experiences when he learns that the mother he loves and the tutor he respected are both betraying his father and him. Masao kept all that to himself, Mrs. Sagara. This accident was the explosion of angry pressures that have been building for some time."

When she reflected, Makiko realized that Masao's abnormal longing to be number one in all things had started at about the time of her first date with Obata. The hardening of Masao's heart toward his mother had been dissipated in the series of incidents involving Soichi Ono.

"Soichi Ono told us everything. Masao blackmailed him. Ono's father works for your husband's company. Masao told Soichi that if he didn't follow his orders, he'd have your husband fire Mr. Ono. Soichi knew, if his father lost his job, he'd have a hard time finding another, because of his serious disability. Soichi's a gentle boy who loves his father. Masao wears the mask of a sweet child and an outstanding student. But he uses his father's position and authority to oppress a person who lacks strength to fight back."

Makiko watched him.

"The fishfood, the fire warnings, all those things were Masao's ideas. Ono got the transceiver and the Molotov cocktail from Masao. Masao may deliberately have made the writing mistakes in the fire-warning leaflets. It's pretty horrible. But, Mrs. Sagara, you are the person who created the horrible face behind the innocent, childlike mask."

Makiko felt a ringing in her ears. To her, the detective's words meant, "It was you who killed the cat, the fish, and Obata."

Just then, she heard the sound of childrens' voices, coming from the garden. She turned. Through the living-room window she saw Masao, Hitomi Sagawa, and a number of their classmates. Evidently they had come straight from school.

"Mama," Masao called through the window. "Today's the first anniversary of the death of Hitomi's cat, Tommy. We're going to have a ceremony at the grave."

The gentle, low sun of winter played on the boy's plump cheeks, turning the down on them to a shimmering gold. A soft breeze ruffled his smooth black hair.

The detective looked out at him and said, gravely, "He certainly is a lovely child, isn't he?"

SHIZUKO NATSUKI

Cry From The Cliff

A graduate of Keio University, where she majored in English Literature, Shizuko Natsuki attracted notice for her first novel, The Passed Death. *She is one of the few female detective writers in Japan, and each year produces an average of one long novel and fifteen novelettes. In 1973 her best seller,* Disappearance, *won the Association of Mystery Writers of Japan Award. Many Japanese critics have predicted that Shizuko Natsuki will become known as the "Agatha Christie of Japan," preeminent in the field of "women's psychological suspense."*

Her contribution to this collection is a bittersweet love story about a strange sculptor and his lovely, sad wife who live near the sea, and a visitor — a fascinating mystery that will clutch at your heartstrings. . . .

I FIRST MET MAIKO NISHIKAWA on an afternoon toward the end of August. The still strong, late-summer sun penetrated deep into the small reception room next to the editorial office. When I entered the room, she was seated close to the wall, where she could be out of the sunlight. When our eyes met, she half rose, then sat back and waited for me to draw up a chair in front of her. She was small and slender, wearing a soft white suit, her attractively cut hair in a delicate line just below her ears. As I presented my card, I said, "Sorry you've made a special trip here. Did you say you've some copies of the *New Art Journal?*"

This magazine had been discontinued. But an architect had written to the "Bulletin Board" column, here at the *West Japan News*, where I work, to inquire if we could find someone with a complete set of issues for 1959–60 who would be willing to sell them to him.

The woman raised her eyes to mine and said, "Yes, I have the ones you want. I'd be happy to give them to you. But, they're very heavy. And I live rather far from here."

Her gaze was cool as she looked steadily at me. There was nothing sensual in her look, nor was it too cold. She seemed intelligent and charming.

"You could send them to us. Of course, we'll pay for the mailing charges."

She glanced at my card lying on the table, then picked it up. There was a kind of excitement in her gesture.

"Shin'ichi Takida. Your name? Did you graduate from the Shuyu High School, in Fukuoka, in 1956?"

"That's right."

"Well," she said. "How about that?"

She looked happy. Her cheeks flushed slightly as she asked, "You remember Sugio Nishikawa? You were both in the same class."

I groped for a moment, but finally recalled his face. He and I had not been especially close friends, but I could see him clearly in my mind's eye. The school we attended was famous in our part of the country. Sugio Nishikawa had been conspicuous as something of an eccentric.

"He's my husband," she said. "Perhaps you've forgotten him, but he speaks of you often."

"No, no. I remember. He was the first student from our school ever to be accepted by the sculpture department of the Tokyo University of Fine Arts. I recall reading that he won prizes for his work while he was at the university. I suppose he's continued as a sculptor?"

"Five years ago he damaged his eyes in an automobile accident. We came back here. The injury wasn't serious. Nothing that would interfere with his work. But it was a bad psychological blow. Lately he's done almost no work. I'm beginning to be afraid he won't get any better."

For a moment, I could think of nothing to say. She lowered her eyes. An unexpected air of heaviness settled between us.

I tried changing the topic.

"You say you live a long way from here?"

"We have a small studio on the beach at Keya no Oto. We're some distance from the nearest town. But, it's quiet there, and the sea is beautiful."

Her tone was brightening again.

Keya no Oto, located some thirty kilometers west of the city of Fukuoka on the northwest part of a peninsula jutting into the Sea of Genkai, is famous for its rugged, exciting shoreline.

"Yes, he speaks of you often. He's not the type man who has many friends. You must have left a deep impression on him."

This surprised me. In high school, Nishikawa had a pale, regular face that always suggested an awareness that he was of the elite. He was on close terms with no one, including me. Since graduation, I'd had no contact with him. After leaving college, I went to work for the *West Japan News*, but remained in the Tokyo branch until I transferred to the Fukuoka main office only five months ago. This was the first news I'd had of any high-school classmate.

A gleam came into the woman's eyes. "I know this is sudden, and I hope you'll forgive me. But I wonder if you'd come to visit us sometime?"

I didn't know what to say.

"Meeting you might give my husband the will to work again. And there are the copies of the *New Art Journal*. Please?"

Her cheeks flushed again, and her gaze was arresting. So, I vaguely agreed to her request. She stood to go, but I invited her to join me for a cup of tea. She accepted without hesitation.

I flagged a taxi and took her to a cool, quiet place some distance from the office. We were there for some time. She talked little, but her eyes seemed to tell me a great deal about her way of life, her unhappiness, her search for something indefinable. At parting, a little flustered at my stupidity, I said, "I don't know your first name."

"Maiko."

Small teeth showed between pale pink lips. We watched each other, and I felt we read something in each other's eyes. We did not understand the true meaning of the word fate.

One Saturday in early September, I drove my small car to the Nishikawa house. Leaving the national highway and driving for a time over rough mountain road, I finally found the desolated little Shinto shrine that was my landmark. I could hear the sound of waves nearby.

As Maiko said, the public beach, caves, and spots tourists visit in boats were about one kilometer from the shrine. There were no houses here. Lines of lofty pines rustled boughs overhead.

Getting out of the car, I heard someone call to me. Maiko smiled at me from a path to the cliff on which I stood. She wore a broad-brimmed straw hat and had yellow rubber zori on her feet. The blue veins were visible in the delicate flesh of her fragile, white toes.

As we came out of the grove of pine trees, the sea opened before us. Far below, waves crashed whitely. Maiko guided me down the steep path leading among boulders and clumps of wild grass to the sea.

"You see that high cliff over there? From the top, the view's wonderful. I'll show you later." Her voice was light as she pointed. The cliff was so high it was necessary to look up. Made of a kind of basalt peculiar to this part of Japan, it was a great column rising toward the sky from a base badly eroded by pounding waves.

The Nishikawa house was built snugly near the sea, almost at the bottom of the path. Though small and old, it had Western-looking white walls and a flat roof that set it apart from the usual fishing-village houses in this part of the country. It seemed to be a weekend house built a long time ago by a person who was both rich and capricious.

Sugio Nishikawa greeted us at the door. I couldn't believe what I saw. Could he have changed as much as this in ten years? He was thin and aged, looking a good ten years older than he was. He combed his hair straight back from his forehead, but it was already thin at the hairline. His skin was transparent. In the past, the high bridge of his nose had contributed to the regularity and artistlike appearance of his face; now it only accentuated sunken eyes and bony cheeks. What struck me most about him was an alteration of general mood. A light of pride had always governed Nishikawa's features. Now he seemed a shadow of weakness and emasculation. Nonetheless, there was a hint of happiness on his face as he welcomed me.

"Good to see you. Thanks for coming."

We shook hands like acquaintances of ten years.

Just beyond the entranceway was a large room with a worn carpet on the floor. Apparently it served as both living room and studio. In a corner was a built-in sofa and table; at the back of the room stood a rattan chair. On the floor, in a semicircle around the chair, ranged various lumps of clay. None of these had definite shape. But the buttocks-shaped dent in the tattered cushion of the rattan chair showed where Nishikawa spent long hours.

He motioned me to the sofa, then sat in the chair, some distance from me. As old friends who haven't seen each other for a long time, we sketched our histories since parting, then ran out of conversation. Names of two or three high-school classmates came up, but neither of us knew anything about them. We hadn't much in common to discuss.

The silence became difficult. I said, "I heard you damaged your eyes in a traffic accident."

I thought I'd gone too far, but Nishikawa smiled weakly. "It's nothing serious. Sometimes things blur, and maybe every ten days I get a bad headache."

To my relief, Maiko came from the kitchen, where she'd been preparing food.

"Sugio's been happy as a child ever since he heard you were coming. But he's not a good talker — probably hasn't let you know how he feels."

I understood. As if unable to suppress his excitement, Nishikawa had been continually toying with a pipe, and stammered a little when he spoke. His attitude made me uncomfortable.

"Shall I show you the house?" Maiko asked.

The request sounded American. Under ordinary Japanese circumstances, it would even have been pretentious. But, coming from Maiko, it sounded completely innocent, and I rose to follow her.

I was surprised to see that the bath was directly next to the studio living room. Beyond a small dressing-room was a blue-tiled bath with a large window looking out on the sea. Below the window were boulders, and several meters farther down, waves beat against the shore. Only the living room and bath faced the sea. At the rear of the house were one bedroom and a small dining-kitchen.

"You'll spend the night of course?"

Maiko's tone was much more intimate than on the day when I'd first met her in my office.

"As you see, we're country. I'm afraid there isn't much to offer in the way of hospitality. But we can get good fresh fish. And then, there's the view of the sea."

Nishikawa had oppressed me. But with Maiko, the entire mood changed. Once again, I felt myself unable to refuse her request.

After dinner, I spent what seemed hours facing Nishikawa across the living room. During the meal, he had taken part in the small talk Maiko engineered. But now he sat in silence, leaning back in the rattan chair with his eyes closed. The only proof I had that he wasn't sleeping was the smile of satisfaction playing over his face.

Somewhat accustomed to the quiet, I enjoyed the moonlight on the sea. From time to time, I heard the humming sound of a motorboat.

Quite some time had passed, when I realized the sounds from the kitchen had ceased. I rose and went to tell Maiko not to stay out of the living room to humor us.

The dining-kitchen was dark. I knocked on the bedroom door, but there was. no answer. Cracking the door slightly, I looked in. There was no sign of Maiko. All was quiet in the bathroom, too. Maiko was nowhere to be found.

I glanced at my watch. It was past nine. She couldn't have gone out to buy anything at this hour.

Somewhat uneasy, I returned to the living room to find Nishikawa just as I'd left him. He swayed back and forth in the rattan chair and wore a look of savoring each second. It was still. All I could hear was the sound of the waves and the occasional humming of a motorboat.

Then the motorboat sound seemed to come nearer. When it reached a point comparatively close to the house, it stopped. After that, I heard it no more. The silence muffled everything.

More time passed; I don't know how long. Then I heard the

soft sound of the front door opening. I went across the room, opened the connecting door a bit. Maiko was there. She wasn't aware of me. She carefully locked the front door, without a sound. After removing her rubber zori, she walked quietly toward the bedroom.

It was night. Sometimes people went out to finish a piece of work they'd forgotten. Sometimes, unable to sleep, they went for a walk. But the thing that made me reject both of these explanations of Maiko's absence was the thick makeup she wore, heavier than what she'd worn during the day. She had drawn pencil lines around her cool eyes, and her lipstick wasn't pale pink, but brilliant scarlet. There was wet sand on her feet.

I closed the door and walked back to the sofa as Nishikawa opened his eyes.

"I think I'll take a bath. Takida, how about you? I hop into the bath, anytime, day or night."

With a motion, I indicated refusal. With a meaningless laugh, Nishikawa opened the bathroom door and went in.

He must have noticed Maiko's absence and her secretive return. He was simply keeping quiet. I concluded this was the most deliberate posture this emasculated man was capable of.

As she promised, on the following bright, sunny day, Maiko guided me to the top of the high basalt cliff. Though the weather was calm and windless, powerful waves hurtled against the cliff base, twenty meters below. It was the kind of sea one could expect at Genkai. In the offing, there were no waves, only an expanse of cobalt-blue water dotted with pale green islands. The two or three hours after lunch, Nishikawa devoted to what he called "work." For this reason, only Maiko accompanied me on the walk. She wore an orange blouse and white shorts and the same yellow zori she'd worn the day before. Though small, she was beautifully proportioned, with legs like a young fawn's. She was very lovely. Seen from behind, her bobbed hair fluttered and she reminded me of an innocent girl who's fond of sports. I found it hard to believe this was the same Maiko who had sneaked into the house the preceding night.

Standing on the cliff, she told me the names of all the peninsulas and islands. Then she laughed. "Forgive me. You're a native of this part of the country."

"Maybe — but I've forgotten these places. I was in Tokyo a long time."

"Tokyo . . ."

Maiko looked raptly at the sea. Her voice was filled with some special emotion.

"Are you from Tokyo?" I asked.

"Yes."

"Your parents still there?"

"They're dead. But I do have an elder sister. I love her very much. I used to visit her often, but now . . ."

Maiko lowered her gaze. I wondered why she didn't enjoy the luxury of trips to see her sister. Psychological, financial? I nearly asked her why she concealed her sadness.

But I turned my eyes away and suddenly saw an elegant building of white walls, near an inlet on the opposite side of the bay. A villa. Partly hidden by a grove of pines, the house looked cool, refreshing.

At the shore by the house was a motorboat; its bright cream hull suddenly filled my entire field of vision and burned itself on my mind.

I decided to spend another night with the Nishikawas. Maiko was eager for me to do so, as on the previous night. I was unable to say no. But I had another reason. Monday morning, I didn't have to be at the office until around eleven. Since I'm a bachelor, there's no one to complain if I stay away from home for a night or so.

Shortly after dinner, Nishikawa retired to the bedroom, claiming he was tired from his first good day of work in a long time. Although there was nothing to show how much or what kind of work he'd done, it seemed certain he was pleased at my staying there. As usual, he was silent, but smiled in a satisfied way when he looked at me.

Alone in the living room, I unfolded the sofa bed and lay down. Moonlight fell on the water. Everything was quiet in the dining-kitchen. After a time, the humming motorboat sound arose from the sea. With closed eyes, I listened as the boat approached, then moved away in what seemed to be a pattern of fixed distance. The repeated rhythm of this pattern finally began to get on my nerves. It was almost intolerable, when the engine stopped. The restored silence penetrated to the very core of my brain. I went outdoors.

I felt it was the same motorboat I'd seen moored by the villa across the water.

I began climbing the stony, upward path. Moonlight bathed everything a pale blue-white. When I reached a point about half-way up, I heard a car engine. Then, at the very top of the path, I saw the car — a white Volvo. A man and woman got out of the car. The woman was Maiko. The man was tall.

Maiko led the way down the path, which was too narrow for them to walk abreast. If she showed any sign of unsteadiness, the man put out both arms to catch her and help her. They were soon well on their way down the slope. I hastened to retrace my steps, since there was no place on the path to hide.

Crouching behind a large boulder beside the entrance of the house, I watched as Maiko almost ran to the front door. I was shuddering with excitement. She seemed completely collected. Then the man arrived. He wore a white shirt with the collar turned up. Since the moonlight was behind him, I couldn't make out his face, but I could see that he was tall and thin.

Maiko turned around. The man's hand stroked her hair and then slipped along her shoulder. His fingers interlaced with her white fingers. Maiko allowed him to touch her lightly, then she pulled free. When she reached for the doorknob, the man did not touch her. After looking at him another moment, Maiko quickly slipped inside and shut the door. The man stood for a moment before the closed door, then turned and slowly started climbing the path.

There had been no embraces, no amorous whispering. But it was all the same to me. I wanted to look away from Maiko's true reason for inviting me "for my husband's sake" and for her eager urging that I stay. As I watched him walk away in the moonlight, I experienced an emotion I was unable to entertain in connection with Sugio Nishikawa. It welled within me. It was jealousy.

Two days later, as I returned to my office from lunch, I noticed a parked white Volvo. I hadn't gotten a good look at the car Maiko came home in that night. It made me uneasy.

I was right to be suspicious. As I watched, a tall man came out of a gun shop in a building two or three doors beyond the car. He had on large, dark green sun glasses and wore a beige shirt with the collar turned up. He carried a hunting rifle in his left hand. Opening the rear door of the car, he dropped the gun inside, then got in himself. With a roar, the car was lost in traffic on the boulevard.

I was certain this was the man who had brought Maiko home that evening.

I went into the quiet cool of the air-conditioned gun shop. Running my eyes over the polished rifles along the walls, I said to the heavy-set man behind the counter, "The man who went out just then. I know him. Does he come here often?"

"Yes. That's Mr. Kusashita, you mean?" The shop owner had a ruddy, pleasant face and smiled as if he liked people. He wore a red bow tie.

"Quite a gun fan, Mr. Kusashita. Been a good customer of mine for about six months."

"Doesn't he have a beach place at Keya no Oto?"

"Yes. But I hear he's originally from Tokyo, He came here to get over a case of asthma, liked it, and stays more here than anywhere else. Even if he's recovering from sickness, he's lucky to be able to do what he wants."

When I returned to work, one of the office girls said I'd received a call from a woman named Nishikawa. She had called a few days earlier urging me to visit them. Since he'd seen me, her husband's condition had changed. He was working and she wanted me to come often to encourage him.

On the phone she was completely the wife who's deeply concerned about her husband. She created a feeling that would only be possible in a woman who believes implicitly in the bond between her husband and an old friend. This hurt me, somehow. Still, I decided that day to visit them again. I had the respectable excuse of wanting to pay them for the copies of the *New Art Journal*. I felt that, if I were being used, it was all right. As long as he understands his part, Pierrot is not really a clown. If I could only see Maiko. But because of work, it was after eight at night when I finally knocked on the Nishikawa front door.

Maiko, dressed in dark blue, greeted me at once. She looked more downcast than usual. I almost believed that look of striking happiness that filled her eyes when they met mine. But probably what I saw was only a reflection of what was in my own heart.

Niskikawa wasn't in the studio-living room.

"He's gone out in the boat," Maiko said, looking in an oddly coaxing way at the dark waters. A fog was moving in over the sea. "He only wants to go rowing on nights like this. He claims he's only relaxed when he's out on the water where it's impossible to see anything."

Maiko prepared something to eat and I sat for a long time in silence, playing with the drink in my hand.

"Are you going to go on living like this?" I asked after a while. And Maiko's eyes spoke to me, just as they had that day in the coffee shop. She seemed deep in thought.

I said, "You're sacrificing yourself for your husband's sake."

She made no reply.

"Are you satisfied with this kind of life? You're not, are you?"

She looked at me. When I felt her glance, a wall inside me seemed to crumble.

"You're giving him everything. Anyway, that's how it looks. But actually, you're betraying him."

"That's not true," she said sadly.

"But I've seen you with him, with Kusashita."

"There's nothing between us. I want you — you of all people — to believe that."

Her lips trembled as she spoke. I wanted to believe her.

There came the sound of a rifle shot from the sea. Then another. The fog seemed to muffle the sounds so they had difficulty reaching us. Something came over me, a sense of foreboding, and I embraced Maiko with all my strength. Her body felt pitiably light as she collapsed against my chest.

"If that's how you feel, it's all the more reason for you to stop living this hopeless way."

"Only a little longer," she said. "Sugio needs this life. Anyway, it'll end sooner or later."

"And then?"

"I'll change completely. I'll become a different person."

Her words were fixed in my mind. The sound of the shots from the sea continued.

"Believe me," she said softly.

I pressed my lips against hers. She kissed me in return. At the same time, a fat tear rolled from the corner of her eye. I believed that tear.

The next day was cloudy, hot, humid. Sometimes a rough wind blew so hard it threatened to topple the little house. We heard that a small typhoon was approaching.

The night before, when Nishikawa came home to find me there, he was in good spirits. But even as late as the afternoon of the next day, he showed no signs of wanting to work. He was more talkative than usual and took pleasure in ridiculing all the generally admired sculptors, one by one. Maiko had wanted me to come to encourage him, but my presence seemed to have the opposite effect.

The typhoon was still creeping our way, but in the evening the wind was strong and steady. The sea swell increased. Whitish clouds rushed across the sky, making things lighter and brighter.

"It's a fine night," Nishikawa said, looking at the sea with feverish eyes. "I feel most relaxed in a storm."

"You going for a boat ride tonight, too?"

I was joking, but noticed that he had changed into the same gray shirt and black shorts he'd worn the night before. I knew I couldn't let him go out. The thing that really disturbed me was the memory of the dull, ominous gunshots from the fog. Before I could speak, Nishikawa said, "No. Since you're here, let's have some drinks."

I agreed. Not that I thought drinking with him would be much fun, but it would keep him home. I suspected Maiko would stay home tonight.

I was wrong. When Nishikawa and I had finished off about a third of the bottle of whiskey I'd brought as a present, I noticed the house was very quiet. Pretending to go to the toilet, I went to the entranceway. Maiko's zori were gone.

Irritation, indignation touched me. After a while, I got the better of my feelings and returned to the living-room. I tried to recall the look in Maiko's eyes when she had said, "I want you — of all people — to believe that." I had believed her. Nothing else mattered. I had to close my eyes to everything.

I had been drinking fast since early evening. Nishikawa held his liquor well. No matter how much he drank, he didn't become flushed in the face. He became paler. Only his eyes glowed with a strange, burning light. From time to time he said disconnected things.

A little after nine, he rose sluggishly.

"Excuse me, but I think I'll take a bath. Sober up. Then we can drink some more."

I nodded and he went into the bath.

A few moments later I heard a sharp woman's cry from the sea. "Help!" Then, "Somebody!" This was followed by inarticulate screaming. Finally there was an indistinct sound of something falling into the sea, of splashing water. This was mixed with the sounds of the wind and the waves, reaching my ears in snatches. I shot up from my chair, then hesitated.

At that instant, Nishikawa opened the bathroom door. He was wet and naked. There was something different in his expression.

"You hear a funny voice, just now?"

It had been no trick of my hearing, then.

"Yes," I said. "Sounded like it came from the sea."

"No. From the cliff. It couldn't be . . ."

His voice choked off. He was thinking the same as I: It couldn't be Maiko.

"I'll go and take a look," I told him.

"Yes. I'll be along in a minute."

I left the house. At first, I looked toward the sea. The boiling sheet of white rain clouds lightened the sky, but the sea was black. High waves crashed and foamed among the boulders below. I could see nothing from the height on which I stood.

I started up the path. Maybe Nishikawa had been right saying the voice came from the cliff. I hurried. I heard my own rough breathing, felt blood pounding in my ears.

Reaching the top, I cut through the alley of pines. Two hundred meters from the small shrine, a narrow path dipped then turned up to emerge at the top of the basalt cliff. It was the same path Maiko had guided me along the day we walked up there. Because the path twisted and turned, it took five or six minutes to reach the cliff edge.

There was no one there. I looked over. The drop of more than twenty meters along the scooped-out cliff face made me slightly dizzy. Looking around, I glimpsed some white thing shining at the very edge of the cliff. I picked it up. It was a small woman's rubber zori with yellow straps. I felt sure it belonged to Maiko.

I noticed something. On one of the straps, was a spot. I looked closer. It seemed to be blood.

"Maiko!" I called out loudly, but the wind and waves obliterated my voice.

I thought of jumping in. But I'd had no experience in high diving. I had no notion what waited for me at the base of the cliff.

Holding the zori, I retraced my steps along the narrow path. My car was parked by the gate of the small Shinto shrine.

The settlement of inns for the Keya no Oto public beach is about a kilometer in the opposite direction from the cliff. It is located on a sandy shore across the peninsula from where the Nishikawa house stands.

The middle-aged officer in the local police station was skillful and expert. Accidents at sea were fairly frequent. He immediately called the innkeepers' labor union and asked them to put out the motorboat they held in readiness. Then he sat beside me in the front seat of my car as we drove back to the cliff. By this time, large drops of rain had begun beating on the windshield.

We arrived at the top of the cliff at the same moment Nishikawa came loping up. He was breathing hard.

"I went to the breakwater," he managed. "But I couldn't see anything."

All three of us rushed to the edge. The policeman trained a flashlight on the blackness, but we only saw dark swelling waters and pounding spray. I explained the situation to Nishikawa, showed him the zori. He collapsed. Wind and rain lashed his white shirt and brown trousers.

I heard a low, smothered groan. It was Nishikawa, pouring out a bitter sorrow.

About an hour later, they found Maiko's body. It was near a cliff, some fifty meters west of their house. She was wearing the dark blue dress and was barefoot. The large fruit knife that remained thrust in her body had been driven into her back, aimed at her heart.

The results of the autopsy were revealed the following evening. She had died instantaneously of the wound in the back. She could not have drowned because she had taken in almost no seawater. Nishikawa testified that the right zori found at the cliff edge was Maiko's. The blood on the strap was Maiko's type. Time of death was established as between nine and nine-thirty. Nishikawa and I had heard the cry about nine-fifteen. From this, it was postulated that Maiko had been stabbed on the clifftop, then pushed over into the sea. The waves and tide carried her body to where it was discovered.

Nishikawa did nothing but wander empty-eyed about the house all day. It was natural I take his place in cooperating with the police investigation. But down to hard facts, I found I knew little about Maiko, except that she went out at night.

Nishikawa could say nothing of any use to the investigators. I couldn't believe he was ignorant of what went on, but he never mentioned anything about Maiko and Kusashita. In a voice touched with grief, he did say that, about six months ago, he and Maiko had each taken out a life insurance policy for ten million yen and had named each other as beneficiary. He said he'd taken this step in hopes of providing for Maiko after his death and that, over his objections, she had insisted on insuring herself, as well.

When Nishikawa wasn't in the room, I told the police about Maiko and Kusashita, hinting the two had been together. The police considered this valuable information. The case was clearly murder, but suspects were so few that the investigators were puzzled and irritated. They would have suspected Nishikawa and myself, but for the fact that we were facing each other in the same room when the cry was heard. Thus, we had an unbreakable alibi.

I soon learned Kusashita was beyond suspicion. He, too, had

an alibi. He hadn't left his house the evening of the murder. Two people vouched for this; his housekeeper and his doctor, who'd had supper at Kusashita's. This exasperated me. Didn't the police know the housekeeper and doctor might easily be bribed?

I decided to act directly on my own.

About an hour after I started waiting, the white Volvo came up the dirt road, which was like a tunnel, shaded by trees and brush. The low-powered engine rumbled as the car climbed the road leading from Kusashita's house to the small shrine. He was alone. I stepped into the road to block the way. Throwing sand, the car jerked to a halt. I glimpsed a hunting rifle in the back seat. Kusashita looked wonderingly at me. I said nothing for a moment.

"You've got a leak in one of your tires."

"What?" He looked doubtfully at me.

"That one," I said, pointing to a front tire. He got out. As he crossed to look at the tire, I moved and gripped him by the wrist.

"I want to talk to you about Maiko."

His face stiffened. It was the first time I'd ever seen him close up. He looked much older than I'd expected. He must have been well over thirty. The skin of his face was smooth and had the bluish-white cast of illness. His eyes were prominent, like those of a person suffering from Basedow's disease, but they were cloudy, weak. Everything about him, from the long nose to the purplish lips and thin, round-shouldered stance, told me he was fragile.

"Let's talk on top of the cliff."

He tried to yank his hand free. A look of panic was in his eyes.

"I have nothing to say to you."

"But I have something for you. I know all about you and Maiko."

Occasional automobiles passed on the road, but we were concealed by trees. I twisted his wrist and he scowled, but stopped resisting.

"You want to talk, let's do it here."

"No. Up on the cliff is better."

He stiffened again at each mention of the cliff. Fear showed on his face. I became certain I was right about him.

"Don't be frightened. I just want to talk."

My throat was tight with anger, hatred. I put my hand on his neck, and he turned, started forward.

A narrow path enabled us to reach the cliff without passing on the larger road. It was evening at sea. A slow wind drew over calm water that glittered red like the scales of a brilliant fish. When we left the path for the clifftop, Kusashita stopped dead.

"We can talk here."

He looked desperate. I felt sure he was afraid to return to the place where the murder had been committed.

"Tell me exactly what your relations were with Maiko."

"There was nothing between us."

"Sure."

"It's true. I met her about six months ago. By the shrine. She spoke to me first. After that, we sometimes went for drives together. On summer nights we'd go out in the motorboat. She almost never talked. I didn't even hold her hand. How can I tell you? She never gave me an opening."

"If that's so, why did you kill her?"

"I didn't kill her," he shouted.

"Yes, you did. You probably talked about killing Nishikawa. But Maiko wouldn't do things like you wanted, and you began to find her a burden. That night, on the cliff, here, you had a fight. You lost your temper, stabbed her in the back, and pushed her into the sea."

"Damn you — none of that's true!"

"Can you keep up this pretense, even at the edge of the cliff? Maybe Maiko's spirit is still hovering here."

I gripped his hand again.

"Stop!"

Beads of perspiration stood out on his forehead. He was afraid.

"I'm terrified of heights. If you take me to the edge, I'll die. . . ."

I pulled at him. The more he resisted, the more he enraged me.

We reached the edge. Kusashita twisted to avoid looking down. I gripped his collar and forced him to look at the sea below.

"This is where you killed Maiko. Admit it."

He did not answer. Feeling him go heavy against me, I realized he was going to faint. I pushed him from me. He sprawled on the ground, panting for breath, staring with unfocused eyes.

I still hated him, but I knew he wasn't putting on an act. His sports car and his hunting rifle were an essential coverup for the weakness of this spineless man. He could never have been bold enough to kill Maiko.

It was an afternoon in late October when I called on Keiko Minegishi, Maiko's elder sister, who lived in a quiet, residential part of Tokyo. It was my first meeting with her. Her husband was traveling on business in Europe, and she'd just had a baby. Circumstances prevented their visiting Fukuoka after Maiko's death. I had found the cream-colored modern house easily from the directions over the phone. When I rang the bell, a middle-aged woman answered. It was Keiko. She was plump, but attractively dressed in a pongee kimono. Though childbirth had robbed her face of some of its color, the cool eyes and the outline from forehead to cheeks reminded me of Maiko. She led me to the living room and I came to the point.

"It's difficult to ask, but do you know of any men in Maiko's life other than Nishikawa?"

She slowly shook her head. "The police asked me the same thing. I know of no one. If there'd been another man, and if it'd been serious enough to change her fate, Maiko would certainly have discussed it with me."

"I understand you hadn't been seeing much of each other in recent months."

"No. But she wrote me often."

"You think she was completely satisfied with her life with Nishikawa?"

"She was satisfied. She tried to believe it, anyway. She vowed she would do anything, endure any life, for his sake." She spoke slowly, raised her fingertips to her eyes, and sat silent for a longtime. I waited. She said, "It was a kind of atonement for her."

Keiko turned her gaze down after speaking.

"Atonement? What did she have to atone for? Atonement to whom?"

"Nishikawa, of course."

"Why?"

"I suspect you know. His eyes were damaged in an accident, and he's been in a bad slump ever since."

"I've heard — but . . ."

"Maiko was driving. A car in front braked suddenly, and she crashed into it. Miraculously, she escaped with only scratches. I'm sure the shock was great for Nishikawa. After all, an artist's eyes are his life. But I think the person most deeply hurt was Maiko, Before then, she was always so bright. Like a sprite. Good at all kinds of sports. In high school, she'd been a champion swimmer. . . ."

Keiko sat perfectly still, looking at the garden as she spoke. I had the painful feeling she could almost see Maiko out there.

She went on. "Shortly after the accident, when they decided to leave Tokyo, Maiko came to say goodbye. She said she was ready to devote her life to her husband. She would put up with anything for his sake. She cried, saying it was the only way she could make up for what had happened. But why did she cry? If she loved Nishikawa, it would have been only natural to give him everything. Before she talked of atonement, she would've seen devotion to him as happiness. I felt she was no longer in love with him. She didn't know it herself yet. She mistook a need for recompense for love. I thought that someday a man would come along and show her the mistake she was making. I was waiting for that to happen, for her sake."

Keiko looked directly at me. Her eyes were wet, but they gleamed with sadness, resignation. They reminded me of Maiko's eyes. I felt strangely tormented.

"You said Maiko had been a swimmer?"

"Yes. An especially good diver. Bold, elegant."

"Diving?" I repeated the word over to myself.

Thick clouds hung over the sky at the Sea of Genkai. The water was harsh black. The basalt cliff, towering into the grayness, seemed sharper than ever. Against my will, I recalled the day of the murder. I opened the door suddenly and saw Sugio Nishikawa seated in the rattan chair, looking at the sea. He slowly turned and looked at me.

"Oh, it's you." He spoke as if I'd been away only a short time. His eyes were lightless, his expression dead. I stood silent behind him.

"With you here, it seems Maiko's still in the house," he said, his voice was a kind of groan.

"All right," I said. "Tell me how you killed her. I understand almost everything, but I'd like to hear it from you."

Nishikawa coughed, looking up at me.

"What are you talking about? At the minute we heard the cry, you and I were here together."

"We were together when somebody cried out. But that wasn't when Maiko was killed."

Nishikawa made no reply.

"You were in the bath. That's why I went out to find what happened. But if you'd really been worried about Maiko, you'd have dressed. You said you went down to the breakwater. But you were gone too long for that. You were the one who first said the cry came from the cliff. And, even if you'd gone to the breakwater, you wouldn't have stayed long. But you didn't turn up till I'd been to the police and come back. Thirty minutes, at least. And you'd changed into a white shirt and brown pants. Why?"

While I was speaking, Nishikawa slumped down. His hands dangled from the chair arms. I couldn't tell whether he was listening. I felt new anger inside me. It was not the passionate feeling I'd experienced against Kusashita, but cold, deep hatred. Lifting his chin, I forced him to look up. He didn't resist, but stared at me vacantly.

"About six months ago, you and Maiko took out insurance policies for ten million each. At about the same time, Maiko first came into contact with Kusashita. That must've been when you planned to kill her and use Kusashita and me in some kind of supporting role."

"You're wrong!"

He spoke clearly for the first time.

"I had no intention of killing Maiko, till that day."

Finally, he straightened up in his chair and said, staring out at the sea, "I couldn't stand the life here any longer. Sitting here, looking at the sea, is no way to calm yourself — it drives you mad. I wanted to go back to Tokyo, where I could be stimulated by other artists and finally get to work again. If I went on the way we were going then, I would've been finished. But I didn't have the means of getting there. This house belongs to somebody else, of course. But if we left it, we'd have no place to live. It's embarrassing, but we didn't have enough money to move."

"Then you remembered about life insurance policies?"

"Maiko said she was willing to do anything, for my sake. No — for the sake of our future together."

"She say she was willing to be murdered?"

"No. Listen. I had no intention of killing her. We were going to make it look as if she'd been killed. You can't collect on a life-insurance policy if death is suicide and occurs one year after the conclusion of the contract. Suicide by a young wife who's known to have no male interests but her husband, would look unnatural. That's why we decided to bring Kusashita into the plan. We didn't intend to lay the blame on him. Sooner or later the police would see they lacked sufficient evidence and would let him go. We only wanted to make it look as if Maiko's murder had been inevitable."

"And you dragged me in for the sake of your alibi?"

"That's right. That's all we had in mind." His voice lowered. "After she met you, Maiko changed. I saw it, but I had no idea you'd make such a deep impression on her."

"Tell me what happened the day of the murder."

"The night before, when I came in from boating, you were here. A typhoon was coming up, the sea rough. Maiko said we should put our plan into action the following day.

"Our original plan was to choose a night when the sea was rough. Maiko would climb the cliff, leave a bloodstained zori at the edge, scream before she dived into the water. I'd be in the bath and would ask you to run on ahead of me to see what happened.

"While you were doing that, Maiko would swim here from the cliff. She'd been a diving champion in high school, and such a dive would be easy. She was a strong swimmer. Even if the sea was rough, she knew she could manage the distance here, about a hundred meters. She'd come here, change clothes, and vanish in the night. She intended to go to Tokyo. A big city swallows up anyone. Maiko thought she would work as a hostess in a club and live alone till I joined her. As soon as I collected the insurance money, I'd go to Tokyo. It might take time, but we felt certain the police would conclude that the body hadn't turned up because of the rough sea. Maiko would then change her name, but stay my wife. And the two of us could start a new life together."

There had been pain in his voice.

"But on the night of her death, Maiko suddenly said she was leaving me. She said she'd go through with everything as planned and that she'd let me have all the insurance money for a new start. Then she asked me to forget about her and our past life. She wanted a new life of her own. That's what she said."

He turned to me.

"I couldn't believe it, you see? She'd been faithful. Maiko had been all mine. On that night, I heard the cry. You went out. I went to the seaside. I thought Maiko might have hidden some dry clothes somewhere and that she'd leave without returning to the house. I waited at the edge of the cliff. I wanted to try once more to talk her out of leaving. She came. I tried to be convincing, but she refused to understand. Her mind was filled with another man. When I saw this, I gripped the knife I'd hidden in my pocket. I would not let Maiko belong to anyone but me!"

"You changed clothes because you were bathed in blood."

He glared at me with flaming eyes. I saw something, then, of the proud, elite Sugio Nishikawa of our high-school days. But it vanished at once. He rose shakily.

"I made one great miscalculation. I'd forgotten that life without her would be intolerable." Nishikawa laughed foolishly. Then he reached to the shelf on the wall, where he found the bottle of whisky he and I had been drinking together that night. "I'm tired, let me have a drink."

With a trembling hand, he poured whisky into a glass. I grasped his wrist the instant before the rim touched his lips. I saw some white powder slowly spreading on the amber liquid. He was suddenly powerful. We fell tumbling to the floor and he still held the glass. It broke, and a splinter pierced my chest.

"Let me die!"

One of his hands fumbled over the floor. I gripped it and

then began throttling him. There was no chance I'd let him die, though. I wanted to drag him before a court just as he was at that moment. I believed that only then would Maiko's spirit find freedom from Nishikawa's spell, and eternal peace in my heart.

KYOTARO NISHIMURA

The Kindly Blackmailer

Kyotaro Nishimura quit his job as a public official to become a writer. While studying his new profession, he held odd jobs — truck driver, insurance salesman, private investigator, guard — all plot grist for his murder mill. In 1965 his Scar on the Angel *won the 11th Edogawa Rampo Memorial Award.*

A good short story should create a uniform impression throughout, and it should gradually build into breathless suspense and then settle in a satisfactory epilogue. Nishimura's "The Kindly Blackmailer" not only does this but also manages to outwit the reader with an unexpected turn. A barber shop is the locale — an interesting place for intrigue and an unlikely background for crime. . . .

A NEW CUSTOMER ENTERED the barber shop. Shinkichi did not know the man. In his late forties or early fifties, he probably suffered from a liver complaint because his face had a strange bluish tinge. He did not make a good impression, but Shinkichi was in a busines that demands courtesy, and, since he liked to talk anyway, he greeted the man with a smile.

Looking steadily at Shinkichi, the man said nothing, but sat in a chair in front of the mirror. Then he yawned slightly as if sleepy. He must be another of those customers who are made drowsy by merely entering a barber shop.

As Shinkichi wet the man's stiff, grizzled hair to make it lie flat, he asked, "Would you like a part?"

The man, with eyes still closed, grunted a low affirmative. Shinkichi, who was naturally inquisitive, thought the bags under the man's eyes indicated a wild way of life. Wonder what kind of work he's in? he thought. Stealing glances at the man's face in the mirror, Shinkichi plied his scissors. He liked trying to guess the occupations of his customers. He usually hit the nail on the head, but this man stumped him.

It was only two o'clock in the afternoon. If the man was an ordinary salaried worker, he would still be at his office. He did not seem the kind to take it easy after retiring from active life. An employee in a store would have seemed more serious. Besides, Shinkichi was familiar with the workers in all the neighborhood shops.

Maybe he's a heavy, he mused. No telling by how he looks. Then, realizing he could not figure the man out, Shinkichi was all the more eager to learn something about him.

"Quite a hot spell we're having. Pretty tiring," Shinkichi said.

"Yeah," the man answered, eyes closed.

"Don't remember seeing you before. Live around here?"

"Maybe." The man's tone was reluctant.

Shinkichi cleared his throat. "Excuse me for asking, but what kind of work d'you do?"

"My job?"

"Yes."

"What would you guess?"

"I've been thinking about it. I can't make you out. I'm usually pretty good, guessing customers' jobs."

"That right?"

"Maybe you work in a bar or something?"

"No. But you'll find out. I'll be dropping in here, often."

"That's very kind of you." Shinkichi nodded respectfully.

After the shampoo, Shinkichi began shaving the man. He steamed his face with a hot towel, then lathered him. The man's eyes remained closed as he asked, "You run this shop all by yourself?"

He was asking the questions now. This made Shinkichi feel he might like to talk after all.

"The wife and I. She's out today. Took the kid to see relatives."

"Just you and your wife?"

"Yes." Shinkichi spoke with a smile and a shrug, as he took up his razor. He lightly pinched the man's skin between his fingers. It was rough and flaccid, the kind of skin that is difficult to shave.

"Shall I trim your eyebrows?"

"Uh." The man nodded as he opened his eyes and looked up at Shinkichi. "Your name's Shinkichi Nomura, right?"

"Yes." Shinkichi looked puzzled. Then he said, "I see — you must've read the name plate on the door."

"No. I've known about you for some time."

"You have? I don't know anything about you."

"Yeah. I know a lot about you."

"That so?"

"For instance, I know that three months ago, when you were driving a light truck, you ran into a little kindergarten girl."

Shinkichi's mouth opened. The hand with the razor remained suspended in air. He paled, and the face of the man in the barber chair seemed to swell strangely.

"The little girl died," the man said slowly, as if he were enjoying himself. "After the accident, you read the papers pretty eagerly. You must know she died."

Shinkichi could say nothing.

"The police didn't pin the crime on anybody. They thought there were no eyewitnesses. But there was one —"

Silence settled in.

"Me," the man said. "You okay? You look pale."

Shinkichi still could not speak.

The man went on. "Oh, don't worry. I'm not going to the police now. Get on with the shave. That soap makes me itch."

"Excuse me," Shinkichi said stupidly and brought the razor close to the man's face. His fingers trembled slightly, and the man grimaced.

"Watch it!"

Shinkichi said nothing, swallowing hard. He gently stroked the razor over the man's cheeks. The roughness of the skin conveyed itself to Shinkichi's fingertips. With a look of pleasure, the man closed his eyes.

"You sold the light truck, huh?"

"Yes."

"I suppose it's safer that way."

"Look . . ." Stopping his hand, Shinkichi stared desperately at the man's heavy face. "Just what d'you want?"

"What are you talking about?"

"You come here to blackmail me?"

The man's eyelids flickered. "When I come to the barber's, I like to sleep. I'm gonna doze now, so be careful." He fell silent.

While he stropped the razor, Shinkichi looked at his own face in the mirror. He was still pale. He looked panicky. Cool it, he told himself. The man said he had no intention of going to the police. If he'd wanted to tell about the accident, there was no reason to wait for three months. It looked as if his story might be true. Without doubt, he had blackmail on his mind.

Shinkichi tried to recall the exact amount of money he had in the bank. Probably no more than two hundred and sixty thousand yen. He was renting the shop. Someday he wanted to have his own place, and that was the reason for his savings. But if this man would forget the accident, he would let him have all the money. He could always begin saving again. Then Shinkichi remembered a motion picture he'd seen about blackmailers. Once they succeeded in getting money, they came back for more. This man was probably the same kind. It would be crazy for Shinkichi to let him know how much he had in the bank. Somehow, Shinkichi finished shaving the man and trimming his moustache.

"Say, now —" the man said, looking at himself in the mirror. "You're pretty good." As he raised his hand to his cheek, his eyes had a lively look. "You been a barber long?"

"Ten years."

"Then I can feel safe. I don't suppose you ever get excited and let your hand slip." The man grinned, but Shinkichi said nothing. For just an instant, when the man brought up the accident, Shinkichi had entertained the thought of cutting his throat.

"Yep, you're pretty good," the man said again. Stepping out of the chair, he examined himself in the mirror from head to foot. He looked satisfied. "From now on, I think I'll always come to you."

"From now on?"

"Yeah. I want to keep up with a man as good at his work as you are."

Looking self-satisfied, the man lightly brushed at his shoulders with his fingertips. "How much'll that be?"

"Four hundred yen."

"Cheap, for such good work." The man took a slip of paper from his pocket, wrote "four hundred yen" on it, and placed it in front of Shinkichi. He said, "I'll be needing these in the future, so I had some printed up."

On the slip of paper were printed *Nomura Barber Shop* and the name *Saburo Igarashi*. Between was a blank line for the amount of money involved in the transaction.

So the man's name was Saburo Igarashi. But the thing that worried Shinkichi was the printed word *Nomura Barber Shop*. The fact that he had had the slips printed indicated the seriousness of the man's intentions. He was going to blackmail Shinkichi over and over. The amount in the blank this time was only four hundred yen. It would grow.

2

A nightmare awakened Shinkichi. During the five days that had passed since the man came to his shop, he'd had the same dream every night. Everything had been taken away from him, and he, his wife, and their daughter were forced to go begging. His body was drenched with sweat. Looking at his watch, he saw that it was almost noon.

When he had gone to bed, his thoughts prevented his falling asleep. Finally, when he dozed, it was nearly dawn. He huddled in bed till late in the morning. But this was no way for a working man to make a living.

Out of bed, Shinkichi washed his face with cold water, and put on his white barber's jacket. When he went into the shop, he found his wife, Fumiko, cutting the hair of one of the neighborhood children.

"You oughtn't to get up if you feel bad," she said.

"Nothing wrong with me."

"But you sweated so much last night."

The mother of the child in the barber chair looked at Shinkichi and asked his wife, "Your husband feeling bad?"

Shinkichi smiled, "No — just a little head cold."

At that moment, the man came into the shop. Shinkichi's

wife, raised in the friendly atmosphere of this poorer part of To-kyo, greeted him brightly, Shinkichi lowered his gaze. The man sat in the empty barber chair. Because he could not avoid it, Shin-kichi approached him. But he had a stiff expression on his face as he said, "Your hair doesn't need cutting yet."

In spite of the disagreeable tone of Shinkichi's voice, the man shut his eyes and said slowly, "Today, all I want's a shave." Then he added, "I could do it myself, but I love your work."

Fumiko, who had no inkling of the situation, said, "Thank you for complimenting my husband's work."

The man opened his eyes. "This the little woman?"

"Yes." Shinkichi lowered the chair.

The man closed his eyes. "She's not only good looking, she works hard, too."

"Oh, I'm not good looking," Fumiko said with a little laugh.

Shinkichi thought, He wants to drag my wife into it.

The man said, "When both husband and wife work together, there's bound to be a nice stash."

Shinkichi's face stiffened. He saw what was behind the man's compliment. There would be plenty of money to extort because both husband and wife worked. But Fumiko took the man at face value and said, laughing, "There's not all that much left over."

Shinkichi did not like this conversation between his wife and the man. He covered the man's face with a steaming towel. If he pressed on the towel now, the man would die. This thought flashed through Shinkichi's mind, but he slowly removed the towel and went to work shaving with a blank expression.

When the shave was finished, just as before, the man looked contentedly at himself in the mirror and took a slip of paper from his pocket.

"How much for the shave?"

"Two hundred yen."

"Fair price," the man said as his pen moved across the paper. Shinkichi flushed as he read what was written there: five thou-sand and two hundred yen.

The man whispered, "Be waiting for you in the coffee shop up the street." Then, with another, self-satisfied glance at the mirror, he slowly left the shop.

Shinkichi shouted, "Goddamn!"

Fumiko, who was giving the child some candy after the haircut, was startled. "What's wrong?"

Hurriedly shaking his head, Shinkichi said, "Nothing." Their daughter was about the same age as the little girl he had hit and killed. He had been unable to tell Fumiko about the accident. "Where's Kaoru?" he asked.

"Why, it's only a little past twelve. You know she never gets home till one."

"Oh, yeah." Shinkichi forced a smile. "I'm going out for a minute."

Entering the coffee shop only three doors away, he found it empty except for the innermost table, where the man sat. He waved to Shinkichi, who approached and sat down. As he did so, the man said, "This's a nice shop. I think it'll be a fine meeting place."

"Meeting place?"

"Yeah. You don't want to do business in front of your wife, do you? I suppose you brought the money?"

"I brought it." Shinkichi drew a five-thousand-yen bill from his pocket and tossed it on the table. Laughingly, the man picked up the money and slipped in inside his coat. He said, "This makes five thousand and six hundred yen I've borrowed from you. I'm keeping track in my little black book."

"Even though you don't intend to repay?"

"Stop your griping."

"You have any idea how much that money means to us? With both of us working, there are times when we don't take in five thousand yen in a whole day."

"Tough —" the man said. "You ask me, you're getting off cheap, if I'm willing to forget about the accident for this kind of dough."

"That kid ran out in front of me, I hit the brakes, but it was too late. There was nothing I could do."

"You think they'll buy that?"

"You were a witness. You know what happened."

"I'm not sure about that. What'd happen if I went to the police and said you were speeding, that you weren't looking where you were going?"

"You shit!" Shinkichi pounded on the table.

The man grinned with satisfaction. He said, "Now, if you'll excuse me," and rose sluggishly, picking up the check. "I'll pay for my own coffee. Thanks to you, I've got a little something in my pocket. Besides, it's too much trouble to write a receipt for one hundred yen."

3

Five days later, the man entered the shop for another shave. Thinking he was just a good customer, Fumiko was happy to see him. This time, he wrote a receipt for ten thousand and two hundred yen. Probably the next time it would be twenty thousand and then forty thousand. At that rate, Shinkichi would be bankrupt in no time. His nightmare would come true. I've got to do something, was all he could think.

He could not complain to the police about being blackmailed by Saburo Igarashi. If he did, his part in the accident would be uncovered. There could be no doubt that Igarashi would tell the law that he had been speeding and reckless. He would be convicted and sent to prison. He could stand jail, but he had to consider his wife and daughter.

After giving thought to his predicament, Shinkichi came up with an idea. Igarashi was blackmailing him because of an accident that had taken place three months ago. Probably somewhere in Igarashi's background there was something shady. Shinkichi was determined to find what it might be. Since he was the kind of man who indulged in blackmail, anything could be true; he might even have a previous record of some kind, or he might be concealing something he did not want exposed.

On the following Monday, a holiday for the shop, Shinkichi visited the office of a private investigator he'd seen advertised in the newspaper. Although the name was flashy, the company was located up a steep flight of steps in a shabby building. The gilt letters on the glass door were peeling. Inside the office sat a small man in his early thirties. His remark that all other employees were out on assignments failed to convince. Entertaining doubts about this unpromising enterprise, Shinkichi said, "I'd like you to investigate someone."

"Personal investigation?" the man asked, opening a notebook on his desk.

"I want to know everything about this person. Even the little things."

"Name?"

"Saburo Igarashi."

"Sounds like an actor. Where's he live?"

"I have no idea."

The man stared blankly.

Shinkichi said, "I know a place he comes to. You could follow him from there."

Shinkichi explained that he would call the investigator the next time Igarashi came to the shop and would ask him to wait in the nearby coffee shop.

"You say you want to find out everything about him. How far you want to go? You want to know whether he has a record?"

Mention of a record upset Shinkichi, but quickly regaining his composure, he said, "I'd like whatever you can find out about him. Everything and anything."

The day after Shinkichi's visit to the investigator, Igarashi came to the barber shop.

"My beard grows fast," he said, rubbing his chin as he moved slowly to the empty chair. He sat down.

With barely controlled disgust, Shinkichi noticed a red handkerchief peeking from Igarashi's coat pocket. After putting a steaming towel on his face, Shinkichi walked to the telephone and dialed. Hearing the investigator's voice, Shinkichi said, "Okay, please," and hung up. When he removed the towel, he found Igarashi looking at him with wide eyes.

Sarcastically, Igarashi said, "'Okay, please.' That sounds like an important phone call."

"A loan from a friend. I knew you'd want money."

"That's an old trick."

"What?"

"No use trying to make me sorry for you. Anyway, so far I've borrowed fifteen thousand eight hundred yen. Working and living the way you do, you must have two or three hundred thousand in the bank. No reason for you to borrow from a friend."

Shinkichi did not reply, but began stropping his razor with a loud, threatening, slapping sound. Igarashi closed his eyes and looked happy. Shinkichi thought, He may have guessed the phone call wasn't to a friend, but he hasn't learned it was to a private investigator. I'll find something in his past — then I'll shut him up. I'll even make him give back my money.

"Where's the wife?" Igarshi asked, eyes closed.

Bringing the razor close to his face, Shinkichi said, "Making lunch, inside. We take turns eating."

"Must be hard when both of you have to work."

"Look, blackmail me if you want. But don't drag my wife or my daughter into this, or I'll kill you." Shinkichi moved the razor back and forth in front of the man's face. Opening his eyes slightly, Igarashi looked at both Shinkichi and the glinting razor.

"I'm not blackmailing you. I'm only borrowing. I even write receipts."

"With no idea of ever paying back," Shinkichi said, spitting out the words.

But Igarashi had closed his eyes again. "Get on with the shave," he said.

When the shave was finished, as a matter of course, Igarashi wrote a receipt for twenty thousand and two hundred yen and gave it to Shinkichi with the remark, "I'll be waiting in the coffee shop."

As usual in the daytime, the coffee shop was empty when Shinkichi arrived. But just inside the door sat the private investigator, reading a newspaper. Shinkichi walked to the table where Igarashi sat and, throwing two ten-thousand-yen bills down, said, "Take the money and get out. It makes me sick to look at you."

"Easy, now. You and I'll be seeing each other for a long time, yet." Igarashi grinned as he rose to leave.

The small investigator made no sign, but followed Igarashi outside.

4

Three days passed before the investigator called, asking Shinkichi to meet him at the coffee shop. With a look of pride and self-satisfaction, he said, "We've checked all we can get on Saburo Igarashi." He took a manilla folder from his briefcase and placed it on the table. Shinkichi reached for it, but said, "I'd rather you told me just what kind of guy this Igarashi is."

"He's fifty-three. A movie actor. Or maybe more accurate, a former movie actor."

"Actor?"

"Yes. He's been on TV a few times. Nothing but bit parts. The way he looks, he was always cast as a heavy — killer, blackmailer . . ."

"Blackmailer?"

Igarashi was putting into actual practice the roles he'd had in the motion pictures and on television. Looking at himself in mirrors must be a habit he'd picked up when he was an actor.

"His acting was old hat. Gradually he was used less and less. Now he's never called at all."

"Then he's hard up for money?"

"Income zero. What else can an old actor do but act?"

"Family?"

"Slightly younger wife, and a son just starting college."

"How can a man with no income send a son to college?"

"His wife works at home. They skin by, but it's thin."

For Shinkichi this was bad news. A man without an income and with a son just beginning college would want all the money he could get. Once a man like that found a soft touch like Shinkichi, he'd go on blackmailing for the rest of his life.

"How about a record?" Shinkichi asked with a flicker of hope.

But the investigator said, "No record. I checked plenty of people who used to work with him, and they all agreed. He might play heavies in the movies, but he's incorrigibly good. Incapable of doing anything bad."

"That's what they know."

"What?"

"Nothing."

Incorrigibly good! Damn the man! . . .

"If he has no record, what about his reputation? No bad rumors about him?"

"Nothing there, either. He liked working in movies, but his lack of talent finished his career. That's all people had to say about him. Oh —"

"What is it?"

"Saburo Igarashi's appearing on the late show on the tube tonight. Picture made ten years ago, called *Kill the Villains*."

This was the report, for which the investigator demanded ten thousand yen. Maybe a knowledge of the true nature of the man was of some value, but it offered no hints about ways to protect him and his family from blackmail. The next time Igarashi appeared and asked for money, Shinkichi would have no choice but to be silent and hand it over.

That night, Shinkichi sat up late watching television. When Saburo Igarashi's name appeared toward the end of the actors' credits, in spite of the foreknowledge given by the investigator, he experienced a shock.

The motion picture was a classic sample of the trival action film. The handsome hero defeated hoods who controlled the town and then married the heroine, an ex-hooker. Igarashi played a cool loan shark who blackmailed the heroine, whom he tried to convince to become his mistress. His acting was poor. The heroine wasn't much. Shortly after his attempt to seduce the heroine, Igarashi was killed by a small-time gunsel. Shinkichi turned the set off at this point.

The investigator had been right. Igarashi was a lousy actor. No wonder he was out of work. But if he was bad on the screen, in life he was a successful blackmailer.

Five more days passed. Shinkichi was expecting Igarashi to come to demand forty-thousand yen, or twice the amount of the last payment. But he did not turn up in the afternoon or evening. As late as closing time, his bluish face had not appeared.

After work, sitting down for a cup of tea, Shinkichi gasped as he saw, in the social-events page of the paper, the photo of Igarashi under the heading "Man Hurt While Saving Child." The picture showed Igarashi, who had a bandaged leg, patting the head of a small child. The article told how he had leaped into the street to save a small child who darted in front of a car. Igarashi was quoted as saying, "I simply jumped without thinking. I only did what anyone else would've done."

Shinkichi couldn't believe that the rescuer of the child was the same man who had been blackmailing him. Shinkichi found it hard to connect a blackmailer and a person who risked death to save the life of a child he had never seen before.

But the photograph certainly looked like him. The name was the same, and the location where the accident happened was on the path Igarashi would follow to reach Shinkichi's shop. What kind of man would take such a fatal risk while on the way to collect blackmail money? In the confusion of his thoughts, Shinkichi saw a faint ember of hope. Maybe Igarashi experienced a change of heart when he saw the near accident. Maybe he'll stop asking me for money!

The afternoon of the following day, however, Shinkichi saw how foolish this had been, when Igarashi, with the same bluish-hued face, limped into the barber shop.

5

"Maybe you thought I was killed in the accident yesterday," he said sarcastically, while Shinkichi was shaving him. "Too bad — because, here I am, healthy as a horse."

Shinkichi held his breath, then said, "How long you going to keep after me?"

"The rest of my life. I like you."

"You like me!"

Shinkichi had shouted the words. Immediately he went silent.

"It's nothing," he said to calm the surpise of Fumiko, who was cutting the hair of a young man in the next chair.

Igarashi closed his eyes and grinned. It was all Shinkichi could do to suppress his passion to smash Igarashi in the face. After the shave, with the gesture of a magician pulling a pigeon out of a hat, Igarashi produced another receipt. On this one was written "forty thousand and two hundred yen."

"Forty thousand!" Although he had suspected the amount would be double the previous one, Shinkichi blanched. Glaring at Igarashi, but keeping his voice low, he said, "You think I keep that kind of money around here?"

Igarashi turned heavy eyes to the clock. "It's only two."

"So what?"

"Banks are open till three," he said with a grin. As he left, he said, "I'll be waiting at the coffee shop."

Shinkichi felt more despair than anger. Once a blackmailer succeeds, he goes on demanding. The price gets higher and higher, since there is no limit to human greed.

Without telling Fumiko, he took forty thousand yen out of the bank and silently handed it over to Igarashi. But he had lost all patience now. He could not go to the police. He had only one course — run from Igarashi. Late that night, without explaining his reasons, he said to Fumiko, "I want to move away from here."

She was shocked. "Why? We've finally got some good customers. It's nice here —"

"Never mind. I hate this place. I can't put up with it anymore."

"But what about Kaoru? She'll have to change kindergartens."

"Look, you don't like the idea, I'll go alone. But I'm going." He shouted it at Fumiko, who paled and said she understood.

"All right. We'll move. But I want to ask you something. Does this have anything to do with that man who's been coming here lately?"

Lowering his eyes, Shinkichi spat out the word, "Nothing!"

Fumiko asked no further questions.

On the following day, the entire family moved to the outskirts of the city. They did not break completely with Tokyo, since they had all been born there and had no home town to which they might return. Since he knew no other trade, before long Shinkichi opened another barber shop. On the day the shop was finally ready, and while Fumiko took Kaoru for her first day in the new kindergarten, Shinkichi was sitting, exhausted, in the barber chair. What with Igarashi's demands, and the cost of the move from the city, the two hundred and sixty thousand yen he'd saved was nearly gone. He would have to start all over putting money aside, bit by bit. The dream of his own shop had been spoiled because of that man. Hearing someone at the door, Shinkichi turned with a smile to greet his first customer. But the smile froze. It was Saburo Igarashi.

Running his eyes over the new shop, he said in a bored tone, "I've spent some time hunting you down."

Shinkichi glared at Igarashi. His lips tightened with anger. Ignoring Shinkichi's emotion, Igarashi sat in the unoccupied barber chair and said in a leisurely way, "Just give me the regular shave.

I've brought the usual receipt."

Silence.

"Well — get with it —"

As if in reflex to Igarashi's words, Shinkichi rose from the chair, got a hot towel, and, mechanically lowering the back of the man's chair, put the towel on the bluish face below him.

When he removed the towel, Igarashi looked at him with wide eyes. He said, "You're kind of peaked. If you're sick, you better get well fast. You're important to me."

"Shut up!" Shinkichi's voice was a sob. He held the razor in his hand. His fingers trembled.

"What you mad about? At last we're together again." Igarashi spoke in a pleasant voice. "I want you to be happy. After all, we're going to stay together now for a long time."

"Shut up!"

"What's got you?"

"I'm asking you to be quiet —"

"Why don't you smile? You're in a business where you have to be nice to people."

Igarashi went on grinning. Shinkichi's face became more and more drawn. He felt sweat breaking out in his armpits.

"You bastard," he whispered.

"Don't get so hot. After all, I like you."

Shinkichi just stood there.

"What a face! Frightening. Oh, I get it. Today's the anniversary of the death of the little girl you killed. Put you in a bad mood?"

Suddenly Shinkichi could no longer hear Igarashi's voice. Just below his eyes, the man's mouth was flapping. His bluish skin wiggled like the flesh of a repulsive mollusk. A disgusting, ugly creature. In his delusion, Shinkichi recalled a blue-black caterpillar he had squashed as a small boy. This was the same caterpillar. If he squashed it, blue juice would spurt out. He had to step on the caterpillar. No! He should cut it with a knife. The caterpillar was still wriggling in front of him. Shinkichi's arm came up with the razor.

"Kill him!"

Everything went red in front of Shinkichi. Then the razor was no longer in his hand. It was slashed deeply into the strained, blue-white throat of Saburo Igarashi. Bright red blood spurted around the razor.

Not knowing what to do, Shinkichi called for help. His voice was ragged. Blood continued to flow from Igarashi's neck. His face was ashen. In a groan, the dying man said, "Tell them — tell them — I moved." These last words were barely audible.

Shinkichi failed to understand the meaning of the words, just as he had failed to understand a blackmailer who risked his life to save a child. Blood continued to flow, but Saburo Igarashi was quite dead.

6

At first, Shinkichi was arrested on suspicion of murder, but later the charge was reduced to manslaughter as the result of severe professional negligence. The police could find no motive for murder. Before they arrived, Shinkichi burned the receipts in Igarashi's pockets and the ones he had kept. No matter how they tried, the police could find no relation between the two men except that of a barber and a regular client. "Just as I had the razor at his throat, he suddenly moved," Shinkichi told them. He recalled the words of the dying man: "Tell them I moved," Why should a blackmailer have been kind enough to provide an excuse for his own death?

The sentence was one year's imprisonment with a three-year suspension; so light that Shinkichi himself was puzzled. Of course, he was forbidden to practice as a barber. But that was to his liking. He would never be able to hold a razor again without seeing blood. He told his wife and child that he was resolved to move back into the city and do hard physical labor. They were happy to return.

As they were making preparations for their second move in a short period, a middle-aged woman whom he did not know came to Shinkichi and introduced herself as Kiyoko Igarashi. Shinkichi paled at the name. Because he did not want his wife to overhear, he invited the woman to step outside to talk. Turning to the woman, who wore a kimono, he said, "Have you come to accuse me of your husband's murder?"

She slowly shook her head. "No."

"Why, then?"

"While we were going through my husband's effects, we found a letter addressed to you. I've come to deliver it," Handing him a thick envelope with his name on it, she ran off. Shinkichi opened the envelope and read:

"I'm writing this because I don't know when you'll kill me.

"I was a failure as an actor. I was such a ham I never got anything but bit parts. As I write this, I am no longer employed by anyone either in movies or TV. But I am fifty-three. Acting is all I know. Now that is gone, and I have nothing.

"Of course, if I were alone, I could solve everything by simply killing myself. But I have a wife and son, who has just entered college. I want to leave them a solid sum of money.

"Fortunately, I have an insurance policy for five million yen. With that much, the two of them can make out somehow. But the problem is that insurance companies do not pay in cases of suicide. Aside from a minor liver complaint, I am in good health. If it is necessary for me to die a natural death, all three of us will starve. The only way out is accidental death, or murder at the hands of someone.

"When I witnessed the accident in which you were involved and found out by tracing your license-plate number that you are a barber, I decided to use you. But, because I hesitated to make use of a stranger, it took me three months to act. Finally, I convinced myself it would be all right because you were the kind of person who was low enough to hit a child and run away.

"Something else made me hesitate. I had no confidence in my acting ability. Because of my looks, I had always been cast as villains, but my acting was so poor people laughed instead of being afraid. I was concerned that, if I tried blackmailing you, you would laugh, too. I studied blackmailing techniques for some time. When I tried them on you, you went pale with fear.

"It is ironic. In thirty years of acting, I never turned in a satisfactory performance. But I succeeded when I tried to be a villain in real life.

"Gradually, however, I found that you are not a bad person. You are ordinary and good. Then I began to suffer for what I was trying to force you to do. That was why I leaped in front of the car to try to save that child. The attempted rescue was really an attempt at suicide. I was certain that, if I died in that accident, the insurance company would have paid. Unfortunately, I did not die.

"You, then, became my only chance. I have continued black-mailing you and have doubled the amounts to increase your hatred for me. Before long, you will kill me. If I die by the razor you hold in your hand, I shall be satisfied. I shall be able to leave five million yen for the wife and son who have long suffered for my sake. And — my final role will have been brilliantly played.

"Please, forgive me.

"I am enclosing the money I received from you up to this date: seventy-six thousand and two hundred yen (including one thousand and two hundred yen for barber services)."

YOH SANO

No Proof

Eight years after he had published his first novel, Yoh Sano, newspa-
perman-turned-writer, was awarded the 18th Association of Mystery
Writers of Japan Award. With Seicho Matsumoto, he represents the
postwar Japanese mystery at its contemporary best. His own witty
nature is reflected in his style, and his superbly refined technique has
no equal.

Yoh Sano's story in this volume illustrates his penchant for unusual
plots and fresh ideas. "No Proof" tells the story of what the press called
"The Mask Murders" — murder by fright, by sudden shock. It is a com-
plex case, in both legal and psychological terms.

Would the verdict of the police inquest be

Non-Criminal Negligence

or

Criminal Negligence

or

Self-Defense

Reader, be the judge and render your verdict. . . .

CHAPTER ONE

Noncriminal Owing to Impossiblity

IN LEGAL TERMINOLOGY, an act is defined as noncriminal
owing to impossibility when, by the very nature of the act, the
end is impossible of achievement. The perpetrator of such an act
is not liable to punishment under the law.

Police Inquest. In attendance:

Inquest chairman — Police Superintendent A.
Inquest vice-chairman — Police Superintendent B.
Criminal investigator — Police Superintendent C.
Chief of the Criminal Investigation Office — Police Inspector D.
Chief of the Inquest panel — Assistant Police Inspector E.
Members of the Inquest panel — Police Officers F, G, H, I, and J.

1

Police Inspector D: "When this case was first made public, the newspapers referred to it as the Mask Murder. As this suggests, it's a rather special crime — that is, a special case of unnatural death. It includes several problems that are difficult to interpret and deal with. We've called you together for this meeting so we can explain what's known about the case so far, and so you can hear directly the opinions of the people who were in charge of the investigation. First, Assistant Police Inspector E, could you outline the facts?"

Assistant Police Inspector E: "The incident occurred at about twelve twenty-five on the afternoon of Monday, January 6th, of this year. It happened on the roof of the home offices of the Chua Business Machines Company.

"Since it was the first day after the New Year's holiday, work was over at noon. Nine members of the business office staff went to the roof to have a group photograph taken. Keiji Nogami, twenty-three, was to take the picture. He was using a Nippon camera of the thirty-five millimeter type.

"Nogami selected the place and set up the tripod. The people lined up, three squatting in front and five standing in back.

"Nogami looked into the viewfinder to focus the lens.

"I should explain that Nogami was using a black cloth to cover his head while he focused. This isn't required with a thirty-five millimeter camera, but Nogami did it for a special reason. While under the black hood, he was putting on a monkey mask.

"Here's the mask. As you can see, it fits the head and is skillfully made to resemble a real monkey."

Police Inspector D: "Officer E, could you put the mask on so we can get an idea of the effect?"

Assistant Police Inspector E: "Sure."

Chairman A: "Terrific. It's the way people look in that movie about the world of monkeys."

Police Superintendent C: "You mean *Planet of the Apes*. Yes. I bet this mask's a copy of the makeup used in that film."

Assistant Police Inspector E: "Wait'll I take it off. There. Anyway, pretending it took time to focus the camera, Nogami put on this mask under the black cloth. Then he said something like, 'Say Cheese!' and poked his head out. He was wearing the mask. It gave the others a start. The shutter clicked. In other words, he was trying to take a photograph of the business department in a state of shock."

Vice-chairman B: "Does he always joke around like that?"

Assistant Police Inspector E: "No. I'll explain it later. But, as you can figure, he got a picture of surprised faces. Later, he voluntarily supplied the film to us. We had it printed. You have the picture there. As you can see, it's very interesting, because it shows facial expressions when something unexpected happens.

"Look at the man on the right in the front row. His eyes are open wider than the others'. He seems to be gasping. And the hand that's been on his knee is raised ever so slightly. The shutter was open for only one-five-hundredth of a second. The hand is arrested. But I was told that, later, it rose to the level of his eyes, where it seemed to move about, as if clutching for something.

"All the others immediately realized they were the victims of Nogami's joke and relaxed. Then they heard a horrible scream. They saw assistant department chief Junsuke Iwatsu, age fifty-three, fall forward. . . .

"This caused quite a commotion. The whole group gathered around Iwatsu and called to him. But Iwatsu was already stretched out straight and was no longer screaming.

"One of the group went downstairs and phoned for an ambulance, which quickly arrived on the scene. Oxygen and heart massage were administered. A neighborhood doctor rushed over and gave camphor injection. But Iwatsu didn't survive. He died.

"The coroner diagnosed the cause of death as acute cardiac insufficiency. Under ordinary conditions, Iwatsu's heart wasn't strong. The sudden shock of seeing the monkey mask must have caused his cardiac muscles to contract violently. This led to what is called cardioplegia, or paralysis of the heart."

2

Police Inspector D: "Thanks. Those are the facts of the case, then, roughly. Although the papers called it the Mask Murder, the word 'murder' is inappropriate, since there is no causal relation between the mask and the death of Junsuke Iwatsu."

Chairman A: "No relation! But he died from looking at the mask —"

Police Inspector D: "Sure, in that sense the mask's the cause and Iwatsu's death the result. In one sense there's a causal relation. But this doesn't constitute causal relation in the legal sense. Legally, a causal relation is recognized only when phenomenon A can be expected to produce result B."

Vice-chairman B: "Didn't Nogami know Iwatsu had a weak heart?"

Assistant Police Inspector E: "He said he knew. Iwatsu was obese. He weighed 78 kilograms and was only 163 centimeters tall. When he climbed steps he panted and suffered from shortness of breath. Other members of the business department noticed this. Iwatsu himself often said he ought to reduce, that his weight was bad on his heart. Nogami must've heard about it."

Vice-chairman B: "Nogami says he had no idea the surprise would be great enough to kill someone. I'm not defending him, but his idea seems to be common sense."

Police Superintendent C: "Yes. Even though a man's heart is weak, there's no reason to think a monkey mask'll kill him. If we interpret this as failure to warn a heart patient adequately and call it negligence resulting in fatality, it'd be foolish to hold a trial. The public prosecutor probably wouldn't issue an indictment. You'd have to make warnings to a heart patient who was confined to bed, but Iwatsu was healthy enough to go to work every day."

Chairman A: "I just remembered something — in a murder mystery about killing a heart patient with a snake. . . ."

Police Inspector D: "I read it, too. *Why Was the Horoscope Open?* by Seicho Matsumoto. But the circumstances are different. In that case, a heart patient tired himself taking part in a hunger strike for three days. When he came home, he wanted to look up something and opened the encyclopedia. Inside he found the skin of a snake, and this shocked him so much he died. Of course, intent to kill was proved against the murderer when it was found out he had deliberately weakened the victim by convincing him to take part in the three-day hunger strike."

Police Superintendent C: "But in court, how could you get a conviction in a case like that, unless the defendant confessed?"

Vice-chairman B: "What do you mean?"

Police Superintendent C: "Can a person die from the shock of seeing a snake skin? Good God. The defense would naturally insist it's impossible. It would be up to the judge. Everything depends on the way the judge sees the matter. If I were the defense attorney, even if the defendant admitted intent to kill, I'd plead noncriminal owing to impossiblity."

Chairman A: "Noncriminal owing to impossibility? But the man's dead!"

Police Superintendent C: "Isn't that just piling up circumstances that have produced an effect? Surprise is basically not a murder method."

Police Inspector D: "Let's get back to the point. First there was thought of interpreting the case as negligence resulting in fatality. This proved impossible. Then we thought of accidental death. But, a new fact turned up. Officer E requested he be allowed to reinvestigate the whole thing. It seems Nogami had a motive for killing Iwatsu, or at least that he stood to profit by Iwatsu's death."

Vice-chairman B: "You mean there's a possibility of suspecting murder?"

Assistant Police Inspector E: "A possibility, yes. Nogami owed Iwatsu nearly one hundred thousand yen. I should like to ask Officer F, who investigated the facts, to report what he learned."

3

Police Officer F: "Actually, I got started on this in a very odd way. One morning on the train, about three days after the death, I happened to overhear two white-collar workers discussing the case. From the way they talked, I got the notion they must be employees of Chua Business Machines. One of them said that, now

Iwatsu was dead, he'd have to go to another bookmaker. This led me to suspect that Iwatsu must've been a horse-race bookie for the people of Chua. I told my superiors about the idea. Then Officer H and I made the rounds of the Chua office asking questions. We questioned Iwatsu's family, too, and found that my impression of the conversation I heard on the train was right.

"It wasn't that Iwatsu really liked horse races. He had heard that bookies made money. After a little research, he decided to try his hand at it, moonlighting a little.

"In May of last year, he borrowed two hundred thousand yen from a home-loan company to use as starting capital. By the end of June, he'd paid back the loan. This means that in about a month, he was already breaking even or better."

Vice-chairman B: "Didn't anybody at the company complain?"

Police Officer F: "The office closes at noon on Saturday. He started taking bets after twelve. This didn't infringe on office work. On Sundays, he took bets over the phone in his home.

"He kept a record of all customers in the kind of notebook college students use, and carried it with him everywhere, in his briefcase. It was in the case the day he died. But the case was private effects and was turned over to the family. They had the notebook when I questioned them."

Vice-chairman B: "What made Iwatsu become a bookie? He have a girlfriend?"

Police Officer F: "Iwatsu had three children, a son and two daughters. The oldest girl's married. The son, who's twenty-one, is a student in the humanities at a large university. He'd like to study abroad. Iwatsu figured he'd make enough money to help him.

"At first the son didn't want to show us the notebook. Claimed it didn't exist. We told him we'd come back with a search warrant. So, he gave in. I think he was going to use it to try and collect from the people who owed his father money."

Police Superintendent C: "How much did he have out?"

Police Officer F: "Most people paid him back with their end-of-year bonuses. The total wasn't much; about three hundred thousand yen. There'd been a race five days before he died. He hadn't closed his records on that yet. He started on a pretty small scale, but this time, a good bit of money was moving through his hands, for a bookie. Of the three hundred thousand he had out, Nogami owed ninety-three thousand."

Chairman A: "He must've been one of the big debtors."

Police Officer F: "He was second. Another person owed Iwatsu ninety-six thousand. With his bonus, Nogami brought his debt down to fifty thousand, but he had lost on a bet of forty-three thousand on the race the first week after New Year's."

Chairman A: "Who's the other big debtor?"

Police Officer F: "A Mr. Onuki, chief of the sales department. He's had debts of nearly a hundred thousand before. But he's always paid off when he won. Besides, his salary's big enough that a debt like this wouldn't cause him much worry. On the day of Iwatsu's death, as soon as work was over, he took a number of people from the sales department to a nearby mahjong parlor. He can't have had anything to do with the case."

Police Superintendent C: "But, even for Nogami, I doubt a hundred thousand's enough motive for murder."

Police Inspector D: "Of course, with the current inflation, one hundred thousand isn't much money. But if your creditor were to die without you doing the actual killing and without your being criminally liable, it might be tempting. A hundred thousand might be sufficient motive."

Police Superintendent C: "Hm. Not for murder. But a motive for action. Kind of, 'Let's give it a try.' If the guy dies, I'm ahead. In that sense, I suppose Nogami had a motive."

Vice-chairman B: "You take a pretty negative attitude, don't you?"

Police Superintendent C: "Not negative. It's a tricky legal point. We've got to be exact in our thinking."

Assistant Police Inspector E: "Well, I think we clearly established that Nogami had what you've called a 'motive for action.' Next we questioned the other employees in the office to find out what kind of opinions they have about Nogami. We learned some strange things I'd like to ask Officer G to explain."

Police Officer G: "Superintendent B asked whether Nogami was in the habit of surprising people this way. Actually, that's an important point. From talking with his fellow workers, we found that what he did on the roof that day was most unusual for him."

Police Superintendent C: "How many people did you hear this from?"

Police Officer G: "All who were having their picture taken that day. They agreed it was unthinkable that Nogami would do such a thing.

"The department chief said Nogami's capable and serious about his work. But he's too negative. The chief was amazed that Nogami did anything like that. He never jokes in the office."

Vice-chairman B: "If that's how he is, I suppose they were plenty surprised by the monkey mask."

Police Officer G: "I'll say. Because of Nogami's personality, suddenly seeing a monkey face come out from under the black cloth must have added to the shock.

"But this made us wonder why he should act like that — on this day, I mean. Did he have some special plan? So, we questioned Nogami directly.

"He said he knows he has a negative personality and that he wants to improve it gradually. In the world of business, there's all kinds of competition. The most important thing is to win the recognition of your superiors. Nogami thought that instead of being retiring and conservative, he'd make a bigger impression if he did something wild occasionally. He made a New Year's resolution to try to change his personality. His first step was to startle his superiors and his coworkers with that monkey mask. At any rate, this is the way Nogami explained it to us."

Chairman A: "At first glance, it looks plausible. But, you think about it, it sounds cooked-up. He probably realized he'd be asked this kind of question and had good excuses ready."

Police Officer G: "Yes. I admit we had the same impression. But when we asked him further, he told us he'd written about it in his diary. He felt that to change his personality, he'd have to act the clown sometimes. He'd have to try to sell himself by being noisy and noticeable. His diary entry for New Year's day mentioned these things."

Police Superintendent C: "What's all that mean? He must've had a reason for wanting to change his personality."

Chairman A: "Wait a minute. This diary entry might be part of the plot. Nogami's ordinarily a quiet man. Suddenly he pulls this monkey-mask thing. He must've realized there would be people who'd think the whole thing odd. So he writes this business about personality change in his diary, ahead of time."

Police Officer G: "It's possible to view it like that. But it turns out someone else urged him to change his personality. A girl in the office named Mitsuko Sakaguchi."

Vice-chairman B: "She his girlfriend?"

Police Officer G: "Well, Nogami likes her. They see a good bit of each other. They went to a movie together on Saturday, January 4th. And the story is that Miss Sakaguchi suggested Nogami buy the monkey mask."

Police Superintendent C: "Sakaguchi suggested? Let's hear more about that."

Police Officer G: "After the movie, the two of them were strolling around and passed the famous Tamagawa toy shop. Mitsuko Sakaguchi spotted the monkey mask in the show window and said if he bought it, carried it secretly to the office, and suddenly put it on, he could give everybody a good surprise. Nogami went for the idea and decided to buy two masks, one for himself and one for her."

Assistant Police Inspector E: "He bought two?"

Police Officer G: "Yes. Miss Sakaguchi said she wanted to wear one. Nogami said he'd give it to her as a New Year's present, and bought two."

Police Superintendent C: "How old is she?"

Police Officer G: "Twenty-four. She's the girl at the far right in the back row."

Chairman A: "Ah, pretty good-looking. Certainly the sexiest of the three girls in the picture."

Vice-chairman B: "Yeah. The other two girls have their faces screwed up with surprise. Sakaguchi looks only mildly surprised...."

Police Superintendent C: "Maybe Sakaguchi knew beforehand that Nogami was going to put the mask on. How about that?"

Police Officer G: "She says he didn't tell her. But when he put his head under the hood, she suspected he'd put it on. That's why she looks less surprised than anyone else in the picture."

Police Superintendent C: "Hm. . . . It's going to be hard to pin suspicion on Nogami. After all, he bought the mask at Sakaguchi's suggestion. It was Sakaguchi who said it would be fun to put the mask on in the office. He doesn't seem to have made preparations for the act himself."

4

Police Inspector D: "We already mentioned the murder mystery by Seicho Matsumoto. In that story, the victim was deadly afraid of snakes. This was why the shock he experienced on finding the snake skin in the encyclopedia killed him. Ordinary people wouldn't die of such a shock. After thinking about this, we began to wonder if anything similar pertained to Iwatsu."

Vice-chairman B: "I see. You tried to find out whether Iwatsu had any special dislike of monkeys?"

Police Inspector D: "Police Officers I and J investigated this, I'd like them to report."

Police Officer I: "At the chief's instruction, we called on Iwatsu's widow and asked if he had any special dislike for monkeys. At first she wouldn't give us a straight answer. She seemed to wonder why we asked. But we were reasonably sure she was hiding something. After we persisted, she finally told us.

"Iwatsu hated monkeys. Perhaps it'd be better to say he was terrified by them. For instance, he wouldn't stay in the room if Planet of the Apes was on TV. He didn't even like to flick past the channel showing it."

Police Superintendent C: "But why did Mrs. Iwatsu try to hide his fear of monkeys? When she heard he died of shock at seeing a monkey mask, you'd think she'd tell the police at once. It seems Officer F might've heard something about this fear in his questioning at the office. But he had to press her to tell him. It doesn't add up."

Police Officer I: "I see what you mean. But in his own lifetime, Iwatsu kept his fear of monkeys a secret from everyone. And his widow tried to hide it from us because she didn't want it to get out."

Police Superintendent C: "What's the need, hiding something like that?"

Police Officer I: "It's a strange story. He had a special reason. His wife was the only person who knew about it. He never even told his three children."

Vice-chairman B: "What was it? Why'd he keep it a secret?"

Police Officer I: "At the end of the war, Iwatsu was a college student. One day, a young man who did side work at the same place said he'd managed to get some monkey meat and would give some to Iwatsu. Iwatsu was happy to accept and went to his friend's place. In those days it was ordinarily impossible to get meat. Even monkey was considered a real treat."

Chairman A: "How did this friend come by the monkey meat?"

Police Officer I: "He was a student at a veterinary school and said he'd been given a monkey used for experiements. They made sukiyaki out of the meat. When they finished eating, the friend asked Iwatsu if he really thought it was monkey meat. Iwatsu asked him what he meant. The friend just grinned and said, 'Well, there's a maternity hospital next door.'"

Chairman A: "What? You mean it was the flesh of a child?"

Police Officer I: "When he heard this, Iwatsu thought so too. He suddenly vomited. He threw up everything he'd eaten right there."

Vice-chairman B: "A lot of funny things happened in those days. Maybe some maternity hospitals sold babies that had died of sickness."

Police Officer I: "There's no way of knowing. When the friend saw the effect his remark had on Iwatsu, he said he'd only been joking, that the meat was really monkey. But Iwatsu went on vomiting. The friend tried to convince him, but after a while Iwatsu left without saying a word. This happened thirty years ago, but it bred deep fear of monkeys in Iwatsu. His wife said she didn't find out about it till years after they were married. He made her promise never to tell. His children didn't know and there was no reason for anyone at the office to know."

Police Superintendent C: It's weird. I can hardly believe it."

Vice-chairman B: "No. You're too young to remember what it was like right after the war. Those of us who are older know such things happened then."

Police Superintendent C: "What I mean is, if such a thing happened, the chain of causes and effects is hard to accept. Why should this breed such deep fear of monkeys in the man that, thirty years later, he'd be killed seeing a monkey mask?"

Police Inspector D: "But the widow's story is true. Officer J found the friend and confirmed the facts. Officer J, tell us about it."

5

Police Officer J: "Mrs. Iwatsu said the veterinary student friend had a name with Funa-something in it. We checked and examined the register of veterinarians and discovered that a Doctor Funazaka who lives and works in Saitama Prefecture is about the right age. We went to Saitama for a talk. He told us that two years after the end of the war, he played a joke of this kind on one of his friends."

Chairman A: "A joke?"

Police Officer J: "The meat they had in the sukiyaki was actually horse meat. Pretending it was monkey is the kind of joke you could expect of a college student. Funazaka expected Iwatsu to be squeamish about the monkey meat. But he'd eaten it completely naturally. Funazaka thought he'd push it a little farther, suggesting it was human flesh. He laughed when he told us. But when he saw how violently Iwatsu reacted, he decided against telling the truth — that it was horse — and to go on insisting it was monkey."

Vice-chairman B: "In other words, Iwatsu was deceived for thirty years?"

Police Officer J: "Funazaka never saw Iwatsu after that and said he didn't know the incident made Iwatsu terrified of monkeys."

Police Superintendent C: "Does anyone at Chua Business Machines have any connection with Funazaka?"

Assistant Police Inspector E: "Far's we know, no. No one in the office, including Nogami and Mitsuko Sakaguchi, had any notion Iwatsu was afraid of monkeys."

Police Superintendent C: "Then there's no hope of establishing any legal causal relation between Nogami's monkey mask and Iwatsu's death. The only interpretation is that thoughtless mischief brought on a tragic effect."

Chairman A: "Why don't we just send a report to the prosecutor? What he does after that's up to him."

Police Superintendent C: "What can we say he's suspected of? Both murder and negligence resulting in fatality are out. If he'd put the mask on in the dead of night and frightened women, we might try for menacing. But this happened at noon. . . . Nobody could've thought Iwatsu would die. Even if we say Nogami had a motive . . ."

CHAPTER TWO
Criminal Negligence

In legal terms, this means a failure to use a reasonable amount of care when such failure results in unforeseeable injury or damage to another.

At restaurant in vicinity of Minato Police Station.

People in attendance at dinner meeting:

Police Inspector D.

Assistant Police Inspector E.

Police Officers F, G, H, I, and J.

Police Officer F: "I'm not convinced about the results of last week's inquest. Nogami had a motive and knew Iwatsu's heart was weak. Maybe he felt he'd be none the worse if he failed, but that he should go ahead and try frightening Iwatsu with the mask. We could at least send the papers to the prosecutor. You agree?"

Police Inspector D: "But like Superintendent C said, what can we accuse him of?"

Police Officer G: "Yeah. But we could've hauled him in on a charge of violating the gambling laws. If we'd grilled him a little, he might've admitted intent to kill. Then we could've reported him on suspicion of murder."

Police Inspector D: "Still, there's something in what Superintendent C Says. Suppose he did admit intent to kill, then what?"

Assistant Police Inspector E: "You mean, noncriminal owing to impossibility? I'm not sure about that. In this case, I think we have what the murder mysteries call 'within the realm of criminal possibility.' Maybe the mask trick wouldn't work. But there was the possibility of succeeding. . . . Can't we interpret it that way?"

Police Officer F: "I agree. I did some study on this noncriminal-owing-to-impossibility thing. I found that legal precedent recognizes this only when the crime's absolutely impossible. In this case, Iwatsu's already dead. Superintendent C talks like he was the defense attorney."

Police Inspector D: "Still, how would it be if we sent the thing in before we were certain and the public prosecutor's boys came down on us? Even if we took it to trial, Nogami'd be almost certain to get off. If you think of it in terms of a man's human rights, you'll see we couldn't send in a report or indict when we're reasonably certain nothing can come of it."

Police Officer H: "Aside from all the tough legal points, I think there's something fishy about this Nogami. Until this year, he never kept a diary. Then suddenly he starts writing about how he's going to change his whole personality. I think it's a trick. . . ."

Police Inspector D: "We brought that up at the inquest. It's nothing but circumstantial evidence."

Police Officer H: "That's not what I mean. I mean, maybe this trick wasn't meant to have any connection with Iwatsu's death."

Assistant Police Inspector E: "I don't get you. What's it supposed to be connected with?"

Police Officer H: "Okay. Iwatsu died when they were having that photograph made. But Nogami didn't expect it to happen. This was part of his plan."

Police Inspector D: "I think I see. You mean he was really planning something else?"

Police Officer H: "In the building where Nogami lives, there's a woman, Masako Hatakeyama. She's thirty-two. She's been married, but she's separated from her husband. Lives alone in an apartment and sells insurance for a living. The building superintendent's convinced there's something between Nogami and this Hatakeyama. Other people in the building suspect the same thing, so it's pretty nearly certain."

Police Officer I: "She good looking?"

Police Officer H: "No, you couldn't call her that. But she's got a sexy body. Nogami's a bachelor. If she'd let him, I'm sure he'd be happy to take her on."

Police Inspector D: "So?"

Police Officer H: "Their building's only two stories high, but there's a clothes-drying deck on the roof. When I visited the building, Mrs. Hatakeyama was hanging out clothes. As I glanced up, I thought, 'She'd better watch out.'"

Police Officer F: "Why? Could you see up her skirt?"

Police Officer H: "No, and anyway, she had on jeans. I mean the railing around the deck's so low. Only about forty centimeters. When I talked with the super, he admitted it and said that in one place the rail's broken. He always warns the tenants to be careful up there."

Assistant Police Inspector E: "Okay, I understand about the railing. But what's it got to do with Nogami?"

Police Officer H: "All right. She's up there on the deck, hanging out clothes. Nogami puts on the monkey mask and sneaks up there, too. When he sees his chance, he taps her on the shoulder."

Police Inspector D: "Yeah. That could give her a shock. She might forget about the low rail and fall off."

Police Officer H: "And what about Nogami? Would this be another case of noncriminal owing to impossibility?"

Police Inspector D: "Not this time. If the woman died, it'd clearly be negligence resulting in fatality. A person ought to know what could be the outcome of surprising somebody in a place like that. Reasonable caution is necessary. It would be a clear case of negligence. Any judge would recognize it."

Police Officer H: "Right. What's the maximum penalty for negligence resulting in fatality? Fifty thousand yen!"

Police Inspector D: "Right. But . . . wait. I get it. He could kill Hatakeyama, and make it look like negligence."

Police Officer H: "That's what I mean. The police would certainly take Nogami's personality into consideration. Nogami'd make it look like negligence, but it'd be possible to interpret the act as murder with deliberate intent to kill. No. If Nogami's a person who doesn't ordinarily joke like that, it would look suspicious. Naturally, it would look like he'd bought the monkey mask as part of the plan to kill."

Assistant Police Inspector E: "Yeah. But if he'd already pulled the mask trick on others, it'd seem to be only one of a series of pranks."

Police Officer F: "And the photography session would be perfect evidence. All the others would testify in his favor. What's more, there's the picture with the shocked look on everybody's face."

Police Officer H: "Then he writes in his diary that he's going to change his personality. With circumstantial evidence like that, the police would decide his joking had gone too far and Hatakeyama's death was the result. Penalty: fifty thousand yen."

Police Officer J: "Hold it. Has Nogami got a motive for murdering Hatakeyama?"

Police Officer H: "A case of man and woman. Hatakeyama's older than he is. She might not want to let him go. There are lots of cases of killings like that. Anyway, that's how it looks to me. I'm not saying we've found out for certain there's been talk of a break between them. But Nogami's fallen for Mitsuko Sakaguchi at the office. Hatakeyama could've been raising hell about that."

Police Officer G: "But would seeing a monkey mask make her fall off the roof? Of course, if she had some special fear of monkeys. Like Iwatsu, I mean . . ."

Police Inspector D: "That mask's very well made. Anybody'd be shocked if he found it suddenly in front of his face. She could fall. Even if nothing happened, the two of them could just laugh it off. . . ."

Police Officer H: "There's another point. Why'd he have to use the mask at all?"

Police Inspector D: "What d'you mean?"

Police Officer H: "As long's no one was around, he could just push her off. Then, when the police questioned him, he could say he'd frightened her when he was joking around with the mask."

Assistant Police Inspector E: "Right. He could simply have murdered her, then faked negligence."

Police Officer H: "Well, there's no proof for any of this. Its just a notion I got when I spotted that dangerous drying deck, I just thought something like this could've been what Nogami had in mind."

Police Inspector D: "In other words, you mean Iwatsu's death may've been a complete surprise to him?"

Assistant Police Inspector E: "But our hands are tied."

CHAPTER THREE
Self-Defense

Self-defense is legally defined as the right to defend oneself with whatever force is reasonably necessary against actual or threatened violence.

Inquest.

Attended by the same people as in Chapter One.

Assistant Police Inspector E: "We've heard a partial report. Now I'd like to outline the facts of the case in a more orderly fashion.

"At six forty-five in the evening, yesterday, an urgent phone call was received at police headquarters. The woman on the phone said, 'I've killed a man.' A headquarters patrol car rushed to the scene, Apartment 215, on the second floor of the Eiko Apartment Building, in Shibuya, Minato ward. Mitsuko Sakaguchi lived there — twenty-four, employed in a commercial firm. On the kitchen floor, next to the sink, lay a man. Mitsuko Sakaguchi was sitting next to him. She was only half conscious. The man had been stabbed in the left side of the chest with a sharp butcher knife and was already dead from loss of blood. The woman was arrested at once.

"For a while after she arrived at headquarters, Mitsuko Sakaguchi, the suspect, was unable to speak because of shock. When she calmed down, we went ahead with questioning. About two meters from the corpse was a large butcher knife. From the blood stains on it, we assumed it was the weapon. Immediately next to the corpse lay a blood-covered rubber monkey mask.

"The condition of the scene of the crime has been recorded in the color photo you have before you. In the lower left corner, you can make out the mask. It's the same kind of mask used in the New Year's photography session."

Vice-chairman B: "It looks like the same mask."

Assistant Police Inspector E: "If you remember, Mitsuko Sakaguchi was with Keiji Nogami when he bought two masks January 4th. She received a mask from him."

Vice-chairman B: "What happened to Nogami's mask?"

Assistant Police Inspector E: "He allowed us to keep it for a while. It was returned to him when the death of Iwatsu was declared accidental.

"To get back, then. When she calmed down, Mitsuko Sakaguchi confessed. The victim was Keiji Nogami. Of course, we didn't need Sakaguchi's confession to find this out. The officers who investigated the scene of the crime knew immediately."

Chairman A: "I think we said Sakaguchi and Nogami were on pretty close terms?"

Police Inspector D: "Yeah, Sakaguchi's supposed to have suggested Nogami try to change his personality. . . ."

Chairman A: "Does it have anything to do with a tangle in their love affair?"

Assistant Police Inspector E: "No. According to her confession, his death was completely accidental. Any rate, she had absolutely no intention of killing him.

"To explain: She invited Nogami to her apartment that evening for supper. They'd gone shopping together after work and arrived at the apartment about five forty-five. Mitsuko Sakaguchi went to the kitchen to prepare dinner. Keiji Nogami was in the next room watching TV. She was preparing a special fish soup that required a large fish head for broth. She was about to cut the fish head with the butcher knife.

"Just then she felt a tapping on her shoulder. Looking around, she saw a monkey standing there. Of course, it was Nogami up to his tricks. But without turning all the way around, she thrust the knife she was holding forward. It penetrated Nogami's chest on the left side. This concluded her statement."

Police Inspector D: "I might add, she said she was thinking about something entirely different when the monkey face suddenly appeared in front of her. She screamed as she thrust the knife into him."

Police Superintendent C: "In court, the defense is sure to claim self-defense. At that moment, she thought she was up against actual or threatened violence and acted to protect herself."

Chairman A: "But actually there was nothing to defend herself from."

Police Superintendent C: "It could be considered self-defense if she thought she was in danger. It would be mistaken self-defense."

Police Inspector D: "Still — you think she had to defend herself with a butcher knife?"

Police Superintendent C: "You mean excessive self-defense? But she said she was holding the knife at the time. If she'd drawn the knife out and then stabbed him again, it'd be excessive defense. But in this case . . ."

Assistant Police Inspector E: "Something doesn't sit right with me. Did she really think she was threatened with violence? I mean, look at that photograph. She shows less surprise than anyone else. She already had one experience with the monkey mask. Now it surprises her so much she stabs a man without thinking. I can't swallow that."

Vice-chairman B: "Yeah. But that time, she suspected he'd put the mask on. This time, she was thinking about something, when suddenly, right before her — the mask. The mask's really well done. I wonder if we ought to register an administrative warning about the way that thing's made?"

Police Superintendent C: "There'd be all kinds of hitches. Might violate freedom of expression or something like that. . . ."

Police Officer H: "Excuse me, but may I say something?"

Police Inspector D: "Sure."

Police Officer H: "Listening to what you said, I get the impression that if an indictment's made, the trial will be a hassle over whether this was or was not self-defense. I think it's possible to take a different viewpoint. I can explain. . . ."

Police Superintendent C: "Different viewpoint?"

Police Officer H: "I mean, all this was planned by Mitsuko Sakaguchi."

Police Inspector D: "Planned? How?"

Police Officer H: "On January 4th, Mitsuko Sakaguchi convinced Nogami to buy two masks, one for her. Then on January 6th, the other incident occurred. But I'd like to call your attention to one point. In this case, an adult man who puts on a monkey mask and taps a woman on the shoulder is killed. None of us doubts Nogami actually did this."

Vice-chairman B: "What d'you mean 'doubts?'"

Police Officer H: "Well, when we hear Nogami put on the mask, we're all psychologically prepared to think, 'Oh, him again.'"

Police Superintendent C: "True."

Police Officer H: "Let's pretend Iwatsu hadn't died when he did. In such a case, we'd have to ask ourselves whether Nogami was the kind of man to play jokes like that. We'd have asked around and would discover he played the same monkey-mask trick at New Year's. Then we'd have thought, 'Ha, he likes to go around surprising people.' We'd have believed her testimony."

Police Inspector D: "One stage is missing from your story, but the outcome's the same, all right."

Police Officer H: "But is it, really? She didn't plan on Iwatsu's death when she worked this out. But, after it happened, she still felt it'd work as she planned. I think this is where she made her mistake.

"Since Iwatsu's death, Nogami must have felt queasy about that damned mask. After all, a person died because he played a trick with it. And as a result he was investigated by the police. Is it likely he'd put the mask on to surprise Mitsuko Sakaguchi when he happened to be visiting her? Doesn't seem right, to me. He was probably nervous about the mask, anyway. I think he would've noticed she was holding a butcher knife. These are the reasons I can't believe what she says."

Chairman A: "All right. What then? You've been talking about a plan. Let's have more."

Police Officer H: "Well, I heard something. At first, I didn't pay much attention. Later, I got to thinking, and started worrying about it."

Assistant Police Inspector E: "What?"

Police Officer H: "Next door to Mitsuko Sakaguchi is a small boy, a sixth-grade pupil. She likes him very much and lets him come to her apartment to play checkers on Sundays. Last Sunday he came. He spotted that monkey mask and asked her to give it to him. She refused. She said she'd borrowed it from someone."

Assistant Police Inspector E: "What's funny about that?"

Police Officer H: "It could be just an excuse for turning the boy down. What worries me is why she refused him at all. She lives alone. If her family was with her, she might play with the mask to amuse them. But what did she intend doing with it? Why did she get Nogami to buy it? She never took it to the office with her. She didn't use it to play with the little boy next door. But when he asked for it, she refused. In other words, she was keeping something for which she had no use."

Police Superintendent C: "Yeah. Kind of unnatural."

Police Officer H: "She just might've had some purpose in getting Nogami to buy it and then keeping it without using it."

Assistant Police Inspector E: "Was that purpose a plan to kill Nogami?"

Police Officer H: "As I said earlier, Nogami must've felt a kind of aversion to that mask. I just believe he never did put it on.

"For instance, let's say while she was working in the kitchen, she called Nogami. When he comes close, she stabs him in the chest with the butcher knife. Then she drops the mask beside the body. Later she says to the police that she stabbed him in sudden surprise when seeing the mask."

Police Superintendent C: "A trumped up self-defense. And to make it work, she had to have that mask."

Police Officer H: "Yeah. That explains getting Nogami to buy it, refusing to give it to the neighbor's boy, and keeping it with her in the apartment."

Police Inspector D: "But did she have a motive for killing Nogami?"

Police Officer H: "I don't know yet. She may've wanted to get away from him. He stuck with her, wouldn't let her go. . . ."

Police Superintendent C: "Then it becomes murder?"

Police Officer H: "In this case, there'd be no punishment if it was self-defense."

Police Inspector D: "We've got to have a winning card. To make her confess, we've got to have some conclusive fact."

Police Officer F: "There were no onions —"

Vice-chairman B: "Onions?"

Police Officer F: "Yes. You've got to have onions to make the kind of fish soup she was supposed to be making. I figured she was going to buy them later. But maybe she had no intention of making that fish soup at all."

Police Superintendent C: "Pretty good, now. You mean the whole fish-soup thing was just a trick? She'd have to work with something like a big fish head to need a sharp, heavy butcher knife. That what you're driving at?"

Police Officer F: "Yes. She must've thought a while before figuring out some dish that'd call for a sharp-pointed, heavy knife like she needed to make a fatal wound."

Police Inspector D: "Great, All right, Officer E. Grill Sakaguchi and question around to find out about her relations with Nogami. What d'you think, Superintendent C?"

Police Superintendent C: "Good idea. Looks like we better follow this up."

Vice-chairman B: "I still think we ought to say something to

somebody about the way that monkey mask's made."
    Police Superintendent C: "But that's a different matter."

SAHO SASAZAWA

Invitation From The Sea

Saho Sasazawa started in the mystery field as a writer of pure detective stories, though his style was more sensual than intellectual. Gradually his reputation changed and he became a leader in the "romantic mystery." Then his style changed again, his mystery fiction is becoming more "hardboiled," with a criminal as the protagonist. He also gained a following outside the detective field in the area of period novels.

"Invitation from the Sea" begins with a mysterious, tantalizing, and anonymous invitation to a luxurious hotel, and develops into a tale closest to his earliest style, with echoes of Maurice Leblanc, Agatha Christie, and Ellery Queen. The journalist detective finds himself in an extremely puzzling situation which he resolves by clever deductions. . . .

AFTER READING THE SHORT LETTER, Sadahiko Kogawa figured it must be a new kind of hotel publicity stunt. Then he changed his mind. There was no reason for a newly opened seaside hotel to use such methods on him. He was neither rich nor famous. At thirty-three, he worked for a top-flight entertainment magazine, but only as an assistant editor. Although he was in no financial need, his income scarcely allowed him to satisfy all of his own desires or those of his wife and three children. if the hotel were out for publicity, they would have sent the letter to one of the higher-ups. Judging from the word "Toto" in its name, this must be one of the chain of prestigious Toto hotels, with plenty of capital behind them. If they desired publicity, they would not have to resort to tricks; they could pay whatever cost to advertise.

The letter was written in an elegant hand that set the whole tone:

July 23

Though this may seem abrupt, I have written to extend to you a heartfelt invitation. I should be pleased if you would consent to spend a most enjoyable night in one of the finest suites in the newly opened Toto Kawazu Hotel, at Kawazu Beach, on the eastern shore of the Izu Peninsula. If you accept my invitation, please come to the hotel by five o'clock in the evening, on Saturday, August 1.

Please present this letter at the front desk. You will be guided to the room. I have taken the liberty of including funds for your transportation.

"The Sea"

Along with the invitation, the envelope contained two ten-thousand-yen notes. Perhaps they intended Kogawa to hire a private car. No name or return address was given, only the words "The Sea." The invitation was from the sea.

Kogawa was undecided what to do. If this wasn't a publicity stunt, who had sent it and for what reason? Though it made him uneasy, it was interesting. Maybe it was only a practical joke played by some intimate friend. After all, the person knew his name and address.

Sadahiko Kogawa decided to accept for three reasons. First, he had received the twenty thousand yen. There was no way to return it. If he ignored the invitation, he would have accepted the money without cause.

Second was the natural curiosity of man. The person extending the invitation seemed to be a woman. The letter asked him to spend a summer night in one of the best suites of a brand new hotel. He could not help entertaining the wishful thought of the kind of night only experienced in dreams.

Third was his curiosity as a journalist. A writer who has worked for years on a weekly magazine specializing in sensational articles comes to have an abnormal curiosity for everything. He develops a sensitive nose for secrets.

About a month ago, his nose for news had led him into something completely unassociated with his work. The editor-in-chief had lectured him about it. A scandal about a famous singer had come up, and Kogawa had hurried to check it out at the Shirahama hot-springs resort in Wakayama Prefecture. The singer was supposed to have disappeared because of a lesbian love affair. While at Shirahama, Kogawa and the cameraman stayed in the Bokiso Hotel, overlooking the sea. Word had it that the singer was at Shirahama, but Kogawa was unable to track her down. The two of them sat in their room drinking until late at night. At about two in the morning, they heard a commotion outside the window. They were on the second floor. The lights that burned all night in the garden brightly illuminated the concrete walkway outside the hotel. Sprawled flat against the pavement lay a young woman dressed in Western-style clothing. Milling around were several guards and men who likely were hotel employees.

Kogawa hurried downstairs. He went out through the service entrance and asked the guard who had found the body, the busboys, and others about what had happened. He learned that the dead woman was Suzuko Kume, twenty-five. She had been staying in room 515.

In her handbag, in her room, were found three suicide notes: one to her parents; one to her younger sister, who was traveling abroad; and one to her superiors where she worked. They thanked the addressees for all they'd done and apologized for the trouble her death would cause. She had decided to kill herself because of an impossible love affair with a man who was married and had children. The handwriting was identified as her own.

The window of 515 was open. She must have jumped.

Although her hometown was Kanazawa, in Shirakawa Prefecture, she had been living with her younger sister in an apartment in Tokyo. The sister worked for a travel agency that sent some of its personnel out with tour groups to act as guides. The suicide had taken place while the sister was in Europe on such a trip.

The hotel log showed that, just before her death, Suzuko Kume had made an hour-long phone call to her parents in Kanazawa. This seemed somehow out of keeping with the mood of a person about to commit suicide.

The suicide notes were in her writing. In her hand she clutched a handkerchief with the initials SK on it, her own handkerchief.

But something warned Kogawa that it was not just plain suicide.

Leaving the alleged lesbian singer up to the cameraman, Kogawa began trying to sniff out the secret behind the young woman's death. After receiving a go-ahead, he went to Kanazawa and talked in detail with Suzuko Kume's parents. Later, he visited the place where she worked and questioned several people there. He learned a few things from them, but nothing that would prove the suicide different from normal. He had, thus, wasted three days on the incident, which brought a scolding from the editor-in-chief.

"Leave stuff like that to the women's magazines. We're in entertainment. If it doesn't concern big stars, it's of no value to us." He repeated this several times.

The unintelligible invitation also had nothing to do with entertainment stars. It might be valueless, but it was impossible to get over habitual insatiable curiosity overnight.

Sadahiko Kogawa had already made up his mind, A week later, at noon on August 1, he faked illness and left the office. He hailed a cab. The driver agreed to drive all the way to Kawazu because Kogawa promised to pay the roundtrip fare.

They traveled along the Tokyo-Nagoya Expressway, then switched to the Atsugi-Odawara bypass. It was a Saturday afternoon and there were long lines of cars at every traffic signal. All along the Hakone Turnpike and the Izu Skyline Drive and finally the shore drive, it was impossible to make any speed because of pleasure drivers. It was sunny and hot outside. Kogawa was happy the taxi was air-conditioned. Looking at the deep blue sea and the clear sky, he found it difficult to believe that so much fuss was being made over the issue of environmental pollution.

After passing several other hot-springs beach resorts, they finally pulled into Kawazu. The undulating green mountainsides seemed to thrust outward into the sea. The town looked cheerful with rows of red and blue roofs. The cream-colored, seven-story Kawazu Hotel was clearly visible halfway up one of the hills. Who could be waiting for him in that building? Why was he invited here? Sadahiko Kogawa was tense as he asked himself these questions.

2

When he presented the letter at the desk, the clerk greeted him politely and called a boy. The clerk seemed almost too polite. This worried Kogawa. It made him think the person who invited him must be very important. Who could it be?

There were many couples and families in the lobby. Children clustered around a large aquarium, admiring tropical fish. The scene seemed to pose no trap. As Kogawa followed the boy into the elevator, he felt sure it was not some kind of trap.

At the fifth floor, they walked down the corridor, thickly carpeted in blue. After several turns, they came to a massive double door with a plaque reading: "VIP Suite." The boy knocked, bowed to Kogawa, then disappeared down the corridor.

Hesitantly, Kogawa touched the doorknob. He was thirty minutes late. He opened the door, stepped inside.

Four people stared at him, seated in the living room. There were two men and two women, unsmiling.

The room was spacious, luxuriously furnished. On the right, a door led to a bedroom; to the left was a Japanese-style room with tatami flooring and a dressing room beyond. At the opposite end, beyond glass windows, was a balcony. The sea lay green-blue beyond. Nearby islands seemed so close one might swim to them. The sky was clear save for light clouds in the direction of Mount Mihara.

Five leather-upholstered chairs were arranged around a large circular table under a chandelier. Four were occupied, one remaining for Kogawa. Making a general greeting, he sat down. He knew none of these people. The chilly mood in the room suggested they were all strangers. Was he in the wrong room?

Presently, three busboys entered with a wagon bearing whisky, sherry, beer. The boys took orders, served drinks, and left without a word. Silence fell again, as everyone sipped drinks.

Across from Kogawa sat a sturdily-built, healthy, refined-appearing gentleman in his mid-fifties. He looked like a company executive. Next to him sat a man of over twenty. His sharp eye and his negative expression concealed his thoughts. Maybe a university student.

To Kogawa's right sat a woman who looked around forty.

Dressed tastefully, in expensive clothes with elegant accessories, she was probably the wife of someone with money. Thin, nervous, she gave the impression of being difficult to deal with. Another woman was to Kogawa's left; physically attractive, in her late twenties, with a beautiful face, though heavily made up. Her legs were crossed high and she wiggled the upper one in apparent irritation. Kogawa could barely keep his eyes off the shapely thighs under the short, hiked-up skirt.

By six o'clock, nothing had happened. Kogawa felt anger. It seemed pretty obvious the others had also been invited. The idea of four hosts was absurd. Suddenly brave, Kogawa turned to the younger woman. "Excuse me. But are you here because you received a strange invitation?"

She seemed relieved. "Yes. That's right."

"Any idea who invited us?"

"No. It's weird, really. I didn't even think I'd come. But the letter said something about a very important personal secret. And," she smiled, "there was the forty thousand yen for carfare. I couldn't ignore it."

"Where'd you come from?"

"Nagoya."

She had received twice as much transportation money as he because she had farther to travel.

The older woman spoke up stiffly. "The same thing's true here. I couldn't understand it. Thought I should ignore it. But it said they wanted to discuss a secret about my husband. The envelope contained twenty thousand yen. It scared me, but I came."

She laid an envelope on the table.

"You came from Tokyo?" Kogawa asked.

"Yes." Her tone was cool.

"I came from Yokohama," the executive type said, smiling brightly. "Asked to spend a pleasant day at the beach. I didn't think twice. Crazy about the sea." He placed his invitation on the table.

Turning to the young man who seemed to be a student and who sat with a blank look on his face, he said, "What about you?"

"Same," the young man replied, rather self-derisively.

"Where'd you come from?"

"Matsumoto, Nagano Prefecture."

"What'd your invite say?"

"Stupid seduction stuff about a romantic night awaiting me. It was the stupidity that interested me. Then, too, I'm stupid enough to welcome a chance for a trip when somebody else pays the way." He drained his glass of beer.

It was clear they all had been invited by "The Sea." The invitations varied from person to person to create a situation where the recipient felt compelled to accept. Kogawa had been invited to spend a most enjoyable night. The young man had been told of a romantic night. Both letters were calculated to stimulate male curiosity. To the older man, the invitation offered the more wholesome attraction of a day on the beach.

Such were not the tactics to use with cautious women. They received invitations concerning personal secrets and secrets about a husband. Including the money, it was a strategy designed to inspire insecurity.

Next, everyone introduced himself. The younger woman was Shinobu Komai, secretary of a company president. The older man was, as Kogawa suspected, an executive in a trading firm in Yokohama. His name was Sojuro Koshikawa. The younger man was Shiro Kayama, a student at Shinshu University. The older woman was the wife of the chief surgeon and head of a large Tokyo hospital; her name was Setsuko Kijima.

Why had these five people, who had never seen or heard of each other, been invited here? What could it mean?

Where was the person who invited them?

3

Oshima island began to fade from view. White mists lay along the horizon; the last light of day reflected on treacherously calm waters. The small town seemed prepared for the night. Only the cars on the highway, miniaturized by distance, continued to hurry.

Glancing at his watch with a yawn, Shiro Kayama said, "Seven o'clock." His face was flushed from two beers.

"I figured it might be a practical joke," Shinobu Komai said. She bit her lip. Light from the glittering chandelier fell directly on her.

Setsuko Kijima moved restlessly. "I'm beginning to consider going home." After two glasses of sherry, she appeared red around the eyes.

Sojuro Koshikawa lifted a plump hand. "Let's wait a bit longer. Be patient — see what comes of this." Like Kogawa, he had been steadily sipping whisky-and-water.

Setsuko Kijima was strident. "Why? this is a silly game to make fools of us all. I haven't got time —"

"I don't agree with you, Mrs. Kijima," Koshikawa said, shaking his head, smiling. "I don't believe it's a game."

"Well, what is it, then? We just sit here?"

"You think we've been brought here for no reason?"

"Yes. I do."

"There's got to be a reason. Why bring five complete strangers here, like this? Whoever invited us has already spent over a hundred thousand yen on transportation alone. No, He's serious and has a purpose inviting us here."

"What purpose?"

"I don't know. We'll have to wait and find out."

"He should have appeared at once, then."

"Yeah. But we don't know who he is. There must be some reason behind it all." Koshikawa was no longer smiling as he raised his drink.

Kogawa agreed that it was no mere prank. It was much too elaborate for that. After all, the person who sent the invitations had spent money to summon strangers from Nagoya, Nagano, Yokohama, and Tokyo. But what attracted Kogawa's attention more than anything else was: If the five had been brought together for a purpose, they could not have been chosen at random. He glanced around, said, "I agree with Mr. Koshikawa. This is no simple joke. Not just anyone would do. Only we five received invitations. There has to be a reason."

Koshikawa nodded heavily in approval. "That's right. It had to be us. He knew our names, addresses, ages, and other things. . . ."

Kogawa became a bit tense. He was suddenly realizing the matter was more serious than he'd supposed.

"We know for certain none of us has any connection with the

other," Shinobu Komai said, looking insecure and all the more attractive. "What can be the reason for bringing us together?"

Kogawa lit a cigarette. "Maybe what you say is true at first glance. None of us ever met, but there may be some connection — something we're not aware of."

Setsuko Kijima said, "I don't get it."

Kogawa ground his cigarette out in a tray, "Maybe it's something we have in common."

"For instance?" Koshikawa leaned forward intently.

"Oh, place of birth. Or maybe friends. Perhaps we all subscribed to the same magazine years ago."

"Can you think of anything you might have in common with the rest of us?"

"No, frankly."

"We might start by looking for something between you and me. I was born in Kanagawa Prefecture. Finished college in Kanagawa Prefecture. I direct a trading firm, have for thirty-one years. I go abroad every year. I like to swim, play golf, scuba dive — anything between us on that list?"

Kogawa shook his head. "Afraid not."

"Well, we could check the front desk," Koshikawa said. He rose, went to the telephone. After asking a number of questions, he returned, shrugging. "No help. Ten days ago, the rooms were booked in the name of somebody called Nakamura. The following day, a representative of Nakamura showed up. He gave some instructions and paid the bill in cash." Koshikawa sat down again.

"I can't beef about how things are," Kayama said, his eyes sleepy. "I can't go back to Matsumoto now. And I can spend the night free in this hotel."

Turning to the young man, Koshikawa said, "I guess we should look for something in common. You like water sports?"

"In the mountains of Nagano?" Kayama said, closing his eyes.

"A river or lake's just as good. Nothing's as much fun as putting on an aqualung and taking a stroll underwater. *Aqualung*'s really a trade name. In America they call 'em scubas. They were developed as special military equipment during World War II by Colonel Cousteau. Bet he never dreamed scuba diving would become a popular sport. The *aqua part of aqualung is . . .*"

"Latin for *water*. And *lung* is English for *lung*."

"Yeah. But it's the lung part that's weak. Its only fault. The amount of time the air in the tank will last is limited. The greater the water pressure, the more air we need to breathe. This means an air tank that ordinarily lasts an hour, lasts only thirty minutes at a depth of ten meters. Twenty minutes at twenty meters. I'm seriously thinking of trying to improve this aspect of the aqualung."

Carried away with enthusiasm, Koshikawa talked on, lighting a pipe, sucking on it after it went out. No one else spoke and he suddenly fell silent, embarrassed.

Shiro Kayama chuckled. The others looked at him. The women seemed hesitant. Kogawa thought for a moment that Kayama was at last ready to reveal himself as the sender of the invitations.

"Everybody's so dense," Kayama said. "It's so simple. Why didn't anyone guess?"

Kogawa said, "You have something?"

Kayama nodded.

"What is it?" Koshikawa asked.

Kayama became serious, looking at them all. "Sojuro Koshikawa, Shinobu Komai, Sadahiko Kogawa, Setsuko Kijima, and Shiro Kayama. Don't you get it?"

No one spoke.

He said, "All five of us have the same initials."

There was a general amazement.

The letters SK.

Then another association with the initials SK struck a note of alarm in the mind of Sadahiko Kogawa.

4

They all sat thinking about the simplicity and undeniable nature of the thing they had in common.

Sojuro Koshikawa asked suddenly, "But why should we all be brought together just because we have the same initials?"

"Must be thousands of people with the same initials," Shinobu Komai said, frowning.

Kogawa was silent. He knew what the initials SK meant. On June 12, at the Bokiso Hotel in Shirahama, Wakayama Prefecture, a young woman had committed suicide. Her name was Suzuko Kume, initials SK. When she died, she had been clutching a handkerchief embroidered with the initials SK. Kogawa had been struck by the letters at the time, since they were his initials, too. When Kayama pointed out the initials as linking the five people in the room, he had recalled Suzuko Kume. It was no coincidence that the person who invited them had selected people with these initials. Something very important related them to each other.

"It's no trick," he said. "It's serious."

They all stared at him.

He went on. "It's true we all have the same initials. But that's only a superficial reason for being here. Something much more important connects us."

"How d'you mean?" Koshikawa wanted to know.

"What we have in common has to do with something we all did in the past. I'm talking about forty days ago. On June 12, we all took a trip to the same place and stayed at the same hotel."

"June 12?"

"Yes, If any of you didn't stay at the Bokiso Hotel, in Shirahama hot springs, that night, please say so."

Kogawa rose and walked to the balcony window. Moths and other insects were thick outside. The room was air-conditioned. Beyond the shore, the sea and sky blended into a vast darkness. He turned to face the room again. They were all staring at nothing. No one denied staying at the Bokiso Hotel that night. Kogawa's guess had been correct.

Shinobu Komai sighed. "How d'you know we all stayed there that night just from the fact that our initials are the same?"

"You probably all recall that, on that night, one of the hotel guests committed suicide by jumping from the window of room 515?"

Kogawa stood behind Koshikawa's chair.

Koshikawa said, "Yes. A young woman."

Kogawa said, "Her name was Suzuko Kume. Initials SK."

"Then why've we been brought here?" Setsuko Kijima said with sudden anger. She was a refined woman, but apparently found it humiliating to be at the mercy of someone else. But she had a point. Why should an unknown person invite them all here just because they happened to stay at a hotel where a young woman committed suicide — just because they had the same initials as that young woman? Kogawa had confidence in his suspected reason. The time he'd thought wasted making inquiries into the history of the young suicide seemed to prove of value. Moving back to his original chair, he remained standing. "I work for a magazine. I'm curious, by nature. At the time of the death of Suzuko Kume, I spent three days making investigations here and there. I probably have more detailed information than any of you. I have an idea about the identity of the person who invited us here." He paused to light a cigarette. They were all watching him.

"Who?" Koshikawa said. "C'mon, who!"

"Probably Suzuko Kume's younger sister. The two of them shared an apartment in Tokyo. But at the time of the suicide, the young sister was traveling in Europe."

Shinobu Komai looked dissatisfied. "But why should the sister do something like this?"

"They lived together. Probably the sister knew Suzuko Kume better than her parents and certainly better than anyone else. Shortly after Miss Kume's death, the sister returned to Japan and made detailed inquiries. Something about the suicide must've struck her as suspicious."

"Suspicious?" Koshikawa said, loudly crushing ice.

"Yes. Something odd or contradictory to what the sister knew from daily association with Suzuko."

"But — what?"

"We all have the same initials as the dead girl. I'd say something suspicious is connected with those initials."

"You know of any connection?"

"Yes."

"What?"

"At the time of her death Suzuko Kume was clutching a handkerchief bearing the initials SK."

"Well — it was her handkerchief."

"Everybody assumed that. But all handkerchiefs with the same initials don't belong to the same person. What about your handkerchief, Mr. Koshikawa?"

"I don't have initials put on my handkerchiefs."

"There are any number of ways to put on initials. Gothic letters, or even letters made up of flower patterns. Sometimes they're printed on, sometimes embroidered. Some use both initials, some only one. My guess is that Suzuko Kume used only the S, in embroidery. Her younger sister knows this. When she heard her elder sister was holding a handkerchief with the initials SK, she was probably astonished. The handkerchief must have belonged to someone else, not to Suzuko at all."

"Then — it was murder. . . ."

"It'd be odd for a person to hold his own handkerchief at the time of death if suicide were planned. Suzuko Kume didn't jump from that window — she was pushed. To keep from falling, she must've grabbed for the murderer's hand and caught the handkerchief, which she was still holding when she struck the ground."

"Then the murderer and the victim both have initials SK."

"Not only that, but the murder took place late at night in a hot-springs hotel. As you all know, hotels of that sort close their doors early. There's no going into or exiting from them late at night. This means the murderer not only has a name with the same initials, but was also staying at the same hotel. The younger sister must've gone to the Bokiso Hotel and found out all the names of people with those initials who were there that night. That's how we five were selected."

"She could get our names from the registration cards. Addresses, everything."

"Exactly."

"But what's her purpose? She invites us here, but doesn't appear. She can't mean revenge on us all."

"The killer is one of us. She's hoping that, as we talk together, we'll solve the question of the murderer's identity."

Kogawa sat down, feeling tired.

Shinobu Komai still kept up the nervous mannerisms with her leg. She had lowered her eyes, unable to conceal her uneasiness. Shiro Kayama sat with closed eyes, as if he were listening to nothing. Sojuro Koshikawa examined everyone's face eagerly. With stiff shoulders, Setsuko Kijima said spitefully, "What a horrible thing! A murderer right here among us."

5

None of them had a clear alibi. Suzuko Kume's sister must have selected them for that reason. All of them but Kogawa had been alone in single rooms. They could have moved freely about the hotel in the middle of the night. Kogawa had been in a twin room with the cameraman, but this was no proof of innocence. There was nothing to show he had not found a way to keep the cameraman quiet, or that the cameraman might even be his accomplice.

Talking about alibis and lack of motive would not solve the issue. They were all equal in terms of advantages and suspicion. Until the killer was identified, they were all suspects.

"This is really stupid," Kayama said clearly, opening his eyes. He slapped the edge of the table, stood up, and pointed at Kogawa, "It's nothing but your fool imagination. Your guesses. There's nothing as meaningless, boring, and worthless as guesses."

Kogawa kept his voice under control. "Okay. It's my imagination. But it's not without grounds. There's something in what I say."

"You're forgetting the most important thing," Kayama said, scowling.

"What, then?"

"The day after the woman's death, I heard the maids say three suicide notes, in her handwriting, had been found." Kayama stared hard at Kogawa.

Kijima nodded. "I heard that, too." She was assuming the role of Kayama's ally.

"Me, too," Shinobu Komai said.

Kayama was much surer of himself now. "Three suicide notes prove without a doubt that she killed herself. It's irrational to claim the woman was murdered in the face of this kind of evidence."

"Let me ask you this, then," Kogawa said calmly. "Is it possible to say with absolute certainty that a person killed himself because suicide notes were found?"

Kayama shrugged. "I don't understand —"

"Well, even after writing suicide notes, is it impossible that, at the last minute, a person might change his mind about killing himself?"

"Well, I suppose . . ."

"Suzuko Kume was one who did."

"You're talking through your hat again."

"No. It's a fact. Just before she died, Suzuko Kume made a phone call that lasted for an hour, to Kanazawa, her hometown. She spoke with her mother. I met both parents and discussed this with them. Suzuko confessed that she'd come to Shirahama with the intention of killing herself. This shocked her mother, who spent an hour talking and finally succeeded in changing her daughter's mind."

"Maybe she promised her mother to give it up. Then, after thinking it over, she decided to go ahead after all."

"Think about it. She had laughed as she talked with her mother and said suicide was foolish. It takes a little time for a person in that frame of mind to become desperate enough again to die. All the more time for somebody who already initiated suicide plans and then broke 'em off. Only six or seven minutes passed from when she promised her mother and hung up, to when she fell from the window."

This was fact. The hotel telephone log recorded Suzuko Kume's call as ending five minutes after two. The guard had seen her fall from the fifth-story window and had hurried to the spot at eleven or twelve minutes after two. At that time, she had no intention of killing herself. She had not had a chance to dispose of the three suicide notes.

"The killer knew nothing about her original plan to kill herself, the telephone call that changed her mind, or the three suicide notes in her handbag. The murderer must have been happy to learn next day about these coincidences, and about the identical initials. These were the factors that caused the death to be declared suicide."

Kogawa blew a cloud of cigarette smoke at Kayama. Kayama sank into his chair, apparently with nothing more to say. But his next step was to reject the possibility of his having a motive. "I just happened to spend the night at Shirahama hot spring on my way to Wakayama to visit relatives. I'd never seen Suzuko Kume. I have no motive for killing her." His tone was softer now.

"What could be the reason for killing her?" Shinobu Kamai asked, turning timid eyes on Kogawa.

"When it comes to that —" He shook his head, then said, "You ask me, the murderer's a woman." He was blunt.

"What?" Shinobu Komai looked startled.

"How d'you mean?" Setsuko Kijima was shocked, too. She went pale. If the killer was one of the five in the room, and a woman, it had to be either Shinobu Komai or Setsuko Kijima.

Sojuro Koshigawa folded his hands on the table. "Mr. Kogawa, what grounds d'you have for thinking the killer's a woman?"

"Because Suzuko Kume let the person into room 515 without hesitation."

"Maybe the door wasn't locked."

"Think of the time. That late at night, anyone would lock the door as a matter of course."

"Then the murderer knocked?"

"It was no time for casual callers. The murderer must have spoken to Miss Kume and said she had something important to discuss. If the voice'd been that of a man, even without thinking of murder, just natural caution, she would've told the man to wait. She would have arranged a date for the following day, in the lobby, perhaps. She wouldn't have opened the door."

"She opened the door because it was a woman, because there was no reason for caution?"

"Sure."

"That all you think?"

"Nope. There's the handkerchief. In other words, throughout the time in room 515, the killer held a handkerchief. Mr. Koshikawa, we take handkerchiefs out to wipe sweat from our faces, but do men generally go around with handkerchiefs in their hands for no reason?"

"I guess not. They take 'em out when they want to use them."

"You see? But women often use them as accessories. You frequently see women simply hold them in their hands."

"That's right."

"Finally, and most important — the relation between the motive and my belief that the murderer's a woman. Suzuko Kume's reason for wanting to commit suicide was the end of a love affair with a married man with children."

"Not exactly unusual —"

"From what I learned, Miss Kume and the man got along quite nicely until the wife found out and caused a row. This is why they started talking about breaking up, but only three or four days before her death."

"You think the motive's connected with this?"

"Finding out about her husband's young lover made the wife mad enough to kill. Since the breakup had taken place only three or four days earlier, the wife didn't know about it. She thought her husband and the young woman were going on as before. She made up her mind to kill the woman, Suzuko Kume."

Koshikawa asked no more questions. The room was heavy with silence.

Shinobu Komai said loudly, "I'm not married. I don't have a husband. I couldn't have any motive!"

They all looked at her, then slowly turned their eyes toward Setsuko Kijima, who slumped in her chair, shoulders twisting as she sobbed.

"If I'd only known he'd broken off with her. No, if I'd known she had come to Shirahama to kill herself over him. None of this would've happened. He said he was going to Osaka. Then the private detective I hired to follow told me the woman had gone to Shirahama. I figured they were planning to meet there. I hurried there myself and took a room at the Bokiso." She leaned on the table now, sobbing.

For some time no one spoke.

6

Setsuko Kijima called the police herself and admitted to murder. Two detectives and a policewoman came and took her away.

The remainder of the group ordered late supper. No one had much appetite. Afterward, over whisky, Sojuro Koshikawa said, "Now, I suppose the younger sister of Suzuko Kume has had her wish."

"She must be happy." Kogawa said, imagining the sister as his type of woman.

A pity the person who invited us still hasn't shown up."

"Maybe we'll see her yet."

"I hope so."

"I'd certainly like to meet a woman who'd do something as crazy as this."

"I agree."

"I have a hunch we'll never get to see her."

"It'd be like her — smart, I mean — not to turn up."

"Let's forget about her. Why not just take what it said on the invitation at face value? It was this beautiful sea that invited us."

"Mr. Koshikawa? You going to spend the night?"

"You bet. I'm going to have a good day on the water tomorrow. Hire a boat and go fishing. Or, maybe diving. How about you?"

"Well, I could."

"Why not? There's room in this suite for lots of people."

"I'm going to spend the night. And I'm going to order anything I want for breakfast. That's why I came all the way from Nagano." Saying this, Shiro Kayama rose and took an erratic line toward the bedroom.

"If you'll excuse me —" Shinobu Komai bowed to Koshikawa and Kogawa and departed. They watched her leave in silence. It wouldn't do to ask a lone young woman to spend the night with three men.

When Shinobu Komai got out of the elevator at the first floor, she was very deeply grateful to Sadahiko Kogawa. She was lucky a man like that had been a member of the group. If he hadn't been there, it would have been more difficult to set a psychological trap for the murderer.

To the man at the desk, she said, "Three people are going to spend the night in the suite. If there's any extra charge, I'll pay now."

"Miss Nakamura, isn't it?" The clerk smiled. "No. We've already been adequately reimbursed."

Shinobu Komai, alias Miss Nakamura, alias Miyoko Kume, left the Kawazu Hotel and walked to the shore. She was not as happy as she thought she would be to have turned the murder of her sister Suzuko over to the police. Somehow, she felt empty.

Her heart was dark and so was the night sea that spread out before her.

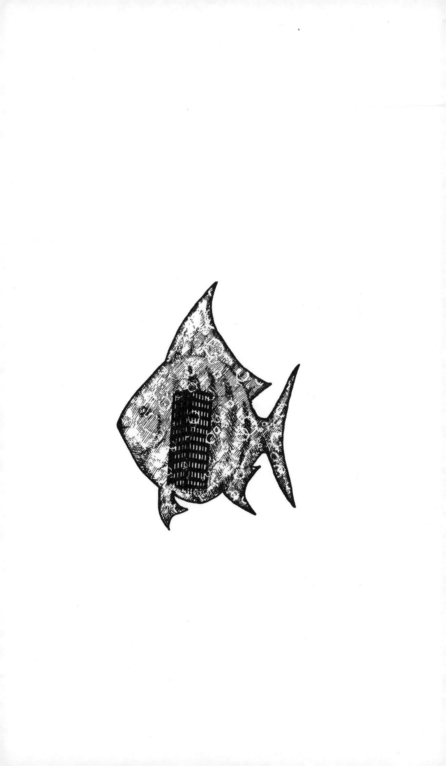

TADAO SOHNO

Facial Restoration

Tadao Sohno was a coal miner in his younger days. Later he worked for the Association of Mystery Writers of Japan and turned to writing suspense stories, specializing in the "romantic mystery."

His tale in this group of modern Japanese detective stories centers on a human skull found in a garbage pit. Newly developed techniques of crime detection do not always contribute to the creation of new tricks or plots in the detective story. Sohno, however, succeeds in this attractive short piece by using the unique idea of facial restoration — putting flesh on a human skull and restoring it to its original state. The story portrays a scientific sleuth named Goro Koike, an investigator of the Western school of R. Austin Freeman's Dr. Thorndyke and Lawrence G. Blochman's Dr. Coffee. But, as detective Miyawaki tells us, "There are things in this world that can't be explained scientifically. . . ."

WHAT IS GARBAGE? It is the remains of dead things. These things that once proved useful in the world and were popular, grow old. They are used up and discarded. Then they die. Waste paper, holey shoes, torn panties, fruit peelings, rotten vegetables, empty cans, wilted flowers — all these things attain the look of having suffered and died.

Of course, the average person does not feel this way. When he sees a garbage heap oozing with the dirty, slimy things that sanitation trucks haul away and dump in such places, he merely turns his head. But Tajiro was different.

For him, garbage was like old friends. As he slowly manipulated the crane from the garbage heap to the hopper, he looked warmly on each piece of refuse. "There, there — I'm going to burn you now. There'll be nothing left but nice clean ashes," he seemed to say as he dropped garbage into the hopper. For five years, Torio Tajiro, forty-five, had been examining garbage from the glass-enclosed operator's cabin of his crane. Sometimes he had regrettably consigned to the incinerator bright, shiny, apparently new things that had found their way into the garbage dump by error. But never in his wildest dreams had he imagined finding a human skull in the pile.

Yet, there it was, caught between the prongs of the grab bucket, teeth exposed and dark, sightless sockets turned toward Tajiro. For a moment he thought, "Must be a toy skull," But, no, there was something definitely unpleasant about this thing. Tajiro stopped the crane and jumped out of the cabin.

2

The telephone call from the Tamagawa Incinerator Plant was received at the Ikegami Police Station. By chance, detectives Miyawaki and Ban were both present. They were sent to investigate.

First they climbed up into the crane cabin and, through the window, determined that the thing was neither toy nor model. They then made preparations to salvage it from the garbage. They placed an old door across the hopper opening and lowered the contents of the grab bucket onto it. The skull had been in a brown paper bag inside a plastic bag. But the bottom had fallen out of the paper bag, and the skull was caught by the projection at its back. It seemed to have been buried somewhere in the bag. Some fairly dry earth still clung to it.

It was unmistakably a real human skull. A bit of soft tissue was still on the walls of the cranial cavity. The detectives assumed that it was not very old. Clearly this was a criminal matter.

The trash that had been in the grab bucket with the skull was kitchen refuse — paper, fruit, vegetable peelings. It was utterly unrelated to the skull, but, just in case, measures were taken to preserve it. The skull was put in an empty kerosene can that happened to be nearby.

Garbage was usually allowed to accumulate for three days in this pit. The skull had been found in the middle layers of the contents. This meant that it had probably been deposited on the previous day. When interviewed, all of the sanitation-truck drivers shook their heads in wonder. They had no ideas on the subject.

Detective Miyawaki said, "These trucks pack garbage down by mechanical force. It's a wonder the bones weren't crushed."

One of the workers in the sanitation department had a different opinion. "No. Things are pressed down, all right. But it's mostly pretty soft stuff."

Another driver added, "Yeah. And things as hard as skulls don't break all that easy."

"Guess you're right."

"Hold it —" One of the drivers seemed to recall something. "I wonder maybe it was the same bag I noticed lying near one of the garbage collection points. I thought how dogs haul things around a lot. I figured I'd just leave it where it was. Then I said, 'What the hell. Might as well pick it up.' I feel pretty sure it was the same bag."

"It wasn't torn?"

"There was a small hole in the bottom. I thought dogs did that. But you couldn't tell what was inside."

"Where was this?"

"Garbage pick-up point at Minemachi, in Chofu."

Miyawaki made a note in his little black book.

3

On a corner in the exclusive residential district of Denenchofu, there stands a quiet house surrounded by a hedge. The name on the gate is Goro Koike, Very few people knew that Goro Koike was an authority on the study of skulls. Though he seemed to be an ordinary private citizen, he was a nonregular staff member of the Police Science Research Institute. More precisely, he was attached to the Scientific Investigation and Forensic Medicine Department of that institute. He was thirty-five and still unmarried. Though considered a bit unusual, he left all household affairs to a housekeeper, Sono Takiguchi, who came daily. Both parents were dead. He had no brothers or sisters or other relatives, and seemed completely alone in the world.

When Detective Miyawaki rang the bell, the watchdog barked.

Sono Takiguchi, elderly, slow, came to the door, then showed Miyawaki into the living room. Presently, Koike appeared. He was a tall, well-built man with short hair. He had a sharp glint in his eyes and a firm mouth that gave him a sober look. He asked Miyawaki to take a chair, then sat on the sofa across the coffee table, He began filling his favorite Dunhill pipe.

"Doctor Koike," Miyawaki said, unwrapping a square cardboard box, "I believe the chief's already told you about this?"

"Yes," Koike lit a match and touched it to his pipe.

"Here's the skull."

Miyawaki spread a piece of paper on the table and placed the skull on it. Koike frowned, examining it through the thick, lavender cloud of fragrant smoke from his pipe. Mrs. Takiguchi brought in a tray with iced tea. Miyawaki took a sip.

He explained. "This case has us stumped. Without knowing what was in it, the driver of a garbage truck picked up the bag with the skull from a regular trash pick-up station. We made some investigations. But with nothing to go on but a skull, there's no way to make any identification."

"Where was the thing collected?"

"We think maybe the vicinity of Minemachi, in Chofu. But we're not even sure of that."

"I read in the paper it was in some kind of bag."

"Yeah. A paper bag inside a plastic bag."

"No clues there, I suppose?"

"No. Neither bag had any kind of marking."

"But you people think it's a murder case?"

"It's the only way to explain it. But it's all dead ends. You're our last hope — with a facial restoration on the skull."

Koike nodded. "Hm. All right, if that's how it is, I'll give it a whirl, do what I can."

"Thanks. I hated to ask you in this hot weather."

They talked of other things for a few moments, while finishing the tea, then Miyawaki bowed and left.

The term "facial-restoration method" was not scientific. Koike had coined it some five years earlier. It simply meant restoring the appearance of flesh to a skull in an effort to recover the identity of the dead person. Although not numerous, successful restorations had been made. Koike had performed over one hundred. But facial restorations in criminal investigations were relatively new. Koike had instituted their use in this connection.

4

After the detective was gone, Koike took the skull to his basement laboratory. Though the room was small, it was comfortably air-conditioned.

Fixing the skull on a stand, Koike sat in a chair and stared at it. Before beginning the job, he wanted to attempt figuring sex, age, and probable facial characteristics.

He came up with the following:

1. The facial area of the skull was comparatively small. In the side view, the development of the parietal eminence, zygomatic arch, mandibular arch, other prominences, glabella, and forehead arch was slight. In other words, the face had probably been flattish and gentle in appearance. These considerations and the form of the front parietal ridge and the mastoid processes suggested that the skull had belonged to a female.

2. The fact that tooth erosion was confined to the enamel and had not extended to the dentine led him to believe the woman had been maybe twenty-two at the time of death.

3. Although most of the soft tissues were gone, a small amount of the pachymeninges and a highly contracted, lumplike bit of the brain substance remained in the cranial cavity. From this, Koike assumed the skull had been buried in relatively dry soil for some four to five months.

With these observations as a basis, he began applying clay to the surfaces. Since the skull preserved the basic form of the head, his general outline was likely to be fairly close to true. A squarish face was not likely to be fleshed round, or a long one to be shortened by the restoration work.

The difficult places to restore were those involving no bone structure: eyes, nose, mouth, and ears. The eye itself and the fleshy sack containing it required caution. The tip of the nasal bone determined whether the bridge of the nose was straight, convex, concave. The point of intersection of an extension drawn from the tip of the nasal bone and a vertical line drawn from the upper region of the nasal cavity determined the height of the nose.

There were more than thirty fixed points for determining the thickness of such fleshy parts as the cheeks. Data was available on average thicknesses for various ages and for margins of error. Using this information, Koike could apply clay where it was needed.

He did not rely entirely on mathematical information, but had to keep morphological inevitability always in mind. Intuition also, was important. For instance, he might have a strong feeling the face had been thin and hollow-cheeked. In other words, inspiration always played a part when he gradually restored a human, living appearance to inorganic, white bones of skulls.

Lighting his pipe, Koike took a break and regarded his unfinished work through spiraling clouds of smoke. What he felt was different from the creative joy a sculptor experienced, though the two emotions held something in common. The attempt to restore the face that the skull once possessed but had lost forever, held a mysterious charm.

In spite of slightly bucked teeth, a general softness and the regularity of the nose suggested that this young woman probably had a very appealing face. Koike addressed her gently: "What kind of predicament did you get into to end up here this way? The police say you were murdered. If that's so, you must be unable to rest in peace. Wait a little, though. With my work, we'll be able to identify you and find the killer."

5

When the work was about seventy percent completed, Koike fell into a desperate slump. He told himself it was a mistake, trying to apply rules to the human face. Like fingerprints, each face was different. The slightest facet of personality could make brothers look totally dissimilar. Whether a person was cheerful, gloomy, cruel, warmhearted, cold, or serious subtly altered the musculature and integument. Phrenology alone could not deal with all possible variations. Health made an immense difference in the appearance of a face. It was work fit only for a god to try to draw from the skull all these physical and psychological elements.

What he was attempting was haughty and foolish.

He hurled the clay to the floor, locked the door behind him, left the laboratory. For three days, he wandered the house, watched television. From past experience, he felt that, while suffering this kind of confusion, he would gradually recover confidence and go back to work. The newspapers were giving the case plenty of coverage. The police said they were resorting to science, and the authority of Doctor Goro Koike. Reading this, Koike suspected that, before long, he would be receiving calls from the Police Science Research Institute urging him to hurry.

But it was a visit from a member of the institute staff that he received one day. A young lady handed him a card with the name Yoshie Sudo and the identification "Research Assistant, Forensic Medicine Department, Police Science Research Institute" engraved on it. He showed her into the living room.

"It's hurry up with the restoration?" he asked.

She laughed. "I'm afraid so."

Though she was not exactly beautiful, she had very pale skin and lovely, bright eyes gleaming under shadowed lids. Her rather flat face gave the curiously sexy impression one got looking down on a woman who lay on her back. Faintly projecting teeth gave the effect of a mouth pouting to be kissed. Her arms, beyond the dark blue of her short-sleeved pullover, were white and smooth. Her breasts were full under her blouse, with no sign of artificiality. A sprinkle of freckles on either side of her nose made her sexiness fresh. She had been walking in the hot sun. As she dabbed perspiration from her nose and forehead, Koike was confused by her attractions.

He was a healthy man in his thirties, living alone. When he needed sex, he went where it could be bought. But this happened seldom. The room was cool. It was only natural that, finding this strongly attractive woman before him on a summer afternoon, he should experience a tingle in his groin.

"But I've come for something else, besides," she said.

"How d'you mean?"

"I'm supposed to come here regularly for a time to learn the basics of the facial-restoration method."

"That so? You mean Forensic Medicine's setting up a special

section?"

"Maybe in the future. Right now, they don't have any plans. I was just told to study what I can with you."

"Of course, the real problem is setting up a proper department for research in the method," Koike said, lighting his pipe. "Right now, all we have is forty percent scientific basis and sixty percent my creativity. I'm doing my best to reverse the percentages." He puffed smoke. "But you've come to study. It'd be wrong of me to say give up, before you've started. I quit working on this project before I was satisfied with what I'd done. Maybe we'd better have a fresh look at it."

He rose and showed her to the laboratory.

6

Yoshie Sudo, a science assistant, revealed no surprise at the numerous skulls lined up on the shelves.

"Have you worked with all these?" she asked.

"Yes. All of 'em turned up in unlikely spots and were unidentifiable. I performed restorations on them, but when no identification could be made, I scraped the clay off."

"But you've made some identifications?"

"A few. Some that were accepted."

"Accepted? It's better when people are properly buried." Yoshie referred to the skulls as people. "All that's left here are people who can never rest at peace in death. You're surrounded by them. Doesn't it frighten you?"

"No. Actually, I have little use for such words as resting in peace. These are just bones. Pure, clean, carbonic substances. No more than lumps of dirt."

"That's not true," Yoshie said sharply. "They're not just lumps of dirt. As long as they have these shapes they can hate and be grateful. They can feel joy, anger, sorrow, and happiness. It's just that they can't show their feelings."

"You sound as if you had some relatives among the skulls," Koike said, with a laugh. "But I suppose there are a lot of spiritualists among you women. It doesn't matter. As I said, the method's more than half nonscientific."

"Is this the skull you're working on now?" She stared fixedly at the skull on the stand.

"Yes."

"Isn't this clamp a little too tight?"

"I don't know."

"It looks as if it hurts around the temples," she said, turning the handle and loosening the clamps slightly.

It was probably just imagination, Koike thought, but the skull looked relieved.

"You're thoughtful for a person so young," he said, shaking his head in admiration. "Maybe you'll be good at facial restorations."

"Don't embarrass me," she said, the tip of her tongue appearing between her lips. "Instead of talking like that, why don't we start our lesson?" She took out a pencil and notebook.

"Lesson?" Koike said. "Very well. We'll begin today with the history of facial-restoration techniques."

There was no text on the subject. Koike's notes were the material. He glanced at them as he spoke to her. She assiduously took down what he said. When she went home, after dark, he did not accompany her.

The following day, Yoshie arrived after noon. He lectured on the general structure of the skull and on standards for judging sex and age. Several times, Koike felt himself go dizzy. He was not ill. It was the indescribable fragrance of Yoshie's body and the milky flesh visible at the open neck of her pullover.

But she wasn't a bar girl. She was a member of the staff of the Police Science Institute. He couldn't make passes at her. He stiffened his jaws and tried to calm a rising excitement.

7

"Doctor Koike? What about the superimposition method?" Yoshie asked as the lesson for the day was drawing to a close.

"Well, there is such a method."

"Could you explain it to me?"

Koike explained the method. A photograph was taken of an unidentified skull. Then photos of missing persons of the same sex and approximate age as the skull were enlarged and superimposed on the skull photo. In some rare cases, the photographs matched. Identification was possible.

"Could you show me an experiment?"

"Experiment?" Koike was surprised.

"Yes. Superimpose my photo on that of the skull you're working with."

"Wouldn't you feel funny?"

"Not at all. I have no feelings about that sort of thing. As you say, the skulls are pure and clean . . . and holy."

"All right. If you like. Of course, you understand that the face of a living person never coincides exactly with a skull. But you're a young woman. You're just right for this experiment."

He took full-front photos of Yoshie and the skull.

"When're you going to develop 'em and make the superimposition?" She asked, sliding her body close in a teasing way.

Laying his hands lightly on her shoulders, Koike spoke absentmindedly. "Soon. But why d'you wear such upsetting perfume? Don't the dreary guys at the institute complain?"

"Shall I be truthful?" asked Yoshie, looking up at him with shining eyes and raising the corners of her mouth. "I only wear it when I come here."

"Really?"

He figured she was just teasing him, but he was flattered.

She said softly, "I have another secret. If you'll walk part way home with me, I'll confess."

"Of course —"

"That'll make me very happy."

"Let's go, then."

When they cut through Tamagawa Park to the shore of the river, the sun was already down and the wind was cool. They walked to the edge of the river and sat down in the grass.

"Well, what's that other secret?"

"I work nights in a bar."

"Ah. And what about the Police Science Institute?"

"That's in the daytime. I'm a kind of female Jekyll and Hyde. You upset to hear that?"

"There's nothing wrong with being a bar hostess. But you're young. You must have a serious financial reason for working so hard."

"Think what you like. But, maybe you could come to the bar

and see what a charming hostess I make. I'd love that."

"Be happy to. Where is it?"

She handed him a box of matches with the name of the bar on it.

"But," she went on, "as long's we have these lessons, we'll have our little daily dates. Drop in some time when the lessons are over. Word of honor?"

Speaking, she lapsed into bar jargon that disappointed Koike. He stuck the matches in his pocket.

One of a pair of approaching, rough-looking drunks called, "O-o-o, real cute! Yeah, a coupla lovers. Let's see you do it once!"

Koike stood and took Yoshie's hand. They walked away toward the embankment. At first, the drunks hurled foul language at them but soon gave up.

8

The third day, they finally got around to the skull Koike had been working on. After explaining everything, he told Yoshie the reasons for his slump. For a time, she sat thinking and tapping her teeth with the pencil. Then she raised her head and said, "Doctor Koike, have you done the superimposition?"

"No, the film's not developed."

"This woman looks a lot like me."

"That's right. She does."

"Then, why not use me as a model?"

"But it's someone else's face."

"It doesn't have to be exact. Here, touch my cheeks. Feel how my teeth are arranged."

She took his hand and brought it to her face. He touched her cheeks, forehead, and jaws. He felt a curious conviction that her bones were very much like the skull. Of course, it was but a coincidental resemblance. Still, everything, even that slight protrusion of teeth, was similar. It was astonishing.

"There is a resemblance," he agreed.

"You see. It's there because, in general, this woman must've had facial features like mine. Why not use me as an image and finish up the restoration?"

"Okay. There's something in what you say."

Stroking her face, Koike could restrain himself no longer.

"Yoshie," he remembered saying. "I want you." After that it was a boil of raging blood.

She didn't pull away, but wrapped her arms around him. The violent kiss was like two animals biting each other. The basement room was locked. No one could enter.

He ripped her clothes off and was quickly naked himself. Her rich breasts rose and fell, the nipples rigid with desire. From her graceful hips to her belly and full-fleshed buttocks, thighs, she was a hot fire.

He embraced her from behind, gripping and rubbing her breasts. Yoshie was breathing fast. She twisted around so she lay on her back under him, welcoming him into her.

The long-stored passions were apparent. He entered her, overflowing with nectar, and she gasped, arching her back. Her white legs clamped tight against his brown thighs. With a sensation of being licked by a cat's rough tongue, the two reached climax.

9

The following day, Yoshie did not appear. Nor did she come the day after that. For three days, Koike was silent, waiting. "She's probably embarrassed," he thought. He was much too shy to call the Police Science Institute to find out. But on the fourth day, driven, he made the call. If he were told her course of study was over, he would visit the bar. He wanted to become her bar customer only as a last resort.

Yuzo Kawamata, an old friend in the Forensic Department, answered. "Oh, Doctor Bones," he said. "How've you been? Finished that restoration yet? They've been on us about that."

"Almost finished. That's not what I called about. Miss Yoshie Sudo hasn't shown up yet. She's from your office. At this stage, we're not finished with her course."

"Yoshie Sudo? Never heard of her."

"Cut the clowning. The assistant from your office. You sent her over here."

Kawamata was head of the department. He would know.

"You must be sleeping," Kawamata said. "We don't have one female assistant here. You must remember that."

Koike could not speak.

"Who is she, anyway?" Kawamata asked.

But Koike had hung up. He knew Kawamata's jokes. He could tell from the man's tone that he wasn't joking this time. Then, who was Yoshie? Why should she go to the trouble of having false ID cards made up?

He went to the closet and took the matchbox from his jacket. On the box was a picture of a red Manhattan cocktail and the name Bar Floydie. The address was 1–3–5, Kamata.

Koike took a train to Kamata and, after checking at the police box and at local shops, finally located the bar in a narrow alley lined with cheap drinking places. The name was flashy and foreign-sounding. The place was sad. The painted letters "Floydie" on the cheap plastic door were peeling. Thinking it was probably too early, Koike went inside. As he'd feared, the stools were upside down on the bar. A man with long sideburns, possibly the bartender, was mopping the floor.

"Sorry, chum — we're not open yet. Mind coming back later?"

"I'd like to ask you something."

The man scowled at him.

"You've got a girl named Yoshie Sudo here, right? A hostess?"

"I don't know, chum. Can't tell what names they use on the job."

"Her real name's Yoshie Sudo."

"Nobody here by that name."

Koike took out the box of matches and showed it to the man.

"These yours?"

"Yeah. So what?"

"You recall whether there was someone by that name working here before?"

"I haven't been here long, myself. I don't know what went on before."

"Who's the woman who runs this place?"

"She won't be here for a while yet."

"Then I'll be back later."

Koike spent time in a coffee shop and returned later on. Now the dim lighting made it look more like a bar. A fat woman of about fifty nodded at him. She was the mamma of the place.

"You the man who was asking about Yoshie?"

"Yes. She here?"

"What's she got to do with you?" the mamma teased.

"I met her in connection with my work. She asked me to drop in here when I was free. . . ."

"Yeah?" She appraised Koike. "She's disappeared. Not here anymore."

"What? Since when?"

"Some time ago. April. It's been over four months. But, c'mon, sit down so we can chat more comfortably."

She led Koike to a corner table.

"What're you drinking? Beer?"

Koike nodded. The bartender brought over a beer, two glasses, and a plate of tiny sandwiches. The mamma poured two glasses of beer and, toasting, drank it off. Then she spoke.

The evening of April 20 had been misty with rain. A young man, who had visited the bar once, sat drinking with Yoshie. He held it well. He had two bottles of beer and three highballs. When the time came to leave, he said he'd left his wallet at the office. The mamma thought of asking for security against his bill, but the fellow didn't have so much as a watchband. He wore a sweater, trousers, and a beret. When asked where his office was, he said in Kamata. The mamma suggested going there with him for the money. But the young man said they wouldn't open again till tomorrow morning. If someone would come to his apartment with him, he had money there. His apartment was on the Ike-gami train line. There was nothing else to do. Yoshie would go with him.

Neither of them ever returned. . . .

Yoshie's things were upstairs in the bar, but there was nothing of value. She had been one of those who move from one bar to another and had nothing but what she stood up in. Not only that, but she had lived upstairs, and borrowed quite a bit from the mamma.

The young man must have been a hostess agent. He made up the story about the money and the apartment to get Yoshie out of the Floydie. The two had worked out a plan, and the man was able to help Yoshie welch on a debt and run away.

The mamma went to the police, but they would make no serious investigation under the circumstances. She'd had to let things go as they were.

Koike didn't touch his beer. He paid and left as the mamma was still asking, "Where'd you meet her? I'm gonna get my money back. Tell me where she is!"

10

On the train home, Koike sat with closed eyes as a single thought ran through his mind. The idea had begun forming when Kawamata told him there was no such woman in the office. Now it was firmer. When he reached home, he began developing the photos he'd taken of Yoshie and the skull.

He locked the laboratory door and lay on his bed for two days, eating nothing, refusing to go out. On the second day, the insistent ring of the phone in the entrance foyer forced him to get up. It was the Police Science Institute wondering when the facial restoration would be finished. Koike promised it within the day. The call snapped him out of his despondent state. He remembered how Yoshie had insisted he use her face as a model. He at last knew why she had appeared in mortal form in his home.

In the laboratory, using his memory and the photo, he reconstructed the face of a woman. He coated its surfaces with plaster and painted it. The result was quite close to the appearance of a living woman.

When Detective Miyawaki received word the restoration was finished, he hurried to Koike's home. All Koike told the detective was that the face of the woman looked like someone who worked in bars. Find out whether a young woman had disappeared from any of the bars in Ota Ward, during the past four or five months. "If you can possibly indentify such a woman, the man with her last is the killer."

"Boy. Sounds better than Sherlock Holmes. If you've hit on this, I'll come to you for lessons."

"Rot."

Detective Miyawaki decided it was only his usual brusque manner that made Koike blanch and wave his hand at the suggestion.

A week later, perspiring from the heat, Detective Miyawaki

came to Koike to explain that he'd been completely correct and that the case had been solved.

Not absolutely convinced, the police had begun working along the lines of investigation Koike suggested. They learned from the police station in Kamata that the Bar Floydie had reported the disappearance of a young hostess. The Kamata police let the matter ride, thinking it just another case of a bar girl's deliberately vanishing to run away from something.

The detective took Koike's reconstruction to the bar, where the mamma was startled. She testified at once that the face was certainly Yoshie. The Ikegami and Kamata police put out a net for a young man answering the mamma's description. Before long, they had him.

He confessed, under questioning. Yoshie had been drunk and pestered him to pay the bar bill. He tired of this, left the train at Ondakesan and forced Yoshie into a dark place, where he strangled her. He then dragged her behind a Shinto shrine and had sexual intercourse with her still warm body. He dumped her into an open trash pit. Then, realizing that if the body were found he could be traced, he used a jacknife to cut off her head.

Working carefully, he got no blood on himself. He took a paper bag and a plastic bag from the trash pit and put the head in them. He stripped the body naked and covered it with mud. Then he buried the clothes and the head in separate locations. It was accidental, burying the head near a trash collection point. Later, a dog dug the bag up and it was collected with the garbage. Acting on his testimony, the police probed the thicket behind the Shinto shrine, and found the headless skeleton. Miyawaki said, "Of course, the facial restoration's excellent. But I'm interested in knowing where you got hints for it. It's amazing."

"I'm ashamed to admit it wasn't detection. It was a dream."

"Dream?" The detective frowned.

"Yes. I saw the same face in my dreams for three consecutive nights."

"Extraordinary." Miyawaki half rose from his chair, staring at the skulls on the shelves. "Then — the victim was standing by your pillow, in a way."

"You could say that. But the face didn't look malevolent. It looked accusing."

"You think so. Well, there's plenty can't be explained scientifically. Now, the case is closed."

"She won't be there anymore. She can rest in peace now." A note in Koike's tone suggested that perhaps he would miss the dreams. But Miyawaki was not a man to note such subtle nuances.

As ghost stories went, there was nothing unusual about this one: revenge by spirits attached to skulls. But the vibrant female body Koike had embraced, the perfume, the sweat, and the thick fluids — these weren't dreams, or supernatural phenomena. Who was she? Why did she take such a roundabout method of suggesting the skull's identity? These nagging questions tugged at Koike. The only clue was the startling resemblance between the woman and the dead Yoshie Sudo. Could they be twins? Sisters? But when he asked Miyawaki, he learned that Yoshie had been alone in the world, just as Koike, himself, was.

One day, the doubt in Koike's mind was forever removed. The newspapers were making much of the case for two reasons. First, the unusual success of the still little-used facial-restoration method. Second, the rumor that the murderer had used the same system to kill and bury many other young women. The photo of Akiyo Sato, the wife of the killer, whose name was Akira Sato, appeared in one of the women's weekly magazines. Although she wore sunglasses and held her head low, Koike saw at a glance that it was the woman.

He found that she lived on the second floor of a cheap apartment house on a back street of Minemachi, in Chofu. When Koike arrived, the door was tightly closed. He rang the bell and heard sounds from inside. He rang again, several times. Finally someone asked, "Who is it?"

"It's me, Koike."

There was no answer. Perhaps she was trying to make up her mind whether to pretend she didn't know him.

Koike said, "Nothing to worry about. I know everything. I've told no one. You want me to, I'll stay quiet. For the rest of my life. I'd just like to ask why you came to me instead of going to the police. That's why I came here."

She spoke, at last. "I'd like to talk about it. But not here. Go and wait on the street. I'll be right there."

"Okay."

Koike went down. The late afternoon sun was blazing on the deserted street. Cicadas singing nearby invited sleep. Koike heard her story in an air-conditioned coffee shop near Ondake-san station.

Akiyo Sato, twenty-three, was the childless wife of the murderer, Akira Sato. When she removed her sunglasses, he saw the familiar little nose and the freckles.

"You want to know why I didn't go to the police?" She spoke tensely, locked in a shell. "I wonder if a man can understand the way a woman feels when she learns her husband's a murderer?" She stared at Koike with cold, emotionless eyes. "Even knowing he'll kill again unless he's caught, he is, after all, your husband."

After a silence, she went on, as if trying to encourage herself. "A horrible killer like this should be taken out of the world as quick as possible. But he ought to be shown the mercy of being turned in by outsiders, not by his own wife. It seems a final consideration. That's what I was thinking."

Koike did not speak.

"About that time, I read that the police were unable to identify the skull and had asked you to make a facial restoration. That's why I worked my little scheme."

Koike realized this was no longer Yoshie Sudo. But he wanted to call Yoshie back. He said, "How'd you find out your husband was the murderer?"

"You must've read about it."

"I'd like to hear it from you."

"Well, it's embarrassing, but . . ." And she told him the following story.

Her husband, Akira, was a pathological sadist, though no one would have guessed it. He got along well with people; only Akiyo knew his secret. When they had sex, he became excited and tried to strangle her. Only when she fought and struck him, did he return to his senses. He would immediately apologize. After this happened a number of times, Akiyo began to suspect that her husband might have a dark background of sex-related crimes. It was a shock for her to learn, upon secret investigation, that he had been in a reformatory for raping a primary-school girl when he was still a boy. Soon after, Akiyo was horrified to read in the papers of a discovery of a skull, apparently that of a young woman, that had been buried for from four to five months, right in her neighborhood.

A little before this, something happened that she still recalled.

One night in April — the cherry blossoms were in bloom — Akira had said to her, "You've been keeping something from me. I find out now that you've got a sister, and maybe even a twin."

"What are you talking about? You know very well there's nobody but my aunt and uncle in Osaka."

"Yeah. Well, tonight in Kamata I met a girl who looks exactly like you."

"Where in Kamata?"

"A bar, called the Floydie, behind the station. A girl named Yoshie. She works there."

"I've never heard of her."

"Hm. Accidental resemblance." He shook his head, "But it makes me creepy to think you might be pulling a Jekyll and Hyde on me, playing a double role."

"Don't even joke like that. And don't get funny ideas about her because we look alike."

"Now, you quit it. One of you is enough. If I play around, it'll be with a different kind of woman." He laughed and the conversation ended.

If the woman whose skull had been found was killed in the cherry blossom season, the timing was right. But there was nothing to connect the two. Akiyo, though, had more than mere suspicion to go on.

One rainy night ten days after the talk about the bar girl, her husband came home drunk. He behaved curiously. No matter what she said, his answers made no sense. In the kitchen, he washed his hands over and over, and with large, staring eyes, checked his trousers and sweater carefully.

Shortly after that, Akiyo went to the Bar Floydie to talk with the mamma. She pretended to be Yoshie's friend, but was prepared to say she'd made a mistake if the girl proved to be there. To hide her resemblance, she wore sunglasses and heavy makeup.

Akiyo's suspicions were well founded. The mamma told her Yoshie had gone out on the rainy night of April 20 with a young man. She had never returned. The mamma's description fitted her husband. It had been April 20 when he'd come home drunk and acting strangely.

"So you found your husband's a sex killer. That clears up everything. But what will you do now?"

"Everything's over for me."

"Don't let it defeat you. The Yoshie Sudo I know is no coward."

"What can I do?" She tipped her head. "I'm still thinking about it. I haven't made up my mind."

"All right. But can we see each other again? After you've made up your mind?"

She said nothing.

"Please — promise —?"

"Yes."

"When you've decided, get in touch. I'll be waiting."

Days passed with no word. Had she made up her mind? On the third day, Koike could wait no longer. But when he reached the apartment building, the Sato nameplate had been removed from the door. The building superintendent said, "She moved. After all, with a husband like that, and everybody knowing all about it. I don't know where she's gone."

Koike walked slowly down the steps and out into the summer afternoon sunlight. He thought, "She'll never come back. Maybe I should have left it a ghost story."

Absorbed in this way, he turned and walked on. The piercing song of the cicadas accompanied him.

MASAKO TOGAWA

The Vampire

In 1962 Masako Togawa, a chanson singer, published A Vast Illusion, *an intricately constructed psychological mystery that won the 8th Edogawa Rampo Memorial Award. Her success as a singer-turned-writer attests to her superb versatility, talent, and efforts, and it characterizes an increasingly modern thinking in Japan.*

Her story, no doubt, will lure you into a phantasmal world where reality mixes with illusion. Her unsurpassed talent is well shown also by the tale's keen sarcasm and words of caution to current society.

"The Vampire" is not "of the ordinary world" — it is an unusual tale about "a living blood bank. . . ."

THERE CAME A TAPPING on the front shutters. At first Jiro thought it was in his dream — but he was awake; it had to be real. The summons from the vampire had come again. It was probably for someone in the AB group. Jiro's guesses were usually accurate. He told himself with confidence, that he had never missed. Of course, he might be recalling only the times when he had been right, completely forgetting all the others.

There were only two people in the AB group: Jiro and Tatsuya Yamane. Jiro hoped Yamane had not gone out. If Yamane weren't here, it would be his turn again.

The tapping on the shutters was peremptory. The vampire must be hungry. He would likely want to suck a couple two-hundred-CC glasses — about equivalent to two half-pint milk bottles.

Jiro had hunches about how hungry the vampire would be. Some great man had claimed that hunches were like nervous reflexes; they developed as a result of experience.

Then Jiro had another notion. It had already been a month since he had been going to the vampire. A month could be very long. During that time, how much blood had been sucked from Jiro? If the vampire took one full half-pint milk bottle every day, in a year, it would amount to something like seventy-three thousand CC's. That would probably be enough to fill a bathtub. It made him giddy to think of having a bathtub full of blood sucked from his body. "We're not even people anymore," he thought. "We're just skin sacks full of rich wine."

Ogata, the dormitory chief, went out, probably to answer the summons. Jiro could hear through the shutters. Long ago, the front door had been boarded up, and the entrance hall was used as a storeroom. This had been done to prevent people running in and out. When messengers came from the vampire, they tapped on the wooden shutters of the large window. The sound of that tapping struck terror in the heart and blood pressure shot up. This made it easier to suck blood.

The shrill voice of Miyota, the female assistant of the vampire, reached Jiro. "The vampire's in a hurry! Two of you, quickly, now." Miyota was over thirty, and single. She painted with bright blue eye shadow and was a sex fiend. If she were here, the situation must be extreme.

Half asleep, Jiro was able to make at least this much judgment as he crawled to the staircase. From the head of the steps, he looked down into the corridor. Yes, just as he'd thought. Ogata had gone to answer the call. Jiro could see his great, swaying, fat body. As big as Ogata was, the vampire should suck his blood. But Jiro was sure Ogata had never been to the vampire, even once.

"Two at the same time?" Ogata said. "How come? The vampire in a bad mood? Have an accident?"

Accidents were frequent on Number Seven National Highway, which passed nearby. Victims, covered with blood, were often brought in. When he saw someone bleeding like that, the vampire could not remain still.

"No accident. A double love suicide."

The words "love suicide" brought Jiro wide awake. It was as if someone dropped him into ice water.

Ogata's voice sounded stupid. "Man and woman?"

Miyota sounded lively, "Yes. The woman was naked. The man stabbed her several times with a butcher knife. Then he stuck himself in the chest and abdomen. I doubt if it's possible to save him." As a messenger of the vampire, she always talked brightly when the conversation was about bleeding. Now she said, "The man's type O. But the woman is Rh-minus AB. That's rare."

Jiro's hunch had been right. His blood was Rh-minus AB. Very rare. Only about one person in two thousand had it. Sometimes the vampire liked to suck blood with a different taste. He probably thought this rare and expensive too, because he didn't often call for it. It had happened just last month.

The vampire had wanted the blood of a newborn baby. But he only sucked the blood of Rh-minus babies. Consequently, Jiro had to make up for the blood sucked from the baby.

As a regular member of the vampire's blood-offering group, Jiro was virtually a prisoner. Because of his special blood type, his health was carefully watched. He was called by the vampire less often than many other members of the group. Otherwise, Jiro's blood would long ago have become weak and yellow. If the vampire sucked out two hundred CC's daily, anybody, no matter how healthy, would soon become anemic and close to death.

Crawling back to his bed, Jiro strapped on his artificial leg. He had lost his left leg from the knee down, in an auto accident. He was long accustomed to this routine. But the vampire detested sucking the blood of physically disabled persons. Jiro did everything possible to conceal his artificial limb.

"Number eight, Tokumoto!" Ogata called. "Number three, Yamane!" He gave orders in military fashion. The person who did not answer loud and clear would be beaten.

Jiro called out loudly, "Coming, right away." And Yamane, number three, murmured something in a barely audible voice. Lately, he'd been having his blood sucked every day. No wonder his face was yellow and lusterless.

Jiro descended the steps, one at a time. Ogata and the assistant dormitory chief, Kurashiki, waited. Kurashiki, a tatooed ex-gangster, acted as a kind of guard. He always sported a pistol or knife where the inmates could see it. He had offered to bludgeon any inmate who tried to run away.

With his chest thrust out as much as possible, Jiro said, "Number eight, Tokumoto. Ready to go." Whenever the vampire called them, they wore white jackets, with red hearts on them. The vampire was fond of ceremony.

When Miyota looked at Jiro's face, she grinned and nodded. She obviously had some plot in mind.

The vampire had a long beak. The end was a tube with a sharp, slender tip. To suck blood directly from their veins, the vampire bent at the waist so the beak came into the proper position.

The vampire was covered all over with long, fluffy red hair. When he sucked blood, the hair turned bright crimson and became as shiny as glass.

To facilitate the sucking, Miyota tied a thick rubber tube around Jiro's arm. Then, just tasting to see if it was all right, she sucked a little blood from the back of Jiro's hand with a small needle-beak that looked like the larger beak of the vampire.

After measuring his blood with a hydrometer, she stroked Jiro's cheek. "Your blood is thick and rich. Oh, if only the others had blood like yours. The vampire would think it delicious. He'd praise you all." Her tone was pensive. "They have weak, yellow blood. It looks watered down."

Jiro said, "But everybody's trying to make their blood as rich as possible. They don't work, you know. They rest all the time, and eat plenty of things with protein in it." He mumbled this as he stared at the patient lying on the white table beside him. It was the girl involved in the love suicide. Just now, she was covered to the chest with a white sheet, but earlier she must have been bleeding from wounds all over her body.

Whenever he saw someone bleeding like that, the vampire lost control and could not calm down again till he'd sucked from two to four hundred CC's from inmates like Jiro.

The vampire came in, dragging a heavy chain that clanked and rattled. Frightened, Jiro fought to avoid looking at the vampire's face. The most dangerous thing was to look into his eyes.

Miyota ran over and began flattering the vampire.

Jiro secretively slipped his hand beneath the white sheet to touch the body of the patient on the table. She was cold, clammy.

But maybe there was no cause to worry; maybe all women's bodies were cold, like corpses. He had no experience. Pulling the sheet back, he saw a large white gauze bandage covering her lower abdomen and her breast. Those must be the places where the wounds were worst. Between her smooth white thighs, he saw a black bush that reminded him of seaweed waving on the ocean floor. Suddenly, he wanted to touch it. Sometimes he had impulses like this, but didn't know what to do about them.

"What're you doing?" Miyota said sharply. She slapped his hand.

The vampire spoke up. "I told you not to use that man. Now you know why. He's dangerous." The vampire rarely spoke. At most he gave short unintelligible orders to Miyota.

When he realized they were talking about him, Jiro went rigid.

"It's all right," Miyota told the vampire. "I'll keep my eye on him. And, remember, his blood is really rich."

The vampire was abrupt. He said nothing. With his hair swaying, he approached and immediately thrust his beak into Jiro's veins. Gradually, the vampire's glass-like beak began to fill with Jiro's blood.

Jiro closed his eyes. Every time the vampire sucked his blood, he became weak in the legs. Some of the inmates became so weak they fainted. But they had to give the vampire their blood. Actually, they were happy to do it. When he finished, the vampire usually gave them a little money. If they did not serve the vampire, they would have to leave the dormitory.

Miyota came over and removed the rubber tube from Jiro's arm.

She said, "Go over there, and rest a while, now."

All Jiro could think of was the earthen color on the face of the girl next to him. Now, a little red had appeared in her cheeks. If everything went well, it might be possible to save her. She had the kind of plump face that Jiro admired.

Miyota led Jiro to a small room on the second floor, where the vampire's assistants rested. Jiro and the other inmates usually lay down in a much more spacious place.

Miyota was kindly. She patted him gently on the shoulder, now, as she helped him lie on the bed. "Tonight, you'll stay here. I still have something for you to do." There was something in her tone. Jiro thought, "No one else knows, but she's going to suck my blood, too."

He didn't like Miyota to suck his blood. It didn't hurt the way it did when the vampire did it, but it made him feel very peculiar.

Miyota went into the hall and returned shortly. On the wall hung an old-fashioned clock. It read three A.M. At this hour, all the vampires in Japan must be busy.

Miyota touched him with her cool hand. Then she went away and when she returned, she had brought him warm milk, and heavily buttered toast. Her voice was gentle. "You feel stronger now?"

Jiro devoured the food while Miyota took off his underwear. When she sucked his blood, she did not use a long beak like the vampire's. Jiro imagined this must be because she was a female.

Now she leaned quickly, and took Jiro's tube directly between her lips.

At first, it tickled, then it made Jiro feel uneasy, strange. He wanted to run away. But he knew if he resisted, Miyota would become hysterically angry. He decided it would be best to be patient and lie perfectly still.

When Miyota had her face buried between his thighs, she looked completely serious. Her lips were hard and probing as she continued to suck Jiro's tube. He thought how her lips probably had no softness in them. At first, he watched her work for some time, but then closed his eyes. He felt as if his entire body were floating on clouds.

He made a short cry. It was a feeling completely unlike the one when the vampire's sharp beak pierced his veins.

Holding the base of his tube with both hands, and making purring sounds, Miyota quickly sucked the overflowing white blood. At that instant, gleaming fangs grew from the corners of her abnormally red mouth. Then she grinned as she looked at Jiro.

Jiro was tired now. He immediately fell into a deep sleep.

On the following morning, Ogata and Kurashiki came to take him back in the dormitory car. Kurashiki was driving. He sometimes invited Miyota to the motion pictures, but she would have nothing to do with him.

Miyota exchanged greetings with Ogata. "He was a little shaky, last night — but I took good care of him," she said brightly.

Jiro knew she was talking about him. It was a secret that she sucked his white blood. And no matter what happened, he would never tell. If he did, the vampire and Miyota would probably kill him.

Slurping the tea she had given him, Ogata asked in his crude voice, "What's with the suicide pair?"

Miyota's voice was lazy. "The man died at four this morning. He cut his own carotid artery with a razor. Odd, it's usually the woman who dies."

"What about the woman?"

"She may get over it. Of course, she's still in serious condition. She may take a sudden change for the worse. Who knows? . . ."

"I suppose her family's coming. Will they pay us for what we put out." Ogata was talking about the blood the vampire sucked from Jiro. His blood was a rare type and probably very expensive. They were always giving out a lot of phony reasons, like, "It costs a lot to find a person with Rh-minus blood."

"Don't you worry. We'll be hearing from them soon enough. The man's parents have already been here. Before long the others will pay, too." Miyota twisted the red lips with which she had sucked Jiro's blood, as she spoke in a crafty voice. She was always in such a good mood after sucking Jiro's blood. She seemed like an entirely different person. There was something indefinable in her eyes, and a smooth quality to her face that hadn't been there before.

As soon as they got into the automobile and drove off, Kurashiki spoke in a frightening voice, "That broad seems to be sweet on you. What she sees in such a damned shrimp, I sure don't know. Maybe she's been playing some fancy games with you, eh?" Kurashiki was interested in Miyota, and this made him dislike any attention she showed Jiro.

"Nothing's happened between us," Jiro said, putting up as much a show of bravery as he could.

"You better be telling the truth," Kurashiki said harshly. He turned and slapped Jiro across the cheek.

Ogata was quick, "Come on, cut it out."

Jiro felt tears welling in his eyes.

2

A week passed, filled with tranquil days. Jiro did not go to the vampire at all, though other inmates in the dormitory were summoned as usual, almost daily, to see how the vampire felt and to have their blood sucked, for which they received money in return.

One day the dormitory chief was in a very bad humor. Jiro was lying on his bed, staring vacantly at photographs of naked women in the gravure section of a weekly magazine with the cover torn off. He heard Ogata scolding Kurashiki in an angry, but suppressed voice.

"Can't you see anything? Why d'you think we have an all-night guard on the dormitory? Just let the newspapers get a load of this, and we're in trouble. If the chairman finds out, you're fired."

"It wasn't my fault. I kept my eyes open. The guy who ran away carried the stories to the papers."

"Why was he able to run away? Because you were damned careless! You got eyes for Miyota, nothing else. That's why it happens."

Jiro heard a loud slap. The dormitory chief must have struck Kurashiki in the face.

Whenever the chief let Kurashiki have it, the latter took it out on Jiro and other inmates. He was not very bright, but he was strong, brawny. It looked like the inmates' turn for a hard time next.

Kurashiki shouted now. "What're you reading?"

They had expected him to show up.

"A magazine."

"What's the date on it?"

Kurashiki lit harshly into number six, an O type who was lying in the next bed and reading a magazine, one that had been given to Jiro by Miyota. There were lots of week-old magazines in the vampire's house, and Miyota would secretly pass them on, but only to Jiro. She thought it would do no harm since all he'd look at would be the gravure sections and the cartoons.

Kurashiki's tone was touched with threat, and sly pleasure. He spoke in a low voice. "This is last week's magazine. It doesn't have the dormitory chief's stamp of approval. You know what'll happen to you for reading things without the chief's stamp."

"Please, forgive me. I thought he'd passed on it."

"Don't lie to me. Who told you to read this? I just want you to close your eyes and lie still in bed. Once in a while, take an hour out to reflect, to think. Think how no damned good you are! Maybe you'll understand how important it is for you to serve the vampire."

Kurashiki was shouting, mouthing the things he'd heard the dormitory chief say. The chief came once a month, and told them the things he'd heard the chairman say, about how useless the inmates were, and how they were being given a chance to serve the world while being born again.

"Who told you you could read this magazine?" Kurashiki said with a growl as he ripped his belt from his trousers, the leather creaking. "Give that some thought."

Jiro covered his ears with both hands as he heard the leather belt striking against the skin of the O type. He did not want to be beaten. He knew that if Kurashiki found out he was getting magazines from Miyota, he would be inspired to greater savagery by jealousy. Jiro slid his own magazine under the cushion that served as a pillow. He hoped Kurashiki hadn't noticed.

The O type was sobbing, but there was neither spirit nor strength in the sound. That morning, the vampire had sucked two hundred CC's of his blood.

Kurashiki was breathing heavily. He had finished punishing the O type. He turned his gaze to the large closet on one side of the room.

"Where're the two A types?" he said loudly, his voice reverberating.

The four or five inmates were as silent as if they'd suddenly been struck mute.

"Don't try and cover up for them," Kurashiki said. "I know where they are. Most of those A types are sneaky worms, always doing things on the sly. . . ."

Kurashiki's grin made it obvious he had some devilish punishment in mind. Jiro began to tremble inside, Kurashiki walked over and hurled the closet door open. In the shadowed depths, they all saw two of the inmates wrapped in each other's arms. One of them had been here some six months; the other had arrived only the week before.

Kurashiki struck the floor twice with his belt. He said, "You guys are forbidden to do anything that'll thin your blood. You know that. Just what've you been doing in there? Playing around in the shadows." Then he shoved his fingernails into the thin, naked, goose-fleshed buttocks of the older of the two inmates.

Both of them had been in a reformatory before. Like the vampire's assistant, the older one enjoyed putting other people's tubes in his mouth.

Kurashiki cracked his belt. He gave a sharp order, "Come out of there, right now!" He laughed shortly. "Carry on with what you were doing out here, where we can all watch."

The two came slowly out of the closet. The older did as he was told and buried his face between the other's legs. The newer inmate didn't know where to look. He blushed, and his face was covered with pinpoints of perspiration.

Kurashiki folded his arms across his chest, glowering at them. The other inmates sat stiffly in silence, not daring to breathe.

"Now, get this. If what you're letting him do to you thins your blood, you'll go three days without food. If that don't make you happy, then begin to exercise some self-control." Kurashiki was threatening the younger inmate. To the older one, he said, "They say you're proud of the way you use your tongue. You damned queer! Hurry up and finish him off. Find out how much spunk this new guy's got left in him. If you don't make him finish fast, you'll go without food for three days. That'll give you time to think on an empty stomach." Kurashiki's voice was cruel.

Jiro closed his eyes and saw nothing but red darkness. If Kurashiki ever found out Miyota sucked his tube, he would kill him. If they tore him apart, he would never tell. He could never tell anyone Miyota sucked his white blood.

The dormitory chief heard the noise. He came hurrying up to the second floor, shouting, "What's going on? Cut out this nonsense." He made a stern face. "Two new girls're moving in today. You've all got to live closer to the rules. Kurashiki — how many times I have to tell you not to punish the inmates on your own. It's important everybody be in good shape when they go to the vampire. Shouldn't use so much energy." He began to calm a little. "Everybody can have two hours a day for reading, and two walks, thirty minutes each. One in the morning, and one in the afternoon. Rest of the time, stay in bed, with the shutters closed — even in the daytime. You've got to rest your bodies, purify your minds."

Jiro felt that the arrival of the dormitory chief had saved him and the others. He wondered who the new girl inmates could be. There had been some girls in the past, but they usually stayed only a week or two. Rumor had it that the chairman took all the young girl inmates to his own house.

The dormitory chief walked over to Jiro. He spoke in a curiously gentle voice. "Number eight? The girl who survived the suicide will be in the bed right next to yours. For rest and recuperation. Look after her for us, will you?"

3

That evening the girl was brought in. She wore dark blue striped men's pajamas. She seemed entirely different from the girl who had lain naked in the vampire's room.

Miyota was with the girl. After she had her lie down, she carefully tucked the bedclothes around her. In a gentle voice, she said, "All right, now. Anything happens, anything at all, you let me know."

The girl did not reply.

Then in a low whisper, Miyota said to Jiro. "She hasn't said a word since that man stabbed her. She may be planning to try to kill herself again. Listen to me, now. I want you to watch everything she does. Don't you dare make any passes. Got that?"

Just then the dormitory chief came in and said, "How's she doing? Still not talking?"

"No. She is conscious and seems to be getting better, though." Miyota tipped her head to one side.

"Wonder if she's lost her memory?"

"We won't know that for a while yet."

"Let Jiro watch her. Anything happens, he can tell us."

Ogata put the white coat of a male nurse on Jiro. The other female inmate was an O type, around forty. The vampire had sucked so much of her blood that she was a little strange in the head. Ogata said she was a useless, squeezed-out stick, fit only for work in the kitchen.

In comparison, the girl who had survived the love suicide received excellent treatment. Every day they brought her three bottles of milk with honey. There was butter in her porridge, and Ogata sometimes came himself to give her nourishing injections. Right in front of Jiro, they would take off her pajamas and insert the injection needle into one of the slimy plump thighs that he remembered well. She had so many knife wounds in her abdomen, chest, and arms, that the thighs were the only places left for the injections.

Jiro looked at Ogata. "What's her name?"

"Don't know. Her number's fifty-one. You know we don't need names around here. You're number eight, right?"

Jiro nodded. To himself, he thought unhappily, "My name's really Jiro."

Perhaps it was because of the milk and honey. In about two weeks, the girl's cheeks were flushed with color. She no longer had the pale, waxen face Jiro remembered from the white table in the vampire's room. Waiting till no one was around one day, Jiro reached down and stroked her soft cheek with his fingertips. He said, softly, "Who are you? The sleeping beauty?"

The girl did not respond. She seemed still unconscious. Slowly, he slipped his right hand under her blanket. He thought how naughty his hand was, but there was nothing he could do to stop it. Under the blanket was a naked woman, like the ones in the magazines. In putting his hand in her bed, Jiro discovered the blanket was soft, fluffy. The ones Jiro and the other inmates had were scratchy and rough. They might've been made of straw. As he stroked the soft blanket, Jiro thought that maybe the vampire's hair felt the same way. Jiro's guesses were usually correct. "Maybe she's the vampire's daughter."

With great caution, Jiro slipped his hand under number fifty-one's pajamas. He was searching for the thighs, where they made the injections when they stripped her nude. He thought how between her thighs he would find that strange, trembling, black bush. The women in the gravure sections usually covered that part of their body with their hands, or a piece of clothing.

Growing bolder, he slipped his hand between her thighs. He was shocked with what he found. Where there should have been something soft and moist, he felt a hard, metal belt. Quickly, he threw the blanket back.

When he'd seen her in the hospital, she hadn't been wearing this thing. Then he had been able to see the black bush, like seaweed gently swaying on the floor of the ocean. Who had put this iron belt on her? Why?

He tried to recall all the pictures he'd seen in the magazines. His memory sometimes worked better than those of ordinary people. Yes. This metal thing was called a chastity belt. He recalled seeing a beautiful woman who was wearing one, twisting her body into odd positions. Was it necessary to protect the vampire's daughter with a chastity belt? His mouth gaped, and with unblinking eyes he stared at the girl, from whose body he had pulled the blanket back entirely now.

"Maybe she's covered with long red hair, too. She's the vampire's daughter, after all." Jiro had already decided that number fifty-one, this large, beautiful doll, was the daughter of the vampire. Slowly he unbuttoned the jacket of her pajamas.

All of her wounds could not have healed yet. Maybe among some of them would be the long red hair that would prove she was the daughter of the vampire. As he thought this, Jiro had an urge to remove her bandages. First, he took the bandage from her shoulder. It lifted easily. But where he'd expected to find wounds, blood, pus, and long red hair, he saw only smooth, flawless, white skin, as lovely as the skin of her thighs. He couldn't believe it.

Trembling, he removed the bandage from her right breast. There, on her belly, and everywhere he lifted the white gauze, was nothing but beautiful, clear, rosy skin. For a while, without knowing what he was doing, Jiro caressed her breasts and felt the nipples grow as hard as berries. She moaned. This was the first reaction she had made, the first time she'd uttered a sound. Twisting her body, raising her arms, she seemed to want something. But Jiro did not know what to do next. He hurried to place the bandages back, buttoning her pajamas and covering her with the blanket. Just as he finished, Ogata, the dormitory chief, came in.

"What're you doing there?" he asked.

"She was moaning for something. . . ." Jiro's voice was a strained stammer. Fortunately, just then number fifty-one emitted a low sound. The dormitory chief shook his head, but did not speak.

4

Out walking one afternoon, Jiro met a man. He was maybe thirty years old, wearing a raincoat with a turned-up collar, and carrying a camera over his shoulder. He approached Jiro and began a conversation. Jiro had permission to walk to a nearby grove of trees and sketch once a week. His pictures were always the same: the vampire, covered with soft, red hair, seated in the middle of a dark, gloomy forest. He did not begin drawing the vampire today, because the skin of number fifty-one had been as white and smooth as porcelain. He had expected wounds. He could not recover from this.

"You one of the new inmates?" the man asked, offering Jiro a chocolate bar.

Jiro looked into his face. The man smiled broadly in an attempt to overcome any suspicion. Jiro could not tolerate people with cameras. When he'd been in the auto accident, people turned cameras on him while he lay bleeding on the gray pavement. He hated them.

"Yes. I'm one of the new ones," Jiro said.

"You're number eight. Jiro Tokumoto. Right? Blood type Rh-minus AB."

"That's right." Jiro spoke hesitantly. He had accepted the chocolate, so he could at least be civil. Dormitory inmates were not supposed to talk with outsiders. But this man seemed to know everything about him.

"How many official spenders are there in your dormitory?"

"Spenders?" Jiro wanted to get away from this fellow, but he was curious. There were some smart-talking people in the dormitory who called themselves spenders; that is, professional blood donors. And the wounded patients. But Jiro always thought in terms of the vampire and his assistants.

The man said, "Never mind, now. Our investigations show there are twenty-two. Two weeks ago, two new women were brought in."

Jiro said nothing.

"Aren't you supposed to talk? It's all right, I won't tell anybody. Anyway, our information's accurate. You don't really want to live in that dormitory, do you? You want to go back to the ordinary world, as fast as you can. Right?"

"No. I like the dormitory," Jiro said. He did not really like the vampire and Miyota very much, and he hated the frightening Ogata and Kurashiki. But it would be the same outside. No matter where he went, there would be people to tease and mistreat him. In the dormitory he had food. He was allowed to do the sketching he loved. And number fifty-one, the vampire's beautiful daughter, was in the next bed.

"That so? You like it, huh? Well, you'll get sick and tired of it before long. Must be a lot of anemic invalids in there, the way they're taking two and three hundred CC's of blood every day."

"I don't know anything about the others."

"You don't talk much, do you? Must be pretty frightened of the people in charge of the dormitory. But we're strong, you know? We're determined to save you and the others."

The man said odd things.

"Tokumoto, there was another Rh-minus spender in the dorm, wasn't there?"

"Spender?"

"Never mind about the word. There was another Rh-minus AB-type inmate, right?"

"I think there was." Jiro's answer was slow. When he considered it, he did remember that on the day when the vampire's daughter was lying on the white table, Yamane, the other Rh-minus had gone out somewhere. It was really Yamane's turn to go to the vampire, and Jiro'd only gone because he hadn't been there. In ordinary matters Jiro's memory operated very slowly, in this way. He didn't like it but there was nothing he could do about it.

"That's right. There was number three, Yamane. . . ." Jiro mumbled as if talking to himself.

"When did he disappear? Don't try to evade me, now."

When this kind of question was put to him, Jiro's memory spun. Of course, it had been the day when the regular order of calls from the vampire was upset. But on that evening, and the next morning, maybe Yamane had gone to the vampire.

"Think hard, now. It was the day two suicides were brought in. Was that the day number three vanished?"

Suddenly the man was holding a microphone in front of Jiro's nose. Jiro began to stutter.

"Ah, the day of the suicide couple . . ."

"Yes. How many CC's they take from you that day?"

"What d'you mean, 'CC's'?" Jiro stared at the man with an owlish expression.

The man was exasperated. "I get it. You don't know what CC's are. Right? Okay, Tokumoto — how much blood did the vampire suck from you that day? The same as always? Or did your legs go numb? Was so much blood sucked that everything went dark?"

"That — that night, when I was sucked . . . everything went dark. I didn't know why. Then I laid down for a bit."

Jiro told how Miyota had put his tube in her mouth and sucked his white blood. Every time Miyota did this, everything went dark, and he passed out.

"What're you talking about? Look, whose side you on, anyway? The hospital records say you only donated two hundred CC's that night. You professional spenders don't pass out when you give that little. Besides, you have a rare type blood. You hadn't been called to donate for more than seventy hours, before that suicide case happened."

The man had lost patience and was irritated. His voice was loud. This made Jiro all the more timid and nervous. He thought, "I'm not lying. The vampire's assistant really did suck my tube and make me pass out."

The man reached out and shook Jiro by the shoulders. "Get hold of yourself," he said. "You guys are having your blood sucked by the Alpha Transfusion Center. The people in charge of the center talk pretty, but they're really collecting your blood to make money. Right? They're in business. They pay a donor four hundred yen for two hundred CC's of blood and sell the same amount for a thousand three hundred. According to last year's records, one million two hundred thousand people offered to give blood. Of this total, only six hundred and eighty thousand were usable. The rest had blood too weak to be valuable. Even when the blood gets so thin, commercial banks go on drawing it for the sake of profit. But this Alpha Transfusion Center is even worse. They keep you people in dormitories and feed you. Then when accidents happen on this highway, the hospitals don't use the stuff in the blood bank. Instead, the transfusion center sends you to the hospital. Last year there were two cases where too much blood was taken from spenders. They died of acute anemia. Why d'you pretend you don't see these things happening? Don't you know it could happen to you?"

The man's eyes brimmed with tears and saliva sputtered from his lips. Jiro couldn't imagine why he was so angry, or even what he was trying to say.

"We're all happy to go to the vampire. He gives us money. When our blood's good, he praises us."

"Oh, damnit. It's no good, talking to you. You're all drop-outs. Give me a straight answer. That night, was two hundred CC's all the blood they took?"

Jiro remained silent.

"Now, listen. That night when the suicide couple were brought in, the woman was bad off. Nobody knows who she is. To save her, it'd require a transfusion of more than three thousand CC's. Without that, she would've died. Hospital records say that all the blood that was taken from you was two hundred CC's. That unknown woman had a rare blood type. Rh-minus AB. Only one person in two thousand has that type blood. It'd be impossible for 'em t'draw that much blood from a bank in one night. If the blood for that woman didn't come from a blood bank, then where did it come from? Spenders, professional donors are the only answer. But if the rules were followed, it'd take fifteen people of Rh-minus AB to provide what she needed. How could any hospital collect that many people with that blood type late in one night? It'd be impossible. The only answer is, three thousand CC's were drawn from your fellow inmate, number three. God, what a horrible thought!"

The man was trembling in a way Jiro thought was exaggerated. At any rate, Jiro understood almost nothing of what he was saying.

"But the inmates sleep under soft, fluffy blankets, and have milk with honey, and buttered bread to eat."

"I don't believe it. You live like prisoners."

"But not that girl. . . ."

"What girl? The one from the suicide couple?"

"Yes. I think she's the vampire's daughter. But she has smooth skin, and no red hair, like the vampire's."

When Jiro told him about the vampire's daughter, the man revealed obvious agitation. Before leaving, he wrote two numbers on a scrap of paper. One was the telephone number of the Bureau of Civil Liberties. The other was the number of a direct line to the production office of a television news program.

"Don't show this to anyone. Anything happens, call one of these numbers — fast. The next person in danger is you. You're a living blood bank, with four thousand CC's of a rare blood type."

The man said this rapidly, but Jiro did not listen. He hated people with cameras. And especially, he now hated this man.

5

"FROM NEWS PRODUCTION STAFF OF AZUMA TV BROADCASTING COMPANY TO PERTINENT OFFICER IN MINISTRY OF WELFARE:

"The Alpha Transfusion Center is employed by the Tahara Emergency Hospital, located on Highway Number Seven, in Fukui, Saitama Prefecture. The location is one where accidents are numerous. Investigations reveal that inmates of the Alpha Transfusion Center are having from five hundred to two thousand cubic centimeters of blood drawn at a time. What is your reaction to this?"

The following was received from the Ministry of Welfare after two weeks:

"The Ministry of Welfare does not permit more than two hundred cubic centimeters of blood to be drawn from a donor at one time. Commercial blood banks must operate according to Ministry of Welfare regulations. The ministry provides guidance and surveillance to this end. But, since the field is wide, it is possible some things have escaped our notice. In the final analysis, we can only rely on the conscientious feelings of people operating facilities of this kind. We investigated the institution in question, but received word from authorities that they are abiding by regulations stating that no more than two hundred cubic centimeters of blood will be drawn at a time. They add that they carefully examine the density of blood before collecting. They further insist all the people who provide blood are in good physical condition and that your accusations are unfounded."

"REQUEST FOR INVESTIGATION TO CHAIRMAN OF FAR EAST RED CROSS TRANSFUSION RESEARCH INSTITUTE FROM NEWS PRODUCTION STAFF OF AZUMA TV BROADCASTING COMPANY."

Reply:

"The incident you mention is beyond our jurisdiction, and it is impossible for us to conduct investigations of such institutions as you describe. I must, therefore, limit myself to explaining our official stand on commercial blood banks.

"A recent questionnaire sent by us to clinics to investigate the ways transfusions are conducted produced the following information.

"Conscientious clinical doctors no longer put much faith in transfusions of stored blood. While realizing the risks involved, they prefer direct mechanical transfusions of the customary kinds. The reason for this preference is the practice of commercial blood banks of providing weak, yellow blood.

"Therefore, it is unthinkable that a clinical doctor could have taken more than one thousand cubic centimeters of blood from a single spender from the Alpha Transfusion Center."

"REQUEST FOR INVESTIGATION TO THE SAITAMA POLICE DEPARTMENT FROM NEWS PRODUCTION STAFF OF AZUMA TV BROADCASTING COMPANY"

Reply:

"Investigation currently in progress."

Jiro opened his eyes. He was lying in bed. Strong light coming through a knothole in the shutters told him the day must be well advanced. When he turned his eyes, he saw the vampire's daughter and her soft blanket were gone. He heard noises from the yard, as if people were playing some game. None of the inmates had ever played sports in the yard before.

He got up to wash his face. Ogata would probably read him a long sermon because he'd slept later than all the others. Group living demanded everyone obey the rules. Fortunately there seemed to be guests in the living room downstairs. Jiro could hear the chairman talking, slowly, demonstrating his dignity.

"Today we're happy to have with us the business manager for medical treatment from the Beta Blood Bank. As you know, we're associated with them. We'll be happy to answer all questions you gentlemen from the television company see fit to ask. But, I would like to say, we want you to realize our work's a contribution to the good of society. You've come a long way to be with us. So before beginning this session, let's have a drink."

Jiro heard the sound of clinking glasses.

"Since you've invited us to be frank, I'd like to start the questioning by asking if it's true you observe the two-hundred-CC regulation?"

"Of course, we do. You have any doubts, check the inmates' health. All they do is play sports, relax, and think. Blood's drawn no more than once or twice a week. This is a social service. We're not out to make money."

"But our investigations show you take three hundred or more CC's of blood from each spender daily."

"Rot. Absurd. Even when we send spenders to the blood bank we check the density of their blood, making certain they pass the mark."

"In these density tests, it's possible to fake results by using somebody else's blood sample."

"Well, some organizations may be foolish enough to try something like that. But we never would."

"We've heard other things. To meet needs for exports of dried blood, haven't you sometimes drawn it as often as twice a day from the same spender?"

Jiro recognized the man who spoke this time, in an angry voice. It was the same one he'd talked with out in the grove.

"You'd better be careful what you say. If you're making wild accusations like this, let me offer you proof you're wrong. The blood production capacity of the human body is limited. It's impossible to take blood from an individual daily, or twice daily. Our blood bank's been exporting dried blood to the United States for nearly ten years. We've never resorted to such practices."

Jiro had come halfway down the stairs, and now he saw the business manager of the blood bank making his speech. Blue veins bulged in his forehead. All Jiro was interested in was the disappearance of the vampire's daughter. He wanted to ask Ogata or Kurashiki where she'd gone.

"Okay. Let us present you with some proof of our own," the angry man said. "A spender from this organization ran away and entered a Tokyo hospital. He'd been forced to give blood every day. His heart was found to have doubled in size. He had difficulty breathing and suffered from edema of the lungs. This means, no matter how hard he breathed, air didn't reach his lungs — water accumulated. He escaped the watch of the people guarding him here, and ran away."

"That's a lie! Somebody's made this up to scare the inmates. We'll be happy to interview this man whenever you like."

"Unfortunately — he died. Writhing in agony. Two weeks ago."

"There, you see? You're telling rotten lies. You don't have a shred of proof."

"There's more. You've experimented with total-exchange transfusions in a case of leukemia involving the rare Rh-minus AB blood type. You've already killed one spender with that blood type."

"You're irritating. We have only one Rh-minus inmate, and he's in the best of health."

There was a shattering crash as the chairman threw a glass at his guest. Jiro decided not to go into the room to ask the whereabouts of the vampire's daughter.

6

Two months passed. The people from the TV company stopped coming around. Suspicious men no longer roamed the dormitory. The tough hoodlums who had pretended to play football in the yard had returned to Tokyo, and the old pale-faced inmates had come back. Only number three never turned up again. On the previous night, the vampire's daughter had been carried in on a stretcher. Miyota hung around all the time, and was especially nice.

She said, "Tonight the vampire's going to come all the way over here to suck your blood."

"You mean, I won't have to go to his house?"

"Nope. Just lie here and wait."

Jiro said, "Why is the vampire's daughter back? She is the vampire's daughter. But when she was here before, I looked in her bandages and I couldn't find any red hair."

Smiling, Miyota tied a thick rubber tube around Jiro's arm. His veins were prominent now. His blood hadn't been sucked for two weeks, and it was very rich.

"Lately all the spenders've been bled so much their blood's turned pink or yellow," Miyota said, speaking more to herself than anything else. "Nice rich blood like yours will make the vampire very happy."

Preparations were completed. After about thirty minutes, the chairman, Ogata, and the vampire came in.

"Let's try one more total-exchange transfusion. Drain out all the useless blood and inject fresh blood."

"It'll be all right this time, won't it? It didn't work right with number three, the other time. After the transfusion, we had a lot of trouble, hiding that body. Those guys from the TV company came pretty close to catching us."

"You boys're getting paid enough for what you do, so shut up! Unless we transfer blood, one of 'em's going to die, anyway. There's no blood available, then pump in saline solution, or anything. We've got to make this exchange."

"You better promise not to do anything dangerous again. We understand she's the daughter of some big wheel. The spenders are nothing but nameless dropouts with nobody in the world. It makes no difference if they're bled to death. Still, we think it's safer to rig a coverup — like that double suicide, or a traffic accident. Then the TV and newsmen won't make a stink. Of course, the guard dropped the ball, let that guy run away and shoot his fool mouth off. This time, let's not try anything fancy. We better work fast."

"You sure it's all right not to give this one an anesthetic?"

"Sure. He's an imbecile. Completely weak upstairs. The long beard has him convinced the doctor's a vampire."

"Okay. No more talk. Get ready for the exchange transfusion. When we've drawn more than one thousand CC's pump saline solution into the spender."

Vaguely, Jiro could hear the vampire and the others talking at his bedside. The return of the vampire's daughter somehow made Jiro feel happy. Miyota took his arm, and the vampire brought his glass beak near. It was a longer glass beak than usual. He kept on sucking Jiro's blood. Jiro broke out in a cold sweat. He went numb in the lower part of his body. He felt dizzy. He could not breathe. He was in great pain. It was not at all the kind of dizziness he felt when Miyota sucked his white blood. When she did that, it didn't hurt this much. The next time he met the man who gave him the chocolate, he'd have to tell him that it hurt badly when the vampire sucked his blood. So much he could not breathe. As he mused about this, Jiro passed into a distant, dark world, from which he would never return.

"REQUEST FOR INVESTIGATION TO THE BUREAU OF CIVIL LIBERTIES FROM NEWS PRODUCTION STAFF OF AZUMA TV BROADCASTING COMPANY. THE ALPHA TRANSFUSION CENTER IS USING MENTALLY RETARDED PEOPLE AS SPENDERS. SINCE THESE PEOPLE ARE INCAPABLE OF MAKING JUDGMENTS ON THEIR OWN, DOES NOT THE ACTION OF ALPHA TRANSFUSION CENTER VIOLATE HUMAN RIGHTS?"

Reply from the Bureau of Civil Liberties:

"We have been strongly advised by the Alpha Transfusion Center that, even if spenders are mentally retarded, the act of offering blood ought to be regarded as a service to society.

"We are unable to remonstrate further with the Alpha Transfusion Center."

TAKAO TSUCHIYA

Write In, Rub Out

Takao Tsuchiya's stories are a blend of pure detection and social aware-ness. He infuses his ingenious plots with insight and humanism. In his more recent work he has shifted from tricks and gimmicks to a deeper realism.

Written Chinese characters, or kanji, *which developed in China and are at present used in both China and Japan, play an important role in the structure of Tsuchiya's contribution to this anthology. Because Chi-nese characters are, however charming, largely a puzzle to most Western readers, we have adapted this story slightly. We're sure you'll agree it was worth the effort.*

Here, Tsuchiya uses a 28-year-old woman novelist as his detective, revealing the events slowly through memories and flashbacks but revert-ing in the end to his earlier style by climaxing the story with a clever plot point. . . .

FOR TWO DAYS, SHUN AKITSU, a teacher at the municipal university, attended a symposium on environmental pollution in Kyoto. On the night of his return to his home in Tokyo, he discov-ered his wife, Misae, dead. She had taken an overdose of sleeping pills and left the following letter, written on ordinary stationery:

"After all, there is no other way. I have been a useless wife to you and, even after my death, I am going to cause you trouble. The idea is bitter and painful to me. I am deeply sorry about Mit-sue, but this is the life I have been given to live. I beg that arrange-ments will be made. Farewell."

The body lay across bedding on the tatami floor of the main

Japanese-style room on the first floor. Misae had put on makeup. At the corner of her mouth was a very small amount of regurgitated food. Otherwise, there were no signs of suffering. In death, her face was peaceful.

When Shun found her, the body was still warm. The police officer who examined her said she had been dead for maybe two hours. It was estimated that she must have taken the sleeping medicine between midnight and two in the morning on the day she was found. At the moment she closed her eyes to take the tablets, her husband had been laughing and talking in a bar in Kyoto. Listening to the officer's explanation of what had probably happened, Shun fell shaken on his dead wife's body. An oddly warm wind was blowing on the night in early January when this took place.

1

The clock on the shelf said that it was eleven. Its old-fashioned dial and folkcraft style had appealed to Misae, and she had bought it on our wedding anniversary last year. I was remembering such things as I leaned against the desk in my study.

Misae's fragrance still lingers, I thought. And yet she has already been dead a week. Probably my mind rejects the idea of being a husband humiliated by his wife's suicide. I requested sick leave from the university. I don't have the self-confidence to face the curious glances of all those girl students. My colleagues, who try to console me, are all thinking the same thing: "I wonder why such a thing happened."

I wondered, too. I was the one wanting to ask why. Why did it happen? Why?

As I reached for a cigarette on the desk-top, I heard footsteps on the stairs. They paused before the study door.

"You still up?"

Startled, I turned. "Misae!"

But the door opened and it was Misae's younger sister, Mitsue.

"Oh. Mitsue," I said with a sigh.

"Did I frighten you?"

"You're so much like her."

"People often used to mistake our voices on the phone."

There were two years between them. In appearance and personality, they were rather different. When I was introduced to them six years ago, I didn't hesitate to choose the older one. Her quiet, gentle face and clear eyes appealed to me. She seemed helpless, the epitome of maidenly grace. Mitsue was larger in body. Her lush beauty made me think of a proud personality that wouldn't suit me.

"What're you doing up at this time of night?" I asked, glancing at the clock on the shelf. "You want something?"

"Could I come in for a minute?"

"Sit down over there," I told her, motioning toward the sofa and chairs in one corner of the room. "But, it's late — I can't talk long."

Since the day of Misae's suicide, Mitsue had been staying in the house. She seemed to think that the words "I beg that arrangements will be made" in the suicide note pertained to her. For this reason, she helped with the housework.

Although she was my sister-in-law, she was still an unmarried woman of twenty-eight. She lived a carefree life alone in an apartment and worked at a small publishing firm. She also wrote novels. I didn't want to cast reflections on her good intentions, but couldn't help wondering what people would think. It worried me.

"Shun," she said, looking into my face.

"What?"

"Something I'd like to ask you."

"All right."

The whiteness of her knees and thighs, visible under her short skirt, dazzled me. I looked away.

"You know the real reason for Misae's suicide?"

"Reason . . . ?"

"Motive, then. The truth behind it — sounds like a novel title. But, d'you know the real motive?"

"True or false, it was all there in the note. She said, 'After all, there is no other way.'"

"Yes, but it's the 'after all' that's strange, if she used a phrase like that, it seems to me something ought to've come before it. Something unhappy, some sudden something. Misae struggled with it. She tried to get away from it. But finally she exhausted herself. I think that's why she said, 'After all, there is no other way,' Nothing in the note explains the 'after all.'"

"Mitsue," I said in a cool voice. "That's a cruel way to talk. You're right, there's no detailed explanation in the letter, but she thought I'd understand her meaning."

"Did you?"

Quite naturally, I was offended. "You understand yourself," I said. "You know last September she had a miscarriage when she was four months pregnant. I scolded her at the time because it was her fault she miscarried. She cried and apologized. But, in about a month, she became neurotic. I did everything I could to cheer her up. But — you know all this. You even said the same thing to the police officer who came to investigate that night."

I recalled the unpleasant scene.

2

Seneca said that suicide is a special privilege of mankind. Other people have said suicide is the ultimate human freedom. But this right, this freedom, exerts tremendous effects on the people associated with the suicide. Misae's death taught me, to my distress, how true this is.

I was upset and disturbed that night. It's scarcely surprising. I had been imagining a smiling wife to welcome me home. Suddenly I was confronted with that shocking sight. The absurdity of being greeted by a corpse nearly drove me mad.

I suspect I was curt and unfriendly to the officer who asked me questions. A relatively old man, he put his arm around my shoulder and said, "Understand, we don't want to be rude, asking these things. We don't like it, but it's regulations. It's unpleasant work."

According to his explanation, all unnatural deaths had to be investigated. In cases of suicide, method and cause should be established. Investigations must be made to determine whether anyone else instigated or assisted the suicide. Attempts should be made to discover suicide notes and to verify them if they are found.

"That's how it is. We hope you'll be good enough to cooperate with us," he said.

I agreed and he began asking about motives, the very topic Mitsue had been discussing.

The officer said, "This suicide note doesn't ring clear to me. How about telling us things in greater detail?"

I was hesitant. "I don't know the actual reason, either."

"Well, recently, have you noticed anything different or strange in the way your wife talked or acted?"

"Well — yes."

I explained the miscarriage in detail. While crossing a street, jaywalking, she'd been struck and knocked down by a child riding a bike. She admitted she hadn't been paying attention. The accident was the result of carelessness.

I'd been looking forward with pleasure to the birth of our first child. From the time I learned she was pregnant, I had been especially attentive to her condition. The miscarriage disappointed me tremendously. I became very angry. This must have hurt her. For a long while, she cried constantly, and would not speak. Lately, she had calmed down, but the topic had remained taboo between us.

The police officer made pencil notes as he listened. Then he said, "So, it was neurosis resulting from miscarriage?"

"It's my guess, yes. I can't think of another reason."

"I see."

I turned and looked at Mitsue. I had phoned her. She arrived some ten minutes after the police officer.

"You're Mrs. Akitsu's younger sister, right?"

"Yes." Her pale face was stiff. I averted my eyes.

"You have any notion why your sister'd want to kill herself?"

"I think what my brother-in-law said is the only possible reason."

Mitsue spoke clearly. I was deeply grateful for her behaving like a true relative.

"In other words, it's the shock of the miscarriage? You think that?"

"Yes. Ever since then, she tended to be dejected. She'd come to my apartment and spend half a day, crying. I'd tell her to cheer up. I'd tell her she could have other babies. I said if she had twins she'd make up for the one lost. But it didn't even make her smile. The shock must've hit her very hard. Even from childhood, she was a fretful person, always easily depressed."

The officer seemed satisfied with this explanation. Then, pointing to the stationery on which the note was written, he asked, "This your wife's handwriting?"

"Yes."

"No mistake," Mitsue said. "I recognize the slender letters, the slant. That's my sister's hand, all right."

I became vaguely angry. Was he suggesting the suicide note was false? If that was the case, Misae had been murdered. But I knew better than anyone that she had committed suicide.

The questioning was stupid. Why did the police conduct useless investigations, like this? They did one thing, however, that won my admiration. They traced the store where she purchased the sleeping pills.

There were two pharmacies in our neighborhood. Since I sometimes took sleeping pills, Misae, who was known at both stores, probably had no trouble buying what she wanted. The proprietor of the store where she made the purchase said she had bought the pills the day before, at eight in the evening, and that she seemed perfectly normal at the time.

Learning this, the officer made further notes, then said, "This makes it a clear case of suicide."

When he'd gone, Mitsue and I collapsed beside Misae's body. I was unable to repress tears. Mitsue sat sobbing. That was a week ago.

I could not understand why Mitsue should so demand the "real motive." What could she be thinking? It was something I could not explain.

3

"Why did you bring it up?" I asked, searching her eyes.

"Something bothers me."

"What?"

"Before we get to that, tell me when you left for Kyoto."

"Thursday, of last week. The conference began in the afternoon of that day and continued for the next day and half of the following day. When it was over, I took the afternoon express train back."

"That means you left Tokyo three days before she died."

"Right."

"What time did you leave the house?"

"Early, I took the seven-twenty express that arrived in Kyoto at ten ten. Plenty of time to make the afternoon conference. But that's got nothing to do with Misae's suicide."

"Maybe it has." There was a challenging look on her face. To avoid this, I looked at the soundless flame of the gas heater. After a moment, she said, "On the day you left, I called here. I hadn't seen Misae for about a month, and I suddenly wanted to visit with her."

"She was home, of course?"

"Yes. But when I asked to come over, she said no. She said she'd be busy both that night and the next day. That was when she told me you'd gone to Kyoto. But, during the call, I heard something. . . ."

I said nothing.

"It was the clattering sound of a sliding door being opened. Then a voice called, 'Misa.' And our conversation was cut off."

"The phone went dead?"

"No. I think Misae put her hand over the receiver. I called her name several times. Then she said, 'Sorry, A neighbor just came. I'll have to hang up now. Good night.' And that was the end of the conversation."

Lighting a cigarette, I said, "I don't get it. I don't see anything strange in the sound you heard on the phone."

"Oh? I think you understand —"

"Don't joke." I felt angry. I know I looked severe. Even if she was my sister-in-law, I didn't relish having a young woman suggest I'm cowardly. Naturally, I don't take such things well.

"Then you don't sense anything in what I said?"

"No."

"I'll explain. The phone's on a shelf in the dining-kitchen. Most of the doors here are on hinges. The only sliding door's the one between the dining-kitchen and the bath. This means the sound I heard was made by somebody coming out of the bath. I could easily hear it, because the sliding door's right beside the phone. . . ."

"In other words, while you were talking, somebody was taking a bath?"

"I think so."

This was something entirely new to me. With a sour look, I blew out some smoke.

"And it was a man's voice that called 'Misa.'"

"Misae said it was a neighbor."

"Yes. But a neighbor would've said 'Mrs, Akitsu' or maybe 'Misae.' But Misa is a name used by only a small number of my sister's school friends."

Another heavy silence ensued. Mitsue was telling the secret that, during my absence, my wife had entertained an old friend and had allowed him to take a bath. My heart was unsteady.

My voice was husky, "I think you know who that man was."

Instead of saying yes or no, she asked, "Have you ever heard the name Mitsu Matoba?"

Mitsu Matoba. Maybe that was Mitsue's answer. I shook my head.

<h1 style="text-align:center">4</h1>

"Mitsu's our cousin, one year older than Misae," she said, glancing down at her knees. "He used to work in a bank in the city, but ten years ago he disappeared."

"Why?"

"Nobody knows. Just disappeared. We advertised in newspapers and employed a private detective, but nothing came of it. The family was resigned to his being gone. Then, last month, all of a sudden, he turned up at my place. He seems to've found my address reading in a newspaper about a short story of mine that won a prize."

I recalled that one of her short stories had been selected by a magazine for a new-author prize. Misae had given me a copy to read. The series of vivid descriptions of love and desire in the story startled me, gave me an idea of the private life Mitsue must lead. It also recalled the fragrance of her white skin.

"I was shocked, seeing him after ten years. I asked him questions about his past life, but he smiled. 'No comment' was what he said. He asked me for Misae's address."

"You gave it to him?"

"No. I didn't like the broken-down, unhealthy look of him. I saw no need telling him anything since he refused to explain his past or even give me his present address. But he must've found her address in my phone directory while I was making tea. The directory was tossed on my desk when I came back into the living-room."

To calm my growing nervousness, I said, "You mean, the voice you heard that night . . ."

As my voice trailed off, she said, "Mitsu was Misae's first love."

I felt wretched, and, as if to drive it further home, Mitsue went on, "They were going to be married. She almost became seriously ill when he vanished. They used to go for walks or to concerts together. Maybe she'd let him kiss her. . . ."

I put up my hand. Her eyes were flaming with a light that might be anger or maybe jealousy.

"Let's leave it at that," I said. "It's already late."

I stood up.

"Just a minute," she said. "I haven't finished."

"I've heard enough."

"But what about the real reason for killing herself? I still haven't heard what you have to say."

She was damned persistent.

"I have nothing to say. No ideas except she killed herself because of neurosis caused by the miscarriage."

"Okay. Let me ask you. The night you found out she'd killed herself, what time did you leave Kyoto? And what time did you get home?"

With a feeling of disgust, I watched her.

5

The police officer had asked me all of this. I had taken the express 310, which left Kyoto at two forty-five. A young instructor from the university traveled with me. We parted when we arrived at five thirty-five, at Tokyo Station, I took the subway to Koenji Station, and walked to my house. It took maybe fourteen or fifteen minutes. I noticed the lights were out. I thought she must have gone shopping, opened the door with my key. I entered the room where I found her still-warm corpse. Thinking there might be some hope of saving her, I called a doctor friend. My hands shook as I dialed the phone. When he arrived, he said she'd been dead for two hours. At his suggestion, I called the nearby police station and then Mitsue's apartment.

The policeman was worried because he thought too much time had passed between my arrival in Tokyo and when I reached home, discovered the corpse, called the doctor. It was stupid. There was no problem. The following question-and-answer exchange took place between the policeman and me:

— You're certain you took the express 310?

— Yes. You can check with Professor Sato. He was with me.

— And you arrived in Tokyo at five thirty-five?

— That's right.

— You took the subway to Koenji and walked from the station to your home. It took you fourteen or fifteen minutes? This means you should've discovered the body shortly after seven. But it was after eight thirty when you called the doctor. There's over an hour you don't account for. What were you doing during that time?

— I didn't take the subway right away. First I thought I might take a taxi. I couldn't find one. I must've wasted twenty or thirty minutes like that.

— I see. Then?

— I gave up and decided to take the subway, after all. But it was suppertime, and I was hungry. I thought I'd eat before going home, and checked for a restaurant in the neighborhood.

— Where'd you eat?

— I didn't go into any of the restaurants. The food at the inn in Kyoto had been greasy. As I walked around, I decided I wanted something very light and that I'd have a bowl of rice and broth when I got home. So I hurried to the subway station. I must've spent an hour or so walking around that way.

I know I'm repeating myself, but the entire discussion was stupid. After all, the real problem is the time when Misae took the sleeping pills. At that time, I was in a Kyoto bar. There were several people with me. I am willing to swear to god I had nothing to do with Misae's suicide. *I knew nothing about it.*

When Mitsue asked me about the time of my return to Tokyo, I felt a sense of animosity and repulsion.

"Mitsue, why do you ask me that? I explained everything to the police. They were convinced. You were there, you heard it all."

"I wasn't convinced."

"What?"

"You hate taxis. You always use the subway or buses. Why would you suddenly, on this one night, decide to look for a cab?"

I said nothing.

"Ever since your marriage, it's been a tradition for Misae to make something special for supper when you return from business trips."

Again I didn't reply.

"I can't believe you'd break family tradition on this one occasion. I think everything you told the police was fabricated to account for the blank hour in your actions."

"Ridiculous!" I hurled the words at her to cover my nervousness. "What d'you think I was doing during that hour?"

"Practically anything. You might've spent time reading Misae's long suicide note."

"The note was written on one sheet of stationery. It took less than thirty seconds to read."

"Oh, no. I think that was only the last page of many, maybe tens of pages, filled with a detailed explanation of why, 'After all, there is no other way.'"

I felt my face go pale. The color drained from her lips.

"What d'you suppose was in the letter?" I said.

"I think it was about Mitsu. I think he came here while you were in Kyoto. He was her first love. It was the first time they'd seen each other in ten years. An old love suddenly materialized out of the blue. He had a dark cloud of his own unknown past around him. He was beaten down and broken. Misae must've felt overwhelming love and pity for him. She clung to him. . . ."

"You're a true novelist. The emotional scenes are very real."

Mitsue's voice was sharp. "Cut it out."

I was quiet, but the cigarette in my fingers trembled.

"After the miscarriage, she lost all composure. She was overly emotional and cried all the time. As if by plan, Mitsu appeared just when she was very weak. There's no doubt the voice I heard that night on the phone was Mitsu, I think you can imagine what kind of time they spent together that night."

I could not speak.

"I suspect Mitsu asked her to leave you and marry him. In the clutch of passion, in the arms of the first man she'd ever loved, Misae probably lost all self-control and agreed to what he asked. She promised to see him again. But after he was gone, she must've turned pale at the thought of her mistake. She realized she'd sinned against you, but there was no way to undo it. In fear and regret, she gradually made up her mind the only way to make recompense was to die. This was the real reason for her suicide, wasn't it?"

Tears trickled across her pale cheeks.

She said, "When I first saw that suicide note, I thought it was strange. It said, 'I am deeply sorry about Mitsue.' But never in my life did Misae call me by my full name. She always called me Miko."

"People don't always write like they speak."

It was a weak attempt.

"No. The name written there was Mitsu, not Mitsue. She was sorry about Mitsu because she couldn't fulfill her promise and marry him, as she deeply wanted to. It was her way of apologizing. But you didn't want anyone else to see his name. You rejected the very idea of his existence. You simply added an e to his name, making it my name. In that way, you altered the entire content of the note. By adding one letter you erased the true cause of Misae's suicide. . . ."

She was brilliant. I was defeated. I spoke from deep down. "Mitsue, why did you say nothing about this to the police?"

She was quick. "No need. Besides — anyway, I love you."

I couldn't believe it. Mitsue loved me; she loved me.

6

Presently, I said, "It's hard to believe. You never gave me any sign."

"That's how I am," she said, smiling faintly. "I think I loved you from the first time I met you. But I couldn't say anything. That's the kind of woman I am."

"I had no idea. I thought you were braver, more worldly."

"Maybe it's because I'm brave that I can't ask a man to love me. When you proposed to Misae, I knew I'd lost. It hurt me. It was so painful I cried all night when I heard about it."

Her words stung. Her love had concealed my cowardly, dangerous act. It was very quiet, now. There was nothing further for us to say. All I heard was the ticking of the clock, and the sound was painful. Suddenly, I felt compelled to tell about that. Now, maybe I could say it — now. . .

I suppressed the impulse. I couldn't put too much confidence in what she'd said. Maybe the love she spoke of was a cover for the plotting of a twenty-eight-year-old woman. Nothing proved she'd remain on my side if I told her about that. No. I had to hide it for the rest of my life.

"Look at the time," Mitsue said, twisting around. Doing this, her short skirt hiked up, revealing the lush white of her thighs. I caught my breath. Desire touched my loins. "It's time for bed," she said, rising to go. "Sorry to've kept you up so late."

"It's all right," I said shortly. "Thanks."

Opening the door and without turning, she said, "I'm not sorry I told you Move you. No matter what happens. . . ."

"Good night."

Her steps faded on the staircase, I released a deep breath.

7

She had guessed correctly. She had discovered the real reason for Misae's suicide. But it was only part, not all, of the truth. There were other, horrible, facts.

Once more, I resurrected all that had happened that night. After arriving at Tokyo Station, I took the subway to Koenji at once. Up to this point, Mitsue was right. Entering the main room on the first floor, I halted abruptly in complete amazement. Lying there were Misae and a man. They were stretched out on the bedding, embracing. When I recovered from the first shock, I knelt by them. Misae was not breathing. The man's breath was deep and regular. At that moment, he was alive.

I'd never seen him before. He had dark skin. He was probably thirty-four or -five. He had taken off the jacket of his black suit, but wore the trousers and a white shirt with a blue bow tie.

I knew right away that Misae had planned a double suicide with this man. In an envelope, I found a thick sheaf of sheets of stationery on which was written Misae's suicide letter. From it, I learned the man's name. Mitsu Matoba.

Relations between him and Misae had been as Mitsue said. But the letter was so confused, so filled with excessive apologies to me that I couldn't understand the psychological course that led to their decision of suicide.

The man had been working as a bartender in clubs and cabarets in Osaka. Although Misae said nothing about it in the letter, from the mood of the room, I sensed the violence of passionate intercourse that had taken place between them on the night after my departure for Kyoto. It was an odd gesture, but I opened the skirt of her kimono and, thrusting my face deep between her legs, sniffed like a dog.

The suicide had been planned. They had bathed, and Misae had put on fresh underwear. The calm way they looked enraged me. I could never forgive them. It was absurd that this stranger should be lying here, embracing my wife. A black anger flooded me. Clenching my teeth, I stared down at them.

At that instant, the man breathed deeply and opened his eyes slightly. I kicked him in the face with all my might. Then I stepped on his throat. A disgusting sound, neither breath, nor cry, burst from his mouth. With both feet, I jumped up and down on his chest. Each time, I heard ripping flesh. Oddly, all the while, I was thinking of a way to get rid of his body.

Afterward, I dragged his limp body into the garden. In one corner, was a place where dead tree roots had been dug up. I took him there.

With a shovel, I deepened the hole. Then I shoved him in, and covered him up. I was sweating when my task was over. But, it was night, and no one passed. The operation took an hour.

I threw away the useless parts of the suicide letter, leaving only the last page. And, as Mitsue guessed, I added an *e* to the man's name, making it her name.

The part about, "I beg that arrangements will be made," referred to burial arrangements. She wanted to be buried together with Matoba. The first part of the letter had said that. I had no intention of complying with such a wish. Instead, I felt I must make it seem she had committed suicide alone. Thwarting their final wish was my revenge. After looking around the room to make certain I hadn't overlooked anything, I phoned the doctor.

The man's body is still buried in a corner of the garden. In the spring I shall plant things there. I wonder what kind of flowers will bloom from that rich soil?

Suddenly, I recalled the words Mitsue had said earlier: "I'm not sorry I told you I love you. No matter what happens. . . ."

That's what she said. "No matter what happens." Surely those words were an invitation. The vivid impression of her white flesh was still fresh in my mind. The smoothness of her thighs. The full breasts. Her room is on the first floor, directly below. I wonder if she is sleeping yet. I was thinking these things as I sat looking at the door that leads to the stairs.

This English translation depends on the resemblance of the names Mitsu and Mitsue. In the Japanese original, however, the names of these two people are Jin-ichi 仁一 and Kayo 佳代. As wise readers can guess, the Chinese characters for the name Jin-ichi are changed into those for Kayo by the addition of horizontal and vertical strokes, as is illustrated above.

YASUTAKA TSUTSUI

Perfectly Lovely Ladies

Yasutaka Tsutsui is one of the best-known science-fiction writers in Japan. His work is characterized by wit and grim but gentle irony.

In Japan, tales of science fiction are often published alongside detective stories, the borderline between these two not being clearly defined. Mysteries themselves now extend into the realm of the thriller or the crime story, so the real purists seem to be returning to the original detective story.

"Perfectly Lovely Ladies" is one of Tsutsui's few tales that can be classified as a detective story. It recounts the drastic manner in which eight wives of white-collar workers deal with the problems of inflation and the high cost of living — a gently grim tale told with the lightness of touch for which the author is so highly regarded. . . .

AS USUAL, at eight in the morning, after her husband and son had gone, Akiko Kamei was alone in the apartment. When she finished clearing the table, she opened her clothes closet.

"What shall I wear?" There seemed nothing suitable.

Last year, she had bought an Yves St. Laurent suit that had been more than she could really afford. But she had already worn it several times; everybody was sure to think, "That thing again." She hated her husband's low salary and her son's high school fees. She hated inflation and especially the recent drastic rises in food costs and the price of good clothing. She envied the wives of shopkeepers. They may have had very little education, but they were doing well and did not want for money.

Putting on a somber suit that she had bought at a sale three months before, Akiko left the apartment building and walked to the train station, thirty-five minutes away. The stores in the shopping district in front of the station had very little merchandise on display. "They're hiding the fact that they're hoarding," she thought.

When she entered the Dig coffee shop, she saw that three of the ladies were already there, seated in a booth in the corner, chatting. All of them were the wives of underpaid white-collar workers who lived in the same apartment building as Akiko. The youngest was Mrs. Kataoka, twenty-eight; the oldest, Mrs. Ise, thirty-five. They were all frustrated in one way or another and were at ages when such things tend to become worse. All of them were lovely. Their manners of speaking and their behavior were comparatively elegant. Their clothes, though inexpensive, were tasteful. In general, they looked like wealthy married women.

Mrs. Suruga was saying, "It's just not fair. Our children — children of people with college educations — can't get into good universities and medical schools because the costs are too high. But the children of mere shopkeepers — who probably never finished high school — get into the best schools because their parents make big financial contributions."

"I know," Mrs. Ise said. "Drives you wild, doesn't it? They say only doctors' children can get into medical schools. No matter how good a boy's grades are, if the family's not filthy rich, it's no good."

Mrs. Kataoka added, "Well, doctors are filthy rich if they're anything. Why, my family could eat for four or five days on what a doctor charges for a simple examination. It scares you to death to think of getting sick. You simply can't afford to go to the doctor."

As they talked, Mrs. Sakata and Mrs. Watanabe entered. Mrs. Sakata looked pale as she said, "My husband may lose his job. The company's cutting back the staff."

Akiko was surprised. "But your husband graduated from Tokyo University."

"He said it's probably because he didn't slip money to the department chief and the section head. Only the rich are going to be left in the company. It makes you sick!"

Mrs. Watanabe sighed. "Makes you worry about the fate of your children, doesn't it? I don't care how hard parents work to put them through good schools, it can all come to nothing."

In the midst of this discussion of apparently unresolved frustrations, Mrs. Urabe and Mrs. Usui, the last of the group, came in. Standing, Akiko said, "Well, ladies, I see we're all here. Shall we go along?"

Each of the ladies put exactly one hundred and thirty yen on the table for her coffee. They did not trifle with even such small sums. Mrs. Usui and Mrs. Urabe, who did not like coffee and did not want to waste money, made it a point always to come together, thirty minutes late. The other ladies tacitly acknowledged what these two were doing.

After leaving the Dig, they went to the station and boarded the now empty commuter train — the rush hour was over. It took only a short time to leave the small urban subcenter where they lived and move into the greenery of the surrounding suburban residential district. The new houses, arranged in rows, had pretty red and blue roofs. The ladies looked out of the train windows with complicated expressions on their faces. They knew that owning an independent house of their own was entirely beyond their means.

They got off the train at the fourth station and walked along the main road, on which there were a few shops, then crossed the highway running parallel with the tracks and started up the gently sloped street leading into a high-class residential district. Luxurious mansions lined the street. After walking for about ten minutes, they paused before the massive gate of a large mansion. On one of the stone posts of the gate was a plate with the name Toba on it.

"This is it, ladies," Akiko said.

Mrs. Kataoka gasped, "My, it's a big house!"

Akiko pressed the button of the interphone directly under the name plate and immediately heard the coarse voice of a young woman: "Yeah? What is it?"

Akiko thought, "It must be the maid. Even maids get arrogant if they work in a place like this."

While entertaining this bitter thought, she addressed the interphone: "Please, forgive me for this sudden disturbance. We're from the Kinryo Primary School PTA. If the lady of the house is in, we'd like a word with her. We have a small request. We are eight ladies from the PTA executive committee."

The Kinryo Primary School was attended by the children of this wealthy district, including those of the Toba family.

"Oh, I see. Please, then, just a minute." On hearing Akiko's refined way of speaking, the voice from the interphone had somewhat improved. Presently, the young woman's voice was heard again: "Mrs. Toba will see you. One moment please."

She had probably decided to see them because she felt it would be difficult to turn away eight members of the executive committee of the PTA from the school her children attended.

As the ladies waited, they closely observed all of the mansions in the neighborhood. Most of them were surrounded by groves of trees that made it impossible to see what the insides were like. A short distance up the slope was one house with wide windows and open lawns. But from the gate, only the massive roof of the Toba house was visible. Throughout the time the ladies waited, no one passed on the road. The neighborhood was truly quiet. The only thing that could be heard was the occasional car horn on the street near the station at the bottom of the hill.

In a low voice, Mrs. Ise confided to Akiko, "I hope they don't have dogs." Mrs. Ise hated dogs.

"They don't. There's no need to worry."

From the small gate beside the main one, the maid, about high-school age, dark of complexion, and dressed in a flashy red one-piece dress, stepped out and said, "I'm sorry to keep you waiting. Please, come this way."

Looking at the red dress, Akiko thought, "That's Chanel. The cut's a little out of date. Must be a hand-me-down from Mrs. Toba."

Conducted by the maid, the eight ladies entered the spacious front garden, which, Japanese in style, was thickly planted with Chinese black pines and ornamented with stone groups and artificial hillocks. The house itself was in a Western style and had a broad front porch.

The entrance foyer had a very high ceiling with an expensive painting on the wall of the landing of the staircase. A glittering chandelier hung in the center of the room. Akiko and the others were shown into a living room immediately next to the front door. It was a large room with a paneled dado, white walls, and a sculpted plaster ceiling. The floor was covered with a Persian carpet in shades of red. There were two sets of black-leather furniture and a grand piano. On one side of the room was a massive Italian liquor cabinet. As the ladies were taking all of this in, Mrs. Toba appeared.

"Good morning, I am Mrs. Toba. Forgive me for having kept you waiting. I should like to say first how much I appreciate all the time and energy you devote to the PTA."

As she spoke, she sat in a chair in front of the marble mantelpiece. She was a beautiful, pale, and intelligent-looking woman who, though not proud, had the manner of speaking and moving that belongs to the innately well bred. On one of her fingers was a diamond of about two carats.

Awed by Mrs. Toba, the eight ladies sat silent for a time, Mrs. Toba asked, "What is it that you wanted to see me about?"

Akiko represented the group: "Please, forgive us for lying. The truth is, we're not from the Kinryo Primary School PTA at all."

Mrs. Toba raised her eyebrows and said, "Is that so? But why did you say so, if you aren't?"

Lowering her head, Akiko explained. "We investigated and learned your two children go to the Kinryo School. We thought that if we told you we were from the PTA there, you'd be kind enough to see us. We really do hope you'll forgive us for this."

"Well. I must admit, it's a bit of a surprise," Mrs. Toba said, looking at the eight ladies. Then, with a shake of her head and a suspicious look, she asked, "But what is your real reason for coming here this way? If it's a contribution of some kind, I'm willing to listen and perhaps even help you in some way."

Akiko's elegant way of talking and the simple, yet tasteful, clothes and educated manners of the ladies left Mrs. Toba's mind completely at ease.

Hesitatingly, Akiko said, "I find this difficult. But, as a matter of fact, we're thieves."

Mrs. Toba's arm fell from the armrest of the chair. "What did you say? You must be joking."

"This is no joke. It's the truth."

At a sign from Akiko, Mrs. Sakata and Mrs. Watanabe rushed to Mrs. Toba's side and pinned her shoulders back and twisted her arms up. Mrs. Urabe and Mrs. Usui took white hemp ropes from their shopping bags. Mrs. Urabe said to the startled Mrs. Toba, "Please don't be angry with us. We're going to have to prevent you from moving your arms and legs. We'll be very gentle so it won't hurt. Forgive us for this."

Still unable to believe what was happening, Mrs. Toba panted as she exclaimed, "But, you ladies! You ladies. You're joking, surely. Of course. You're such lovely ladies. . . ."

"We're quite serious, you know. Please, don't hold it against us." Mrs. Usui tied Mrs. Toba's wrists. "I really don't like having to do this to you, you understand?"

Mrs. Urabe tied her legs together, and Mrs. Sakata and Mrs. Watanabe tied her body — she was wearing a Jean Patou suit — to the chair.

"Come this way, please, ladies." Leaving Mrs. Sakata and some of the others in charge, Akiko led three of the ladies out of the reception room. They had to tie up the maid, who would certainly be in the kitchen, preparing tea for the guests. They tiptoed down the corridor leading from the entrance foyer. There were doors on both sides. On the right was a library. To the left, a bedroom. The kitchen was at the end of the hall on the left.

The maid, who was preparing tea, was startled when she sensed someone else in the room. She whirled. "What d'you want here?" she asked, staring at the ladies with distrust.

Akiko thought the girl was probably both young and ill-bred. If she began fighting back, it might be very difficult to pin her down. Smiling, Akiko approached the maid and said, "I'm sure our visit is a lot of trouble for you. Forgive us, and let us help you."

"No thanks, I can manage," she said, putting the kettle filled with hot water on the table. Seeing their chance, Akiko, Mrs. Kataoka, and Mrs. Ise forced the maid into a chair. Mrs. Suruga, who had already taken out the rope, approached and bound the girl's wrists.

The girl shouted, "What're you doing?" and shook her legs violently. "What the hell is this? Lemme go! Lemme go, damn you!"

Wrapping the rope around the girl's body and tying her to the chair, Mrs. Suruga said, "My, she has a loud voice. There, there, now. Be still. Won't do you any good to struggle like that. You'll just hike your skirt indecently."

Unconcerned, the girl threw her legs about and twisted wildly. "Thieves! Untie me — untie me —"

Akiko said, "Just sit still like a nice young lady."

"What're you talking about? Thieves — thieves!"

Sighing, Mrs. Kataoka said, "You're certainly noisy. Believe me, it's better for you if you stay quiet."

Mrs. Ise said, "Yes, that's true. I'm afraid she leaves us no choice."

Working together, the two ladies fashioned a noose out of a length of rope and slipped it over the girl's head. The maid gasped. Her eyes bulged as she looked around. Sensing something bad, she tried to break free from the rope. Her voice was rough with fear. "Stop, please. Don't kill me. Don't kill me."

"It'll be over in no time," Mrs. Suruga said sympathetically, holding the girl's legs. "Be patient."

"I don't want to die," the girl screamed, her voice rattling, Akiko looked at her face and smiled wryly.

When the rope was around her throat, the maid opened her mouth and sobbed, revealing decayed teeth. "I'm afraid!" she whimpered.

Mrs. Kataoka, who belonged to a large Buddhist organization, said, "There's absolutely nothing to be frightened of, my dear. You're simply going to be with the gentle Goddess of Mercy."

"I'm still young," the maid sobbed.

Her tearful, terrified face was so ugly that Akiko had to look away as she cautioned her: "There, now. You're going to die. Why not behave with a bit more dignity and feminine decorum?"

"But, I want to live." Her face was sticky with tears and saliva.

"She just can't resign herself, can she?" Akiko said, giving Mrs. Kataoka and Mrs. Ise a signal. "Ladies, please."

Mrs. Kataoka and Mrs. Ise pulled on the ends of the rope with all their might. Blood congestion caused the girl's face to swell like a red-black balloon. The veins on the sides of her fleshy nose protruded. She arched her back, and her eyes swelled wide. The two ladies continued pulling the rope. The maid's head slumped forward.

The four ladies immediately began looking for things.

Taking a package from the refrigerator, Mrs. Kataoka said, "Why, Mrs. Kamei. I wish you'd look at all this meat. Nicely marbled, too. Must be top-quality serloin."

All the ladies examined the beef.

"A kilogram at least."

"Yes. I'll bet it sells for twelve hundred yen a hundred grams."

"But if we divide it among eight people, there won't be much to go around."

"It's frozen, too. We'd have to thaw it in the range before dividing it."

"I'll tell you what. I won't have any of the meat. I'll just have some of these," Mrs. Ise said, taking shrimps out of the freezing compartment.

"Oh, what nice fat shrimp!"

"There are six of 'em."

"I think I'll have the shrimp, too."

"A little beef'll be fine for me," Akiko said. "I think I'd better call the other ladies," She went along the hall to the living room and spoke to them, "I'll be all right alone here for a while. You go on into the kitchen. The others are dividing beef and shrimp."

"Did you say — beef?"

"Wonderful!"

The four ladies hurried to the kitchen. Looking sadly up at Akiko, Mrs. Toba said, "Why do you do this? I simply can't figure it out."

Akiko sighed. "This probably sounds rude to you, but, even if I explained it, I doubt that you'd be able to understand. You live such a comfortable life. I really envy you."

"Did you have some special reason for selecting my house?" Mrs. Toba said, puzzled.

"No. We only learned that your husband is a famous surgeon and the head of a hospital; that your children attend Kinryo Primary School; and that, until two in the afternoon, you and the maid are alone here. Then we discussed it among ourselves and decided we'd pay you a call — if you were good enough to let us in. We had no bad intentions. . . . But, perhaps that's not the way to put it. Let's say we have nothing against you." Akiko approached and looked into Mrs. Toba's beautiful face. She could smell expensive French perfume. "By the way," she said. "We'd like some cash. Would you be good enough to tell us where you keep it? Cash is all we want."

"It's — it's in the top drawer of my dressing table in my bedroom. There should be some more in a black Hermes handbag in the den — but —"

"Thank you, very much." Akiko bowed her head. "I'm not flattering you when I say you're a very gracious lady. We won't take anything but cash and a few trifles, like foodstuffs."

In the kitchen, seven ladies were busily opening cupboards and pantries and taking out canned goods and vegetables.

"My goodness, just look at everything."

"My dear, I wouldn't touch the canned tuna if I were you. Mercury poisoning, you know."

"You're quite right. I won't have that. But there're plenty of other things. Here's some very nice canned ham and some excellent canned crab."

"I think I prefer the canned asparagus."

Mrs. Suruga opened a cupboard. "Oh, how grand! Sterling. A whole set, and all of it pure silver."

"Yes," cautioned Mrs. Usui. "But we mustn't touch things like that."

"Of course. We make it a policy not to receive anything that could be detected and traced." Mrs. Suruga bit her lip as she spoke. "But it's killing not to have it."

"Oh, look at all these onions."

"Yes, my dear. And those are a special imported kind. Very delicious. From the way they're wrapped, I'd say they were delivered directly here."

"We must remember to set aside a portion for Mrs. Kamei."

The ladies gathered around the kitchen table and, chatting merrily, divided the food into eight equal parts.

None of them so much as looked at the inert body of the maid.

Mrs. Urabe entered the living room and said, "My dear Mrs.

Kamei. We've received all of the food and divided it into eight parts. Now some of the ladies would love to see the underclothes of the husband and children."

"Excuse me, but where might you keep your husband's and your children's undergarments?" Akiko asked Mrs. Toba.

Mrs. Toba's eyes were glazed. "The fresh things are in the basket in the laundry room. If you're interested in my underclothes, they're in the wardrobe in my room, though I'm embarrassed to say you'll find nothing very fancy there."

"You're very kind. Now, Mrs. Urabe, if you'll be good enough to take my place here for a while . . ."

"Yes, of course, my dear."

Akiko went to the kitchen. "Ladies, Mrs. Toba is going to let us have some underclothing. This way, now."

The laundry room, which doubled as a dressing room for the bath, was at the end of the corridor. All of the ladies formed a group around the large basket in which they found a stack of new underclothes.

"My, these look warm. They're knitted."

"My husband is heavy. I wonder if these will fit?"

"Let me see. Her older boy is in the fifth grade, isn't he? That means these should fit my boy."

"Heavenly days! Mohair underwear. Her husband must really hate the cold."

"If no one else needs those, I'd love to have them. My husband's still young, but he's very susceptible to cold."

"A word, ladies," called Akiko. "Don't choose any socks with flashy patterns, or someone will put his foot in it."

"That's very good." All the ladies chortled.

After dividing the underwear and the laundry soap and toilet paper, the ladies moved into the bedroom. The abundant space and the uniform dark green color scheme brought sighs of envy. The ladies lived in small apartments, where they sometimes shared sleeping quarters with their children.

Akiko pulled out the top drawer of the dressing table and found one hundred and twenty thousand yen.

"Oh, dear — I thought there'd be more." The ladies exchanged glances. "Divided among eight, it's only fifteen thousand apiece."

"Just a minute, dears," Akiko said, and left the room.

The other ladies opened the wardrobe drawers to examine Mrs. Toba's underthings.

"Oh, how pretty!"

"Made in Paris, all of them."

"These panties cost twenty thousand yen a pair."

"Oh, look — the lace and silk things in this drawer were all made in Switzerland."

"Ladies, what d'you think? Would this slip look good on me?"

"Oh, yes. Wonderful."

In an almost tearful voice, Mrs. Ise lamented, as she opened and looked into a jewel case, "What a pity. We can't let her give us this kind of thing."

"The temptation's too great, my dear. You mustn't even look."

"Too true. Just look at this closet. Oh, I wish I'd never opened it."

All the ladies rushed to the closet and looked at the racks of expensive clothes, which caused them to sigh, all in unison.

"Goodness! Mink."

"And here's a leopard coat!"

Akiko returned with Mrs. Toba's handbag. "I found sixty thousand in here. There are some credit cards and a check book, but they don't do us any good. In the maid's handbag in the kitchen there was another twenty thousand."

"For heaven's sake. What's a maid doing walking around with that much money?"

"Ladies, here's something nice." Mrs. Watanabe pointed to some large paper shopping bags with the marks of exclusive dress shops on them. She had found them in the closet. "We could put the things we received in these."

Akiko said, "But, we mustn't use anything with conspicuous markings."

All of the ladies took out the shopping bags they had brought with them. In these and in the more somber of the shopping bags from the closet, they carefully packed the spoils of their forage. They walked out of the bedroom, each with a bag in either hand, and returned to the living room.

As the group's representative, Akiko said, "We've caused you a great deal of trouble and we apologize. But now we have received everything we came to receive."

"Have you ladies done this often?" Mrs. Toba asked, staring with genuine amazement at the women, who certainly did not look like thieves, yet who were so skillful at their work.

Akiko stared at Mrs. Toba. "You mean you don't know? A lady like you living in a big mansion like this must read the papers. The odd robberies that have been causing such a stir lately. Well, we're the ones."

"Oh, I know about that." And the moment Mrs. Toba spoke, the blood drained from her face. "But you can't mean you are the ones who mercilessly kill people and steal nothing but cash and some worthless trifles."

Relieved, Akiko said, "I'm delighted you said it yourself. I was desperately trying to think of a way to break it to you."

Then, placing her bags on the carpet, from the pocket of her suit, she pulled a straight razor that she had found in a bathroom of the mansion.

"To ask you to give up your life after having already asked you to give us so many other things is very difficult."

Mrs. Toba's face was white as paper and she trembled.

"Then, I — I'm going to die? Here? Now?"

"My dear Mrs. Toba. It grieves me to have to take the life of a person as lovely as you," Akiko said with emotion. "But you must realize we cannot let anyone in the outside world know about the existence of an eight-lady group like ours. I will do it so your lovely face won't be disfigured and so the pain will last but an instant."

Mrs. Toba was crying. "I — I must die for a little over a hundred thousand yen and a small amount of food? It's too awful!" She was sobbing now.

"Mrs. Toba, Mrs. Toba. Please, get control of yourself. Be brave and die beautifully, not like the maid we strangled a little while ago."

Mrs. Toba ceased weeping. "Then she's already been killed?" Suddenly, she laughed in a cackling way. Then she sang a phrase of a festive song. In shock, Akiko and the others took a step back. Then Mrs. Toba regained composure and nodded solemnly.

"Forgive me for being rude," she said. "I am now prepared.

Only, a few minutes ago, I am afraid I wet my panties."

In a voice filled with sympathy, Akiko said, "Small wonder."

"I have a favor to ask," Mrs. Toba said. "When I'm dead, will you be good enough to change my panties for me?"

Her stoic calm touched the ladies, all of whom simultaneously said, "Oh," in low voices.

"But, certainly," Akiko said. "I'll be personally responsible for that. This proves to me that you are indeed the great lady of a fine house. Shall we, then? . . ."

Akiko moved quickly to Mrs. Toba's right side, gripped her black hair in her left hand and pulled her head back.

"Hail to the Buddha Amida." As Mrs. Toba murmured this, Akiko cut a single line across her white throat with the straight razor.

A spray of fresh blood flew from the wound with a sound like rain. The strong spurting lasted for some ten seconds and then diminished. All of the ladies complimented Akiko on her skill.

"It was splendid."

"You're improving all the time."

"Yes, I am. Thank you. Lately I manage without getting any blood on my clothes." Akiko was slightly bashful.

"She was a true lady, wasn't she?"

"Yes, but she was a little strange."

"I don't agree. She was a fine lady."

The ladies left in staggered groups of twos and threes, so as to avoid attracting attention. Akiko was the last to go. She closed Mrs. Toba's staring eyes and changed her panties. Then she took a look around the living room to make certain no evidence had been left behind. Finally, she took a long look at the two-carat diamond on the hand of the corpse.

Neither her low-salaried father nor her low-salaried white-collar husband had bought her any jewelry except a plain wedding band. But, sighing, she shook her head resolutely and looked away from the sparkling stone.

Picking up her shopping bags, Akiko left the Toba house. That night when she and her husband made love, she was probably going to be highly passionate. She was always passionate on these nights.